Susan Meier is the author of over fifty books for Mills & Boon. *The Tycoon's Secret Daughter* was a Romance Writers of America RITA® Award finalist and *Nanny for the Millionaire's Twins* won the Book Buyers' Best award and was a finalist in the National Readers' Choice awards. She is married and has three children. One of eleven children, she loves to write about the complexity of families and totally believes in the power of love.

A MISTLETOE KISS WITH THE BOSS

BY
SUSAN MEIER

MILLS & BOON

First Published in Great Britain 2016
By Mills & Boon, an imprint of HarperCollins*Publishers*
1 London Bridge Street, London, SE1 9GF

© 2016 Linda Susan Meier

ISBN: 978-0-263-92023-9

23-1016

CHAPTER ONE

WHEN THE ELEVATOR bell rang in the lobby of the upscale Paris hotel, Kristen Anderson's heart thumped. She spun to face the ornate wrought iron doors, her whole body shivering in anticipation—

Two middle-aged American women got out.

She didn't have time to sag with disappointment, because someone tapped her on the shoulder and asked her a quiet question.

In French.

Which she didn't speak.

She turned around to see a man dressed in a suit, undoubtedly the desk clerk.

Speaking English, because her native Grennadian was nearly unheard of, she said, "I'm sorry. I don't speak French."

The elevator bell dinged again. Her head snapped toward the sound.

In perfect English, the desk clerk said, "May I ask, mademoiselle, your business in our hotel?"

She pointed at the tall, broad man exiting the elevator. "I want to see him."

She took two steps toward Dean Suminski, chairman

of the board and CEO of Suminski Stuff, but the clerk caught her arm.

"No, mademoiselle." He shook his finger like a metronome. "You will not disturb a guest."

Walking toward her, Dean Suminski shrugged into a gorgeous charcoal-gray overcoat. His eyes were down. She guessed that was his way of ignoring anyone who might be around him. But she didn't care. Getting him to visit Grennady and consider it as the place to relocate his company was her mission for her country. Approaching him was also practice for when she had to deal with men like him on a daily basis after she started her charitable foundation. One desk clerk wouldn't stop her.

"Sorry, Pierre." She pulled her arm out of his short, stubby fingers. "Someday I'm going to build schools in third world countries. I have to learn to be brash."

She spun away from the clerk and shouted, "Mr. Suminski!"

He totally ignored her.

"Mr. Suminski! I know that's you. I've seen your face on the internet."

He walked to the door.

She scurried after him. "I just need two minutes."

Out of the corner of her eye, she saw the clerk point at a man behind another discreet desk. He nodded and bounded toward her. But Suminski walked out the door and she stayed on his heels, catching him when he stopped in front of a limo.

"Seriously. Two minutes. That's all I need."

In the silence of the crisp early December morning, at a hotel set back, away from the congestion of Paris's main thoroughfare, she heard his annoyed sigh and was surprised when he faced her.

"Who are you?"

With his dark eyes locked on her face, Kristen froze. His black hair was perfect, not a strand out of place. His high forehead, straight nose and high cheekbones could have made him a king.

When she didn't answer, he said, "Fine," and began to turn away.

"I'm Kristen Anderson," she said, her voice coming out louder than it should. She sucked in a quick gulp of air and calmed herself. When she spoke again, it was quieter, smoother, and with authority. "Gennady would like you to consider moving your company to our country."

He faced her again. "Prince Alex would know I wasn't interested."

Prince Alex was the husband of Kristen's boss, Princess Eva. As executive assistant to Grennady's future queen, Kristen knew Alex had immediately said no to considering Suminski Stuff as one of the tech companies being recruited to boost their flagging economy. But their options had run out. Dean's was the only company left.

"So that's why you weren't put on the list?"

He smiled. But the movement wasn't warm or friendly. More sarcastic. Almost frightening. "There's a list?"

"There was. It's dwindled."

"To no one, I'm guessing, if they sent you to barge in on my day."

She swallowed. Those black eyes were just too intense—like they saw every damned thing going on in her head. She'd read that he was shrewd, uncanny in his ability to judge his opponents. Orphaned at four, raised by a cold grandmother who hadn't wanted him, he'd played video games to amuse himself. At fourteen, he'd gone to business school because he'd taught himself to code and didn't need any more instructions in computers. He was brilliant. He was arrogant. He was also their last chance.

She opened her hands in supplication. "If you could give me two minutes of your time, I could persuade you to visit and make an assessment about whether or not you might consider, perhaps, moving your company to Grennady."

"That's a lotta maybes and mights and perhapses."

"It's possible you're not looking to move."

"I'm not."

"You should be. Grennady is a beautiful country with a diverse labor pool."

He scowled, and really just scared the hell out of her. Tall, broad-shouldered, and blunt, he made her blood tingle with fear. And she had the feeling he did it deliberately. Maybe this was why Prince Alex didn't want him in their country? And maybe she had overstepped in contacting him. Grennady might be desperate to find an employer who could keep their younger, educated residents at home, but Suminski Stuff wasn't the answer.

She stepped back. "You know what? I'm sorry I bothered you. Have a nice day."

He shook his head. "You're gonna give up that easily? I had higher hopes for you."

Her face scrunched in confusion. "What?"

"You obviously flew from your frozen country to Paris where you don't even speak the language." His head tilted. "I heard you tell the clerk. You also didn't mind running after me, shouting in a quiet lobby. That takes some guts. But when you finally had my attention, you backed off." He almost smiled. "Too bad."

He turned to leave, but she caught his arm. "What would you have done, if you were me?"

He laughed. "So now you want me to teach you how to dicker?"

His dark eyes held her gaze. She swallowed down her fear because, damn it, why should she be afraid of this guy just because he had money? And was big. And handsome. And had a terrifying way of looking at her.

"I don't want you to teach me to dicker. I want you to listen to my pitch for about fifteen minutes."

"Before you said two minutes."

"That was if I didn't show you some pictures."

He looked at the blue sky, then back at her. "All right. Get in the car. I'm on my way to the airport. You've got the entire drive. Give it your best shot."

Hope burst inside her. Maybe he wasn't so bad, after all? "Really?"

He motioned to the black limo awaiting him. "Here's lesson one. Don't question good luck."

The driver opened the car door and Kristen slid inside. Warm leather seats arranged in a semicircle greeted her.

Dean Suminski eased in beside her. A few seconds passed in silence as the driver got behind the wheel. Dean spent the time texting.

As the car pulled away from the hotel, Kristen said, "So I'm assuming you already know a little bit about Grennady?"

"I own controlling interest in a big company. I know who's managing the world's oil. I met Xaviera's Prince Alex a few years back. When he married, I did my research."

"Why would you care who he married?"

He sniffed a laugh. "Would you put your money in oil stocks if the region was unstable?"

"That has nothing to do with Alex getting married. Besides, that region's always unstable."

"Let's call it controlled instability because of people like Prince Alex's dad, King Ronaldo. As long as Ronaldo is happy, he's strong. I needed to make sure Alex's marriage didn't rock the boat."

She supposed that was true. "So you know that our country's every bit as well ruled as Xaviera."

"Your country nearly had a coup at the beginning of the year."

"Nearly. King Mason was on top of things."

He made a noncommittal sound.

"But, just for the sake of argument, let's pretend he wasn't. He is now."

"True."

"We're going through something that could be described as a renaissance, and you could be part of that."

"I'm rich. I don't need to be part of anything."

His phone rang. He slid it from his breast pocket. "Very few people have this number. So if someone's calling it's important." He clicked the button to answer. "Hello?"

A pause.

"Maurice! Je m'excuse. Mon voyage a été coupé court..."

French again. Damn it. She knew two languages. The language of her country and English. It was becoming clear that she would have to fix that, if she wanted to run an international charity.

As he went on, holding a conversation in a language she didn't speak, she looked at the luxurious interior of the car. She'd ridden in limos with the princess, of course, but this felt different. She wasn't the scampering, scrambling employee of an important person, doing her job to make Eva's life easier. She was the one talking to the important person.

She was more than getting her feet wet with this guy. He took her seriously.

She felt herself making her first shaky step into the life and work she really wanted. Though she loved being Princess Eva's assistant, she had a degree in economics and a plan to change the world. When she was in high school, her pen pal Aasera had been one of six kids, living in Iraq. Her brothers had been educated, but she and her sisters were not. So she'd sneaked her brothers' books. When they discovered, she'd begged them to teach her to read and write, and they did.

She had been brave, determined. She'd often said her country would be a different place if women were educated, and she'd intended to make that happen. But she'd been killed by a suicide bomber, and in her grief Kristen had vowed to make Aasera's wish a reality.

Today, she was finally beginning to feel she could make that happen.

Dean hung up the phone. "Sorry about that."

"It's fine."

The words were barely out of her mouth before his phone rang again.

He waved it at her. "Sorry. I have to answer."

This time he spoke fluent Spanish. Not wanting to appear to be listening in, though she couldn't since she also didn't speak Spanish, she looked at the beauty of Paris outside the car windows. The curved arches. The ornate buildings. Happy people bundled in scarves and warm coats, sitting on the chairs of sidewalk cafes, in spite of the December cold.

She almost couldn't believe she'd been courageous enough to take her own money and track down Dean Suminski, but here she was, in Paris, trying to influence him as an equal—or at least as someone who deserved his support. It filled her chest with pride and her stomach with butterflies, but after three years as Eva's assistant, she was ready to move on.

Dean talked so long that the city gave way to a quieter area, and then the buildings became fewer and farther apart. Suddenly a private airstrip appeared. Eight or ten bright blue, gray and tan metal hangars gleamed in the morning sun. Around them were five jets that ranged from a sleek, slim, small one to a plane big enough to hold the entirety of Grennady's parliament.

Dean Suminski continued talking as the limo stopped in front of one of the smaller, sleeker jets. He talked as the driver opened his door. He talked as he motioned for her to get out of the limo and as he followed her out and onto the tarmac.

Finally, he clicked off the call. "This wasn't my fault. As I said, any call that comes in on this phone is important. Normally, I don't feel the need to make amends, but if you want, you can fly to New York with me. That gives you almost nine hours to make your pitch."

Her eyes bulged. It was one thing to take a few steps toward her dreams, quite another to cross an ocean. "Fly to New York?"

"You don't have time?"

"I…" She didn't want to tell him she'd used her own money to travel to Paris and couldn't miss her flight home the following morning. She didn't want to tell him that her boss and her husband were at Prince Alex's island home of Xaviera with his family, at the end of their vacation celebrating American Thanksgiving with Princess Ginny and Queen Rose. She didn't want to admit that Princess Eva didn't know where Kristen was, and hadn't authorized her talking to him. She wanted to surprise them with a visit from Dean Suminski in January, as a way to thank them for being so good to her, but also to show them she could get a job done. So that when she left their employ to begin her charity, they'd be her first backers.

But she was also proving to herself she had what it took to be more than an executive assistant. If she couldn't persuade Dean Suminski to visit Grennady with an eye toward relocating, would she be able to persuade benefactors to put up the millions of dollars she would need for her schools?

"Once we get to New York, the plane will turn around and bring you back home."

Probably in time for her flight. Or she could simply tell Dean Suminski to instruct the pilot to take her back to Grennady. "That's generous."

His eyes turned down at the corners as he frowned. "Generous?"

"Well, you could leave me at the airport."

"I could." He glanced away, then looked back. "I know I have a reputation for being...well, not a nice guy. But you don't need me to be a nice guy. You want time to make a pitch. I'm offering it. Consider this an early Christmas present."

It suddenly struck her that he must be interested. He hadn't told her to get lost at the hotel. He'd offered her time in his limo, though that hadn't worked out. But here he was again, giving her a chance to sell him on her country.

"Thought you said you weren't thinking of relocating?"

"Thought you said I should be."

CHAPTER TWO

"YOU SHOULD."

Dean Suminski studied the pretty girl in front of him. Blonde with pale green eyes and a generous mouth made for kissing, she wore a simple black wool coat over black pants and sensible shoes. Normally, he would have had his bodyguard deal with anyone who approached him, but she reminded him of himself ten years ago, when Suminski Stuff was in its infancy. When he wore simple, practical clothes, hoping he didn't stand out for his lack of sophistication, and when he was trying to raise money from investors to start his business.

Still, he hadn't gotten this far by being stupid. He'd texted his executive assistant and told her to get everything she could on Kristen Anderson of Grennady, and that's what the call in Spanish had been about. This woman really did work for Princess Eva.

If Grennady's royal family had sent her to him, there was a reason. He might not want to be part of a renaissance precipitated by a near coup, but he wouldn't mind having a desperate country at his mercy.

He said, "All right. I'll admit that the most popular places to locate a corporation in the United States are getting crowded." He speared her with a look, delving deeply into those pretty green eyes, knowing she wasn't very experienced at negotiating and wondering why a princess would send *her*. Surely, more astute negotiators or even public relations people would do a better job.

Especially since he knew Alex Sancho, Princess Eva's husband, didn't like him.

Her eyes brightened. "So there is a chance you'd relocate?"

The sparkle in her eyes hit him like a punch to the gut, surprising him. Those soft green orbs were little mirrors to her happy soul. And that lush, kiss-me mouth? It took a stronger man than he was not to notice its plump fullness.

Still, he shouldn't be looking. He only dated sophisticates. Women who took lovers, who weren't seeking happily-ever-after, as this bubbly, obviously naïve woman would be.

But the feeling in his gut wouldn't go away. It kept telling him that something about her was important. And he should pay attention.

He pointed at the plane. "Let's not get ahead of ourselves."

She preceded him up the short stack of steps into his jet. When she gasped, he laughed.

"The princess never takes you on her jet?"

"Up until last year, she didn't do much government business. Actually, she didn't even have bodyguards."

He raised his eyebrows. "Are you going to waste these next few hours gossiping?"

"No." She waved her hands. "Sorry. I know your time is precious."

"Let's just buckle in and you can start your pitch once we're at cruising altitude."

As he spoke, his second-in-command and best friend,

Jason Wilson, stepped into the corridor from the office in the back.

Short, twenty or thirty pounds overweight, but looking expensive and self-assured in his three-piece suit, Jason said, "We have a problem."

Dean motioned for Kristen to take a seat and buckle in. "I suppose we do if you flew the whole way to Europe rather than phone me."

Jason caught Dean's arm and moved him to the back of the plane before he whispered, "While you were in meetings yesterday, I got word from a few investment firms that our stock's about to be downgraded and they're going to advise investors to sell."

Forgetting all about Kristen Anderson, he gaped at Jason. *"Sell?"*

"Tech Junkie ran an article about you. They suggested that the new product is late because we don't have one."

"That's absurd!"

"Oh, it gets worse. They said you're so far removed from real life and so far removed from real people that it's a miracle you came up with the original operating system and games that you did. They claim being out of touch with real people means you can't figure out what they want because you're not one of them."

"How I live has nothing to do with my abilities."

"Not according to the pundits quoted in the article. They say your reign is over. That you had five or six good ideas and exhausted them."

The urge to shake his head at the stupidity of some people was nearly overwhelming. He was a genius, for crying out loud. Of course he didn't live like a normal person.

"I spent my childhood poor, looking for ways to entertain myself. I know software. I know games."

"They say that's what got you here. But your ideas are gone."

He tossed his hands in frustration. "We have a fantastic series of games in the works!"

"In the works for three years. Too long in this market." Jason snapped his fingers. "Everything's all about speed these days."

"The series has to be perfect before I can even talk about it, let alone roll it out."

"Then you're pretty much screwed." Jason's gaze strayed to Kristen. "Who's that?"

He didn't like explaining himself to anybody. Not even his best friend—especially since he wasn't entirely clear why he was willing to hear Kristen Anderson's pitch. Every time he looked at her, he got a "there's an opportunity here" feeling. Which made no sense since Alex Sancho was married to her boss. Couple that with the way he kept noticing all the wrong things about her, and being around her was tempting fate. Which was absurd. He did not tempt fate, push envelopes or even take risks. He was cautious. That's why he was rich.

Yet here she was in his jet.

He held back a wince as he said, "She's a girl I met at the hotel."

Jason's eyes widened. "Really?"

Deciding to let honest and genuine Kristen explain this, he turned and started up the aisle to the four plush seats. "Kristen, this is Jason Wilson, my second in command."

Kristen jumped off her seat and extended her hand.

"Kristen Anderson. I work for Princess Eva of Grennady."

Jason's gaze walked back to Dean. *"Prince Alex's
wife's assistant* is your new girlfriend?"

She laughed. "No. I'm not his girlfriend. My country
wants your company to consider relocating to Grennady."

The pilot's voice came over the speaker, advising pas-
sengers to buckle seat belts and get ready for takeoff.

Dean caught the gaze of Kristen's happy green eyes.
An unwanted tingle of attraction zipped through him,
but so did that damned feeling that she, somehow, was
important.

He said, "You buckle in," then he faced Jason. "Let's
take this discussion to the office."

He followed his friend down the aisle to the compact
room. As they fastened their seat belts, Jason said, "So,
who is she really?"

Dean focused his attention on his cantankerous buckle
so he didn't have to look at Jason. "She told you. She's
from Grennady. Her country wants us to consider lo-
cating there."

Jason's eyes narrowed. "You don't *like* her?"

He did actually. Even if he paid no attention to the
"she's important somehow" feeling or the way her physical appearance kept tempting him, she was smart and
ambitious. She was also totally inexperienced, but that
might be why she was such a curiosity. She wasn't a
shark. She wasn't a schmoozer. She was too naïve, clearly
too green to be either of those. She was just a woman
trying to do a job. If the royal family had an agenda in
sending her, he didn't think she knew it.

"If you're asking if I want to take her out, the answer
is no." He might be attracted to her, but he didn't date.

And she was too naïve to fit the role as his lover. "I told her I'd listen to her pitch in the car, but got caught up in a phone conversation with Stella. So I told her I'd listen on the plane. When we land in New York, the plane will turn around and take her home."

Jason said, "Okay, fine," as the jet taxied. "As long as this mess with investors comes first."

"Of course."

When they were in the air, climbing to cruising altitude, he and Jason began a discussion of how to combat the *Tech Junkie* article. But in hours and hours of studying schematics, employee reports and his own damned business plan—which was shot to hell because the schedule was now almost two years behind—all they could come up with was a stopgap measure: contact the most influential brokerage firms and ask them to delay advising their clients to sell to give Suminski Stuff time to get the games to one more set of beta testers.

They made a list of firms to call when they got to New York, and created a script of what they would say, but Dean knew brokers were right to be concerned. The games they'd been working on had had one setback after another because the series was too ambitious. No one really knew how far away it was from rollout. The staff had gotten tired, worn down, and everything was now taking longer than it should.

He'd been warned. But he'd gotten arrogant. *His* staff could do anything...

Or so he'd thought. And now they were in trouble because he couldn't even give a hard date for when it would be ready for another round of beta testing, let alone a hard date for when it would be for sale.

When the script was ready, Jason scrubbed his hand across his mouth. "So this is what we say?"

Dean shrugged, then leaned back in his comfortable chair. "Yes. If the brokers listen to us, I think we'll buy about six weeks. But we're going to have to do some hand-holding. And at the end of that six weeks, we have to have something—even if it's only a date for when it can go into beta testing again."

"Christmas is smack-dab in the middle of those six weeks. Then New Year's."

"So we'll cancel Christmas."

Jason laughed. "We can't cancel a holiday."

"No, but we can cancel vacations and leave."

"They'll hate you."

"Yeah, well, I'm not feeling warm and fuzzy toward them right now, either. Three years they've been working on this. If anybody's got a right to be disappointed, it's me."

The pilot announced that it was time to buckle in for landing and Dean wasn't surprised. The flight to New York had felt like the shortest of his life because he'd spent it figuring out how to keep investors from dumping his stock, when, really, if he was one of them he'd drop his stock like a hot rock.

He and Jason buckled in. The jet landed and taxied to his private hangar. They unbuckled their seat belts and stepped into the aisle only to find Kristen Anderson facing them, looking furious.

He squeezed his eyes shut. *This* was why he didn't deal with people. He wasn't considerate. He had a one-track mind. Right now his company was in danger of total failure. He didn't have time to listen to a pitch for something he neither needed nor wanted.

"Sorry. I'd say you could have the limo ride to my office to chat, but then you wouldn't be able to turn around and fly home."

Her pretty face softened a bit. "I'm okay with that. Just have your plane take me back to Grennady instead of Paris and I'll be fine."

Dean started to say, "Okay," but Jason caught his arm. "She can't have the limo ride. You have to start making those calls the minute we step off this plane. I'm guessing you'll be spending the entire day talking. After that there's the Christmas gala."

"I can miss that."

Jason sniffed a laugh. "Really? After you spend an entire day convincing brokers that the company's solvent and you're fine, not some prima donna genius who doesn't understand real life, you think you can miss an event where you actually mingle like a normal person? The one that opens the season? The one that *everybody* goes to?"

Damn it. Jason was right. The speculation of why he hadn't attended the party of the year could undo all the hours he'd spend making those telephone calls.

He unhappily caught Kristen's gaze. He hated messing up the way he had with her. He didn't make mistakes. And even when he did, somehow or another, the situation turned out okay, as if his instincts could see the future and know there was a reason he'd done whatever unusual thing he'd done.

But not this time.

There was no "reason" that he'd strung her along except that he had an odd feeling in his gut every time he looked at her. And now he had to brush her off.

"I'm sorry, Ms. Anderson. It appears I really don't

have time to talk to you. It's best you take the plane back."

"Seriously? I just sat patiently for *hours* and you won't even listen for fifteen minutes?"

The word *sorry* was on the tip of his tongue again but he swallowed it. Technically this wasn't his fault. "You orchestrated this. I told you I was a busy man. You took a risk and it didn't work out."

Jason caught his arm, but he addressed Kristen. "Just hold on for one second." Then he faced Dean. "Can I talk to you in the back?"

Dean reluctantly followed Jason to the aisle in front of the office.

"We sort of have a weird opportunity here."

Not following how or why, Dean said nothing.

"We want to counteract that article. We want brokers and big investors to see you as a normal guy, and be comfortable that you're not worried about the situation with the new games."

Dean quietly said, "Yes."

Jason nudged his head toward the front of the plane. "So why not take her to the party tonight?"

Dean laughed. "What?"

"No one's ever seen you date. You keep your relationships private. The press has been dying to catch you with a woman. But more than that, a date makes you look normal. Happy even. Who knows? The next article might come out speculating that the rollout is late because you're preoccupied with your new girlfriend. It's a chance to totally spin this mess in our favor."

Dean glanced up at Kristen. His heartbeat slowed. The sweet tingle of attraction rolled through him. Attending a party with her was exactly what his hormones wanted. "She is pretty."

"She's more than pretty, Dean. She's gorgeous. The kind of girl everybody expects you to end up with. She, personally, might not have breeding, but she works for a royal family. She's on the periphery of the jet-set crowd, good-looking enough to attract someone like you. The connection is logical. We'll send her out with Stella to get something for the party. Shoes, dress, whatever the hell she needs. Then she's on your arm tonight."

"I'll have to listen to her pitch. Right now," Dean said emphatically. "I'm not stringing her along and I'm not going to let her think I'm using her."

Jason shook his head. "Your honesty is going to bite you in the butt one of these days."

"Yeah, but my arrogance will save me."

Jason slapped his back. "Whatever."

Dean led Jason to the front of the plane. "I'm going to listen to your pitch right now."

Her eyes widened. "You are?"

"Yes. But then I'd like to hire you to do something for me."

"Hire me?"

"Yes." Though he and Jason hadn't discussed paying her, with all the strange feelings tumbling through him when he was around her, he needed to make sure they kept this "date" in perspective. He also wouldn't ask Kristen Anderson to go to the party with him as a favor. Favors implied that he'd be indebted to her. He was indebted to no one. "I'll pay you a hundred thousand dollars to go to a party with me tonight."

She laughed.

He waited until she realized he was serious.

Wide-eyed, she asked, "Why would you do that?"

"You heard a bit of the discussion about my company hitting a bumpy patch?"

She inclined her head in acknowledgment.

"Well, I believe it will make me look a little more—" He wouldn't say "normal." Refused. Being a genius took him out of the normal column, but that didn't mean he didn't understand kids. Especially lonely kids. He had been one. He knew how to entertain them. "—approachable if I go to tonight's gala happy. Having a date will make it appear that everything's fine."

She just looked at him.

"Stocks are funny things," Jason said. "They sometimes rise and fall on rumors. How a company's leader is perceived dictates how much money people are willing to risk."

Dean frowned at Jason. "She has a degree in economics. I'm pretty sure she knows that." He faced Kristen. "What I really need to counteract that article is for people to perceive me as a regular guy. Dating is something a regular guy does."

"And if I say no, you won't listen to my pitch?"

The odd feeling rolled through him again. The feeling that something about her was significant. Holding the gaze of her pretty eyes, which were serious this time, he knew he had to be fair with her.

"No. Regardless of whether you go to the party with me or not, I'll listen to your pitch. But if you decide to come with me, we'll make arrangements to get you something suitable to wear, and we'll put you up in a hotel suite. Party's not until eight. You can get some sleep so you'll be fresh and happy for tonight. Then tomorrow you're back on this plane, on your way home."

"For a hundred thousand dollars?"

"I'm not paying you more than a hundred thousand dollars for a date."

"I don't want more. In fact, I, personally, do not want the money. But I am in the beginning stages of setting up a charity that will build schools in third world countries. I think what I'd really like is a commitment from you to put computers in those schools."

Disappointment flooded him. Just like everybody else, she wanted something from him. She might be on an assignment from Princess Eva and Prince Alex, but *she* had an agenda too. There was nothing special about her.

Still, he was accustomed to people wanting something. Everybody in his life wanted money or a favor or a recommendation of some sort. So what if she was no different? He didn't know why something about her had caught his attention. Maybe hormones mixing with jet lag? Disappointed or not, he was accustomed to this.

"When will the schools be built?"

She bit her lip. "I don't know. I'm in the planning stages of the charity itself. I don't really know when I'll have an actual school."

Jason touched Dean's arm to prevent him from replying. "So what you want is a promise in writing—"

"An agreement. I want this to be a normal charitable contribution. Not money given to me personally. But a charitable contribution."

Dean nodded. "Okay, we'll write an agreement that states I will put the first three hundred computers in your soon-to-be-developed schools."

"Yes."

He held out his hand to shake hers. "Deal."

She took his hand. "Deal."

CHAPTER THREE

STELLA TURNED OUT to be a thirtysomething hipster with short hair and big glasses, a long sweater over black leggings and tall boots. Standing in the middle of a huge dressing room in an exclusive boutique, Kristen watched Dean's assistant frown at the red dress she'd asked the shop manager to bring in her size.

"Sweetie," she said, then took a sip of her designer coffee. "If I were you, I'd get a black gown. Something I could wear again and again. When you've got a rich man footing the bill, you shop smart."

The boutique manager rolled her eyes.

Kristen winced. "I just want something acceptable. I don't want to break the bank."

Stella sniffed. "Dean Suminski's bank can't be broken." She motioned Kristen back into the curtained-off section of the dressing room. "Try the black one I picked out."

Kristen stepped between the two colorful strips of fabric that blocked off the changing area. When the boutique manager arrived with the black dress, she shrugged out of the cute red gown and into the elegant black one.

"Oh."

She hadn't meant to comment, but the tiny squeak

had slipped out. Black satin, sleeveless and formfitting from her chin to her hip bones, the dress flared out from thigh to floor and made a beautiful swishing sound when she moved.

The boutique manager, Jennifer, sighed. "I hate to call that little twit out there right, but this dress is perfect."

They found black shoes of an appropriate height, so the dress wouldn't need to be hemmed, and stunning white-gold earrings and necklace that sparkled against the simplicity of the dress. Then Stella had Dean's driver take them to a hotel on Broadway, where she was led to a suite.

"Get a nap," Stella said. "I'll be in the front room when your dress and shoes are delivered. I'll arrange for a hair-stylist and someone to do your makeup."

"I have makeup in my purse."

"That big, black ugly thing? I wanted to burn it."

"My purse might be old, but my makeup is fine."

"You'll be photographed. *With my boss.* It's my job to make you look perfect for tonight. You will not be wearing over-the-counter." She shooed her into the bedroom. "Get that nap. Your body's about ten hours ahead of ours. You're probably exhausted. I won't have you looking tired in photos."

Feeling like a wayward child, Kristen walked into the bedroom, hating to admit that bossy, opinionated Stella was right. She was tired. But she was also happy. Going on one date was a small price to pay to get the computers she'd need. Aasera would have been so proud.

Plus, it wasn't like she'd accepted a date with Dean Suminski for real. She didn't have to fawn all over him or make goo-goo eyes. She also wouldn't have to laugh at his jokes, since he didn't make them. He was as serious as a person could be. Probably because he was a genius.

That thought caused her face to scrunch. She had no idea what a girl going out with a certifiable genius was supposed to do. But she could be polite…actually, she could be friendly. Which was probably what Dean Suminski really needed—a buffer. Someone outgoing enough that his seriousness wouldn't be so off-putting.

She could handle that.

As she slid under the covers, she remembered that Dean's friend Jason had said something about her job being to make him look normal. So that's what she should focus on doing. Behaving normally, so he would too.

She would do her best, even if he had declined her offer for him to visit Grennady and consider it as a place to relocate. He wasn't planning to move his company, he'd said. So she'd had no choice but to accept that. But at least she'd tried. And he'd really listened.

She had to give him points for that.

She woke hours later when bossy Stella walked into her room with her iPhone blaring Spanish music. "It's one of my Zumba tapes," she explained, proudly displaying her trim body. "I'm sure you have an exercise regimen to be so thin and fit."

"No," Kristen said, rolling out from under the covers. "Tossing hay keeps me fit."

"Tossing hay?"

"For the cows. Not just for them to eat, but for their beds. I live on a farm."

Stella's eyes widened. "No kidding. A real farm?"

"You have farms in the US."

"Yeah, I know. I've just never seen one. Or known anyone who lived on one," Stella said. She pointed to the bathroom. "Get your shower and be out in ten minutes. Hairdresser is already here. Makeup artist is on her way up."

Kristen walked into the bathroom and gasped. Everything was marble or glass. Eight showerheads peeked out at her. Fluffy white towels were arranged in baskets like bouquets. The soap smelled like heaven.

Too bad she only had ten minutes to enjoy it all. She couldn't even try the jets. Too much temptation to linger. She simply washed in the sweet-smelling soap and cleaned her hair with shampoo the scent of oranges.

After wrapping her wet head in a towel, she slid into the fluffy white robe on the back of the bathroom door. She stepped out into the sitting room of her suite to find at least ten people all talking at the same time.

When they saw her, everybody shut up for about three seconds, then started talking again.

"Who told her to wash her hair?"

"I like her eyes. I think we can go bold with them."

"I want to see the dress before I even think about makeup."

"We should do an updo."

"Does she have jewelry we should consider?"

Like an orchestra conductor, Stella raised her hands, then made a chopping motion. "Everybody shut up." She turned to Kristen. "You…in the chair."

Kristen walked over to the salon chair that had materialized in her sitting room while she'd been sleeping, sat down and turned herself over to the professionals.

Almost two hours later, Stella helped her slip into the black gown. She fastened her sparkly white gold necklace, then gave her the earrings. When they were in place, she handed Kristen a box.

"This is a gift. From Dean. He doesn't like to make a big deal out of these things, but he appreciates your help tonight."

As she took the box, a weird feeling enveloped her. It was one thing to keep the gown she'd need to help pull off his charade. Quite another to take a gift.

"I can't accept this."

Stella sighed. "You have to. He wants you to wear it tonight." She held up her hand. "Wait." Racing to a table by the door, she picked up another box. "These first."

She opened the box to find long black dinner gloves. "Gloves?"

"It's white tie," Stella explained, helping Kristen pull on the elbow-length gloves. "Way more formal than black tie. When I realized we'd forgotten them, I called the boutique and had these delivered. Open the gift."

Silky black gloves fumbling with the lid, she opened the second box and gasped. Her gaze jumped to Stella. "I don't care if he wants me to wear this, I can't accept it."

Without missing a beat, Stella took the diamond bracelet out of the box and slid it over Kristen's left hand and onto the glove. Sparkling against the black silk, the bracelet nearly blinded Kristen.

Stella laughed. "See why he bought this for you? When he saw the dress and gloves this afternoon—"

"He was here?"

"He was busy calling brokers, but I texted pictures." She shook her head. "He approves everything. Every detail. Anyway, when he saw the gloves and realized all your other jewelry was just white gold, he insisted on the diamonds."

"I can't keep them."

Stella laughed. "It isn't a request. Or an option. The

bracelet is a necessary part of your outfit that becomes a thank-you gift. It's not my place to change that. If you don't want the bracelet, fight it out with Dean."

"I will."

Dean arrived in her hotel room at eight and Stella stepped back as if she were presenting Kristen as a completed project, not a person.

He took in the fancy upswept hairdo the stylist had given her, and then his gaze skimmed from the top of her dress to the tips of her toes. If another man had looked at her like that, she probably would have shivered, but his gaze was cool, efficient.

"She's perfect."

Stella beamed. "Of course she is." She grabbed her coat and purse. She said, "You two kids have fun," and then she left the hotel room.

Kristen sucked in a breath. "So I'm okay?"

"I already said you were perfect," he said, his voice businesslike and efficient. "Let's go."

Uneasiness wove through her. From his extremely chilly behavior, she had the odd sense that she'd done something wrong. But she hadn't. She'd agreed with everything he'd asked, including a stay in New York City that she hadn't planned on, a shopping trip and a Christmas party.

How could he be upset with her?

She picked up the black satin wrap that matched her gown and walked to the door with him. They rode down in the main elevator of the exclusive hotel in complete silence.

In the lobby, employees nodded and said, "Good evening, Mr. Suminski. Ms. Anderson," but other guests ignored them. They stepped outside into the cold December air and, glancing at her skimpy wrap, Dean rushed her into the limo.

She slid onto the seat. He slid on beside her. The limo pulled out into traffic.

The silence continued.

She peeked over at Dean who wore a black tux, white shirt, white vest and white bow tie. He looked clean and expensive and smelled divine. And for the first time it hit her that she was really on a date with him. One of the richest, most handsome men in the world.

The whole freaking world.

Her throat tightened. Her nerve endings buzzed. Right at that moment, sitting next to him, his money and social status took a backseat to his good looks. Never in a million years would a farm girl from Grennady ever date a guy like this. Not that the men in Grennady weren't handsome. But there was something about Dean Suminski that made her tingle. He was so pulled together and so smart, and those penetrating dark eyes of his were like onyx.

Of course he was also distant with her. Maybe not angry, but not exactly a guy who looked like he was on a date with a woman he liked. And it was her job to fool the world into thinking they were a couple. A happy couple.

She cleared her throat and said the first thing that came to mind. "So it really is white tie?"

He faced the window, clearly unhappy that he'd have to speak. "It's funny what rich people will think up to distinguish themselves."

"You're one of those rich people." She held up her arm, displaying the bracelet. Since he was angry anyway, they might as well settle this now. "By the way, I can't keep this."

He turned to her with a frown. "The bracelet?"

"Yes."

"Why not?"

"Because it's not right."

"You're helping me."

"We have a deal. Ten minutes after we shook hands, I signed the written agreement for *computers* in exchange for this date. No bracelet."

"The miracle of technology. I call my lawyer. He writes a simple, no-nonsense agreement, emails it to me and I print it. Everything goes at the speed of light these days."

She almost laughed at the way he tried to fool her. "Don't change the subject. As it is, we're equals. You start giving me bracelets and everything changes."

He tilted his head. "How so?"

"It makes our relationship personal. Plus, it's expensive. I don't need it—or want it."

When he only stared at her, she sighed. "Our deal should be professional. Things get messy when you mix personal things into business. I don't like messy."

He studied her face for a few seconds before he said, "It sounds like you've had a little experience in this."

She said nothing.

"If you want me to understand your point of view, you have to explain."

"I had a boyfriend who used me to get to the princess."

He studied her face again. "Taught you a lesson, huh?"

"And not a fun one." Actually, the idiot had broken her heart into a million pieces, made her feel like a fool and caused her to decide love wasn't for her. She would put her whole heart and soul into making Aasera's dream a reality because that had purpose and meaning. Love?

She wasn't sure it existed, except for a few lucky people like Princess Eva.

"He used me to get to my boss, and when I figured it out, he said he wanted to marry me." She shook her head. Though it had been years, it still hurt. "It was ridiculous how simple he thought I was. It taught me never, ever mix business with pleasure."

He said, "Humph. I learned that lesson the hard way too."

"You did?"

"It's why Prince Alex hates me and why I also have a very strict policy about not mixing business with pleasure."

"That should make tonight easier. I don't want anything from you beyond what we've already agreed to." She laughed lightly. "Except maybe a good time. I haven't been out in forever."

He nodded. The stern expression on his face softened. She swore he almost smiled.

"At the end of the evening, I'll take back the bracelet."

She said, "Good," but she got a weird feeling, as if there was some kind of subtext to everything he said, and she didn't have the code for it.

The inside of the car grew silent again. She wondered what had happened to him that he'd learned the lesson, especially since it involved Prince Alex. Had the prince approached him for a favor? Or used him? She couldn't picture Prince Alex using anybody. Ever. It didn't make sense.

She waited a minute, hoping Dean would resume the conversation and explain, but of course he didn't. Curiosity wouldn't let her brain rest. And the limo was so quiet. Too quiet.

"So what happened?"

He peered over at her. "Excuse me?"

"What happened? Who used you?"

"I don't talk about my private life."

"You might not, but knowing why Prince Alex dislikes you would really help me when I have to explain to the princess that I approached you."

His gaze swung to hers. She didn't know if it was surprise or annoyance she heard in his voice when he said, "Princess Eva didn't send you?"

She shook her head. "It just didn't seem right that you weren't on the list of companies to try to woo to our country. Grennady is desperate to bring jobs for young people. And here you were with this great company and nobody was showing you what we had to offer. I was trying to do something good. I didn't know Prince Alex doesn't like you. When Princess Eva finds out I approached you, I'm screwed."

"Maybe you shouldn't tell her."

She shook her head. "Not telling her would be a lie of omission. I can't be dishonest."

His eyes narrowed as he studied her face. "Which means you knew you'd be telling them eventually. So you probably had an explanation in mind. Why not use that?"

She shrugged. "My endgame was to be able to tell them you'd be visiting in January to consider our country as the new home for your company. And they'd be so happy that they'd be glad I took the risk."

"I'm not coming to your country."

"Well, I know that now. And I know that has something to do with your feud with Prince Alex—"

"It's not a feud. He doesn't like me."

"Well, that's just shocking, considering your sparkling personality and all."

He laughed. "As if Alex Sancho is better."

"He adores my princess. He works as hard as any employee in the palace. He's kind to the staff. So, yeah. He's a good guy."

Dean sniffed. "He might be the happiest prince in the world now, but he wasn't always a good guy."

"I know that at one time he was sort of a playboy, gambler. I'm guessing the same is true with you. That you weren't always this dry and stuffy. I'm guessing that whatever happened between you and Alex, it happened when you were young—" she sneaked a peek at him "—and foolish."

He grimaced. "I was foolish, all right."

She groaned. "Tell me, so I know how to apologize to the princess and her husband for overstepping."

"Just say you're sorry."

"Please."

"No."

CHAPTER FOUR

THE NOTE OF finality in Dean's voice told Kristen the conversation was over. To seal the deal, his phone rang.

Miffed that he always got his way, she turned her gaze to the window. New York City was a sort of blur as the limo sped down the street, then they stopped at a traffic light. Not only could she see the lights and tinsel, ornaments and pine branches that decorated streetlamps and buildings, but the city itself was huge and modern.

She'd noticed that on her shopping trip that afternoon, but New York City was such a far cry from Grennady that it once again stole her breath. The crazy feeling that she was in over her head tried to sneak in and ruin her confidence, but she wouldn't let it. She might not be experienced, but she was educated.

And she had a goal to make Aasera's wish a reality. She would have to be tough enough that one city or one guy's opinion wouldn't shake her. She also had to be able to face the princess and her husband on her own, to apologize to Alex for doing something he hadn't wanted done.

She straightened her shoulders, sat taller in the limo seat. She could not—*would not*—fail because she let her confidence waver. She could do this.

When Dean finally hung up the phone, she didn't care what had happened between him and Prince Alex. Taking responsibility for this trip and responsibility for contacting the one person Alex hadn't wanted to be contacted was another step in her growth as a businessperson. Dean would probably call that lesson three, clean up your own messes.

Rather than endure the oppressive silence or let him think she was brooding because he wouldn't tell her why Alex hated him, she said, "The city's already decorated for Christmas."

"Yes. We seem to start earlier every year." He paused then said, "Have you never been to New York before?"

She turned from the window to face him. His serious dark eyes caught hers. The now familiar tingle skipped along her skin as they studied each other.

He was so gorgeous that it was hard to believe no woman had snapped him up. Of course his personality did leave a lot to be desired. He might be so handsome that she sometimes lost her breath when their eyes met. But he was a grouch. Her job tonight was to make him seem normal—maybe even likable. She had to remember that task and do it, not lose her breath or wish he was different.

"I haven't been very many places. Except for university, I've been a homebody."

"Yet you want to start a charity that would technically be global."

His tone wasn't demeaning, more like curious, so she answered honestly. "This thing that I did with you," she said, pointing from herself to him and then back again. "It was like the first step in getting myself out of my shell and into the real world."

"Ambitious."

She laughed, glad he was no longer grouchy, just his usual stiff and formal. "Most people wouldn't think a flight to Paris would turn into a trip to New York. You're giving me a crash course in how rich people operate."

"Glad I can be of service. I want to do as much for you as you're doing for me. The more professional we keep this and the more equitable our deal, the easier it will be to manage."

"Lesson number four?"

"No, that relates back to lesson two. Don't mix business and pleasure."

"Right."

He frowned. "What was lesson three?"

"Clean up your own messes. I figured it out myself. Your disagreement with Alex has no bearing on the fact that I went behind the backs of the royal family to meet with you. So I have to own up to it and apologize."

"Good point." He peered over at her. "So we're officially counting them now?"

"The lessons?"

He nodded.

She laughed. "Sure. Why not?"

"You do recognize that this evening is four or five hours of me introducing you to important people. Potential contacts. You'd do well to make a good first impression and remember names."

"I never have a problem making a good first impression."

He smiled a real smile. "I have no doubt about that."

Fissions of pleasure skipped up her spine. If he continued being nice like this, the physical thing she felt for him might morph into a total attraction. Especially since the way he kept gazing into her eyes told her he was attracted to her too.

The limo stopped. The driver opened the door for them. Dean got out, and reached in to assist Kristen. The warmth of his fingers closing around hers caused her chest to freeze. Tingles rained down on her like snowflakes.

He gave a soft tug that brought her out of the limo and almost into his arms. Their eyes met and held. They might not want to mix business with pleasure, but the electricity humming through her made her wonder what it would be like to be on a date with him for real.

Crazy. Weird. Odd.

Those things popped into her head first. He might be good-looking, but he was also a genius who spoke his mind, always thought he was right and always wanted his own way. Those traits didn't make a good boyfriend—or date.

She pulled back, as he pulled back. Almost as if they'd both taken those two seconds to ask the question, *What if they acted on their attraction?* and both decided against it.

Dean put his hand on her elbow and turned her toward the hotel. They walked into the stately lobby and were directed to the elevator that would take them to the ballroom several floors up. When the doors closed, he immediately took his hand off her elbow and stuffed it in his pocket.

Those few seconds after he'd helped her out of the limo, when they'd stood face-to-face, a mere fraction of an inch apart, his whole body had tensed with wanting her, and he'd suddenly seen that his gut wasn't telling him she was somehow important. It was telling him he was a lot more attracted to her than he'd thought. Not because her eyes were pretty or because she had a long sloping back that led to the most perfect butt he'd ever seen. He *liked* her. *Her*.

She'd had hutzpah enough to question him about the situation with Alex. She'd easily confessed her fear about how she would explain approaching him to her boss. Then she'd admitted it was her own mess, and she'd clean it up.

He couldn't remember the last time anybody was so honest with him. So open. And the fact that he liked it confused him. He was a need-to-know person, who lived in a need-to-know world. Yet hearing about her, her background, her situation, pleased him.

Even so, starting something with her was wrong. He did not do relationships. Especially not with innocent women. So he stopped the pleasant hum buzzing through him.

The elevator door opened and her gasp of joy took his gaze to her face. Her green eyes sparkled. Her lush lips lifted into a glorious smile.

"It's so pretty."

To him the decorations were fairly standard. Evergreen branches outlined the arch doorway that led to the ballroom where white poinsettias in short fat fishbowls sat as centerpieces on round tables covered with red linen tablecloths. Crystal glasses sparkled in candlelight. White lights twinkled overhead like stars.

Putting his hand at the small of her back, Dean nudged her out of the elevator. "It's about normal." He frowned. "Your princess must take you nowhere."

"I'm a background person. But I'm changing that.

And I appreciate this opportunity to step out of my comfort zone."

There was that honesty again. So pure and so simple, it almost made him relax. But that was absurd. Not only was getting involved with this woman out of his life plan, but also his company was in trouble. Instead of constantly being drawn into wondering about unwanted feelings, he needed to use this time to assure people that he wasn't out of touch. He was in control.

"Dean!"

Dean and Kristen turned toward the sound of the booming voice owned by George Perkins, the party's host. A tall, striking man, with snow-white hair and probing blue eyes, he held out his hand to Dean. "So glad you could come."

Dean said, "The pleasure is mine, George. Thank you for inviting me." He smiled at George's wife, who stood beside him. Petite and pretty, Lorraine glowed with happiness.

"Good evening, Lorraine." Then he turned to Kristen. "Kristen, these are George and Lorraine Perkins, our hosts for the evening." He faced their hosts and said, "This is my guest, Kristen Anderson."

Kristen shook hands with George and Lorraine. "The decorations are wonderful."

Lorraine brightened even more. Toying with the extravagant diamond necklace at her throat, she said, "Thank you. It's always a debate. Simple and elegant or over-the-top. This year I went with simple and elegant."

Kristen said, "Everything looks perfect."

A middle-aged couple walked up behind them and Dean took Kristen's elbow. "We'll see you inside," he said to George and Lorraine, as he guided Kristen into the ballroom.

"You should have told Lorraine you liked her necklace."

Dean stopped. "What?"

"Lorraine kept playing with her necklace. She clearly loves it. Noticing it would have pleased her."

Dean laughed. "Really? You want a guy to notice a necklace?"

"It couldn't hurt. Women love compliments. Plus, George probably bought it for her. Noticing would have made him happy too."

"Are you trying to tell me how to behave?"

"Sort of."

"Well, stop. I know what works for me in social situations and what doesn't."

"I think Jason disagrees with you."

He grabbed two flutes of champagne from a passing waiter. "Jason worries like an old woman."

"Maybe. But you must have agreed on some level or another or I wouldn't be here."

"You're here for appearances."

"Right. You want me to look normal, so you'll look normal." She tapped her index finger on her chin. "Hmm. That actually makes my case, doesn't it?"

He sighed. Though her logic was a bit twisted, she was correct. Jason wanted him to appear happy and she was happy. "Just don't say or do anything I'll regret."

"Fine. But if I'm supposed to be myself, I'm being myself."

She accepted the champagne from him and gazed around. Dean took the time she was preoccupied to study her dress, her fancy upswept hair. He almost told her she looked really pretty, but swallowed back the words. He already knew his attraction to her was stronger than he'd thought. Not complimenting her was part of his "don't tempt fate" policy.

He wondered what she'd think if he taught her that rule—don't tempt fate—and burst out laughing.

She pivoted to face him. "What?"

"I just thought of something when I looked at you."

Her face fell in dismay. "I look funny?"

He sobered. "No." The words *you're beautiful* almost popped out of his mouth, but he caught them again. "I told you, you're perfect. Stella did a perfect job." He quickly scanned the tables and said, "This way. My invitation says we're at table thirty-one."

As they searched for their table, they said hello to various couples and exchanged pleasantries. Dean introduced Kristen to everyone, but he didn't really pause long enough to talk with anyone, finally understanding Jason's strategy. He'd already called all the brokerage houses. He didn't need to say any more. What he needed to do was look calm and confident, happy to be out with a pretty girl.

When they paused to say hello to Mr. and Mrs. Norman Jenkins, Kristen said, "Mrs. Jenkins, your necklace is beautiful. Is it an heirloom?"

The tall, thin woman beamed. "Why, yes. It belonged to my grandmother."

"It's stunning." Kristen turned to Dean. "Isn't it?"

He stole a peek at her. It might be weird for him to compliment a necklace, but Kristen pulled it off easily and had also put him in a position where he could simply agree and probably look like a nice guy.

"Yes. It's beautiful."

Mrs. Jenkins caught Kristen's hand. "It's so kind of you to notice. These days everyone seems to be captivated by new and shiny." She pressed her hand over the brooch-like necklace, which—surrounded by untold carats of diamonds—sparkled like a bonfire. "I prefer old and familiar."

Norman Jenkins chuckled. "Which is why she's still married to me."

Kristen laughed. Dean smiled. Having Kristen with him really did ease him more naturally into conversations, especially since he'd realized he shouldn't talk about business.

The Jenkinses walked away happy, and Dean let Kristen take the lead in all their chats, and allowed her to compliment to her heart's delight. He drank his champagne and took another glass for himself and Kristen. He even found himself laughing once or twice.

Right before dinner, the Kauffmans sidled up to them. A bubbly young couple who owned a PR firm that Suminski Stuff had used a time or two, and who had just had their first child, Pete and Belinda were more his age than most of the attendees.

After Dean introduced Kristen, she said, "We'd love to see a picture of your son. Wouldn't we, Dean?"

Trusting her, he said, "Sure."

The Kauffmans whipped out their phones. Belinda was the first to get her pictures up for viewing, and she handed her phone to Dean. On the screen was the oddest face he had ever seen. Bald head, bugging eyes, spit bubbles in the corners of the little boy's lips.

He honestly wanted to say something nice but his tongue stuck to the roof of his mouth.

Kristen smoothly said, "Oh, he's adorable! Such big eyes!"

Following her lead, Dean said, "Yes, big eyes." But ten minutes later, when the new parents were finally out of earshot, he turned to Kristen. "You deserve some kind of an award for keeping a straight face while looking at that kid."

She laughed. "He was adorable."

"No. He wasn't."

"Sure he was. All babies are cute in their own way."

"If you say so."

"Oh, Dean, life isn't about symmetry or perfection. It's about what makes a person unique, and that little boy's eyes were spectacular."

He said, "I guess," but what she'd said made real sense. Not just because the baby with the big eyes and bald head did look happy, but because he'd met all kinds in his world. Superstitious programmers who had lucky T-shirts. Marketing people who wore the latest fashions, and accountants who were never out of their suits. It took all of them to make Suminski Stuff successful. In spite of her naïvety, Kristen Anderson was pretty smart.

Relaxing another notch, he motioned her in the direction of their table, but she didn't make a move to walk toward it. She peered at him. "You haven't spent a lot of time around kids, have you?"

"No. And I plan to keep it that way."

"Really? You don't want to have kids of your own someday?"

"I wouldn't know the first thing about being a father."

"I've heard it comes naturally."

He gestured again for her to walk. "Not when you didn't have one to be an example."

Her face filled with sympathy. Apology filled her green eyes. "I'm so sorry. I forgot your parents were killed."

"It's fine."

She shook her head. "No. It's not fine. I should have thought that through before I made such a careless comment."

"Don't worry about it. It's hard to remember every little detail of somebody's bio."

"But that's an important one."

"Not really. I'm over it."

She held his gaze, her sympathetic eyes sending an odd feeling through him, a knowing that if he'd talk about this with her she'd understand.

"You're not over it or you wouldn't be so sure you don't want to have kids."

He laughed to ease the pressure of the knot in his chest, the one that nudged him to say something honest when he couldn't be honest. He'd never told anyone anything but the bare-bones facts of his childhood. And one woman with pretty eyes—no matter how much she seemed to be able to get him to relax—wouldn't change that.

He stuck with the rhetoric that had served him well for the ten years he'd guided Suminski Stuff. "Being over it has little to do with the decision not to have kids. I don't just lack parenting skills, I also have an unusual job. In the past twenty-four hours I've been in two countries, crossed an ocean. There's no place in my life for a wife, let alone kids."

She caught his gaze and gave him the most puzzling look for about ten seconds, and then she finally said, "You know, that just makes you all the more a challenge."

"A challenge?"

"Sure." Her smile broadened, a bubble of laughter escaped. "Every woman wants to be the one who tames the confirmed bachelor and turns him into a family man."

She said it in jest. Her laugh clearly indicated she was teasing. But he could picture them in the master bedroom of his Albany estate, white curtains billowing in the breeze from open French doors. White comforter on a king-size bed. Her leaning on pillows plumped against a tufted headboard. Holding a baby.

His baby.

He shook his head to clear it of the totally absurd thought.

She pointed to a discreet sign on a table only a few feet away. She said, "Thirty-one," and started moving toward it.

He breathed a sigh of relief. Not that the vision was gone, but also that she'd finally started walking. They reached their seats and he pulled out her chair for her.

She sat. "I want lots of kids."

He sat beside her. The discussion might not have changed, but it had shifted off him and to her. That he could handle. "While you're globe-trotting for your schools?"

"There are ways around that. Like nannies. And my mom." She laughed. "I don't have a doubt that she'll be a hands-on grandmother."

His breath stalled as a memory of his own grandmother popped into his head. If she'd been "hands-on" it had been with her palm to his bottom when she'd decided that he'd misbehaved.

He rose and shook hands when another couple arrived at their table, working to bring himself back from the memory of his grandmother paddling him for spilling milk when he was five or asking for a baseball mitt when he was seven.

But as he frantically struggled to block his bleak, solitary childhood from his brain, Kristen said, "I can't imagine not having my own family. I mean, I love my parents and all, but I want a crack at being a mom. Teaching someone everything I know."

An empty feeling filled him and on its heels came an envy so strong it was a battle not to close his eyes. She must have had a wonderful childhood. But being jealous was stupid, pointless. He'd gotten over his hollow beginnings years ago. Being lonely had forced him to entertain himself, and that ultimately had made him rich. He was pragmatic about his past. So, it shouldn't make him feel bad that his childhood had been crap. Just as it shouldn't make him jealous that Kristen was so confident in her decision to have kids. Or make him wonder how much fun the family she intended to create would be.

Dinner was served, a very untraditional meal of steak and vegetables. To his surprise, Kristen ate with gusto. While the wives of his counterparts pushed their food around their plates, Kristen ate every bite of her steak and was on the edge of her seat waiting for dessert. Crème brûlée.

Then he realized they hadn't fed her all day. He'd had a sandwich and fries delivered to his office as he'd made all his calls to brokers, but he'd forgotten to tell Stella that Kristen hadn't eaten. And skinny Stella was known to skip meals.

He leaned over and whispered, "I'm sorry we forgot lunch."

Her head tilted as she smiled. "I slept the day away. I was fine."

Her pretty face made his breath stutter again. Her smooth, pink skin glowed in the candlelight. Her genuine smile warmed him. She wasn't faking having a good time.

And hadn't she said she needed a good time?

Ignoring the odd happiness that filled him when he realized he'd done something to please her, he motioned to her plate. "You were obviously starving."

She frowned. "You think I was starving because I ate all my steak?" She burst out laughing. "I eat like that all the time."

Her laugh made him laugh. Muscles he hadn't even realized were knotted untangled. She really was the most honest, most open person he'd ever met. He might feel the need to fight all the crazy feelings she inspired, but he simply could not help relaxing around her.

Gina McMurray, wife of Tim McMurray, leaned across the table. "I didn't mean to eavesdrop but, oh, my God, I would love to eat like that."

Sherri Johnson said, "Me too. I can't, though. I'd blow up like a cow. What's your secret?"

Kristen said, "Good metabolism probably. But my parents own a dairy farm. I still do my fair share of the chores."

Sherri nodded. "When I ran around after my kids, I didn't have to worry about weight, either."

Gina said, "I guess it's all about moving."

As the women chatted, Dean glanced over at Kristen and let her work her magic. He now trusted her enough not to worry about what she'd say or how she'd say it. He liked hearing her tell their tablemates about her life.

She was *interesting.* She worked for a princess, lived on a farm very different from anything he'd ever experienced and had a degree that she intended to use to start a charity that built schools. While she did all that, she wanted to have kids, and teach them to be citizens of the world.

It was no wonder he liked her.

She was amazing.

George Perkins walked on stage and took the microphone. He wished everybody a merry Christmas and announced the dancing would begin. All the men at his table asked their wives to dance and Dean knew it would look odd if he and Kristen didn't join them on the floor.

He rose and held out his hand. "Shall we?"

She smiled. "I'd love to."

He led her to the dance floor and took her into his arms, where she fit perfectly. She was the right height for him. She was pretty. She had just enough sophistication that it didn't impinge on her natural, innocent charm. She ate when she was hungry. She wanted to have kids. She wanted to change the world.

All his crazy feelings around her came into focus, and he nearly stopped dancing. She wasn't just amazing. She was the perfect woman for him. *Of course he was attracted to her. Of course he wanted her.*

If there was such a thing as the woman of his dreams, it was Kristen.

Happiness mixed with a knowing that expanded his chest with a fierce need to kiss her, and his heart with a longing to keep her—to never let her out of his sight—that he'd never felt before.

It also explained the unwanted vision of her with his child, the way he could relax with her and why he couldn't stop staring at her face.

Some crazy, romantic part of himself wanted a future with her.

But it was all for nothing.

Not only did he have a really crappy upbringing that meant he had no idea what a real family looked like, no idea how to be a husband or a father, but there was also the matter of why Alex Sancho hated him.

If that wasn't enough to make him all wrong for her, he had a one-track mind. His company. Even if she found him as attractive and interesting as he found her, she should run like the wind away from him.

Once she got to know him, she probably would.

He stepped back, sliding his hands down her arms until he could take her hands. "I'm suddenly very, very tired. Let's go back to the table."

Her eyes sought his as her lush mouth, her perfect, oh-so-kissable mouth twisted in confusion. "We aren't going to mingle?"

He once again used pragmatism to overcome her questions.

"I might mingle later. I'm not sure. Jason just wanted me to put in an appearance. I think we've done more than that."

Before she could say anything, Dean caught her hand and began to maneuver through the crowd, toward their table, pulling her with him. Regret wobbled through him, but he wondered why. This was his life. And he was essentially happy with it. He was a rich man, doing work he loved. He wouldn't feel bad that he was attracted to a woman he couldn't have. He had many, many things to be grateful for.

They didn't quite get to their seats before Winslow and

Julia Osmond, who owned one of the biggest brokerage houses in New York, ambled up to him.

"I see your stock is hanging tough."

"Thanks to you," Dean agreed. He'd had a good chat with Winslow that afternoon. Even though he'd created an informal "no talking about business" rule for this party, this was a chance to reinforce what he'd said.

Kristen tapped his arm. "I thought we agreed no shop-talk tonight."

The gesture was sweet, familiar, and longing whispered through Dean again. Longing for a life, a relationship, things he'd never wanted before. It was confusing. Frustrating. Ridiculous.

Winslow Osmond said, "I got the same lecture." He smiled at Kristen. "Where did you two meet?"

"Paris."

Julia Osmond said, "Oh, how romantic."

Kristen laughed. "Somewhat romantic. We actually find ourselves on opposite ends of a business thing. I work for Princess Eva Latvia of Grennady."

Julia caught her arm. "Oh, darling! Didn't she just marry that gorgeous prince from Xaviera?"

"Yes. Alexandros Sancho. They're in Xaviera right now at the end of a vacation celebrating American Thanksgiving. Alex's brother Dom is married to an American and his dad married Princess Ginny's mom, Rose."

Winslow laughed. "Now, that's going to be a compli-cated family tree." He faced Dean. "What business does your company have with Grennady?"

Dean's gaze slowly meandered to Kristen, then back to Winslow. When in doubt, go with the truth. If he and Kristen were alone, that would be lesson five.

"Kristen would like me to consider relocating my company there. Unfortunately, I'm not in a position to even consider it."

"Why not?"

Dean sort of laughed. "We are in a bit of a hurry to get that series of games ironed out. As I told you in our phone call today, I *will* be beta testing the new version by mid-January. I'm not going to disrupt people who are already stalled."

Winslow glanced at his glass of whiskey, then back at Dean. "You've never considered that a change of scenery might do them good?"

When Dean frowned, Winslow said, "Maybe their creativity would return if you sent them to a country that's known for fresh air and fresh snow. Somewhere they can get outside and do something physical that will revitalize them. Grennady sounds like the perfect choice to me."

"Where are your offices?" Julia asked.

"Manhattan," Winslow answered for Dean. "His employees fight to get into the city, then they're in a high pressure situation trying to fix or finish a product that's obviously in trouble, then they fight to get back home." He caught Dean's gaze. "No rest for these guys and gals."

Dean recognized a criticism when he got one, but he smiled at Winslow. "That's certainly an interesting observation."

"That's not an observation. It's a fact." Winslow clasped Dean's shoulder. "You know what? A few of my associates and I are having lunch tomorrow. It's our little Christmas celebration. I'd love to have you and Kristen join us."

"Oh, well…" Dean fumbled for an excuse, but his

mind went blank. He couldn't ask Kristen to stay another day, could he?

"Oh, come on. You want to miss the chance to talk to CEOs for some of the biggest companies in the city?" Winslow winked at Kristen. "If nothing else, you should want to show Kristen off."

Kristen laughed. "It sounds fun."

Considering Kristen's response approval of a sort and not wanting to miss the opportunity, Dean said, "Have your staff send me the restaurant name and time."

Osmond slapped him on the back. "You bet."

As he and his wife walked away, Dean turned to Kristen. "If you only answered that way to be polite, I can show up alone. It's not a big deal."

But Kristen glanced behind her, watching Winslow and his wife mingle into the crowd. "He's pretty influential?"

"He is the definition of *influential*. If you look in the dictionary, his picture would be beside the word *influential*."

"Then we should go."

"Seriously? You don't mind staying in New York another day?"

She laughed lightly. "Tomorrow's Saturday. It's fine." She frowned. "Except." She looked up and into his eyes again. "Will I be able to wear the black pants and white blouse I flew over in?"

Regret surged through him that he'd put her in an uncomfortable position. Luckily, he could fix it. "We'll get you new clothes."

"Stella?"

"No, this time I'll take you. We'll have breakfast, then go back to the boutique where you got this gown."

"Okay."

She was such a good sport that he almost felt guilty taking advantage of her. Except he needed her. And she *was* a good sport. "I swear tomorrow at three you'll be on your way to the airport, and in the air headed for Grennady by five."

But the assurance that he'd get her home the next day didn't stop the nagging feeling in the pit of his stomach.

Their deal wasn't balanced now, and he hated owing someone.

CHAPTER FIVE

THE NEXT MORNING, Kristen woke, showered and dressed in her simple white blouse and black pants. She'd carefully hung them the day before so they weren't wrinkled, but this was day two of wearing the same clothes, and she had to wear these home. She might have to rinse out her blouse when she returned.

As she stepped into the sitting room of her suite, her hotel phone rang.

Confused, she picked it up and cautiously said, "Hello?"

"It's Dean. I'm in the hotel dining room. I've ordered coffee. Come down when you're ready."

The sound of his voice made her heart light, but she squelched the silly feeling that had started the night before by reminding herself that she'd fallen desperately in love with Brad, a man who had also used her. She'd ended up hurt and disillusioned. Just because Dean was coming right out and telling her he was using her, it only made him marginally better than Brad. Or maybe not better. More like honest. Especially since the way he'd pulled away from her on the dance floor had all but proven she was safe with him. A man who didn't want to touch her didn't want to get involved with her.

And she shouldn't want to get involved with anybody,

either. Especially not such a difficult man. She was about to embark on the journey of a lifetime. Beginning an international charity, something with the potential to change the world, would be all-consuming. She didn't have time for a romance until her schools were off the ground.

She took the elevator to the lobby, found the restaurant and walked to the table where Dean sat. He rose and her stomach fell to the floor.

Wearing jeans and a comfortable olive green sweater, he barely resembled the angry man she'd met the morning before in Paris. He looked young, approachable. And if the smile on his face was any indicator, he was very happy to see her.

The joyful feeling bubbled up in her again, the sense that there was nowhere she'd rather be than with him. Because it was true. He was so handsome in that sweater and jeans. And he looked happy...

How was she supposed to resist that?

He pulled out her chair. "I hope you slept well."

"Since I'd napped all yesterday afternoon, I was glad to have had a few glasses of champagne to make me drowsy."

A waiter walked over and poured Kristen a cup of coffee from the carafe already on the table.

Dean said, "I'll have the bacon and eggs breakfast." He faced her with another smile. "Kristen?"

She could barely say, "I'll have the same." Her heart did a crazy dance in her chest every time he smiled at her. She tried reminding herself of Brad, but it didn't help. With Dean's face a study in happiness and her attraction to him tapping on her shoulder, the giddy feeling rolling through her wouldn't let anything negative in.

As the waiter walked away, happy Dean faced her again. "I realized last night that your attending another event with me warrants another agreement." He pulled a document from beside his plate. "This is a second agreement that takes the place of the one we signed yesterday. Instead of a hundred thousand dollars' worth of computers, it's now two hundred thousand."

Her eyes bulged. "Two hundred thousand dollars' worth of computers?"

As she took the agreement from his hands, she realized *this* was why he was so happy. He wasn't smiling because of her. He wasn't happy to see her. He was happy that their deal wasn't lopsided. By giving her more computers, he was no longer accepting a favor. They were even.

All the crazy feelings rumbling around inside her stopped instantly.

She glanced up at him. "You don't like owing people, do you?"

His head tilted. "Because I'm continuing our arrangement?"

"Because you won't let me do you a favor."

He shrugged. "This relates more to the 'don't mix business with pleasure' rule."

"Nope. I think we've entered new rule territory. You don't like anyone doing anything for you."

He fiddled with his linen napkin. "Good business people keep things balanced. The revised agreement is simply a way to do that."

"Sure it is." She paused for a moment as the waiter brought their bacon and eggs, then said, "And what about the clothes you're buying me?" She caught his gaze. "And the bracelet you didn't take back last night. If you want everything even and balanced, then I'm going to have to pay you for the clothes. And God only knows what I'll owe you for the bracelet."

He shook his head. "The clothes and bracelet are the cost of doing business."

She scrunched her face. "What cost of doing business?"

"You are here at my request. You cannot wear the same clothes every day. Hence, it's my responsibility to clothe you."

"You are a piece of work."

He frowned. "Because I like to keep things balanced?"

"Whatever you call it. It's kind of weird. And don't think I'm not noticing that you always have to win arguments."

"I win because I'm right."

She picked up her fork and began eating, deciding she wasn't even going to try to debate that. But after the first delectable bite of toast, for some odd reason or another she pictured him as a child, a genius in an elementary school filled with ordinary kids, and she laughed.

"I'll bet that attitude worked out really well on the playground."

He shook his head. "It didn't. That's how I met Jason. When things would turn ugly, he would race over and run interference before somebody decked me or before I hit someone. He was also smart enough to direct me to a few YouTube videos that taught me how to fight." He smiled again. "I got pretty good."

And how was she supposed to not laugh at that? "How long were you in public school?"

He chewed a bite of toast, obviously pondering that. "Every year until somebody finally figured out I might be a genius. At thirteen, I took a test that proved it and instantly got offers for scholarships for university. I spent one year at MIT and in the end decided that wasn't for me."

He'd *discarded* the Massachusetts Institute of Technology? "Seriously?"

"The thing was, I already knew everything I needed to know about computers. As a kid, I'd bought a few books, torn apart a few motherboards and I was up to speed. But I didn't know anything about business." He shrugged. "So that's what I studied. I knew I wanted to work in this field, but not as a grunt. I wanted to own the company. So I needed to study how to run one."

And he'd figured all this out at fourteen. "Smart."

He laughed. "Exactly."

She let that settle in for a second, her mind wrapping around the double meaning and not able to let it go. "Did you just make a joke?"

"I guess I did."

And he seemed genuinely surprised. Which was equal parts of cute and breath-stealing. She'd seen him relaxing with her the night before. She'd noticed him staring at her as if he couldn't look away. He was every bit as attracted to her as she was to him. And he wasn't after money, or an introduction to the princess. If anything, he *didn't* want to meet her royal family. He needed her to pretend to be his girlfriend and if anything he was more than honest about it.

It was getting harder and harder to see him as someone like Brad. And harder and harder not to see how he relaxed around her, how he talked to her, how they clicked.

They finished their breakfast and walked outside into

the sunny December morning, where his limo awaited. In a few minutes, they were back at the boutique, where Jennifer, the store manager from the day before, happily greeted them. Kristen hadn't seen the price of her gown yesterday afternoon, but she guessed that if Jennifer got a commission, it had been a hefty one.

"Good morning!"

Dean said, "Good morning. We're going to an important lunch in a few hours, but our trip was so unexpected that Kristen didn't have time to pack. So we'd like to see everything she'll require for an upscale lunch."

Jennifer all but bowed. "Of course."

Dean shoved his hands in the pockets of his black leather jacket. "I was thinking in terms of something like a suit."

Kristen balked. "A suit? What am I? Seventy?"

"A suit is appropriate," Dean said, glancing around at the various styles of clothes they offered.

"A sweater dress can be just as appropriate."

"It's a business lunch," Dean argued.

"Not really. It's a Christmas lunch with friends or a bunch of guys you hope to make your friends," Kristen countered, deciding this was one argument he was not winning. "And besides, I'm not a part of your business." She almost said, "I'm supposed to be your girlfriend," but she caught the way Jennifer was looking at them, her wide eyes speaking of her curiosity. So, she smiled and said, "I'm your girlfriend."

Dean's expression shifted from determined to confused.

But Jennifer seemed to love that tidbit. "This explains so much about yesterday," she said enthusiastically. She faced Dean. "From the things she chose while she was with Stella, I know that you can trust her taste." She turned to Kristen. "And I agree with you. The right sweater dress will be more than appropriate."

She motioned to the dressing room. "Give me two seconds to pull my three favorites."

Dean scowled.

But as Jennifer walked away, Kristen laughed. "Who would you rather do business with? Someone who cowers or someone who knows what she's doing?"

He sighed and brushed his hand in the direction of the curtained-off changing area. "Just go get ready to try on the dresses."

She slipped into the mirrored room and removed her pants and shirt. Jennifer stepped in holding three sweater dresses.

"The red," she said, hanging it on the first hook, "Because I think you'll look beautiful in it. Blue because it's a little more sedate for Grumpy Pants out there. And black because I know his type. He'll pick the black because he doesn't want anyone looking at you."

Kristen's face flushed with color. "He's really not possessive."

"Oh, honey, they're all possessive. But if you don't believe me. Start with the red, give him the heart attack he wants to have, move on to the blue and go to the black. He'll pick the black."

Doing as she had been told, Kristen slipped into the red dress. The soft knit clung to her curves, but not obnoxiously. It just looked like a pretty dress.

When she stepped out of the dressing room, Dean's back was to her. She said, "Here's dress one," and he turned around.

* * *

Seeing Kristen in the red dress, Dean swore his heart exploded. It nicely cruised her curves but not indecently. It was a pretty dress that complimented a gorgeous figure. And it came to her knees. There was nothing to be upset about.

But blonde, green-eyed Kristen was certainly heart-stopping in the striking red dress. Then he realized it wasn't the dress. It was Kristen. In anything other than black pants and a white shirt, she was going to be a knockout.

He tried to say something, but his tongue was stuck to the roof of his mouth.

Jennifer laughed. "Let's try the blue one."

She shooed Kristen into the curtained off room and in a few minutes Kristen returned in the blue knit dress.

"Wow." Okay. He'd tried to stop that but couldn't. The blue dress somehow highlighted the pale green color of her eyes and made her look spectacular. "That's…" He cleared his throat. "Very pretty."

Jennifer smiled. "Okay. On to dress three."

This time, Kristen emerged in a black dress. It looked simple and elegant. Yes, it still accented the same perfect figure, but not quite so enthusiastically.

"I like this one."

Jennifer laughed, but Kristen said, "I like the red!" Her eyes narrowed. "And you liked the red too."

He sucked in a breath. He'd been struck speechless by the red. She'd have had to be blind not to see that. "I did."

"Then why are we picking the black one?"

"Because I don't want Winslow or his friends to have a stroke."

She sighed. "Okay. You know what? I'm going to buy

the red one for myself." She picked up the tag from the sleeve, glanced at the price and her mouth fell open. "Or not. I don't think my parents paid this much for our last cow."

A laugh burst from Dean. "If you really want the red one, I'll buy the red one too. But I'm asking nicely for you to wear the black one to the lunch."

"I can't let you buy the red one," she mumbled, turning to walk into the dressing room again.

"Well, you're going to need something to fly home in. You can't wear those black pants and white shirt again."

The curtain flew closed in a resounding swish. She was mad.

She was mad?

Why?

He approached the closed curtains and called out, "I'm happy to buy the red dress."

"Just stop." The order came from behind the curtain. "I have plenty of clothes at home. I don't need the red dress and before you get to harping about what I'm wearing home, I am not going to let you pay God knows what for a pair of blue jeans."

Ignoring her, Dean motioned to Jennifer to get a pair of jeans, knowing she'd have Kristen's size from choosing the dresses that day and the gown the day before. Then he pointed at the sweaters.

When she returned, he whispered, "Add shoes or boots and socks...whatever else she's going to need to stay this extra day."

Jennifer disappeared into the racks as Kristen walked out. Her chin high, she headed toward the cash register. "I do not want the red dress."

He said, "Fine."

She stopped, faced him. "You're losing an argument?"

"No. I'm simply not arguing over something stupid. I was happy to buy you the dress as a thank-you."

"Wouldn't we have to draw up another agreement for that?"

He sighed. "I'm not that bad."

"No. But for a guy who talks about balance you certainly don't see my side of the story."

"And what side is that?"

"That I don't want to take gifts. I have some pride. And I have a job. I can afford to buy my own clothes. I just can't afford to buy them in this shop."

"Okay."

Her eyebrows rose. "You're losing another argument?"

He shook his head. "No. I'm doing what you told me to do. I'm seeing your side of things."

"Good."

"Good."

He directed her to walk to the checkout, where Jen stood beaming. He guessed she worked on commission.

She scanned the tag on the black knit dress and a black wool coat. "I noticed that your coat is hip length and to wear a dress you'll need a longer one." She smiled hopefully. "I picked the most useful, inexpensive coat we have."

Kristen nodded.

Jennifer scanned the tag of a pair of black stilettoes. She looked up at Kristen. "I remembered your shoe size from yesterday. The shoes you wore under the gown had such a small heel. I think you'll need these."

This time Kristen sighed.

Dean quietly said, "I don't know a lot about women's

shoes but we've trusted Jennifer so far. If she says you need the shoes, you probably need the shoes."

Kristen rolled her eyes.

Jennifer shoved the shoes into a shopping bag, then picked up a pair of jeans and a bright red sweater.

"I hope those are for Stella."

He cleared his throat. "You know you need something to fly home in."

She eyed the red sweater.

Dean saw the flicker of longing that sparked in her eyes before she could bank it, and he said a word he didn't often say. "Please." What was the point of having money if he couldn't spend it to make someone happy?

She faced him. "It's not a gift? It's not you saying thank you to me? It's a necessity?"

He nodded. "Absolutely. Unless you want to wash out your blouse in the sink of your hotel room."

"I'd considered it."

"And it would dry wrinkled."

She drew in a breath. "Okay. I do feel a little slimy in these clothes."

"Good. I mean, not good that you're slimy. Because you don't look slimy. Good that you can get a shower and fly home refreshed."

Kristen rolled her eyes and looked away.

A strange relief poured through him, followed by something he almost didn't recognize. Pride. She'd really wanted that sweater and he'd bought it for her. It gave him the most amazingly wonderful feeling.

As Jennifer lifted the sweater and jeans off the counter and slid them into the bag, a black lace bra and panties revealed themselves.

The store clerk winced. "You did say to get everything she needed."

His heart kicked against his ribs. He could see tall, slender, nicely endowed Kristen in the black bra and panties…and the black stilettos. He tried to say, "Maybe another color would be better," but it came out, "Navy anubber color would 'e 'etter."

Kristen looked at him through her peripheral vision. "You don't like black?"

Good God, he loved the black. But he realized that he'd have to sit through an entire lunch with several influential people, knowing she had black lace panties and bra under that dress.

He tugged at the collar of his sweater, but said, "Get whatever color you want."

She faced Jennifer. "I'll keep the black."

He had his chauffeur drive them to her hotel and carried her bags up to her suite for her. She opened the door with her key card and let him enter first.

"Where do you want these?"

"The chair will do."

He set the bags on the chair and headed for the door. "I'll be back in about two hours."

She nodded and he left breathing a long sigh of relief. He would go to his penthouse, take a cold shower and return a calm man, who would not, absolutely would not, remember the sexy black lace panties and bra she'd have under that sedate dress.

CHAPTER SIX

DEAN WAS QUIET when he picked Kristen up at her hotel room at noon. The drive to the restaurant was also quiet, and Kristen was glad. It wasn't that she was angry about him buying her clothes. It was that he was so flippant about doing everything he wanted, but anything she did had to be part of an agreement.

When they walked into the restaurant, Dean didn't even say his name. The maître d' smiled and waved him forward, leading them to a private room in the back. Decorated for the holiday with evergreen branches bathed in white twinkle lights and a sophisticated poinsettia centerpiece on the large round table, the warm space welcomed them.

As Winslow had said, the group was small. Eight men in dark suits like Dean's. Eight women in everything from elegant skirts and jackets to slimming sheaths. In her black knit dress, Kristen fit in as if she belonged there.

But she didn't. She and Dean entered to a conversation about European vacations, and Kristen suddenly felt like a bumpkin. She was twenty-four, the executive assistant to a princess, who did have a degree, and who wanted to start a foundation that would build schools—but who knew no one. She'd been nowhere…

Well, except to Paris, where she'd picked up with this gorgeous, crazy, somewhat obsessive-compulsive guy, and was now pretending to be his date.

As Dean made introductions, she smiled and said, "It's a pleasure to meet you all," reminding herself that this was part of her new reality. She had to learn to schmooze prospective donors, speak intelligently about her cause and find support.

Dean pulled out her chair and she sat. He sat beside her.

Mrs. Arthur Flannigan, a woman who looked to be in her eighties, leaned across the table. "Julia tells me you work for Princess Eva of Grennady."

"Yes, I'm her executive assistant."

"Sounds exciting."

Kristen laughed nervously. Everybody assumed that because she worked for a woman who would someday be a queen, she had a fantastic job and glamorous life. But it was Eva who traveled while Kristen stayed behind and kept up with emails.

"Some days my work is exciting. Other days, it's just like any other assistant's job."

Dean slid his arm across the back of her chair. "Kristen is about to leave her post to begin organizing a charity that will build schools in third world countries."

Mrs. Flannigan's eyes lit. "Really? That's quite an undertaking."

"Having worked for a princess," Dean said, "she's up on world politics. She knows what she's getting into."

Kristen sat a little taller. Not only did it feel right to have his arm around her, but also he seemed genuinely proud of her. She might not travel, but she did know world politics. Working for Eva had taught her a lot. Now she just had to figure out how to use it.

"I hear your company is in a spot of trouble," Mrs. Flannigan said, changing the subject as she smiled at Dean.

He shrewdly returned her smile. "Nothing I can't handle."

Winslow leaned toward Mrs. Flannigan. "Kristen and Dean met because she flew to Paris to get time with him to persuade him to relocate Suminski Stuff to Grennady."

Mrs. Flannigan's face brightened. "Really? Well, my dear, you are quite the adventurer."

All the pride she'd felt fled as her chest tightened. No matter how much she'd seen working for Eva, she wasn't really an adventurer. She was a shy woman with a big goal, who milked cows and baled hay. And being in this room, with a small group of influential people, she suddenly wondered about her sanity. How the hell did she ever think she could start a charity that would change the world?

Dean's arm slid from the back of her chair to her shoulders. The reassuring feeling that she wasn't alone pumped air back into her lungs and restarted her breathing.

"She's not much of an adventurer, but she's got a heart of gold and I'm watching her grow more confident by the day. I have no doubt she can do this."

His belief in her revived her confidence. But she also realized this was the second time he'd spoken as if he knew her. Or at least knew things about her. The first time had been the day they'd met, on the plane, when he'd told Jason about her economics degree. He could

have looked that up. He could have also guessed she was
growing in confidence from the changes in the way she
dealt with him since she'd first approached him in Paris.
But her heart of gold? How would he know that?

They spent three hours with the business people and
their spouses. It had surprised Kristen to learn Mrs. Flannigan, not Arthur, was the owner of the brokerage firm
that didn't want to downgrade Dean's stock. They wanted
him to get his prototype to another round of beta testers
and roll it out, which was why Winslow had invited him
to this lunch.

The group had ideas for how Dean could jump-start
his staff's creativity. Winslow had even suggested that
Dean should consider temporarily moving the team to
Grennady, if only for the next six weeks or so, to get
them away from the daily grind and hopefully motivate
them. Especially since it would give him a chance to investigate a permanent move.

Kristen's ears had perked up at that, but Dean had
blown off the idea. By the time they got back into the
limo for the drive home, her head spun. First, she knew
Winslow's idea was a good one. Why not send the Suminski Stuff team to Grennady to finish the project?
Then she and Princess Eva would have tons of time to
persuade him to move there permanently. Except Dean
didn't like Prince Alex. Or, as Dean had said, Prince Alex
didn't like him. Second, she hadn't forgotten the way
he knew things about her and dropped facts at the oddest times. And while part of her itched to ask him about
that, her mission for her country was more important.

"You should move your people to Grennady for the
next six weeks. Let them celebrate Christmas on our

snow-covered ski slopes and get refreshed enough that they can finish your project."

"It will take more than ski slopes to get my people moving. Winslow was being optimistic when he suggested that."

"Or maybe he's right."

"You just want me in your country for six weeks so you can give me a hard sell."

She should have realized he would see right through that and winced. "Would it be so bad?"

"I already told you Alex hates me."

"Why?"

He caught her gaze and smiled. "Must be my sparkling personality."

He'd made another joke? She struggled not to gape at him.

"You're a nice guy." Even as the words came out of her mouth she knew she meant them. He was a nice guy. A good guy. A very, very smart guy. But a guy who was deep down, very nice. "Something happened between you and Alex."

When he didn't answer, she sighed. "You have a best friend that you've kept the whole way since middle school. You must have looked me up on the internet because you know things about me, and you remember them enough to get them into the right places in the conversation. That's not just smart, it's considerate. I'm thinking your reputation for being mean is highly exaggerated."

He peeked over at her again. "Or maybe you bring out the best in me."

In the silence of the limo, their gazes locked. Her heart stumbled in her chest. The warmth of connection flowed through her. Even as it filled her with wonder, it scared her to death. They were using each other. He was buying her things she didn't want. They were making friends under false pretenses. So why did they keep having these odd, intimate moments that felt honest?

Dean quietly said, "You did really well at that lunch. I sometimes see your confidence dip, but it shouldn't."

"And how would you know?"

"For starters, you have a natural poise. But I also talked to a few people. Everyone says you're full of energy and dedication." He frowned. "Though I have to admit I am curious about the cause you chose."

She said nothing, a little tired of the way he knew so much more about her than she knew about him.

"You're not going to share?"

"I'll tell you that story, if you tell me a story about you."

"Okay. Go ahead."

"Oh, no. I know this scam. I'll tell you how I chose my charity and suddenly the limo will be at the hotel and you'll stay Mr. Mysterious."

He laughed. "Mr. Mysterious?"

She shrugged. "That's how you look to me. If it isn't in your bio, I don't know it."

"All right. I'll go first. What do you want to know?"

"I want to know what happened between you and Alex."

He winced. "Right for the jugular. You couldn't settle for hearing the story of how I was a poor kid, raised by a grandmother who was too tired for another child, who got underwear for Christmas?"

She knew he'd meant to be funny, but once again she could hear the sadness in his voice and picture him as

a little boy, alone, quiet. She was suddenly very grateful Jason had come into his life, and wished with all her
heart that he had other people in his life, so many that
he'd never be alone again.

"I can guess what you went through as a child." Her
gaze crawled over to meet his. "But it's hard for me to
understand how Prince Alex dislikes you when he loves
everybody."

"I tried to steal his girlfriend."

Kristen couldn't help it. She laughed. "That's not
enough to make him hate you."

"It's a much longer story." He took an exaggerated
breath. "He had a girlfriend, Nina, who was the daughter of a Saudi prince I was schmoozing for funding when
I first started out. Nina came into her dad's office one
day when I was there. She smiled at me, and the prince
thought this was a good opportunity to get his daughter away from Alex, who, at the time, was a gambler."

"Her dad wanted you to put a wedge between them?"

"Actually, her dad thought she and I were better suited
for each other. And though he didn't say the words, he
more or less tied his investing into my company to me
hanging around Nina, trying to steer her away from
Alex."

"That's awful."

"It isn't, when you remember that Alex wasn't a nice
guy. He was the spoiled prince of a filthy rich country.
He had access to more money than God and did what
he wanted, including take Nina for granted and ignore
her most days."

Though it was difficult to picture Alex that way, Kristen had to admit she'd heard those rumors.

"At first, I just started showing up at the places Nina

frequented. Bars. The marina. A club or two. Then she accepted a date." He cleared his throat. "I fell head over heels in love with her, but she was only using me to make Alex jealous. And it worked. He stopped gambling, started paying attention to her and proposed."

Kristen's heart sank, as little pieces of things began to fall together in her head. Not just about Dean being an inexperienced kid hanging around jet-setters, who now had a rule about not mixing business with pleasure, but also about Prince Alex. She remembered the princess telling her that Alex had had his heart broken when he was younger, when his fiancée had died.

The magnitude of the loss almost overwhelmed her and she whispered, "Nina died, didn't she?"

Dean quietly said, "In a boating accident after an argument with me. For a while Xaviera's royal guard investigated me, but I was nowhere near the dock or her boat. But I'd been with her that morning. She called me to have breakfast with her, to let me down easy, and she'd told me about the engagement, showed me the ring. I was flabbergasted and confused, and she admitted to using me. Young and stupid, I argued that she loved me, but she disabused me of that notion really quickly. She loved Alex. I had been a pawn. I felt like an idiot." He met her gaze. "I *was* an idiot. Then I heard she'd been killed driving her boat recklessly, and I fell into a depression so deep I thought I'd never come out. Not just because she was dead but because I was so crazy about her that I didn't see she was using me. It was humbling and humiliating because the story got around really quickly. I left Xaviera. Hell, I left Europe. I came back to New York, licking my wounds and vowed it would never happen again. None of it."

"I'm sorry."

He sniffed a laugh. "You had your wake-up call with the boyfriend who wanted an in with your princess, but mine was a lot costlier. A lot harder to handle. In some respects, I don't think you ever recover when someone so young dies."

"No, you don't. I'm starting the school project because of a friend who died. The schools were her dream."

He frowned. "Your schools are someone else's idea?"

She nodded. "Yes." The limo pulled up to the curb outside her hotel. Kristen continued anyway.

"Aasera lived in Iraq. Her brothers were educated but she wasn't. She begged them to teach her to read and write and they did. She said it opened up a whole new world for her and she decided that she wanted to create schools for girls."

"And you picked up her crusade?"

"After she was killed by a suicide bomber."

"Oh, I'm sorry." Dean reached across and took her hand. "There aren't a lot of people who can say they understand and really mean it." He held her gaze. "But I do."

She could see in the depths of his dark eyes that he did understand, and she felt another one of those clicks of connection. This one more important than attraction or likes and dislikes. They'd both suffered a tragedy that had changed them. It was no wonder she kept feeling they meshed.

"I do this to honor her, but also because knowing her, hearing about her dream, I learned how important it was." She shrugged. "Her cause is now my cause."

The shrill sound of Dean's phone invaded the quiet. He winced. "It's the one I have to answer."

She nodded, glad for a few seconds to pull herself

together before they said goodbye. Because this was it. They no longer had a reason to stay together. She'd gone to his party and lunch and both were over. Winslow Osmond wanted him to take his team to Grennady, but he didn't see the value in doing that. This time tomorrow he'd go back to being the ruthless businessman he always was and she'd be home, getting ready to step onto the world's stage as a founder of an organization that built schools.

After she got out of this limo, she'd never see him again.

Dean clicked the button to answer his phone. "Dean Suminski." He paused for a few seconds, then said, "Mrs. Flannigan. What a pleasant surprise. What can I do for you?"

He paused as the older woman talked. Suddenly feeling awful, missing Aasera, confused by all these feelings she had around Dean, Kristen buttoned her coat and slid across the seat to the limo door. Why prolong the inevitable? She barely knew him, and what she'd discovered only proved he was married to his business. And, really, she should be okay with their parting. She'd need all her mental and emotional energy to start her charity. Neither one of them had time for the other. Why belabor the issue with a goodbye in a busy hotel lobby?

Just when she would have opened the limo door, Dean caught her hand again.

"We'd love to. Seven tomorrow. We're looking forward to it."

She faced him as he clicked off the call. Though she hated the way her breath stuttered when he held her hand, happiness filled her at the possibility that this wasn't goodbye.

"You have another event?"

"Yes and no. *We've* been invited to a private dinner with the Flannigans." He smiled. His dark eyes lit with pleasure. "She wants to talk to *you* about your schools. Tomorrow night at seven."

CHAPTER SEVEN

"Oh, my gosh! She wants to talk to *me*?"

Kristen looked at him, her stunning green eyes wide with excitement and he laughed. "You'll do fine." She drew in a long breath. "I had a few hiccups in my confidence today." She caught his gaze. "But you helped a lot."

A wave a pleasure flowed through him, but he didn't let himself wallow in it. He might be with Kristen for another party, but he wouldn't indulge the emotions he experienced around her. Especially the relief he'd felt sharing his story about Nina. Not because he didn't like the feelings she inspired in him, he did. He liked them too much. Keeping his distance was for *her* protection.

"Here's what we'll do. We'll have Stella take you shopping tomorrow morning to get you an appropriate dress."

She gasped. "She's going to have to take me some place inexpensive! I can't afford the clothes in Jennifer's boutique."

He shook his head. "Whether you understand it or not, this dinner tomorrow night also works for me. While you talk with Mrs. Flannigan, I get a chance to chitchat with Arthur. She might own the business, but he's got influence over her." He smiled. "Actually, I owe you for the fact that your charity is getting me extra time with them."

"You just won't let this go, will you?"

"Not if you're about to pay for things that are helping me out." Deciding the time for teasing was over, he sucked in a breath. "Seriously. Thank you. I need this extra time with them, and you and your charity are providing it."

"Well, the dinner is supposed to be for me so I'm getting benefit too. That means there'll be no more agreements drawn up."

He drew a cross on his chest. "I promise."

Still in the limo, they placed a call to Jennifer at the boutique. Dean told her they needed a cocktail dress for the following night, and that Kristen would be in the next morning to look for one with Stella.

"Anything special I should pull for her to try on?"

"Just something pretty. We trust your judgment." He caught Kristen's gaze and smiled. "And make it red."

Kristen laughed as he clicked off the call. "Very funny."

"I'm getting much better at being funny."

She said, "You are," as Dean pressed the button for the chauffeur, who came around and opened the door.

Kristen got out and he followed behind her. He walked her into the hotel lobby and almost escorted her to her room, but the feelings he'd been having around her all day kept growing. Now they were committed to another evening out. He needed the time with the Flannigans as much as Kristen did—so he couldn't pass up this chance.

But as he spoke with Mrs. Minerva Flannigan about dinner Sunday night, he'd had the oddest sense they really were becoming a couple, and though he knew it wasn't true, there was a part of him that wished it was.

That was the real reason he couldn't walk her upstairs.

He knew as surely as he knew his own name that if she gave him any sort of encouragement at all he'd kiss her. And then what?

Date?

Marry her?

The vision he'd had of him and Kristen in his master bedroom at his house in Albany filled his brain, and his chest tightened. How could he picture himself with a child when he had no clue how to be a father? How could he picture himself with someone as wonderful as Kristen when he was a stodgy workaholic who would get so involved in his projects and his business that he sometimes slept in his office?

How could he get involved with Kristen when he knew it would end…and knew, quite painfully, how paralyzing it was when a relationship ended. Nina might have died, but when she broke it off with him she'd outlined a hundred reasons they were wrong for each other, crushing his soul, reinforcing his beliefs that he shouldn't get involved in a real relationship.

His feelings for Kristen were wrong. He would stop them.

The elevator came. She stepped in and waved goodbye as the door closed, and he got back into the limo and headed for the sanctuary of his penthouse.

The limo stopped at his building, and he slid out and walked toward the glass revolving door, noticing an odd number of paparazzi hanging around. They came to attention when they saw him. One or two even snapped a picture. But neither of those things was unusual. First, the flirtatious daughter of a hedge fund manager lived in his building and she was a tabloid darling. Paparazzi were always around. Second, those who snapped pictures probably wanted a new file photo of him. God knew, there was nothing interesting about him walking into his building alone.

He breezed through the lobby, pausing only to say hello to the doorman. He used his code to get the private elevator to start and in a few seconds the door opened on his penthouse.

The whole place had been done in black and white, with berry-toned throw pillows and accent pieces. He wouldn't know a berry tone from a hole in the ground, but his decorator had told him that berry colors were all the rage, so that's what he'd gotten.

He ambled into his bedroom and the walk-in closet, and chose black boots, blue jeans and an oatmeal-colored sweater, the color of which he also wouldn't have known if Stella hadn't told him when she showed him the array of sweaters she'd chosen for him that winter.

He didn't know fashionable colors. He didn't put his own touches on his houses and condos because he didn't really have homes. He had places he stayed. He was cold. Emotionless. And that was reason number seven hundred and forty-one why a nice woman like Kristen should stay away from him.

It was also reason number one that Nina had said she could never fall in love with him. Never really want to be with him.

He was cold. Not heartless. Just distanced from the world because of his genius and the way he was raised. He really didn't know how to connect.

Not wanting to think about Nina or Kristen anymore, and the yearning for something he knew he couldn't have, he grabbed the four newspapers he had delivered every morning.

Sitting on his sofa, he rifled through until he got to the *New York City Guardian*. He flipped it open but one section popped out and slid to the floor. The society pages. Without thought, he bent to pick it up, but there on the front page, bigger than was comfortable, was a picture of him and Kristen.

And he was laughing.

The photo itself confused him, reminding him of how differently he behaved with her. He slowly brought the paper up from the floor, staring at the picture first, then reading the caption.

Is the Iceman of Suminski Stuff falling in love?

His gut clenched. His gaze jumped to the article that detailed the troubles with his company and the article in *Tech Junkie*.

Crap.

But the worst were the closing lines.

Could the confirmed bachelor billionaire be dating someone? We doubt it. He has enough money that he doesn't have to meet women the old-fashioned way.

If innuendos could kill, he'd be dead right now. They'd all but suggested he'd hired Kristen.

And he had.

He dropped his head to his hands, then called his driver and told him to be in front of the building in ten minutes. After slipping into his black leather bomber jacket and gloves, he scooped the paper off his sofa before heading for the elevator.

Outside his building, as his limo pulled up and he raced to the door, the whir of cameras followed him.

Damn it.

In the bathroom of her suite, Kristen stood in the fluffy white robe debating. Shower or bubble bath? The room came equipped with any supplies she could possibly need, and though the shower gel was nice, the bubble bath crystals smelled divine. It was a sinful, wonderful, guilty pleasure to have the rest of the afternoon and all of the evening to herself to do what she wanted, and she was taking full advantage.

She chose the bubble bath, started the water and poured in the crystals, which instantly became irides-cent foam. Immersed in bubbles, she closed her eyes. Unfortunately, as she sank into the water she thought about Dean.

After hearing his story about Nina, she realized she knew *nothing* about being used. Brad was a man who wanted money and power, and he did what he had to do to get it. Unashamedly. Almost embarrassingly obviously. If Kristen had opened her eyes, she'd have easily seen it.

But using an inexperienced nineteen-year-old to make another boyfriend jealous? Kristen couldn't even imag-ine what Dean had felt when Nina had told him. It was no wonder he had so much pride. And no wonder he dis-liked mixing business with pleasure, given that it was Nina's father who had set them up as a condition to giv-ing Dean money.

It was perfectly understandable that the situation had scarred him. This also explained his need for agreements and rules. She actually admired him for pulling himself together as much as he had. In the years that followed

Nina and her father using him, and a world leader hating him, Dean had built an empire.

So she couldn't feel sorry for him. He certainly didn't feel sorry for himself. But she also couldn't stop herself from coupling his difficult beginnings—losing his parents, being raised by a grandmother who didn't want him—to being publicly humiliated when he tried to get funding.

It was no wonder he not only noticed but understood when her confidence wobbled.

Sunk neck-deep in bubbles, she almost cursed when the phone rang. Not sure who it might be, since she'd called her parents and given them her hotel room number in case anything happened, she got out of the tub, slid into the fluffy terry cloth robe and grabbed the extension in the bathroom.

"Yes."

"It's me. Dean. Can I come up?"

She grimaced. "Now?"

"It's important."

"Okay. I'm just getting out of the tub. Give me five minutes."

She hastily dried, dressed in the jeans and red sweater he'd bought for her to wear home, and combed out her hair. Because it was an unruly mass, she twisted it into a bun before she walked into the sitting room. A few seconds later, there was a knock on her door.

Expecting Dean, she opened it.

He handed a newspaper to her. "I'm sorry."

She glanced down at it and saw it was folded to display a picture of them printed on the first page of that section.

"Oh-oh."

"It's not a big deal, except they suggest that I hired you to date me."

She laughed. "They're sort of right."

"Yes. They are." He ambled into her sitting room. "We have a written agreement that proves it."

She really liked the way he looked in the leather jacket and boots. Though a suit gave him an air of power, the jacket, jeans and boots made him look strong, male, virile.

She pulled back from that train of thought before she had to fan herself. "So we have an argreement? No one will see it."

He scrubbed his hand down his face. "No, no one will see it. But this is the kind of gossip I don't need when my company's in trouble."

"Really? I don't understand how it relates."

"I look like a lunatic."

Because she'd just run through all the attributes of how he "looked" she thoroughly disagreed. But even though Kristen herself never had to worry about the press, Princess Eva did. Like it or not, think it was funny or not, Kristen understood.

"You know, you didn't hire me for tomorrow night's dinner."

He sucked in a breath. "So?"

"So it kind of, sort of, is a real date."

His eyes narrowed. "What are you getting at?"

"Well, if we went out—right now for instance, when, again, you're not paying me—and saw some sights and then got dinner, we would officially be dating."

"And if someone saw us—like the photographers following me—then we'd look official."

She shook her head. "No. Get into the spirit of this. We won't *look* official. We *will be* dating."

He met her gaze. "Oh."

She sighed. "Thanks for your enthusiastic response."

"I'm sorry. I just don't date."

"And you wonder why the press prints crazy articles about you?"

He laughed.

She smiled. "See? Dating me is not so bad. Especially since I come with a shelf life. I have to go home sometime."

"No ugly breakup."

"Exactly."

He pondered that for a second before he said, "Grab your coat. We're going to Rockefeller Center."

Since she was wearing jeans, she got her old black wool coat from the closet by the door. "Sounds promising."

"Every tourist goes there. They have a big Christmas tree."

"Fun!"

He pulled in a breath. "I suppose."

Kristen shook her head, but didn't scold him about being a Scrooge. Knowing his story, she could easily see why all this would be new to him.

Out on the sidewalk, a couple of guys in winter jackets—trying to be inconspicuous about holding cameras—followed them to Rockefeller Center. Obviously, they were members of the press Dean was so worried about.

She didn't have to point them out. She was fairly certain Dean saw them, but he pretended he didn't. So she

pretended too. When he started talking about her charity, she let him.

"You're going to need a board of advisors."

She skipped along the sidewalk, working to keep up
with his long strides. A light snow began to fall, and she
inhaled deeply, suddenly homesick for fresh snow, her
mom's homemade gingerbread cookies and the way the
sun dipped at about three in the afternoon, making the
world a silent, peaceful place. Even on a Saturday, New
York City was mad, noisy, filled with life and energy.

"I know I'll need advisors. In fact, I'm counting on
advisors helping me through the things I don't know."

"If Mrs. Flannigan ponies up anything over five hundred grand, it will be a subtle indicator that she wants
on that board."

She stopped walking. "Five hundred thousand dollars?"

He shrugged. "As I said, she might be angling for a
seat on that board. I'd give it to her."

"You better believe I will."

Her silly answer made him laugh and she slid her arm
beneath his to nestle against him, whispering, "This is
for authenticity."

He glanced down at her. "Oh."

Their gazes held. His dark orbs held a wisp of longing that tugged at her soul, but he said nothing. So she
took that for agreement and stayed close as they made
the few blocks' walk to Rockefeller Center.

When she saw the enormous Christmas tree, she
gasped. "It's beautiful."

Decorated with multicolored lights, the huge tree was
festive and happy, and again filled Kristen with a longing for home. She knew she'd be back in Grennady for

the holidays, but right now she was missing all the fun of prepping. All the cookie baking. All the decorating.

"This tree is why Rockefeller Center is a big tourist attraction."

She saw people ice-skating in the huge sectioned-off center. Her longing for home doubled. "There's skating!"

"That's reason two that this is a tourist attraction."

"Do you count everything?"

His head tilted in confusion. "Count?"

"Keep track."

He laughed. "I suppose I do. I think it's the way my brain files things."

She said, "Interesting," but her attention was again caught by the skaters. The snow picked up, but she didn't feel cold. Having grown up in a Scandinavian country, she was more than accustomed to snow and temperatures much colder than what New York City offered. The swish, swish, swish of the skaters as they whirled by filled her with homesickness.

"I think we should skate."

He blanched. "No way in hell."

"Why not?" She glanced at him and the leather jacket over his warm sweater and jeans. "We're both dressed for it. There's a sign over there that says they rent skates." She bumped his shoulder with her own. "It'll be fun."

"Not with three reporters following us. I do not want a bunch of guys with access to important media outlets to see me fall on my ass. I don't want to look like an idiot."

"You won't look like an idiot. You'll look like someone who likes me enough to try something new. Then speculation will go from 'did he pay her?' to 'who is this woman who has him trying new things?'"

He shook his head. "You know they're about to in-vestigate you, right?"

She shrugged. "You did."

He sighed.

"And what did you find? That I'm a nice, simple girl. Your search didn't hurt me. Didn't affect me. So I let it go." She smiled. "Not everything has to be life-or-death. Let's just have fun. The photographers following you will see that. They'll investigate me and find nothing and poof they'll disappear."

"You're such an optimist."

She turned to him and studied his face. "You know, I'd say you're a pessimist but I don't think that's true. I think so many crappy things happened to you that you're just careful."

"Careful enough not to break my ankle."

"See? There you go. Deflecting again because that's how you stay away from subjects that are too painful. But you don't have to worry. I won't ask you to talk about Nina anymore. I won't ask about your childhood. But I do want to skate. I'm in a new country unexpectedly, for longer than I thought, and I'm just a little homesick."

If she'd argued or tried to get her own way, Dean would have easily beaten her. But what kind of a Scrooge would he have to be to deny her the chance to get over her homesickness?

He sighed. "I'll check out the skating schedule and see about skate rental."

Her entire face brightened. "Really?"

"Yes. But don't think I'm trying anything fancy. And no holding my hand."

"We're supposed to be dating."

"I don't want to look weak on the ice."

With that he walked away. Because it was an odd time of the day, they could actually get into the next round of skating. He called her over. They rented skates. Within twenty minutes they were on the ice.

After a few minutes of wobbling, working to get his balance, knowing photographers were documenting his efforts, Dean finally found his footing. The first time he glided along for more than a few feet, he burst out laughing.

"All right. It's fun."

She skated a circle around him. "I told you."

"You actually use the same core muscles to balance yourself as you do for snowboarding."

She gaped at him. "You snowboard?"

"Used to. I had to learn to do a lot of things to be in the places where I could accidentally run into the wealthy people I thought most likely to invest in Suminski Stuff."

"You make me feel like I should be grateful Mrs. Flannigan invited me to dinner."

He stopped skating. "You should."

"I am."

Silence stretched between them as they studied each other. Skaters glided around them, reminding him that he was stopped, staring at her, taking in that earnest face and those beautiful eyes, and reporters were probably noticing.

She quickly caught his hand and pulled him into the fray. "Let's get out of everybody's way, and then I'll drop your hand."

He almost wished she wouldn't. The connection to her felt so nice, so normal, that it should have scared him.

Instead, it filled him with the sense that he could trust her to take him places he'd never been.

They skated into a rhythm and she dropped his hand, but he scooped hers up again.

Her gaze flew to his.

"We are supposed to be dating."

She nodded and smiled as she skated in front of him. "Wanna do a trick?"

"Getting bored with just plain skating?"

"Sort of. But I also think I'd rather get my picture in the paper for doing something cool, than for looking like two spectators who didn't know what they were doing."

He laughed nervously. "Seriously? You're going to make me do a trick?"

"A simple one." She grabbed his other hand so they stood facing each other, both hands tightly clasped. Then she shifted them so they were skating sideways and that movement became a circle.

He imagined that from the spectator area they looked cute, fun. And they probably did pose a much better picture. But as the world whizzed by and he grew more comfortable, with her and with his skates, he started to laugh. For the first time in weeks, he wasn't thinking about his company or his troubles. He wasn't thinking at all.

Except to realize that he really did trust her.

Kristen noticed the change in him immediately. She stopped their circle and dropped one of his hands so she could pull him behind her. When they got enough speed, she led him into a figure eight.

He called, "Now I think you're showing off."

"Nope. Showing off would be teaching you how to do a spin or maybe a lift."

She expected his face to freeze in horror. Instead, he said, "I could probably spin."

She pulled him out of their third figure eight and guided him to stand beside her. "You like being good at things."

"Don't you?"

She shrugged. "I like doing the best I can."

"Same thing."

She said, "I suppose," but she understood what he meant. As a genius, his version of doing the best he could undoubtedly meant that he had to be perfect. It was why he didn't want to fall on his face in front of reporters, why he stayed out of the public eye. People were always watching him. Maybe hoping he'd make a mistake.

When their ninety minutes were up, they left Rockefeller Center, walked a bit more around that section of the city and had dinner at an out-of-the-way Mexican restaurant.

She buttoned her jacket as they walked out onto the now snow-covered sidewalk. Christmas lights decorated shop-front windows and doorways. Snow sat on evergreen branches like icing on sugar cookies. Without hesitation, he took her hand and she couldn't stop a smile.

It was one of the best dates of her life.

Still, she knew it didn't mean as much to him as it did to her. He might be having fun. He might even be enjoying her, but having heard the story of Nina, she more than suspected he'd vowed never to let himself get close to a woman again. He'd probably even made a rule.

When they reached her hotel lobby, she expected him to say goodbye at the elevator. Instead, he stepped inside with her.

Wonderful hope filled her tummy with butterflies. "Walking me to my door?"

"There were three photographers in the lobby."

Disappointment rumbled through her. "Oh."

But when they got to her door and she turned to say good-night, he had the most baffling expression on his face. She recognized the longing. The end of this date should be a kiss. But the confusion in his eyes told her he wouldn't even kiss her cheek.

"What's wrong?"

He drew a long breath and looked away. "Nothing." But when he turned back to her again, his dark eyes had sharpened. The muscles of his broad shoulders tensed beneath his smooth leather jacket. He took a fraction of a step toward her.

Her breath stalled. He *was* going to kiss her.

She took a fraction of a step toward him, drawn by an unknown instinct inside her that seemed to know exactly what to do.

His eyes stayed on her face. One of his hands came up, as if he were going to put it on her shoulder or maybe her waist to nudge her closer.

Her heart did a rumba in her chest. She smiled hopefully.

But his hand stopped. He took a step back and ran his fingers through his hair.

"Good night."

Disappointed, she whispered, "Good night," but he just stood there. She thought for a second that he might be hanging around because he didn't want to leave and did want to kiss her. Then she realized he was just being a gentleman, waiting for her to go into her room.

She quickly slid the key in the lock and let herself inside. She said, "Good night," again, hoping she didn't look like an idiot, then closed the door behind her.

But no matter how hard she tried to talk herself out of it, she couldn't let herself believe it was okay that he didn't kiss her.

She had wanted him to kiss her.

Very much.

She told herself that was trouble, reminded herself of his story of Nina and how her now favorite genius had probably made a rule to protect himself, and even suggested to herself that no matter how they manipulated this agreement of theirs, they were using each other.

But she still wanted him to kiss her.

CHAPTER EIGHT

"DEAN TOLD ME you need a cocktail dress and that I'm to take you to lunch."

Eyes squinting, Kristen eyed the time on her cell phone and saw it was already ten o'clock.

She sat up. "Yes. I'm sorry, Stella. I got up late or I'd be dressed by now."

"No sweat. I'm in the lobby when you're ready."

"Thanks."

Kristen got out of bed, showered and put on the red sweater and jeans again. Then she called the front desk and made arrangements to have her black pants, white shirt and underwear cleaned that day. Housekeeping promised her clothes would be back in her room by that evening and she thanked them. Now there'd be no arguments about how she "needed" more jeans and a new sweater. She would fly home in the clothes she'd been wearing in Paris.

She met Stella in the lobby. They took Dean's limo to the boutique and found Jennifer waiting, ready with three red cocktail dresses. She tried on all three and chose a simple red lace sheathe.

Stella said, "Now we just need new jeans and sweater."

Proud of herself, Kristen smirked and said, "For what?"

"Dean said something about you needing clothes to go home in."

"The clothes I wore over from Paris are being cleaned by the hotel." She smiled. "I'm fine."

Stella gaped at her. "Are you nuts? The man is willing to buy you an eight-hundred-dollar sweater. Take it."

"I don't need it."

Stella sighed and looked at the ceiling as if seeking guidance from above.

Kristen firmly said, "I don't need it and I don't want it. End of discussion."

Shaking her head, Stella said, "Whatever."

They had Jennifer send the red dress to her hotel and left the boutique for a restaurant.

The snow from the day before had been shoveled away, but steam rose from the grates in the sidewalk, mixing with the frigid air and swirling toward street vendors who stood huddled by food carts.

"Where do you want to eat?"

She pointed at one of the carts. "A hot dog would be fine."

"No. Dean said to get you a proper meal."

Kristen laughed. "He's probably the bossiest guy I've ever met."

Stella snorted. "You don't know the half of it." She pointed at the door of an Italian restaurant. "Do you like Italian?"

"Everybody likes Italian."

"Great." They took the three steps down into the lower-level restaurant and found there was no wait.

Seated at the round table, holding her menu, Stella said, "So you're okay with another date?"

"Are you asking for Dean or are you curious?"

Stella leaned forward. "Dean sounded as if he believed you were perfectly happy with tonight's dinner. That's what makes me curious."

"The dinner is actually for me. Mrs. Flannigan wants to talk about my charity."

Stella peered over her menu. "Well, good, then. Dean's a difficult man even for pretend dates. I'm glad to see you're getting something out of this deal."

"You mean aside from a gown, two dresses, a sweater, jeans, boots, a black coat and two pairs of black heels." She paused, then cursed. "Damn it! He still hasn't taken back that bracelet."

Stella laughed. "Lighten up. To Dean that's not even pocket change."

The waiter, a short Italian man who must have come directly from Italy because he spoke with a wonderful accent, took their orders.

As he scampered away, Kristen refused to let the subject of the bracelet die. "I've got to get that bracelet back to him."

Stella leaned forward again. "Why do you care? The man's a surly bastard. He fires employees and drops lovers like the rest of us change shoes. The only person he really talks to is Jason."

"He talks to me."

Stella gasped. "Oh." She considered that for a second, then gasped again. "Oh, no! I think I see what's going on here." She shook her head fiercely. "Sweetie, do not let that man get his hooks into you. You are too nice of a girl. And if you really want to start that charity you told me about the other day, you can't have your reputation sullied by having dated Dean."

Annoyed, Kristen said, "First of all, he's not that bad. From what I saw at the Christmas party and our lunch with his friends, he talks when he has something to say. At yesterday's lunch he was a virtual chatty Cathy. Second, dating one guy isn't going to ruin my business reputation."

Stella put her elbow on the table and rested her head on her closed fist. "Okay, I take the reputation thing back. And change it to the reality that he *could* ruin you with a broken heart. He is as hard-nosed as a businessman gets. Do not let a few nights out fool you into thinking he's nice or he likes you."

Fiddling with her napkin, Kristen said, "I'm not that stupid." But she'd wanted him to kiss her the night before. Really wanted it. And from everything Stella was saying, she didn't know him. She had been dealing with a guy who was at first grouchy, then standoffish, then nicer and nicer, more open, willing to take a risk ice-skating. A guy who was either growing comfortable with her or changing...or something.

The picture of Dean, sitting in the limo beside her, saying, *Maybe you bring out the best in me*, popped into her head.

What if she did bring out the best in him?

But what if she didn't? What if he really was a snarky guy who needed her, so he was acting the way he had to, to keep her here in New York, available for appearances at his beck and call?

Oh, that made so much more sense than to think a farm girl from Grennady could tame the New York City genius superstar.

* * *

When Dean came to Kristen's hotel room to pick her up at seven, she was ready to go. Wearing a red lace dress, with her yellow hair swirling around her in big, loose curls, she looked amazing.

But he'd almost kissed her the night before, so tempted he nearly lost the war inside his head, even though he knew kissing her was wrong. They had a deal. They weren't really dating in spite of the fact that they'd set it up to look that way. He could not kiss her.

Tonight, he would be smarter.

He picked up her black wool coat from the back of the sofa and opened it so she could slide it on.

"Thank you."

Was it just him, or had that thank-you seemed a little clipped?

He opened the door for her. She stepped into the hall. "Thanks again."

That one was definitely stiff, too polite. Not Kristen at all.

"You're welcome." He paused, then said, "Is something wrong?"

"I'm fine."

She wasn't fine.

"Did Stella say something?"

The elevator arrived. They stepped inside. Standing face forward, Kristen said, "Stella and I had a great time."

"Well, you certainly picked out a nice dress."

"Jennifer picked it."

The chill of her voice and the way she wouldn't look at him sent a sprinkle of apprehension up his spine. Stella could have told her a million things, all of which would make Kristen back off.

But she should back off. He didn't date. He took lovers. She didn't fit that category. She'd be wise not to get close to him.

And he would be wise to let her do whatever it was she felt she needed to do to protect herself.

They drove to the Flannigans' in complete silence, and, for once, it felt odd. He almost pointed out the decorated storefront windows, remembering how she'd loved the Christmas tree in Rockefeller Center, but held back, respecting her obvious wish to keep her distance. But the more he held his tongue, the more the decorations popped out to him. Fat Santas in store windows. Elves. Bright Christmas ornaments. He hadn't really looked at decorations since the year his grandmother gave him fifty bucks and told him to buy himself a gift. She didn't want to decorate. Didn't want to bake. Didn't want to go out at all. Because Christmas was a holiday created by stores to get people to spend money.

So he'd taken his fifty bucks to a pawnshop and bought some poor sap's old computer. To stave off the sadness of missing his parents and wishing Christmas was real, he told himself his grandmother was right. Christmas was a sham. For foolish people who could be duped.

The limo pulled up to the Flannigans' building. Dean and Kristen said nothing walking into the building lobby, nothing as the doorman—who had them on an expected-visitors list—walked them to the elevator and used a key card to allow the elevator to take them to the upper floor and the Flannigan residence.

As the elevator opened on the stunning foyer and a

beaming Mrs. Flannigan and Arthur, Dean started to sweat, worried how Kristen's unhappiness might affect the evening. And her charity. If she was quiet with Mrs. Flannigan, the potential donation could go sailing out the window.

Worse, it was his fault because Stella had probably told her he was a bastard.

Because he was.

She stepped out of the elevator into Mrs. Flannigan's hug. "Let John take your coats."

As Mrs. Flannigan said the words, her butler stepped forward for Kristen's black wool coat and Dean's charcoal-gray overcoat.

As Kristen slid out of hers, Mrs. Flannigan gasped. "Oh, red! You look so lovely in red. I remember those days. I used to love to wear red."

Kristen laughed. "Used to? I'm sure you're still stunning in red."

Mrs. Flannigan hooked her arm through Kristen's and led her down a long hall, into a high-ceilinged living room replete with art. Furnished with simple ultramodern sofas and chairs, the room got its beauty from famous paintings hung on walls and sculptures scattered about. Red velvet bows and evergreen branches hung over paintings, a nod to the holiday.

Kristen said, "Your home is lovely."

"Thank you. Some people," she said, her gaze sliding to Dean, "use decorators. I prefer to make my home my home."

Though Mrs. Flannigan and Arthur looked at him, Kristen kept her gaze averted.

She did that the whole way through dinner, through the discussion of her charity and the promise of a sizable donation from Mrs. Flannigan. Kristen mentioned inviting her onto her board of advisors, and, as Dean had predicted, her eyes sparkled with approval as she happily accepted the position and volunteered to find other board members.

"Who will also make donations," Mrs. Flannigan promised. She tossed out a few names, people famous enough to make even Dean's head spin, but when that discussion was over she turned to Dean.

"Now that our real business is out of the way, I think you and I need to have a chat."

The way she looked at him sent fear rattling along his nerve endings. She had too much life and energy to remind him of his grandmother, but she was so influential on Wall Street that one word from her could send his stock into a free fall.

Seated on her sofa, with after-dinner drinks, he crossed one leg over the other and leaned back on the cushion as if totally unconcerned.

"So chat."

"Winslow was right about you taking your staff somewhere now—right now—to motivate them to get this project done. I've had my assistant investigate Grennady and it's quiet. Peaceful. But the country still has enough things for your employees and their families to do that it could be like a working vacation."

"It sounds great, but—"

"No buts, Dean. This time next month my word isn't going to be enough to stave off the inevitable."

"I know that."

"So you have no choice but to try something different."

"I'm just not convinced that taking them out of their work environment will jump-start their creativity."

"Look at it this way, keeping them where they are hasn't worked in three years. I'm going to be bold enough to suggest that you have nothing to lose."

Kristen unexpectedly reached out and took his hand. It shocked him that she'd think he'd need support for what was, essentially, a simple business conversation. Then he realized how sweet it was—especially considering that she'd been protecting herself all night.

When she thought he needed her, she was there for him.

No one had ever been there for him.

It didn't matter that she mistakenly believed Mrs. Flannigan's stern voice somehow cowed him. It hadn't. No one cowed him. What mattered was she took his feelings into consideration over her own.

An indescribable feeling invaded his chest. A warmth that rose until it filled his blood and every happiness-starved cell in his body.

All the feelings he'd had skating returned. Especially the sense that his world was opening up and he could trust her.

He couldn't follow the feeling. He wouldn't risk hurting Kristen. But for once in his life he wanted to soak it in.

The conversation shifted to a painting over the marble fireplace. Kristen and Mrs. Flannigan walked over to it, with Mrs. Flannigan telling the story behind the purchase.

Though he spoke with Arthur, Dean let his gaze follow Kristen around the room, knowing she wasn't fak-

ing her interest in the art, or her immediate love of Mrs.
Flannigan.

And he suddenly, desperately wanted to kiss her. Even
more desperately than he had the night before.

The evening wound down. As they made their way
up the hall toward the foyer with the elevator, John approached them, holding their coats. Dean helped Kristen
with hers before putting on his own.

"Oh, look at this," Mrs. Flannigan said, pointing at a
huge spray of flowers on the hall table. "You're not exactly under the mistletoe in that arrangement, but you're
beside it." She nudged Dean. "If you wanted to kiss her,
Arthur and I wouldn't mind."

A rush of need swooshed through Dean's blood-
stream. It was the perfectly logical way to get the kiss
he'd wanted for nearly two days. He'd already vowed he
wouldn't get involved with her, wouldn't hurt her…but
didn't he deserve one kiss?

Of course he did.

Kristen laughed. "Mistletoe has to be overhead for it
to be a legitimate reason to get a kiss."

Then she strode toward the elevator, Mrs. Flannigan
following behind, chuckling, and Arthur behind his wife.

Dean glanced at the flower arrangement, then looked
up at the group, all of whom had their backs to him. And
he did something he had never done. He pilfered some
mistletoe.

In the limo, Kristen went back to being quiet. He let
her because it was the right thing to do. They drove up
Fifth Avenue, Christmas decorations glittering in the
frigid night air, and he took a long drink of air. The same
decorations that had reminded him of his past twinkled

in the light of the streetlamps and unexpectedly warmed his heart, even as apprehension tugged at his soul.

His time with Kristen was almost at an end. And he had some decisions to make in the few minutes left of their drive to her hotel.

He debated a couple of things, but in the end, he knew Mrs. Flannigan was simply too powerful to ignore. He was going to have to take his staff to Grennady. He fingered the mistletoe in his overcoat pocket. But to keep things simple and protect Kristen, he also had to cut Kristen out of the picture.

They got out of the limo and for the first time in two days there was no paparazzi following them.

Kristen noticed too. "No press?"

"It's late and cold, and we gave them enough pictures yesterday to keep them happy."

She said, "Ah," as he held open the door for her.

They walked to the elevator in total silence and waited for it to arrive in equal silence.

She gave him a confused look when he followed her inside, but he said nothing. When the elevator reached her floor, he walked out with her, staying as quiet as they had in the limo.

At the door, she turned to him with a polite smile. "Thank you very much for this evening. Heck, thanks for introducing me to Mrs. Flannigan. She's wonderful. Perfect. I know that with her help my charity will be up and running in about half the time it would have taken me alone."

He smiled. "Probably even less than that. She's very powerful." He smiled again. "And she likes you."

"I like her too."

Pride for her surged through him. Not because she was

great, but because she was honest. She genuinely liked Mrs. Flannigan, and with her assistance Kristen probably would changes the lives of hundreds of thousands of women, maybe millions, over her lifetime.

"You'll make a good team."

"Thanks."

For the first time all night, she looked him in the eye. The effect was instantaneous. Dean's heart swelled again. His breath froze in his lungs.

And he knew this had to be the last time he saw her. If he let her stay in his life, he wouldn't be able to resist this pull.

Digging her key card out of her purse, she said, "I'll be in touch when it comes time for the computers."

"Good."

She turned to open her door, but he stopped her. "Not so fast, Cinderella. You want me and my company in Grennady, and it looks like you've got us there."

Her eyes widened. "Really?"

"You heard what Mrs. Flannigan said."

She frowned. "Yes, but everybody's been saying that and you didn't appear to have taken any of them seriously."

"Mrs. Flannigan's a brilliant businesswoman. And she wields a lot of power. Not taking her advice would be like asking her to downgrade my stock."

"So you're moving your company to Grennady?"

"Temporarily. If my staff can finish this project before the first of the year, I will consider a permanent move."

"But that's three weeks! And Christmas is in there!"

"Yeah. Bad luck for you. If I were you, I'd be on the phone tonight, finding office space. And I hope you have a strategy for handling Prince Alex because once we get to Grennady I'll be dealing exclusively with the royal family."

That was how he planned to circumvent his unwanted feelings around Kristen. He would simply push her out of his life by working only with King Mason or Princess Eva. He had it all figured out.

But that didn't mean he didn't recognize that something wonderful was passing him by. He'd never before felt the way he felt around her. He knew he wasn't made for what she wanted or needed. But he also knew what he felt for her was special. *She* was special.

And he couldn't walk away without a kiss.

He fingered the chunk of mistletoe he'd taken from Mrs. Flannigan's huge display. His heartbeat slowed as his brain cleared. He deserved at least one kiss. He wasn't the guy who would get the girl. He wasn't a guy who was going to have a happily-ever-after—

But surely he was entitled to one little kiss from the first woman who made him think happily-ever-after might exist.

And even if he wasn't, he was taking one.

He pulled the mistletoe from his pocket. "You said this only works if it's overhead...right?"

Her gaze jumped to his.

He raised his arm, putting the mistletoe directly above them before he put his hand on her shoulder and stepped closer. Her eyes widened, but he didn't give her time to ponder or protest. He dipped his head and pressed his lips to hers.

CHAPTER NINE

SURPRISE AND INSTINCT caused Kristen to lift her lips and kiss him back. He took advantage and nudged a bit, encouraging her to open her mouth. When she did, he deepened the kiss and all the breath stalled in her lungs. His lips were smooth and sleek, his kiss experienced.

Desire whooshed through her. Her brain stopped. Wonderful urges spun through her. She shoved her hotel room key into her coat pocket, stepped closer and smoothed her hands up his silky shirt, over his shoulders until they met at his nape. Another half step eased her body against his chest.

It was heaven. As his hungry mouth took hers, and his hands slid down her back, then up again, the whole world slimmed down to just him and her, and spiraling sensations that made her feel dizzy and warm and just a little confused.

Then he broke the kiss and stepped back, away from her.

Kristen stared at him. Her heart beat crazily. Her thoughts sambaed. The mouth he'd just kissed so thoroughly couldn't form words.

"It was really nice to meet you, Kristen Anderson.

Good luck with your charity. When the time comes, let Stella know and you'll have your computers."

She watched his long-legged stride take him down the hall to the elevator, her entire body shimmering.

The man had kissed her! And not like some soulless nerd, like a poet—a love-starved poet.

Her brain couldn't sort it out. He'd barely wanted to hold her hand the day before. He'd absolutely walked away from a kiss at this very same hotel room door. But tonight after she'd all but ignored him, he'd kissed her.

She didn't know what to think, except that his parting words were definitely a goodbye.

She tried not to read too much into the wistful way he'd said goodbye, and the puzzling sadness that tightened her throat as he turned a corner and disappeared from view. Each was for nothing. They both knew how this worked. No matter how attracted he might be to her, men like him didn't date ordinary girls.

They also didn't deal with assistants—even if said assistant was executive assistant to a princess. As he'd said, he'd be communicating with the royal family from here on out. When she needed her computers, she'd be talking with Stella. She'd never see or speak to him again.

She shook herself to force away the sadness that brought, and opened the door to her suite. If he and his staff planned to be in Grennady the next day, and he intended to communicate with the royal family, she couldn't spend her time wondering about a stupid kiss and a sexy, interesting, but patently unusual man. She had some calls to make.

She tossed her coat onto an available chair and found her phone. After calculating the time difference between midnight in New York and middle of the day in Xaviera, she dialed.

Princess Eva answered on the second ring.

"Kristen?"

Eva's voice was soft and sweet, but there was a thread of steel that ran through it. She might be a wonderful person, but she was a future queen. A strong woman destined to rule a country.

"Please don't fire me."

"Fire you?" Eva laughed. "You're the best assistant I've ever had. What could you have possibly done to be fired?"

She took a long drink of air to steady her nerves, then said, "I've been watching you and Alex try to entice a tech company to Grennady."

"Yes."

"I also know your list had dwindled. There was no one left to contact."

"That's a subject we intend to revisit in January."

She swallowed. "Well, you may not have to. I approached Dean Suminski—"

"Of Suminski Stuff?"

"Yes."

"Oh, no! Alex hates him."

Kristen said, "I know."

"Then why would you approach him?"

"At the time, I didn't know Alex hated him. I just thought maybe you and Alex didn't think we stood a chance with him."

"Oh, Kristen!"

She paced into the bedroom of the suite out of the area that reminded her of Dean helping her with her coat, talking about the press, and them deciding they could "date" for real. All of that was just so confusing. In a couple of days of being with Dean Suminski, she'd really grown to like him. But he didn't want anything to do with her.

Otherwise, he wouldn't be saying goodbye...would he?

"I'm so sorry. But I swear I didn't know there was bad blood between them until Dean told me when we were on our way to a Christmas party—"

"You went to a Christmas party with Dean Suminski? He's in Grennady?"

"No, we're in New York."

Eva gasped. "What are you doing in New York?"

"It is a long, long story, Princess." Kristen fell to the huge king-size bed, realizing how odd this whole thing sounded. But, one step at a time, it had all made sense.

Even her feelings for him.

Inch by inch, he'd shown himself to her, and inch by inch she'd fallen for the man she genuinely believed he was deep down inside.

"I'd intended to start this explanation off with an apology for overstepping, but I now know I more than overstepped. It just seemed wrong that we never approached Suminski Stuff. So I found Dean in Paris."

"Paris?"

"I called in a favor to get the name of his hotel, and he agreed to give me five minutes in the limo ride to his airstrip, but that didn't work out. So I was going to fly to New York to have time with him while we were in the air, but his friend was on the plane, waiting for him. He told Dean his stock was being downgraded." She sucked in a breath. "His company's in trouble. He intends to fix it. But he has to get his latest game series to beta testers the first of the year to prove Suminski Stuff is still viable. Anyway, we were having dinner tonight with Mrs. Flannigan, a woman who owns a huge brokerage firm, who told him to get his staff somewhere quiet and peaceful and get this project done."

"Dinner tonight? Are you dating this guy?"

She winced. "Yes." And it had been her idea because she hated the way everyone misinterpreted him, but more because she'd wanted to date him for real. She liked him.

"You may see it in a newspaper. So, yes, we were sort of dating. But we did it so the press wouldn't think he'd paid me to go to the Christmas party because he sort of had."

"Kristen!"

"It's not what you think. In exchange for me being his date for an important party, we signed an agreement for him to provide the first hundred-thousand-dollars' worth of computers when I start my schools."

Eva's voice softened. "So you're leaving us to start your charity?"

"That was the point of the dinner with Mrs. Flannigan—"

"Is this Minerva Flannigan?"

"Yes. She's the first of my board of advisors."

Eva's voice softened. "She's got a great business mind. She's the perfect choice to be on your board of advisors."

"And of course I want you on the board too, Princess."

Eva laughed. "My ego is not so fragile that you need to pamper me."

"But I really do want you on this board."

"Then I am honored."

"But I'm also not going anywhere yet. Dean Suminski and his staff will be in Grennady tomorrow evening, our time. He needs office space. Though I could easily get it for him if I had a couple of weeks, he needs it tomorrow and I don't have that kind of clout."

"Okay. Getting a company like Suminski Stuff into Grennady could be really good for us. Alex has been a ruler too long to let a ten-year-old problem keep him from doing the right thing, but that doesn't mean we'll poke the bear. As long as we keep Alex away from Dean Suminski everything should be fine."

"But he expects to be dealing with the royal family."

"And he will. He'll deal with me. I have some thoughts on how to get office space. So I'll make some calls." Princess Eva paused. "And, Kristen?"

"Yes?"

"Be careful with this guy."

Kristen laughed. "Right." But remembering the way he'd kissed her shot that odd longing through her—even though she knew he had no intention of seeing her again. The way he said goodbye proved that. And she should be glad. Rich guys didn't marry commoners. They used them. Hadn't one heartbreak been enough?

She was smarter than to long for something that made no sense.

"He's got to be the grouchiest man on the face of the earth. I think I'll be fine."

"So the accident changed him?"

"Accident?"

"Dean was a very happy sort of party guy, until Alex's girlfriend was killed after Dean—" Eva paused. Her tone went from conversational to royal in one indrawn breath. "Actually, Kristen, if Dean didn't tell you, then let's not poke that bear, either."

"He told me."

"Then you understand how sensitive this is."

"Yes, ma'am."

"I'll call in some favors to find Suminski office space. Our vacation is over in two days. There's no sense in cutting it short now. You can handle Dean and his staff for two days, right?"

Kristen said, "Yes, ma'am," again, but she hung up the phone with the oddest feeling in her stomach. Dean might think he wouldn't see her again, but Princess Eva had just put her in charge of him.

She tried to stem the crazy bubbly feeling behind her ribs, but she couldn't. Dean might seem like the coldest man on earth to the rest of the world, but he'd confided in her, laughed with her, kissed her.

She did not want to let him go.

Dean's jet landed in Grennady four hours after the plane carrying Kristen, Stella and the portion of Suminski Stuff staff who were working on the series of games. Jason was staying in New York to do some PR and some hand-holding, so Dean had met him for breakfast before he'd flown out. But he'd been glad to have the excuse of meeting Jason, so he didn't have to spend a long flight with Kristen, tempted by another kiss, wishing circumstances in his life were different. Because his life wasn't different. It couldn't be different. He was who he was.

And damn it! Though he'd had a rough beginning and made one huge mistake involving Alexandros Sancho, he was basically a lucky guy. Mostly because that mistake with Alexandros had taught him some hard lessons. He now did nothing without forethought. Lots of forethought.

Kissing Kristen might have been the most impulsive thing he'd ever done, but it hadn't been thoughtless. He knew he'd never see her again. Even though they'd soon be in the same small country, there was a chasm of protocol between them. He'd deal with her boss because that was the level he was on. She'd deal with Stella because that was the level *she* was on. Nine chances out of ten he wouldn't even see her in passing.

He'd reasoned all that out before he'd kissed her and he'd been fine with it. But he hadn't counted on her lips being so soft or her kiss being so tempting. He hadn't counted on his head spinning and his hormones begging to take over. Still, he'd kept control. He'd stepped away like a gentleman.

And he'd eliminated a long plane ride with her by leaving for Grennady much later than his staff, and now here he was alone...

In the middle of the night.

In the frozen tundra.

Good God, it was cold!

And dark. Darker than he'd ever seen.

Of course, having grown up in the city, accustomed to streetlights, car lights and neon signs, he hadn't really been exposed to darkness.

He looked up and simply stared for a few seconds. The twinkle of a million stars, light-years away, almost stole his breath—which wouldn't be too hard to do since it was a visible puff of freezing air every time he exhaled.

Crap! It was cold!

And they'd lost a day. Considering time difference and travel across an ocean, it was late Monday night, early Tuesday morning, depending on how you looked at it. He was cold, late, and he'd had to force himself away from the first woman who'd really interested him in ten years. This trip was off to a fantastic start.

He wasted no time racing to the limo that awaited him. But instead of the driver opening the door, Kristen appeared at his side and pulled the latch to offer him entry.

"Good evening."

He had to shake himself to keep from staring at her. He'd meticulously planned it so he'd never see her again. Yet here she was.

He took another freezing breath to give himself time to recover from the shock, to stop the tingle that sprang to his lips, to fight his eyes from drinking in the sight of her. To get himself back into work mode. To remember she was an underling to the people with whom he'd be dealing for the next six weeks. And to speak normally.

"Evening? That's what you call this?"

"Actually, it's the dead of night. I went with *evening* because I thought *good night* would sound too much like goodbye—" She stopped abruptly and winced.

Internally, he winced too. They'd already had their goodbye in the form of a really great kiss. And just the thought of that kiss kicked his heart into high gear again.

Recovering quicker than he did, she smoothly motioned him inside the white limo. "We like to think of the darkness as cozy." She smiled. "Just wait until Christmas."

Her smile made him want to smile. But he refused. He had no intention of getting involved with this woman— for her sake, not his—and no intention of being a bundle of emotion around her. He would speak logic, behave logically and he would be fine.

When they were inside the limo, he pointed at her parka, thick mittens and the knit hat that hid her pretty yellow hair. "You can laugh because you're all bundled up."

"You'd think a genius would be smart enough to realize he was traveling to one of the coldest countries in the world and dress appropriately."

He displayed the arm of his overcoat. "This is a winter coat."

She shook her head. "You're going to need something a little warmer."

"I'll call Stella."

Kristen put her hand on his wrist before he could pull out his phone. "She broke her leg."

Dean was so focused on how naturally, how easily she touched him, and how normal it felt to have her touch him, that he almost missed what she'd said. When it sunk in, he said. "Stella broke her leg?"

"Walking on the tarmac to get to the big jet, she lost her balance and fell. While we waited for the ambulance that took her to the ER, she insisted the flight go without her. When she's well enough to travel she said she'd catch up."

Dean sighed. "She needs to stay in bed for a few days, not fly across an ocean. I'll call her later and make sure she stays right where she is."

"Are you going to be okay without your right hand?"

"She's not my right hand. She's my people person."

"She talks to people for you?"

Dean peered at her, not sure if she was kidding. Jason had insisted he needed a date for the Christmas party to make him look normal, but they'd spent almost three entire days together. Surely, she didn't still think he was a social misfit. Though her having that wrong assumption might work to prevent her from getting the wrong idea about the kiss, it didn't sit well with his pride. He couldn't let her believe there was something hugely wrong with him.

"No. She takes care of things that involve other people. Like, when you needed a gown, she helped you get one. The employees needed to be rounded up and at the airport for their flight here, she arranged it."

He sighed, suddenly realizing the hole that would be left without Stella. "She was the one who would have been getting lift tickets and rental cars and all those things for the twenty people and their families we brought here." He rubbed his hand across his mouth. "We're screwed."

"Your staff is smart enough to get their own lift tickets. And if they aren't, I have an entire palace staff at my disposal. With Eva and Alex in Xaviera for another two days, they're all yours. I'm happy to be your liaison."

His gaze crawled over to hers. So much for getting himself away from her. The royals were out of town, which he now remembered her telling him. Stella was out of commission. Until he got to know the palace staff, he needed her.

And he wasn't going to let his own personal longings get in the way. "Thank you. I appreciate the help."

"It's our pleasure. Even if Grennady only turns out to be a good place for your company to finish this one project, we want you to remember us fondly."

Right. His plan was exactly the opposite. She tempted him to want things he knew he couldn't have. So he intended to forget her, and everything about her.

"You want us to remember that your country didn't suit us so we left?"

"No. We want your employees to remember skiing and snowboarding. Sleigh rides. Hot cocoa. Hot toddies.

Snuggling in front of fireplaces. We want them and their families to go home and talk about what a great time they had here."

He sniffed a laugh. "Leave it to you to find the bright side."

"Being in charge might be new to me, but I'm not stupid, and all of a sudden the timing feels right. Like I'm stepping into my destiny."

"Destiny." He snorted. He hated when people talked that way, as if some big hand would nudge them along, open doors, keep trouble at bay. She might be smart but that darned naïvety of hers was going to get her into trouble if she didn't put a lid on it. "Don't think destiny. Think to do list. Think organizational chart. For a charity like you're proposing, you'll need accountants and tax people, all of them versed in international law."

She laughed. "I haven't just kept a princess on track for three years, there's also the matter of that little degree you know I have. I'm more prepared for this than you think."

"You have a fanciful streak, as if you assume everything's going to automatically work out."

Her gaze ambled over and snagged his. "I got you here, didn't I?"

Desire slammed into him like a punch in the gut. She was tempting when she was sweet, but damned near irresistible when she was sassy.

He sucked in a breath and brought his briefcase to his lap so he wouldn't have to look at her when he spoke. "Technically, Mrs. Flannigan got me here."

"Yes, but it was a stroke of luck that I was with you every time you saw her."

"No, it wasn't luck. It was a bunch of things coming

together. I took you to a Christmas party where Winslow invited us to lunch. You had told him you were pitching your country to me. He brought it up to Mrs. Flannigan. No magic. No destiny. More like logical steps. Everything had a purpose and a reason. Stop thinking about magic and destiny and start using this." He tapped her head. "And things will go a lot easier for you."

"I bet you're a real barrel of laughs at Christmastime."

He turned his attention to his briefcase, opening it as if he had something important he needed to read because once again he just couldn't look at her. "If I choose not to celebrate that particular holiday, I think I have good reason."

"Yes, you do. I'm sorry. I spoke thoughtlessly."

She looked so apologetic that he felt bad—for her. But he was the one who'd needed the reminder about mixing business with pleasure. If *he* wasn't so damned attracted to her, *he* wouldn't have fallen into such a complicated conversation. He would have told her what he needed. Told her yes or no. And the discussion would have stayed on track the way it should have.

"Look, it appears we're stuck working together for two days, so let's agree to stop trying to be friends and just do our jobs."

She gave him a funny look. "But you kissed me."

He sighed. Why was he not surprised her honesty wouldn't simply let that go?

"I know. I thought I was never going to see you again, so it wouldn't be a big deal. It was a nice way to end a nice weekend."

Her eyes softened when they met his. "A really nice weekend."

His pulse scrambled. It had been one of the nicest

weekends of his life and to see she felt the same made him want to kiss her again. But he couldn't have her and she shouldn't want him.

"So let's leave it at that. A nice weekend." He rifled through the documents in his briefcase, pretending to be looking for something. "Right now my priority— and yours since you're my liaison—is to get this game to beta testers on January second. Forget about kisses, forget about the whole weekend. Hell, forget about Paris. Let's pretend we just met."

"Okay." She reached into her pocket. "You'll need this back, then."

The bracelet he'd given her fell into his briefcase. He'd told her he'd take it back, but actually having the damned thing almost fall into his lap sent a zap of weirdness through him. He'd bought that for her. He didn't want it back. It didn't feel right taking it back.

But if they were going to keep this strictly professional, he couldn't say any of that. He had to accept the bracelet.

"Great. Thanks. Are you sure you don't want it?"

"Totally."

He tucked it in his overcoat pocket and the weight of it felt like a rock. No one had ever returned a gift. He wasn't even sure what to do with it.

As they reached a hotel that looked more like a Swiss chalet, Kristen said, "The princess had to pull some strings, but we emptied the entire hotel and it's yours."

"Mine?"

"Well, yours and your employees'. You have the penthouse suite on the third floor. The first and second floors each have twenty rooms, so you've actually got an extra room or two. Just in case."

"So I'm in a hotel with my staff?"

"You'll be fine."

He shook his head. If Stella had booked this hotel, he would have accepted it on faith. Which was why they never fought or got personal. She did something. He accepted it.

So if he wanted to have an uncomplicated relationship with Kristen for the next two days, that's what he needed to do with her too. Not engage her. Just trust her judgment.

"Okay. Whatever. When do I see our work space?"

"Actually, your work space is the hotel's two first-floor meeting rooms."

He gaped at her. "We're working in the same space where we're living?"

"I thought you'd like that."

He blew his breath out on a sigh. Winslow had said to shake things up. So, sure. Why the hell not? "I might."

"It'll be very convenient. Staff has already been briefed on the fact that there's only about six hours of daylight. Most have decided to use the daylight for family time and work when it's dark."

This he could not handle. "I've gone along with your conference rooms and having my employees and their families underfoot in my hotel…but eighteen hours of dark?"

She laughed. "It's winter in Scandinavia. Anybody who knows geography knows we don't get much daylight."

He struggled with the urge to close his eyes in frustration. He supposed he did know that. He simply hadn't put it all together.

"Look on the bright side. If your employees work when it's dark, that's eighteen whole hours a day."

He sniffed a laugh. "You are such a dreamer."

She climbed out of the limo. "Yeah, well, you're pretty much the opposite."

Of all the answers she could have given that was the last thing he'd been expecting. "That's it? I call you a dreamer and your best shot is to call me the opposite." He shook his head. "I'm absolutely going to have to teach you how to fight."

She smiled and pivoted toward the entryway. "Maybe I don't want to fight. Besides, that would take us back to you giving me lessons on how to handle myself in the business world. We just agreed to pretend we'd only met tonight. We can't go back to those lessons."

She walked into the hotel and he blew out another exasperated breath, staring at the starry sky.

Being with her, pretending he didn't like her, was going to kill him.

Wʜᴇɴ Kʀɪsᴛᴇɴ ꜰɪɴᴀʟʟʏ got to bed, she slept like the dead. She woke around nine, just as the sun was coming up.

Curious about what she'd been doing the past few days, her family asked a million questions. She'd phoned them the day she'd flown to New York, in the limo on the way to the boutique to get her gown for the Christmas party with Dean, but they'd never heard of flying across an ocean with someone just to make a pitch. So she filled them in on the details of her trip and the weekend that followed, but her mom had trouble taking it all in.

"He's a busy man, Mom. People ask him to go places like lunches and dinners and I was his date for the weekend so I went too. But now we're in Grennady and everything's back to normal," she said as she grabbed a piece of cheese and headed for the door. "I can't do a darned thing to help him meet his deadlines, but I am in charge of making sure he and his crew are happy over the next two days. With his assistant in New York, I'm not sure what that's going to entail, but I need to be on-site."

She rushed out of her mom's kitchen and headed into town, to the men's shop where Prince Alex had bought his coat the first time he'd come to Grennady with Princess Eva, and realized he was horribly underdressed.

Stefan Steiner, a tall blond with big blue eyes, greeted her when she walked in. "Kristen! How can I help you?"

"The royal family has a visitor. An American."

"Oh, sounds interesting."

Dean was interesting, probably the most interesting guy Kristen had ever met. But he didn't want anything to do with her except a professional relationship, and she didn't want to push him into admitting he had feelings for her. Though he did. She knew he did. That kiss *told her* he did.

And she recognized that if he was avoiding whatever was happening between them it was because he'd gotten his heart broken by Nina. She'd cheated him, used him, then dumped him.

And died.

Was it any wonder he was so careful about his feelings?

There was absolutely nothing Kristen could say or do without stepping on incredibly private territory, and if she pushed him he probably wouldn't talk anyway.

Realizing Stefan was waiting for an answer she said, "He's a businessman, only in Grennady for a few weeks trying to get some work done."

"Now? When we're about to celebrate Christmas?"

"He's American."

Stefan laughed. "Last time I heard, they celebrate Christmas in America."

She ambled toward a circle of parkas. "Not this guy. He's all about the work." Because his life had been difficult. Marred by tragedies that molded him into someone cool and precise with haunted eyes. But she couldn't dwell on that, couldn't wonder about the scar on his heart that might never really heal, or the days and nights of anguish he'd spent before he'd built his walls. Because when she let her mind go in that direction, she longed for him to talk to her, to get it out and see that he could be happy.

"So it's my job to make sure he doesn't have to worry about anything else." She picked a sturdy navy blue coat. "I think this is what he needs. I'm just not sure of the size."

Stefan joined her at the rack. "How tall is he?"

She glanced over. "About your height."

Stefan nodded. "Shoulder width?"

She frowned.

"How broad is he?"

"Well, he's…" She lifted her hands until she had them in a sort of circle the way they had been when she slid them to his nape when he kissed her. "This big."

Stefan eyed the shape made by her arms and told her the size Dean probably wore.

She shrugged. "Sounds good to me."

He helped her find warm gloves and a fur-lined bomber hat with flaps to cover his ears.

She nodded appreciatively. "He's probably going to need boots too, but I won't even venture to guess that size."

"Yes, especially since you didn't kiss his feet."

Kristen felt her face color but she innocently said, "What?"

"You think I don't recognize the arm placement of someone kissing a man?"

She grimaced. "I guess you do."

He leaned across the counter. "Don't worry. My lips are sealed."

"Thanks. Because nothing's going to happen between us. Like I said. He's all about business." And no matter how haunted his eyes, she absolutely had to respect his wishes.

She signed off on the purchases, charging them to the royal family. Stefan told her to have Dean phone him with his boot size, and he'd have a pair delivered to his hotel.

She lugged the enormous bag out of his shop, passing familiar bakeries, groceries and restaurants on snow-covered streets that wafted with the scents of cheese, breakfast meats and breads. The frosty air nipped her nose and turned her breaths to puffs of smoke as she wove through gaggles of happy, chattering tourists.

In the lobby of the hotel the princess had procured for Dean and his staff, she stomped snow off her boots. After a quick chat with the desk clerk, she took her big package down the hall to the first meeting room.

Much larger than a conference room, more the size of a classroom, the space had round tables scattered throughout. Covered in white tablecloths as if prepared for a banquet, they weren't suitable for a bunch of computer geeks who would be working to find and fix the problems in software.

Given that it was light out and most of the Suminski Stuff staff were on the ski slopes with family, the hotel had plenty of time to put some workstations in there and maybe a sofa or recliner or two. She would remind them of that as soon as she gave Dean his coat, hat and gloves.

A few feet down the hall, she found the second meeting room. From the doorway, she could see this room was set up the same as the first. Round tables with white tablecloths, each surrounded by six chairs.

The only difference was this room wasn't empty. Dean Suminski sat alone at one of the tables. Dressed in jeans and a sweater, with his hair causally mussed, he looked the way he had at Rockefeller Center. Memories of skating, holding hands, nestling against him as they walked up the busy New York City street slid through her brain, almost making her sigh with longing.

"In case you can't interpret the expression on my face, this empty room does not please me."

She laughed, though her heart jerked a bit. It was hard to believe that this guy currently being so cool with her had held her hand, built her confidence, introduced her to Mrs. Flannigan and made sure she had private time with her. And even harder to believe she had no choice but to go along with him.

"It's your employees' first day here. They may decide not to work at all today. I told you last night that they intended to take at least the daylight hours for family time. Your people need a break."

She hoisted the big bag containing his parka onto one of the round tables. "I bought you a few things."

One of his eyebrows quirked.

"Now you understand how I felt in New York when you kept buying me clothes."

"I told you that was the cost of doing business."

"Well, consider this a welcome gift from the royal family."

She pulled the hat out of the bag and tossed it to him, then the gloves, then the parka.

He caught the first two easily, but barely managed to grab the big coat. "I won't be going outside."

"You're here for six weeks. If nothing else, you'll tire of the hotel food and want to go to a restaurant. That coat you have won't cut it." She handed him Stefan's business card. "You'll also need boots. All you have to do is call Stefan and give him your size. He'll send the right boots to the hotel." She smiled hopefully. "Let's try everything on."

Hugging the big parka, Dean sighed in resignation and rose.

She took the coat from his hands and motioned for him to turn around. When he did, she held it open and guided the sleeves up his arms. After he shrugged into it, she smoothed her palms along the shoulders, straightening the fabric, recognizing it was a perfect fit.

But as her hands moved from his spine outward, she realized she was touching him. Essentially, rubbing his back. Because she liked it. She liked the feel of him, the look of him. Even the haunted expression in his eyes tempted her to ask him a million questions because she *wanted* to know him.

He turned his head and caught her gaze. "Having fun back there?"

She grimaced. "Sorry. I was just straightening things, making sure the coat fit."

"Right. And my lips accidentally bumped into yours when I kissed you."

His sarcastic wit would have surprised her, except he'd been making jokes all weekend, as he'd relaxed with her. She reached for the fur-lined navy blue hat with flaps that could be pulled down over his ears. Before he realized what she was about to do, she went to her tiptoes and plopped it on his head.

She burst into giggles. "You look like a Russian." But she quickly sobered. She really didn't know a damn thing about this guy she was so drawn to. "Are you Russian? With your dark hair and eyes, it wouldn't surprise me."

He gave the straps of the hat a tug to yank it into place. "I'm half Polish, half Irish."

"That's a strange combo."

He shrugged. "I'm sort of happy with it. The Polish part of me makes me resilient, and I've never met a Saint Patrick's Day that I didn't like."

The corners of her mouth tipped up into a smile. "There you are being funny again. You should let more people than me see your sense of humor."

"Oh, really? And what do you think Winslow would have done Friday night if I'd cracked jokes when my company was in trouble?"

"Maybe thought you were human?"

"Or thought I wasn't serious. Or thought I didn't realize how much trouble I was in."

"Well, I don't care." She reached up and linked the two straps of the hat under his chin, securing them in their catch. "I like it when you're funny."

He caught her hand to stop it. "You shouldn't."

Once again they were standing incredibly close, almost as if they couldn't help themselves. "Why are you so determined to ignore what we feel for each other?"

"Because I'm not anybody's knight in shining armor, Kristen."

"Only because you were hurt."

"And that turned me into the kind of guy who isn't made for relationships."

He didn't have the look of longing that usually came to his eyes when they stood this close. For a few seconds, she missed it, and then she understood what he was saying. Away from the trouble that threw them together in the first place, he was in control again.

And maybe he didn't like her as much as she'd thought.

She cleared her throat. "Now that you have a coat,

you should go out. Go find your people on the ski slopes. Have some fun."

"Yeah, Dean, maybe you should."

Kristen whipped around to see Dean's right-hand man, Jason, standing in the doorway. Dressed in a colorful sweater that made his twenty or so extra pounds all the more obvious, he sauntered into the room, holding a cup of coffee.

Dropping her hand, Dean said, "What are you doing here?"

"Stella's down for the count." He shrugged. "She's got a few days of really good drugs for the pain and then six weeks in some sort of boot thing, then a few weeks of rehab."

Dean winced. "Ouch."

"Yeah, she says 'ouch' a lot." He laughed. "Anyway, I thought you might need me. So I flew over."

"Thank God." Dean breathed an insulting sigh of relief, as if Kristen didn't cut it as his assistant. "I do need you. *This* is where the royal family decided we should work."

Jason didn't answer. He glanced at Kristen.

Kristen held her breath. One wrong word from Jason and she'd be looking for another place for them, and she didn't have the clout of a princess.

Jason glanced around, took a sip of coffee and said, "I like it."

Dean scowled.

Kristen's heart about exploded with relief.

"Winslow Osmond said the staff needed a change of scenery, but I was thinking maybe we need a change in the way we're doing things too," Jason said. "What can it hurt to have all the key players in the same room?"

"They could kill each other."

Jason shrugged off his boss's concern. "Or they could learn to work together." He ambled over to Dean. He pinched a bit of the sleeve of the parka. "What's this?"

"A coat, gloves and some hat thing," Dean said, peering at Kristen as if the coat and hat had somehow ruined his life.

Jason nodded. "I like them." He caught Dean's gaze. "So technically you *could* go skiing."

Dean just looked at him.

Jason faced Kristen. "Truth be told, he's not a skier. But he used to be hell with a snowboard."

"*Used to* being the operative words," Dean said.

But Kristen pictured a much younger Dean, in a cooler coat and a trendy knit cap. Having seen him laugh, she guessed he'd probably laughed on the slopes, that he'd loved the challenge of the snowboard and the rush of speed as he flew down winding hills. Once again her heart ached that one tragic episode in his life had taken a probably happy young man and turned him into someone afraid to live.

Jason smiled. "You know what? You might not want to jump on a snowboard today, but you should get out and see the town." He turned to Kristen. "Your capital is amazing."

Kristen said, "Thank you. Most of the buildings have been around for centuries."

Jason nodded. "You don't see craftsmanship like that anymore." He pivoted to face Dean. "You need to go out and see some of this." Then back to Kristen. "Kristen, would you take him?"

Kristen said, "I can't," at the same time that Dean said, "We have work to do."

Jason waved both hands. "Oh, garbage, you two. You'll work tonight. Or tomorrow when our wayward staff is scheduled to be here. Go now, while you still have—" He glanced at his watch. "What? Four hours of sunlight?"

"That's about it," Kristen agreed.

"Good." He faced Dean. "It's not so long that you'll get bored. But it's enough time to see some of the sights. And clear your head. Get some fresh air into those lungs."

Dean's scowl grew.

Jason faced Kristen. "Whether he understands it or not, he's going to want to compliment your king and princess when they return from their holiday in Xaviera. Give him a little bit of a history lesson so he can speak intelligently."

"No. I'm not going anywhere."

CHAPTER ELEVEN

DEAN'S REFUSAL RANG through the quiet work space. Jason took a step back, as if he knew he'd pushed too far.

But Kristen sucked in a hard breath. Dean had hurt her, and he'd done it deliberately, but he decided that's what she needed to see. The demanding, difficult side of him that everybody thought was the real him.

She turned and headed for the door. "If you need anything I'll be in the palace."

He didn't say goodbye. He didn't say anything. He waited for her to leave, and then he faced Jason. "Get maintenance back here. I want this room and the one up the hall ready for work when that blasted sun goes down."

With that he exited, heading up the hall to the elevator that would take him to his penthouse suite. When the door opened on the modern space with red sofas and black and white accent pieces, he wrestled out of the big coat he didn't want and threw the damned hat at the cold fireplace.

He wasn't just angry that Kristen kept pushing him to be the person he was deep down inside. He was angry that he couldn't be that guy.

He got on the phone and made some calls and forgot all about Kristen Anderson. But when the sun went down and his employees began returning, laughing, happy, more enthusiastic than he'd seen them in weeks, guilt set in. When an hour went by with everybody getting along, making accommodations for each other in the unusual work space and sharing ideas for what they should do next with the games, the guilt tripled.

Winslow and Mrs. Flannigan had been right. They needed this time somewhere different, somewhere they could relax, somewhere their creativity could be nurtured. Kristen had found him, essentially had made this four-week getaway possible, and he'd thanked her by treating her like dirt.

After dinner with her family, Kristen went upstairs and opened her laptop. Mrs. Flannigan had given her a list of people to consider for her board of advisors but before she approached anyone she wanted to know a bit about them.

But reading resumes for and articles about people who were wealthy because they were brilliant, only reminded her of Dean. How she'd wanted him to be the playful guy she'd uncovered in New York and how he'd bitten her head off. It hadn't taken a real yelling session. She'd gotten the message from the way he'd said no to a tour with her.

It had stung, though. Because deep down she believed he liked her. And it stung even more, because deep down she had more feelings for him than she'd let herself admit.

The sound of sleigh bells penetrated the haze of her thoughts, then two male voices, and she frowned. Her family's farm was far enough off the beaten path that no one "accidentally" drove or walked by. She rose from her desk and looked out the window.

At the edge of the road was a pretty red sleigh decorated with yellow flowers and green leaves. The driver sat on the bench seat, holding the reins of a chestnut mare. Dean Suminski sat in the backseat.

She spun around and raced out of her room and down the stairs to the front door, so thrilled to see him that she didn't care why he'd chosen a sled to come to her house. She hadn't been wrong about his feelings for her, and that, once again, quadrupled her feelings for him.

With a laugh, she whipped open the door. "What are you doing?"

Walking up to the porch of her parents' house, he wore the big blue parka and the hat, with the flaps over his ears. He angled his thumb toward the sleigh. "This is an apology."

Her heart stumbled. The great Dean Suminski apologized? "For what?"

"I was a bit nastier in my refusal of a tour of your capital than I wanted to be."

Her heart stuttered. "A bit nastier? Did you intend to be nasty?"

He sighed. "No. I just felt overwhelmed."

She could have said, "Overwhelmed by what?" and forced the issue that he was having trouble with the fact that he wanted to be himself around her. Except he was here. Outside the door of her parents' house…with a sleigh! He *wanted* to see her. He didn't need to say the words. And she didn't need to push for them.

"So is everything going okay at the hotel?"

"Yes." He nodded at her white sweater and jeans. "You're freezing without a coat. Go get one. We'll talk while we ride."

He turned and began walking back to the sleigh. She

spun around, raced into her house and grabbed her coat, hat and mittens.

Her mother, a tall, thin blonde wearing a colorful apron over jeans, walked into the front hall. "Kristen? Did I hear you talking to someone?"

"Dean Suminski, the guy I went to New York with… he's here with a sleigh."

Her mom frowned. "The man working at the hotel?"

Sliding into her coat, she nodded.

Her mom said, "You should invite him to dinner."

Kristen froze. Invite him to dinner? Have him meet her parents? That would probably freak him out. "Didn't we already eat?"

"I didn't mean tonight. I meant tomorrow or Friday," her mom said with a laugh. Then she shooed her out the door. "Go. Have fun."

Kristen raced out onto the big front porch of her family's old farmhouse and down the three steps to the snow-covered sidewalk. Dean stood by the sleigh. When she reached him, he helped her climb inside, then pulled himself in behind her.

The air was crisp, the night freezing cold, but, God help her, to her it felt just plain magical. Every step he took was a step closer to him being the man he was supposed to be, the man who could love her.

She slowed her thoughts. Told her brain to settle down. He was a broken man. A man who'd grown up without love, whose first love had used him. She wasn't going to wave a magic wand and he'd be normal again. His wounds might be healing, but he would need time to learn to trust again.

Still, she knew her heart was racing ahead of things because she had feelings for him far beyond anything she'd ever felt. If she wanted this, wanted him, and she did, she had to take her time. Give him a way to get to know her enough that he'd trust her with his heart. Not rush. Not nudge. Just enjoy the sleigh ride.

After all…he was here, wasn't he?

Spreading a thick blanket over both of their legs, he said, "I actually learned how to drive the sleigh from the internet. YouTube."

She glanced over, saw he was serious and laughed. "So why aren't you driving?"

"Clyde up there," he said, pointing to their driver, "knows his way around the countryside. I don't."

"Good point."

Powdery snow muffled the clip-clop of the horse's hooves, but caused the sleigh blades to make a *swoosh, swoosh, swoosh* noise as the sled moved along. A light in the front illuminated twenty or so feet ahead, but otherwise her world, her county, was dark and silent.

Dark, *freezing cold* and silent.

The kind of cold where two people who shouldn't like each other, shouldn't belong together, could snuggle under a cover and get to know each other.

She slid her arm beneath his, nestled close, seeking his warmth but also basking in the chance to touch him.

"So tell me more about what you did today."

"Being this far away from the US and being plunged into darkness more hours of the day than any human being should have to endure has had an odd effect on me."

She cuddled closer. "Let's not forget that it's cold."

He stiffened, but he said, "It is cold." Then he slowly relaxed beside her, as if he couldn't deny he wanted the closeness too, and using the cold as an excuse made that easier. "But it seems to work. The employees came back today more energetic than I've seen them in months."

He leaned back, relaxed. Saying all that out loud seemed to have helped it to sink in that everything was working out.

"I'm glad we could help."

"It's just…" He turned to look at her. "Unexpected."

She couldn't have said it any better herself. What was happening between them was unexpected. But maybe that was part of the attraction. She was an unsophisticated country girl. He was a guy who had pulled himself up by his talent and his genius and made himself one of the most important men in the business world. But they clicked.

They rode through the silent night for about twenty minutes with her prodding him with questions, getting him to talk about his work.

"Jason thinks I should stop the US calls when the team comes in off the slopes. And forget about Asia until we get home. He says the team wasn't just energetic because they'd had fun on the ski slopes. He thinks they respond positively to having me around." He stole a peek at her. "Normally, I'm in my office four floors above them and they work on their own. Today, I spent time in the meeting room, asking questions, giving suggestions." He shrugged. "It was fun. Like the old days."

"Maybe you *should* spend more time with them."

"I haven't touched that part of the company in years."

"That's interesting since they've been stuck for years."

He shook his head. "If you're hinting that they need me, don't. I've hired the best in the business. They don't need me."

"And yet…here they are…stuck."

He sniffed a laugh and she let the subject die, knowing she'd gotten her point across.

As the night got colder, their blanket drifted higher, to their chins. She reveled in the way he talked, the sound of his voice, the quiet trust. The sleigh turned around, headed back, and she knew she had only another twenty minutes.

When he asked how her day had been, she returned the favor of being honest with him the way he'd been with her. "When the princess is away I'm bored. I have nothing to do but check her email a few times a day to make sure nothing that comes in is a crisis." She peeked at him. "And as small as we are, we get a crisis about once every ten years."

He laughed. "Too bad you can't code."

"Really?" She knew he hadn't intended to take them down this road, but this was the heart of why she always wanted to be around him and why he'd brought a sleigh to her house in the dead of night. And maybe it was time they talked about it.

"You think it's a bad thing that we're different?"

He faced her, held her gaze for a few seconds.

When she couldn't take the honest scrutiny anymore, she whispered, "Admit it. Part of the attraction is that we're nothing alike."

He looked around her frozen countryside. "We might have been raised differently and have two different ways in which we want to change the world." He met her gaze again. "But we both want to change the world."

"So? That just means we're enough alike that we understand each other, but different enough that we're interesting."

He shook his head. The sleigh silently swooshed to a stop in front of her parents' farmhouse.

"Maybe. I don't know."

He appeared genuinely perplexed. She supposed if someone tossed a monkey wrench into her life she'd be confused too. But even with the totally baffled expression on his face, he was handsome, strong. She couldn't resist leaning forward and touching her lips to his. She stayed there a second, giving him time to respond and he did. Under their blanket, his hands came up to her shoulders to pull her close so he could deepen the kiss.

And she realized this was what she'd been waiting for her whole life. The magic prince she didn't believe existed wasn't a guy on a white horse; he was someone who understood her. Someone she understood. An equal.

She broke the kiss and slid out from under the cover, bolting out of the sleigh before he had a chance to get out into the cold when he didn't have to.

They were falling in love. Real love.

She turned and waved. "I'll see you tomorrow."

Then she pivoted around and ran into her house. Her blood racing. Her knees a little weak. But her heart happy as well as terrified.

They clicked. That's why everything felt so different when they were together.

But she had only four weeks to get him to see it.

And even if he did, he'd have to brave a whole new world of communication and honesty. He might not be capable of having the kind of relationship she needed.

CHAPTER TWELVE

THE NEXT DAY Dean woke feeling happy, refreshed. Jason joined him in the penthouse suite for breakfast.

After room service wheeled in their cart, Jason said, "So where'd you go last night?"

Dean kept his attention on his tablet. He'd pulled up *the Wall Street Journal* and was reading the highlights of the day's financial news.

After he finished the article, he glanced up at his friend. "Believe it or not, I hired a sleigh."

Jason laughed. "Sleigh?"

"I figured I owed Kristen an apology for barking at her yesterday when she was trying to be helpful." He shook his head in wonder. "I never knew darkness could be so appealing."

"You've lived too long in the city," Jason said, lifting the lid off his plate of eggs and pancakes. "When we get back home, we'll start scheduling more time for you in your Albany house."

Just the thought of the Albany house made him smile. He knew it was because of the vision he'd had of Kristen in that house, on his bed, with his child. Though the vision didn't scare him to death or confuse him as it had the first time he thought it, it did fill him with questions.

Was that what he was doing with her? Falling in love so he could have something he wasn't even sure existed? The sleigh ride hadn't been as romantic as it had been warm, nice. Then she'd kissed him and, of course, everything that had been warm and friendly suddenly became hot and steamy.

He'd thought of her the whole way back to town, thought of her when he woke up and now he was thinking of her again.

He just liked her. Everything about her.

Even her freezing cold country.

And it scared him to death.

He'd liked everything about Nina too. Even her sweltering hot country. When it came to falling in love, he had no guidelines, no common sense. He'd been gobsmacked when Nina told him she'd been using him to make Alex Sancho jealous.

So what would he find out about Kristen? That she had used him to get to know Mrs. Flannigan? That being connected to him gave her a stature that would help her establish herself in his world and easily get the money she needed for her charity?

Because there was something.

There was always something.

A few minutes later, the suite phone rang. Not knowing who would have the number, he didn't answer. Embroiled in a discussion of marketing techniques in Asia, Jason didn't even acknowledge that the phone had rung.

But after Jason left to go do some sightseeing, Dean checked with the front desk. They had indeed taken a message from the call he'd ignored.

"Kristen Anderson called. She'd like you to join her

family this evening for dinner. Seven o'clock. She left a number."

Dean said, "Thank you. I won't need the number." Because he did not intend to go to that family dinner.

But all day long he thought of the white farmhouse he'd glimpsed when his sleigh had swished up to her sidewalk. He thought about the fact that it was so far out in the country and wondered about the people who lived there...

And the people who had raised Kristen. What kind of parents were so strong that they raised a daughter who took up the cause of a pen pal who'd been killed? What kind of parents raised a child to be so open and honest? Did she have brothers and sisters?

In the end, he waited until the very last second, until it was too late to call and say he was coming. So late, he barely got a cab.

He arrived at her house, bottle of wine in hand—the suggestion of the cabbie—and knocked on the door, wondering what in the hell he was doing.

The door opened. A tall, blonde woman smiled broadly at him. "You must be Dean Suminski." She opened the door a little wider. "I'm Joan, Kristen's mom." She motioned for him to enter, then turned and called up the stairs, "Kristen! Your friend is here."

As Dean stepped inside the old-fashioned foyer, Joan faced him with a smile. "I hope you like roast beef. We're not fancy here."

Feeling odd and awkward, he said, "That's great," just as Kristen came running down the stairs. She stopped when she saw him and their gazes met.

She wore jeans and a white sweatshirt. Her hair fell around her in loose curls. But her smile was huge, luscious. As if seeing him made her the happiest woman in the world.

Now, how the hell was he supposed to resist that?

"I'm so glad you came."

"Yeah, well, I'm sorry I didn't call."

"There was no reason to call," Kristen's mom said, taking his arm and guiding him through the short hall that led to an unexpectedly modern kitchen. "We don't stand on ceremony here."

He walked up to the center island that was cluttered with pots and pans, utensils and dishes used to make the dinner. The hardwood floors sparkled. The other counters were neat and tidy. A table in the adjoining dining area had been set.

Kristen said, "I'll set another place."

As she scrambled to gather plates, Kristen's mom nodded at a stool by the center island and he sat.

"Kristen's dad should be in any minute," Joan said, rifling through a drawer. She pulled out a corkscrew and handed it to him with the wine he'd brought. "You do the honors." She turned to the dining area. "Kristen, would you also get wineglasses?"

He opened the wine as Kristen retrieved wineglasses from a cabinet with a glass front. She set the four glasses on the counter, then smiled at him.

Warmth invaded his heart. Warmth and ease and a kind of comfort he'd never felt before.

The back door opened and an older man entered, a teenage boy on his heels.

"This is Kristen's dad, James, and her youngest brother, Lars. Lars, Jimmy, this is Kristen's friend Dean. He's the man who brought his company here for a bit of a rest while they work."

He didn't question that they knew about him. He would expect Kristen to tell her family about her work. Given the relaxed atmosphere of the kitchen, he would expect that she talked about everything in her life with her parents, and that they talked freely with her.

"It's a pleasure to meet you."

The big man walked over and clasped his hand. "It's a pleasure to meet you, too. Kristen's been all about trying to get a company here to Grennady, especially since her other brother, Brian, is studying computer science at university."

Dean peeked over at Kristen who blushed. "She never mentioned that."

Her gaze met his. "I didn't want to unduly influence you."

That made him laugh. Really laugh. The kind of laugh he experienced with her in New York. "Are you kidding? You stalked me to Paris, wouldn't get off my plane in New York until I listened to your pitch. And now you're trying to say you didn't want to influence me?"

She winced. "All right. Maybe a little."

Kristen's father and brother went upstairs to wash up for dinner. Dean poured the wine. He sat at the center island while Kristen cleared the counter and her mom put the finishing touches on dinner. By the time the men returned, dinner was ready to serve.

They spent the meal discussing Dean's company, Kristen's charity and the possibility that Lars would be going into computer science too. They sat around the table, eating chocolate cake for dessert, finishing the wine, talking like old friends, not worrying about clearing dishes. Until at nine o'clock when Kristen volunteered to drive him home.

He realized that her parents probably had to get up early the next morning and took his jacket when Joan brought it from the newel post on the stairway in the foyer.

"I can get a cab."

Shrugging into her coat, Kristen said, "Nonsense. It's not that far."

Then she smiled that smile again, the one that made him feel warm all over, the one that made him feel very much a part of her life, and the one he couldn't resist.

They got into her little car and he let her have her concentration to maneuver out of the farm's lane and onto the snow-covered main road.

"Your family is really nice."

"Yes. They are. We're just average, normal people, living life." She peeked at him. "I appreciate you being so nice to them. My mom really wanted to meet you. She was thrilled you accepted her dinner invitation."

"She's a great cook."

"Hey, I made those potatoes."

"Then you're probably a good cook too." He took a breath, considered for only a few seconds, then said, "My Gram had been a really great cook in her time, but the older she got the less she wanted to cook." He shrugged. "We ate a lot of pizza."

"As a little kid you probably liked that."

He laughed. "I did."

"Other stuff, not so much."

"I just always felt left out. She wouldn't let me sign up for Little League, or even after school activities. Said we couldn't afford the fees and insisted there always were fees. If there were parent-teacher conferences, I knew she wouldn't go. It's why it took so long for anyone to recognize that I was gifted."

"It sounds like she was just overwhelmed."

"She was."

"It also sounds like you forgive her."

"In a weird kind of way, there was nothing to forgive her for. Even as a kid I recognized that I was a burden."

"That's not a very nice way for a kid to feel."

He shook his head. "No."

"But you're over it."

"Most of it." He shrugged. "Lots of it. But there are some things you can't get over. All you can do is adjust."

"Nothing wrong with that."

No. He supposed there wasn't. He also couldn't believe how free he felt talking about this with her.

When she pulled the car into a parking space in front of the hotel, he glanced around, confused. He'd thought she'd drop him off at the door. Instead, they were in the back.

He turned to ask her why they were parked, just as she stretched across the seat and kissed him. Quick and light, her lips brushed his, and then she pulled back again.

"Thanks for coming tonight."

He laughed. "You're welcome. That's the first time anybody's ever kissed me as a thank-you."

Her head tilted. "Really?" She leaned forward and kissed him again. "Now you've been kissed twice as a thank-you."

This time he didn't let her pull back, he caught her shoulders and kept her right where she was so he could deepen the kiss. He had absolutely no idea what was happening, but if this was love, he really liked it.

After a few minutes, he realized he was necking in a car—in a hotel parking lot, with a woman he really liked who was nothing like any other woman he'd ever gotten involved with—like a horny teenager.

He took her shoulders and set her away from him, back on the driver's side of the car.

"That was different."

She laughed. "Really?"

"All this is so normal for you. So easy—"

"You think? You think I just go around kissing random guys?" She laughed gaily. "It's every bit as unusual for me as it is for you. And maybe even really poor timing for me since I'm at the beginning of the project I hope will be my life's work."

He sobered. "I'm sorry."

She laughed again, then shook her head. "Seriously, you need to work on thinking before you talk. I'm not saying this is a bad thing. It's a good thing. What I'm saying is that what we feel comes with complications." She stretched around again so that she could look into his eyes. "My family's putting up our Christmas tree on Saturday afternoon. I'd love for you to come."

Sitting so close, staring into her eyes, all he could think to say was, "Yes."

She pulled back. "Take the next few days to think things through." She put the car into gear again and drove up to the hotel door. "I'll see you Saturday."

Dazed, confused, he said, "Okay," as he got out of the car. But he understood what she was saying. The timing was wrong for them. Plus, he had issues. He might not be tumbling headfirst into love as much as he could be tumbling headfirst into disaster.

* * *

Saturday afternoon, Kristen was surprised when the doorbell rang and Dean stood on the front porch of her home, holding two bottles of wine.

Her heart spun crazily. She absolutely hadn't expected him to come to her house again. She believed he'd talk himself out of it. First, though he'd been comfortable with her family, she could see him returning to his hotel, picking the evening apart and finding a million things wrong with him getting to know her parents and brother. Second, she was positive he'd decide his work was more important than an afternoon off. Third, they were going to decorate a tree and Christmas was not his favorite holiday. Fourth, she was very sure what he felt for her confused him.

But confused or not, he was on her porch.

"Come in."

He stepped into the foyer, handed her the wine and shrugged out of his jacket, which he casually hung across the newel post again.

"You brought extra wine to help you get through this, didn't you?"

He laughed and brushed a quick kiss across her mouth. "Sort of."

Though his answer didn't surprise her, the quick kiss did. She couldn't imagine what he felt for her, that the man who didn't even like talking to people was willing to take himself this far out of his comfort zone for her.

She led him into the kitchen, where they grabbed four wineglasses, then into the living room where a huge blue spruce sat in the corner.

Dean said hello to her family, then uncorked the wine and poured, not really looking at the tree or the decorations that were strewn all over the chairs, sofa and coffee table.

She picked up an ancient ornament and presented it to him. "I made this in kindergarten."

His eyes narrowed. "Is that a—?"

"Toilet paper roll? Yes. Covered in glitter and tinsel, but it's still a toilet paper roll."

He laughed.

Lars picked up his corresponding roll. "Mine."

Dean laughed again. "It's nice that you saved them."

Kristen's mom said, "We like to remember Christmases past."

Kristen's gaze flew to Dean. But he hardly responded. If she hadn't known to look for the quiet indrawn breath, she wouldn't even have known the comment had affected him.

Still, she'd seen the breath. But though she knew walking through a family's Christmas memories might be difficult for him, she also knew he needed to do this. He needed to stop avoiding the holiday that gave most people pure joy and get involved, so that someday he'd feel a part of that joy.

"Grandma Anderson lived with us till her passing when I was in high school. She loved to make nut rolls."

As her father reached to loop a string of lights over the tree, he said, "There was nothing like warm nut roll on Christmas morning."

"With a glass of milk," Lars agreed.

Dean set down his wine and walked over to the tree. Standing on the opposite side of her father, he caught the strings of lights when her dad tossed them, placed them on a branch—as her father had been doing—and guided them back to her dad.

Knowing there was no time like the present, Kristen said, "So do you have any special memories, Dean?"

Kristen's mother's eyes widened and her dad's head jerked toward Kristen, but she knew this was what had to be done. Face the elephant in the room head-on.

Dean quietly said, "No." Working with the lights, he kept his gaze averted. Still, Kristen knew this was the best thing for him, so she persisted.

"I told my parents about your parents."

Apparently finally figuring out what Kristen was doing, her mom jumped in saying, "That was tragic and difficult for you."

"Yes. It was," Dean said.

"Worse that your grandmother was too old to care for you," Joan said sympathetically.

With all that out in the open, Kristen knew it was time to shift gears. "But that's over now. And you have an entire holiday of traditions to investigate and experiment with. Lars, why don't you get a tray of those fruit horns Mom made this morning?"

Not needing to be asked twice, Lars raced out of the room.

Dean looked up at her mother, his head tilting as he studied her. "These cookies are good?"

"These cookies are excellent," Kristen's mom answered without a hint of humility. "Christmas baking is my specialty. If you like banana nut bread, you'll be thrilled when you eat mine."

Dean laughed. "Okay. Bring on the cookies."

Kristen breathed a sigh of relief. With Dean's past now acknowledged, Dean didn't have to pretend anymore. Kristen would have been thrilled that her idea had worked out, except in New York, she'd seen Dean noticing Christmas decorations, being part of Christmas celebrations.

He had been ready to not just acknowledge there was a Christmas, but also to ease himself into it.

But she was falling in love with him—and he'd been hurt, used in the worst possible way. A few Christmas cookies and an afternoon decorating a tree wouldn't be enough to get him past Nina.

He might never get past Nina.

And then what would she do? Be in love with a man who couldn't trust enough to return her feelings?

CHAPTER THIRTEEN

On Monday morning, the royals had been back for three days and were settled in. Rumor around the palace was that Dean had been invited to dinner Sunday night, and that he and Alex had been cordial. No one expected them to become best friends, but for Grennady's sake, Kristen was glad they'd made a peace of a sort.

Around noon, Kristen's intercom buzzed. She pressed the button. "Yes?"

Eva said, "Kristen, could I see you in my office, please."

"Of course."

When she walked into Eva's office, Prince Alex rose from his chair beside Eva's. He smiled. "Sit."

Confusion rumbled through her, but she sat.

Eva said, "We understand you and Dean spent time together while we were away."

"Yes. I mentioned to you already that he needed a guest for a Christmas party and when he brought his staff here I kept our relationship going to make sure he and his staff were comfortable."

"He told us that he's advising you on your charity, specifically talking about your board of advisors."

"He told you that?"

"Yes. We had a very good conversation." Eva reached out and took Alex's hand. "This isn't an easy situation for any of us. But ten years have gone by, and Xaviera's Royal Guard, headed by Alex's brother, absolved Dean of any guilt in the death of their mutual friend. It was time to let go."

Kristen sat back on her seat. She tried to picture Dean's reaction to that and couldn't. The royals might not blame him for Nina's death, but Nina had used him.

"Which was how the conversation naturally flowed to you and your charity. Dean is very impressed. We've always been impressed with you. And now that everything seems to be falling into place, Alex and I would like to offer our suggestions on that too."

"I'd love to hear them."

"We also want to be one of your first benefactors. As soon as you have your corporation and bank accounts set up, we'll be donating a million dollars."

Kristen's face fell. "Thank you."

Alex said, "We also think it's time for you to quit your post here."

Something inside of Kristen blossomed to life. For years she'd been dreaming, researching, and the day was finally here. She was going to do something important not for herself but for the world.

The thrill of it shimmied through her and she sat up taller in her chair. "Yes. It is. Thank you."

"So as of today, you're free." Eva laughed. "Which means I now have to give you a formal invitation to the reception we'll be hosting tonight for Suminski Stuff. Because you were the one who got them here, we'll feel it's only right you attend the reception—as yourself, not an employee anymore."

Kristen rose. "Thank you, ma'am."

Eva rose too. "Sweetie, you can call me Eva now. After all, if I'm on your board of advisors, I'll sort of be working for you."

The reception that night hosted by King Mason to honor the guests from Suminski Stuff was as formal as a ball, just a lot smaller. Kristen dressed in a pink lace gown she'd bought for the royal Christmas Eve party the year before. She wasn't one to care about wearing the same dress twice. She'd actually seen Princess Eva do it. Plus, now that she was officially on her own, every cent she spent had meaning.

The princess straightened the cap sleeves of her gown. "You look perfect. Very smart. Are you ready for this?"

Kristen laughed. "I think dealing with Dean prepared me for a lot of it."

Eva said, "Hmm… I hope you're being careful with him. His upbringing made him ruthless. That's not something a man gets over or forgets. It's part of who he is."

"I'm fine with him. In fact, I like him."

"Like him?"

With everything happening so fast in her life, Kristen decided it was time to take another plunge. "He's very different with me than he is with other people. He's been to dinner at my house, helped my family decorate our tree."

"Oh, my gosh." Eva's eyes widened. "You're in love with him."

Kristen winced. "I think. Yes."

Eva shook her head. "Just be careful."

Eva's gown swished as she led Kristen from the staging area to the receiving line for the reception. Eva's father, King Mason, a tall, fair man stood with her mother, Queen Karen, who wore a black velvet gown and a diamond necklace—her gift from her husband for being so understanding about why he'd left her out of the details of their near coup the winter before.

The king saw Kristen and Eva entering, and a smile blossomed on his face. He took both of Kristen's hands. "I understand congratulations are in order."

She bowed. "Thank you, Your Majesty."

"The queen and I would also like to add a donation to your school project."

Humbled, she bowed again. "Thank you, very much."

Queen Karen hugged her. "Don't thank us. You're the star. Mr. Suminski using our country—even if it's only for short-term projects—is huge for us." She smiled. "And we have you to thank for that."

Kristen laughed. "I just took things one step at a time."

King Mason said, "Then that's what you keep doing."

They entered the reception room and took their places in the receiving line. Two butlers opened the wide double doors, offering entry to Dean first, who bowed to the king and queen, shook hands with Alex and Eva, and took a place next to King Mason, as the evening's official guest of honor.

Then the doors were opened and Dean's employees entered. Wide-eyed with amazement and curiosity, they glanced around the ornate reception room. Other dignitaries and guests filtered in, including the ones Princess Eva wanted Kristen to meet.

As Dean shook hands and talked of software and stock prices, Kristen spoke to the same guests, making plans to meet potential advisors and benefactors for lunch or dinner.

In what felt like a flick of a switch, her entire life changed.

Because Dean was with the king and queen, and Kristen was with the princess and Alex, their paths didn't cross until after dinner when the king and his wife mingled and Eva and Alex danced.

Kristen saw Dean standing off to the side with Jason and she walked over.

"Hello, again."

Jason all but bowed. "Hello, again, to you too. It's quite a night for you."

She laughed. "I've been building to this for years. I wasn't always giving a big push for my schools, but raising money and looking for people to help find real estate, teachers, textbooks was always in the back of my mind." She took a long satisfied breath. "Now it's a reality." She turned to Dean. "Would you like to dance?"

Jason laughed. "Look at her. Her first official event as a leader and she's already bold enough to ask a guy to dance." He turned to Dean. "This is going to sound so odd, but you know who she reminds me of? Nina. Now there was a woman who was bold."

His comment seemed out of place to Kristen, but she knew Jason and Dean had history. What he'd said probably made sense to Dean. Even if Kristen had no clue what he meant.

Dean put his drink on the tray of a passing waiter. In her pink dress, with her hair piled high on her head, Kristen looked as regal, as elegant as Princess Eva.

But she was more than royalty. She was an honest, open, wonderful person. Someone who liked him. Someone he liked—and trusted. She was nothing like Nina.

He smiled. "I'd love to dance."

They walked out onto the dance floor and he smoothly took Kristen into his arms. As always, she felt like an equal. In a weird kind of way, she'd always been his equal.

No, if he remembered correctly, the night of their first Christmas party, in New York, he'd realized she was the woman of his dreams. The woman who could be his partner. Smart and sassy enough to keep him on his toes and beautiful enough to hold him spellbound, Kristen Anderson was everything he wanted.

And this was his moment.

"So how was your day?"

He laughed because her question, everything about the night felt right. Actually, a part of him was a little giddy.

"I snowboarded."

Her eyes widened. "On your own?"

"Yes." He smiled. "I took one of the buses that runs to the slopes and rented a board."

A laugh bubbled up. "No kidding."

"On the slopes I had some interesting revelations."

"Sounds serious."

He spun her around to change that mood. What he felt for her was serious, but it was also fun. Spontaneous. Wonderful. Snowboarding for the first time in a decade, he realized he'd already pushed through the hard stuff. Meeting her parents. Talking about his situation in front of them. Decorating a tree with her family. Eating cookies. And he knew that with everything in their relationship moving at the speed of light, he shouldn't stop what was happening between them. He should grab this opportunity and run with it.

But he wouldn't tarnish that by being ominous. He liked wonderful. He could get addicted to wonderful.

"My revelation wasn't serious as much as it was true. Coming to terms with everything with Prince Alex at dinner last night, I felt like I was knocked back to the place I was ten years ago."

She frowned. "Ten years ago? When you were starting out?"

Her question reminded him of Jason's comment that she reminded him of Nina. It was ridiculous. She was nothing like Nina. "When I met the Saudi prince I wasn't so much starting out as I was collecting capital. I knew I was good at what I did. I was also learning to have fun." His eyes met hers. She might be "nothing" like Nina, but they did have the common denominator that they'd both pushed him out of his comfort zone to have fun. "You reminded me that I like to have fun."

"Everybody likes to have fun."

"Yeah, but some of us need to learn how to do it." Kristen had brought him into her family. Nina had eased him into her social circle.

She smiled. "Well, you caught on really quickly."

His chest pinched with a pleasure-pain. This was why he liked her. And what made her different from Nina. Kristen didn't flirt. She didn't have to flirt to make him feel good about himself, or life, or her. All she had to do was make him feel normal, worthy, honorable…and she did that by being herself, letting him be himself.

So though there were similarities between her and Nina; there were also differences. Big differences. "I like having fun."

"But…?"

"No but. Just a statement." He blamed Jason's stupid

comment for the fact that he was fumbling for what he really wanted to say. That she was warm. That she was honest. That she was everything he wanted.

The music stopped and they drifted out of their dance hold, but he didn't let go of her hand. He needed to take her somewhere out of the ballroom. Somewhere they could talk. As he glanced around for a doorway that might lead to a private alcove, there was a commotion at the entry, and then King Mason strode to the stage, carrying a baby.

He took the microphone. "For those who don't know, this is James Tiberius Sancho." He kissed the little boy's cheek. "He's my daughter's nephew by marriage. Dom and Ginny Sancho's son."

Dark haired, dark eyed, the child was as cute as a kid could be. The people clustered around the stage testi-fied to that with their "Aw, isn't he cute," and "What a beautiful little boy."

Dom and Ginny stood only a few feet away, proud, beaming parents, with Ginny's mom and Dom's dad, the King and Queen of Xaviera, now also married, looking on like the happiest grandparents in the world.

Kristen laughed. "That kid is going to be one spoiled child."

Dean slid a glance to her. "Yeah, well, he *is* going to be a king someday."

"His parents will make sure he's raised right," Kristen said with authority. "Dom looks all cool and sophis-ticated, but he's got a father's heart."

A father's heart.

Dean's throat tightened. He had absolutely no idea what that was. Nina might have been able to ease him into her social group, and Kristen might be able to ease him into her family, but no amount of "easing" could make up for the shortcomings that counted.

Kristen tugged on his hand. "Come on. Let's go say good-night."

Dean tugged her back. "To a baby?"

"Sure. He's a sweetie. I've met him a few times when Dom and Ginny visited Eva and Alex."

She tugged again.

He tugged her back again. "But there's so much family around him already."

Kristen laughed. "That's the way they like it. The Sancho men were alone for so long that they love being surrounded by people. They especially love showing off Jimmy." She smiled. "Come on."

He almost took a step. Almost. But something held him back. From the corner of his eye, he saw Jason approaching.

Relief rippled through him when Jason said, "What's going on?"

Kristen said, "We were just going to say good-night to Jimmy."

Jason laughed. "Cutest kid I've ever seen. But Dean and I really need to talk about a thing. So why don't you go and we'll catch up later."

He saw Kristen hesitate. Inside him, a small battle ensued. He wanted to go with her. He wanted to take this step. But he couldn't and he thanked the heavens Jason needed to talk to him.

Kristen walked away and Dean turned to Jason. "So what do we need to talk about?"

"Nothing." He laughed. "I could just see that you needed rescuing."

"That obvious?"

"Nah. I just know you. Kids freak you out."

Dean stuffed his hands in his trouser pockets. "Yeah, well, I'm going to have to get over it." He nudged his head in Kristen's direction. "I really like her."

Jason snorted. "Of course you do. She's gorgeous. And just like with Nina, you're in love in two weeks." He batted his hand. "You're so predictable with a certain kind of woman. You like them strong and smart. But it almost seems that subconsciously you pick somebody you really can't have. Nina was already taken, and this one—" He pointed at Kristen. "Is moving on."

Confused, Dean faced Jason again.

"You didn't hear that the royal family gave her the boot today?"

"What? They fired her?"

"No. No. They gave her the 'shove the bird out of the nest' dismissal. Rumor has it they also contributed to the tune of a million dollars."

Pleasure for her shimmied through him. "That's great."

"It's fantastic. For her. And who got her to this point? You. You introduced her to Mrs. Flannigan. Just like you gave Nina the way to get to Alex, you gave Kristen the way to get to know the people who could set her on the right course."

Dean's blood ran cold. "Are you saying she used me?"

"I don't think she did it deliberately. I don't think she realized the kind of clout that you have, but the genie's out of the bottle now. She's gotten her introductions and literally millions of dollars of funding. She doesn't need you anymore. And you still have weeks of work on a failing project."

Dean stood frozen, trying to link the things Jason said

to Kristen's behavior and he just couldn't do it. True, he and Kristen were in two different places with their careers. But there was no law that said they had to be in the same place.

He wanted to support her. He wanted her to support him. "She's exactly where she needs to be."

"And so are you."

Dean frowned. "Excuse me?"

Jason took Dean's shoulders and turned him to face Kristen, who stood by King Mason, playing peekaboo with Jimmy. "Look at her, Dean. She is in her element. She is going to travel around the world and build schools. And what she needs is some big blond guy name Sven to hold down a fort at home. Maybe run the family farm. So that when she comes home, she will see her beautiful, well-adjusted babies and rest up before she has to go to Africa or Asia or South America."

"That's ridiculous."

"What's ridiculous? You don't think she deserves a nice home, the family she wants?" He waved a hand. "Forget it. Forget I said anything. You want to mess with the life of a woman who's finally got her act together, who deserves to have the family she wants, who worked damned hard to get there, then who am I to stop you? Just remember you were in a car behind Nina, chasing her down, refusing to take her no for an answer when she jumped into that boat. You might have been cleared of any wrongdoing, but you're in no way an innocent."

As Jason said the words, Kristen approached, her smile broad, her eyes gleaming.

Jason said, "You should be mingling with your staff, making them feel welcome."

Jason's assertion that Dean was to blame for Nina's

death was like a knife in Dean's heart. He hadn't been chasing her. True, he'd followed her from the restaurant, but once he realized she was going to the marina, he pulled together his pride and turned around. He'd been cleared of wrongdoing because Nina had driven five miles knowing he wasn't chasing her.

The fact that Jason would bring it up—would make him remember—put a chill in his blood again.

"The staff is fine."

Jason shrugged. "Okay. Whatever. If you want to lose what you have I'm not going to take the blame."

Jason shifted away about the same time Kristen reached Dean. He felt the rush of happiness that she was near, but Jason's comments rang in his ears. His company had teetered on the brink of failure for months after Nina's death.

And now here he was with Kristen. A woman on the edge of having everything she wanted. It infuriated Dean that Jason would connect Kristen and Nina, and, worse, suggest that he would ruin Kristen's life.

Because he could? Because that's who he was? Or because Jason knew, just as Dean knew, that his upbringing didn't lend itself to Dean being the most understanding, most easy-to-live-with guy in the world.

She said, "That baby's a doll."

Everything about her seemed to glow. And he suddenly saw what Jason saw. Not a comparison between her and Nina, but a comparison between *himself* and Kristen. Kristen was right now as he had been when he met Nina. She looked strong, but looks could be deceiving. Inside of everyone taking their first shaky steps was the potential to screw up royally.

As he had with Nina.

Jason wasn't worried that Kristen was using him. He was worried that if Dean hurt Kristen, she'd spiral out of control as he had after Nina's death...and she'd lose her dream.

She caught his hand, as naturally, as perfectly, as if they belonged together, and crazy fear raced through Dean.

What if he hurt her?

What if something he said or did ultimately hurt her enough to destroy her dream?

Some people really did only get one shot at life.

What if he ruined hers?

"So Dom and Ginny took the baby to their room. They'll leave him with a nanny and be back, but I think it's so cute that they are hands-on parents."

He did too. He imagined that being raised by a nanny could be as cold and unhappy as being raised by a grand-mother who didn't want you.

So he couldn't even think he'd work out his fears of being a bad father by hiring help. Help wasn't what a kid wanted or needed. Love was. Love from a parent.

His blood ran cold at the truth of it. He slid his hand out of Kristen's.

"I...um...need to mingle with my staff."

Her smiled grew. "Great. I'd love to meet them."

He took another step back. "No. I'm fine. You mingle with your potential benefactors."

"I've already mingled. I talked with everyone in the receiving line." She grinned. "Any more talk and I'm going to look obnoxious."

She could never look, act or be obnoxious. She was too honest. Too open. And he was nowhere near that.

He was grouchy, lonely, driven. And two weeks in

her company couldn't change that. Just as two weeks in her company couldn't possibly cause them to fall in love.

He took another step back. "I don't want you to come with me."

Her eyes brimmed with confusion. "What?"

"Look, I get it that you're excited. I get it that things are going your way. But this is my company, my legacy. I don't want or need your help."

He let the words fall out, deliberately cruel, to chase her away, but also to remind her that she didn't really know him. And getting to know him would be stupid because, in the end, she wouldn't like the person she would find.

He took another step back. "Goodbye, Kristen."

He said it the same way he had the night he'd first kissed her, intending it to be the last time he saw her. Except this time, it wasn't an easy decision. This time he knew her enough to recognize what he was giving up.

He took one last look at her face, one last long glance into her pretty green eyes, and walked away.

CHAPTER FOURTEEN

THE REST OF the reception was a whirlwind for Kristen. Though she'd told Dean she didn't want to make a nuisance of herself with potential benefactors, everybody seemed interested in her cause. Everybody had advice. Start a blog. Do a Kickstarter campaign. Get on Facebook.

By the time she was free enough to look for Dean, he had gone.

She didn't understand what had happened. One minute everything between them was perfect. Warm. Romantic. But also casual, like two people so in tune they didn't have to work at getting along. And the next he was running away from her.

Telling herself not to make a big deal of it, she went home that night, took off her pretty pink gown and fell into a restless sleep. The next morning, she went to the hotel to see him, but he was already working. When she stopped by the meeting room, he had Jason tell her that he was too busy to be interrupted.

"We're at a pivotal moment," he said, smiling patiently. "I finally got him working with staff. *He* told me that there were to be no interruptions." He peered at her over his glasses. "From anyone." He smiled benignly.

"It's best that you don't come back. He's a busy man, who really doesn't date. Now that he's made up with the royal family, he'll be dealing with them."

Her heart about pounded itself out of her chest. If it hadn't been for their dance the night before, she might—*might*—have wondered if he hadn't used her to pave the way to make up with Prince Alex.

But that was absurd.

Wasn't it?

She hadn't done anything to facilitate him talking to Eva and Alex—

Except bring him to Grennady.

And tell the princess he was in Grennady two days before they returned home so that Eva had time to get Alex acclimated…

So that by the time they did meet, both Alex and Dean were in a good enough frame of mind to make amends rather than sling accusations.

The truth of it settled in on her, made her breath shiver and her heart hurt.

Once again, she'd been taken in by somebody who used her.

And like an idiot, she'd fallen in love with him.

Except all she had was Jason's word that he didn't want her around.

So that night, she waited until she knew Dean had gone back to his suite. Standing in a quiet corner of the hotel lobby, she watched as he stepped into the elevator for the penthouse. Then she used the house phone to call him. He answered on the second ring.

"Hello?"

"Hey, it's me, Kristen. I stopped by to see you before but Jason said you were busy."

"We're on the verge of being ready to ship the games to beta testers."

"That's great."

"So you can understand why we don't want any interruptions. I appreciate everything you did for me with Alex and Princess Eva, but we have work to do now."

He hung up the phone and Kristen just stared at the receiver in her hand shell-shocked.

He really had used her.

It had physically hurt Dean to disconnect the call. But he knew this was for her own good. He deliberately led her down a path where she'd draw some wrong conclusions about him and his intentions, to prevent her from trying to get back into his life.

She was a good person and he was a bad bet.

But every day it hurt a little more. Christmas decorations once again looked tarnished. Taunting. He didn't want to hear Christmas music. Didn't want to eat Christmas cookies. Didn't want to see even one Christmas tree. He might be busy, but he was also alone, empty. And he felt the way he had when he was six or eight or even ten. The world around him was celebrating, happy. And he was alone.

Within a few days the bugs in the games were nearly gone. They tested and retested, found new bugs and fixed them, and by Christmas Eve morning, they were done.

He gave the staff the option of going home for Christmas but everyone unanimously said no. They wanted to spend Christmas in the winter paradise they'd grown to love.

Dean almost took the plane back to New York, but the smart businessman in him couldn't miss the Christmas

Eve ball being thrown by the royal family. Grennady had brought his staff back to life. Grennady had saved his company. As a thank-you, he'd made an informal agreement with Princess Eva to bring his staff to Grennady two times a year for corporate retreats. Though it wasn't the commitment she had hoped for, it had given her the idea to entice other tech companies to do the same. He would not be so rude as to walk out on celebrating with the royal family who—in spite of all odds—had become an asset to him.

But he also couldn't stay in the penthouse an entire afternoon, waiting for the hands of the clock to move far enough that he could dress for the ball. So he put on his parka, caught the bus to the resort and snowboarded until his feet were tired and his nose was frozen.

He found new trails, bypassing the ordinary routes usually taken by tourists and suddenly found himself in the most pristine, peaceful valley he'd ever seen.

He reverently swooshed down a small slope to the center so he could take it all in, the mountains, the blue sky, the silence, but when he slid down the final hill, he realized he wasn't alone.

Prince Alex stood staring at the mountains.

He turned to go, but Alex said, "I hear you back there. This isn't my personal mountain. You're welcome to stay."

Dean winced. "Are you sure?"

Obviously recognizing Dean's voice, Alex turned to face him. "It's you."

Alex might have forgiven Dean, his country might have made an alliance with Dean's company, but he'd also told Dean they'd never be friends.

Which Dean totally understood. He quickly said, "You stay. I'll go."

But Alex shook his head. "No. As I said at dinner the night you came to the palace, we can't avoid each other." He laughed. "Especially not now when you've made agreements with my wife."

Dean took one foot off his board and used it to flip it off the ground and into his hands.

Alex frowned. "Still a pro I see."

"It was kind of like riding a bike."

"Good."

"Yes, thank you."

The world became eerily quiet. It was odd seeing Alex in a parka rather than a dark suit or a tux. Dean said, "This is a far cry from the Mediterranean."

Alex gazed around at the wall of mountain on the horizon. "Yes. It is. But it's beautiful here. In a lot of ways, Grennady feels more like home to me than Xaviera."

"Princess Eva is a wonderful person."

"Most of the people in Grennady are wonderful. They're kind. Loyal. Fiercely protective of their own."

"Why do I get the feeling you're trying to tell me something?"

"Because Eva and I are worried that you're going to hurt Kristen."

Dean winced. "You don't have to worry about Kristen. I scared her off at the reception last week."

Alex took a cautious step toward him. "You did?"

Dean shook his head. "I shouldn't tell you this, but it's easy to see Kristen's the kind of woman who wants everything. Not just a career but kids. A family. I'm not that guy."

Alex frowned. "You don't want a family?"

He did. He desperately did. After two visits with Kristen, her brother and her parents, he wanted a real home, real Christmases, a wife to share his dreams, kids to give his life warmth and meaning…

Dean raised his hands. "What difference does it make? She wants something I can't give her."

"You can't have children?"

"No." He shook his head. "It's not that. I didn't have much of a childhood."

"Being a genius?"

"And being raised by someone who was tired. I had no father. No male influences. And my work takes up most of my time. Kristen deserves somebody named Sven who will be what she needs."

"So you scared her off?"

He shrugged.

"Well, this explains why she's barely spoken this week."

Dean's heart thumped. "You've seen her?"

"We tried to set up two meetings but she wouldn't come. Said she was busy with Christmas prep with her mom and we accepted that." Alex's eyes narrowed. "But that wasn't it. She was probably at home licking her wounds."

Dean said, "I'm sorry."

"Really?"

"Of course. I love her. Everything about her. But she deserves better."

Alex put his hands on his hips and sighed heavily as he looked at the sky for a few seconds. "You are a crazy weird man, Dean Suminski. I shouldn't help you but I'm going to."

"Help me?"

He took a long breath, glanced at the mountains, then looked at Dean again. "It doesn't matter if you think you're made to have kids or not, marriage material or not. If you've found someone who makes you want all those things, then you don't let the chance go by."

Alex shifted his ski poles. "You work things out. You talk about things. And in the end, everything comes together."

Hating that assessment, Dean scoffed. "Like destiny? Or maybe magic?"

Alex laughed, pushed his goggles over his eyes. "It isn't magic. It's work." Using his poles he swooshed himself down the slope, then stopped and in a spray of snow faced Dean again. "It's a lot of work," he called up the mountain. "But it's worth it. Don't let your chance pass you by. Because if you really love her, and I think you do, you're going to regret it."

Kristen had all but decided not to go to the royal family's Christmas Eve party when her mom appeared in her room. "You're not dressed."

Kristen sat up on her bed, saw her mom in a bright red Christmas gown and her eyebrows rose. "You are dressed. What's up?"

"Your dad and I were invited to this year's Christmas party too."

"Really?"

"Something about my position with you in your charity." She sat on the bed and nudged Kristen's shoulder. "Thanks for putting your mom on your board."

Kristen laughed. "You're one of the smartest people

I know. You might not be able to make a million-dollar contribution, but I think we need you."

"So, since I'm such a smart person, I'm going to give you a piece of advice."

"I'm not going to the party."

"I know you don't want to see Dean, but your days of cocooning yourself in here because you're upset over a guy dumping you are done. You don't have that luxury. You need to go to this party." She rose from the bed. "Even if you go late, you need to go. If nothing else, you need to show your benefactors that in spite of being upset you will do your job."

Kristen sighed.

Her mother headed out the door. "Your dad and I are leaving now. We don't want to miss a minute. I'd thought we'd all ride together but we don't want to wait for you to dress."

She laughed as her mom disappeared from sight, but when she was gone, she squeezed her eyes shut. Her mother was right. She needed to put in an appearance. She needed to look strong and happy because her charity was coming together. She couldn't let losing one man, one man who had used her, cause her to crumble.

She had to be strong.

Unfortunately, because she'd convinced herself it was okay to stay home, she hadn't shopped that week and she had nothing to wear.

She suddenly missed Stella.

Then she saw the black gown hanging in the back of her closet. Memories of how fun that party had been caused her heart to stutter and she almost decided she couldn't do this. She couldn't see Dean. She couldn't face the fact that he'd used her.

But as quickly as she thought that, she realized she had to see Dean. She had to prove to herself, to him and to everybody that nothing would keep her from doing her duty for her charity.

A quick trip through the receiving line at the royal family's Christmas Eve party gained Dean entrance to the ballroom. Huge silver and gold ornaments hung from the high ceiling with tinsel that arched between each bell and ball and then looped over to the next. Glittering crystal vases held red rose centerpieces on the round tables. The table for the royal family was awash with twinkling white lights. Replete with the scents of roast goose, good wine and sweet treats, the room smelled like heaven.

Dean saw every style and color of gown, glittering necklaces and every hairdo from simple to fancy. But he didn't seen Kristen, and he wondered, as Alex had said, if he hadn't let his chance pass him by.

He'd thought through everything Alex had said and knew he was right. Dean did love Kristen. He was afraid. But he'd spent most of his childhood alone, then ten years unable to trust, and he couldn't do that anymore. He wanted everything Kristen had to offer.

When he still hadn't seen her at dinner, he glanced at the entry one more time, worried that he'd hurt her enough that she'd decided to miss this ball. King Mason had made a Christmas toast. Dancing had begun. She'd be here by now, even if she only intended to put in an appearance for her royal family's sake.

When he saw her parents mingling without her, his breath stuttered and the truth settled in. She wasn't coming.

Jason walked up to him with two flutes of champagne. "Here. We need to toast."

"Toast?"

"Our success today. With that game going to beta testers a week early, I think we proved we're everything we said we were."

Dean laughed in spite of himself. "I guess we did."

"I thought I'd lost you to the pretty blonde, but in the end you came back stronger, if that's possible."

Dean's brow furrowed. "Wait. What?"

"You and Kristen. The thing between you was pulling you away. I had to put a wedge between you."

Dean just stared at him for a second. "First, you didn't put a wedge between us. You said some things that made me realize I might not be good for her. But in the end it was my choice." Not that he was proud of it, but he didn't like the idea that Jason seemed to think he controlled him. "Second, if you ever do anything like that again, you'll be fired so fast your head will spin." Even as he said that, he wondered what he was still doing at this party. He handed the champagne glass back to Jason. "Now, I'm going to go find her and fix this."

Oddly, Jason trying to take credit for breaking him and Kristen up only made Dean stronger. Maybe he'd needed to think through everything he had in the past week before he could make a real commitment. Maybe he'd needed to run back to his fortress of work to realize it was a cold, empty place without the woman he loved. Whatever the reason, he was back now. Stronger. Smarter. He would win her back.

Just when he was ready to get his coat and call a cab to go to the Anderson farmhouse, the ballroom doors opened and Dean's head snapped toward them.

Wearing the black dress she'd worn in New York, the one Dean had bought her, Kristen stepped into the ball-room. All the feelings from that night came tumbling back to Dean. How she'd fit with his crowd of friends. How she'd relaxed him enough that he could mingle and enjoy the party he'd been dreading. How he'd known from the second he'd taken her into his arms to dance with her that she was his other half. The woman of his dreams. His perfect partner.

He didn't let two seconds pass. He raced over to her. "Kristen."

She turned slowly but didn't say anything. Her green eyes caught his gaze. But there was no sparkle in them. No warmth for him. No welcome.

"I'm sorry."

"Sorry things didn't turn out better for you? I can't imagine how since you seem to have gotten everything you want. Your game went to the beta testers today. A week ahead of schedule. Rumor has it you're not wor-ried about a new set of comments because this time the team got it right. You don't have to move to Grennady... Though you have a free pass to return for corporate re-treats anytime you want. You have access to our labor pool. You're basically giving us nothing and getting ev-erything...and all it took was making a fool of me to get it." She raised her chin. Her dull green eyes filled with hurt. "If you'll excuse me."

She took a step away from him but he caught her hand. "I know this looks bad."

She laughed. "Looks bad?" She shook her head as if his audacity amazed her. "Get lost."

She wrangled her hand out of his and slid into the crowd. Sidling up to an American couple, she accepted their warm greeting and began to talk animatedly, probably about her charity.

Remorse tightened his chest. Not that she didn't need him, but that he'd needed time to think this through, to realize not just what he wanted but that he could be what Kristen wanted. In the moment, he'd felt he was being noble. Now he realized he hadn't had the right to make the decision to end their relationship by himself.

And even if he couldn't win her back, he couldn't let her go through life thinking any part of this was her fault.

He marched over to her. "Excuse me," he said to the Americans, who smiled politely. "But Kristen owes me this dance."

She said, "I don't—"

But he didn't give her a chance to finish. He tugged her along to the dance floor where he took her into his arms.

"I'm not just sorry that I treated you badly after the reception. I love you."

The words hung in the air as Kristen stared at him and little things settled into his brain. Like the way she felt in his arms and the way he felt in general. He wasn't playing a role. He wasn't doing what was expected. He was simply being himself.

And that was why he loved her. She wasn't just wonderful. She was the one person with whom he could be himself. His real self. The person he longed to be.

Kristen saw the second he realized what he'd said. Though part of her wanted to yank her way out of his arms and leave him, the other part melted. She knew how huge this was for him.

Unfortunately, he'd also hurt her and he would hurt her again if she let him.

She couldn't let him.

"My whole point in walking away was to save you from getting hurt."

"Too late for that."

"I hurt myself as much. But not for the reasons you think. It hurt me to know you were hurting. And that sort of messed up my whole plan."

Curiosity overwhelmed her and her gaze met his. His brown eyes were soft, almost happy. She wanted to deck him.

"In trying not to hurt you I hurt you."

"You don't need to spell it out. I got it."

And she was softening again, mellowing to him. Not because he deserved her kindness, but because there was something about him that meshed with something in her. If either one of them believed in destiny anymore, she'd think they were cursed. As it was, she wondered if her hormones weren't out of whack to make her believe she belonged with this crazy man.

"You see, I thought that the fact that I can't be a good dad would either keep us from having kids or mess up our lives if we did have kids."

She almost stopped dancing. "What?"

"I meant what I said about loving you. And loving you meant that I wanted everything you did...even kids."

She did stop dancing. "And you saw far enough ahead to worry about what would happen if we had kids?"

He nodded.

"You didn't stop to think you could look up father-hood on YouTube?"

To her surprise, he burst out laughing. "Never thought

of it. The idea of having a child or two or three paralyzed me and all I could think was how unfair that was to you." He sucked in a breath. "But there's more."

The music stopped. Some couples left the floor. New couples meandered on.

He took her hands. "You're at the start of your life, a wonderful career. I worried that I would drag you down."

His hands holding hers felt so right, so good, but she couldn't let herself give in. If they had a relationship, they had to be equals.

She carefully said, "You don't seem worried now."

"Because I finally realized I wouldn't hold you back. In some ways knowing me might actually help you." He grinned. "I did introduce you to Mrs. Flannigan."

A laugh bubbled up. She raised her eyes to his. "So you love me?"

He rubbed his chest. "A lot, if the pain in my heart is any indicator."

She stepped close. The music started again. Couples waltzed around them, but they didn't move. "Love is actually a very happy thing."

He snorted. "I'd never have guessed."

She laid her hands on his chest, flattened them against his silk shirt. "I have so much to teach you, grasshopper."

He laughed.

She let her hands slide up to his shoulders.

His soft brown eyes caught hers. "You don't hate me?"

"I love you. But we're going to have to make a pact. You don't get to make decisions for me. We talk about things."

He smiled. "Okay."

Her hands finally met at his nape. "Okay."

A second went by, then two. "You could kiss me now."

He laughed, dipped his head, pressed his lips to hers and Kristen's heart sang. The love of her life was a strong, opinionated, sometimes arrogant man, but she had no doubt she was his equal.

He broke the kiss. Couples danced around them. He shoved his hand in his jacket pocket. "We need a little something to seal this deal." He pulled his hand out and dropped a diamond bracelet into her hand.

She gasped. "My bracelet!"

"Aha! I knew you liked it!"

She bounced to her tiptoes and kissed him. "Of course I liked it. I just didn't want to take such an elaborate gift from someone I didn't know."

"You think you know me?"

"Oh, I think we're going to spend the rest of our lives getting to know each other." She rose to her tiptoes to kiss him again. "But that's what's going to make our lives interesting and fun."

He took her hand, led her off the dance floor, and Kristen nestled against him. They hadn't had the most conventional courtship, but once-in-a-lifetime love had nothing to do with normal, ordinary things.

She had no doubt she and Dean Suminski would change the world...

Because together they were stronger than they were alone.

* * * * *

"Are you just trying to butter me up before the trial starts?"

He grinned. "Is it working?"

"Nope. I'm not so easily swayed." She feigned affront, but in the face of his smile, it was hard to hold the pose, and she ended up laughing instead.

He reached up, brushed a tendril of hair off her forehead and tucked the lock behind her ear. His touch lingered on her cheek, and she leaned into it. "Too bad."

"Why?" She could barely whisper the word. The desire simmering inside her was a living, breathing thing, overpowering every sane thought she'd ever had, pushing her closer to him.

"Because if you weren't Lindsay Dalton, lawyer, and I wasn't Walker Jones, owner of Just Us Kids, I think—" his gaze dropped to her lips, then back up to her eyes "—we could have been something."

"But we are those things," the sensible part of her said, even as the rest of her was telling that sensible side to shut up, "and we can't be something."

"In the morning, I would agree with you. But right now—" his thumb traced over her bottom lip and made her breath catch "—why don't we just pretend none of that exists. Just for tonight. Just for now…"

* * *

Montana Mavericks:
The Baby Bonanza—
Meet Rust Creek Falls' newest bundles of joy!

MAVERICK VS.
MAVERICK

BY
SHIRLEY JUMP

First Published in Great Britain 2016
By Mills & Boon, an imprint of HarperCollins*Publishers*
1 London Bridge Street, London, SE1 9GF

© 2016 Harlequin Books S.A.

Special thanks and acknowledgement are given to Shirley Jump for her contribution to the Montana Mavericks: The Baby Bonanza continuity.

ISBN: 978-0-263-92023-9

23-1016

Printed and bound in Spain
by CPI, Barcelona

New York Times and *USA TODAY* bestselling author **Shirley Jump** spends her days writing romance so she can avoid the towering stack of dirty dishes, eat copious amounts of chocolate and reward herself with trips to the mall. Visit her website at www.shirleyjump.com for author news and a booklist, and follow her at Facebook.com/ shirleyjump.author for giveaways and deep discussions about important things like chocolate and shoes.

To the family I was born into and the family
of friends I have found along the way—thank you
for always having my back and for the steady supply
of belly-deep laughter and warm, sweet memories.

Chapter One

Walker Jones's mother would tell anyone who would listen that her oldest son came into this world ready to argue. He was a carbon copy of his father that way, she'd say, another man ready to debate everything from the color of the sky to the temperature of the room.

So it was no surprise he'd grown up to fill his father's shoes in the boardroom, too.

The elder, Walker Jones II, was a formidable opponent in any corporate environment, though his advanced age had warranted a decline in the number of hours he worked. Walker III had stepped in, doubling the company in size and reach. That desire to take over the world had led him to do the one thing he thought he'd never do again—journey back to small-town America to defend the family business interests.

Walker had grown up in Oklahoma, but as far as he could tell, Rust Creek Falls and Kalispell, Montana, where the courthouse was located, were just copycats of the kind of tiny spit of a town that Walker tried to avoid. Lord knew what his brother Hudson saw in the place, because to Walker, it was just one more Norman Rockwell painting to escape as soon as humanly possible. He'd spent as little time as possible here a few months earlier when he'd opened his first Just Us Kids Day Care center. Basically just enough time to unlock the door and hand Hudson the keys. The day care center was a tiny part of the much larger operation of Jones Holdings, Inc., a blip on the corporate radar.

Walker had no intention of staying any longer this time around, either. Just long enough to deal with a pesky lawsuit and a persistent lawyer named Lindsay Dalton. The attorney worked in her father's office. Probably one of those kids handed a job regardless of their competency level, Walker scoffed. He figured he'd make quick work of the whole thing and get back to his corporate offices in Tulsa ASAP.

Walker strode into Judge Sheldon Andrews's courtroom on a Friday morning, figuring he could be out of town by sunset. The lawsuit was frivolous, the charges unfounded, and Walker had no doubt he could get it thrown out before the arguments got started.

Walker shrugged out of his cashmere overcoat, placed it neatly on the back of his chair, then settled himself behind the wide oak defendant's table. He laid a legal pad before him, a file folder on his left, and a row of pens to the right. Props, really, part of sending a message to the plaintiff that Walker was ready for a fight. Perception, Walker had learned, was half the battle. His lawyer, Marty Peyton, who had been around the courtroom longer than Walker had been alive, came in and took the seat beside him.

"This summary judgment should be a slam dunk," Walker said to Marty. "These claims are totally groundless."

"I don't know if I'd call it a slam dunk," Marty whispered back. He pushed his glasses up his nose and ran a hand through his short white hair. "If Lindsay Dalton is anything like her father, she's a great lawyer."

Walker waved that off. He'd gone up against more formidable opponents than some small-town lawyer.

"And for another, this is about sick kids," Marty went on. "You already have the court of public opinion against you."

"Sick *kid*, singular," Walker corrected. "She's only representing one family. And kids get sick at day care centers all the time. Kids are walking germ factories."

Marty pursed his lips and sat back in his seat. "Whatever you say. I hope you're right. You don't need this kind of publicity, especially since you're planning to open five more locations this year."

The new locations would bring the day care division up to twenty-two locations, throughout Montana and Oklahoma. A nice dent in the western market. "It'll be fine. We'll dispense with this lawyer and her ridiculous suit before you can say hello and goodbye." Walker straightened the pens again, then turned when the courtroom door opened and in walked his opponent.

Lindsay Dalton was not what he'd been expecting. Not even close.

Given the terse tone of her letters and voice mails, he'd expected some librarian type. All buttoned up and severe, with glasses and a shapeless, dingy brown jacket. Instead, he got a five-foot-five cover model in a pale gray suit and a pink silk shirt with the top two buttons unfastened. Not to mention heels and incredible legs.

She was, in a word, fascinating.

Lindsay Dalton had long brown hair in a tidy ponytail that skimmed the back of her suit and bangs that dusted across her forehead. Her big blue eyes were accented by a touch of makeup. Just enough to draw his gaze to her face, then focus it on her lips.

She smiled at her clients just then—a young couple who looked like they'd donned their Sunday best—and the smile was what hit Walker the hardest. It was dazzling. Powerful.

Holy hell.

He turned to Marty. "*That's* Lindsay Dalton?"

Marty shrugged. "I guess so. Pretty girl."

"Good looks doesn't make her a good lawyer," Walker said. She might be a bit distracting, but that didn't mean his lawyer couldn't argue against her and get this case thrown out.

She walked to the front of the courtroom, not sparing a glance at either Walker or Marty, then took her seat on the plaintiff's side, with her clients on her right. An older woman, probably a grandma, sat in the gallery with the couple's baby on her lap. Lindsay turned and gave the baby a big grin. The child cooed. Lindsay covered her eyes for a second, opened her hands like a book, and whispered "peekaboo." The baby giggled and Lindsay repeated the action twice more, before turning back to the front of the courtroom.

It was a sweet, tender moment, but Walker knew full well that Lindsay Dalton had arranged to have the baby here, not for silly games, but to garner some sympathy points.

The door behind the judge's bench opened and Judge Andrews stepped out. Short, bespectacled and a little on the pudgy side, Judge Andrews resembled a heavy Bob Newhart. The bailiff called, "All rise," and everyone stood while Andrews gave the courtroom a nod, then took his place on the bench.

"You may be seated," he said. Then the bailiff called the court to order, and they got under way.

This was the part Walker liked the best, whether it was in courtroom or in the boardroom. That eager anticipation in his gut just before everything started. Like two armies squaring off across the battlefield, with the tension so high it charged the air.

"We're here on your motion for a summary judgment regarding the lawsuit brought by the plaintiffs, represented by Ms. Dalton, correct?" Judge Andrews asked Walker's attorney.

"Yes, Your Honor."

The judge waved at the podium. "Then, Mr. Peyton, you may proceed."

"Thank you, Your Honor." Marty got to his feet and laid his notes before him on the table. "This lawsuit, brought against Mr. Jones's day care center, is a waste of everyone's time. There is simply no legal or factual basis for the suit. Ms. Dalton is trying to prove that her client's child caught a cold at the center, but there is no evidence whatsoever to support that claim. Germs are a fact of life, Your Honor. They're on any surface we touch, and no one can prove that the Marshalls' child contracted a common cold because of her time in day care. Why, for all we know, one of the Marshalls could have brought the germs into their own house. All it takes is one sneeze from a stranger or contact with a germ-infested surface in a public place. Surely Ms. Dalton can't blame Mr. Jones's day care center for the world's inability to reach for a Kleenex at the right time."

That was a line Walker had given Marty in their meeting last week. It seemed to amuse the judge. A smile ghosted on his face then disappeared.

"Your Honor," Marty continued, "there are no cases holding that a day care center is legally responsible when a child who spends part of her day there comes down with a cold. Frankly, it's a frivolous claim, and we're asking that the court enter summary judgment in the defendant's favor, dismissing this case."

Judge Andrews nodded at Marty, then turned to Lindsay Dalton. "Ms. Dalton?"

Lindsay got to her feet and smoothed a hand down the front of her jacket. She took a moment to draw in a breath, as if centering herself.

She was nervous. *Good*, Walker thought. He had this thing won already.

"Your Honor, Mr. Peyton is greatly minimizing the situation at hand. This was not a common cold, not by any means. We intend to prove that Mr. Jones's day care center, Just Us Kids, has been grossly negligent in cleanliness, resulting in a severe respiratory syncytial virus infection for Georgina Marshall, the then three-month-old child of Peter and Heather Marshall. The Marshalls entrusted Mr. Jones's day care center with the care of their precious child, only to end up sitting by her hospital bed, praying for her to overcome the bronchitis that developed as a result of her exposure to RSV."

Walker fought the urge to roll his eyes. *Precious child? Praying?*

"Your Honor, RSV is a respiratory infection," Marty said, standing up again. "It's marked by a cough and runny nose. Just like the common cold."

"Georgina stopped eating," Lindsay countered. "She lost two pounds, which for a baby of her size is a dramatic weight loss. The hospital she was in didn't see this as a common cold. They saw it as a life-threatening illness. A life-threatening illness caused by Mr. Jones's negligence." With those words she turned and glared directly at Walker.

As if he was the one neglecting to mop the floors and wipe down the toys every night. Walker had barely stepped inside the day care center in Rust Creek Falls. He'd left his brother Hudson to oversee the business and hired a highly experienced and competent manager to help run the place. He had no doubt that Just Us Kids was running as smoothly as a Swiss watch.

He was busy enough maintaining the corporate interests. He had oil wells in Texas and overseas, the financial division expanding in the northeast, and then these day care centers, all started in small towns because his research had shown they were the most in need of child care resources.

Ms. Dalton rushed on. "Your Honor, I invite you to read the medical charts, which we filed with the court in opposition to the defendant's motion for summary judgment. Those alone will prove how close the Marshalls came to losing their only child."

Marty got to his feet. "Your Honor, does the Marshalls' counsel really need to use words like 'precious'? All children are precious, and no disrespect to the Marshalls, but their child is no more precious than anyone else's. Can we stick to facts, without the flowery language?"

"The facts are clear, Your Honor," Lindsay said. "The Marshalls' baby contracted RSV as a direct result of staying in Mr. Jones's day care. As did many other children—"

"This case is only about the Marshalls," Walker interjected. "It's one family, not a class action."

She wheeled on him and shot him a glare. "They merely want justice for the pain and suffering their daughter endured."

Code for *give us a big settlement so we never have to work again.* Walker bit back a sigh. He was tired of people who used the justice system to make a quick buck.

"The child is healthy now," Walker said to the judge, despite Marty waving a hand to silence him. "This was a short-lived illness, and again, not traceable to any one contaminant. To blame my day care center is casting a pretty specific net in a very large river."

The judge gave him a stern look. "Mr. Walker, I'll thank you to leave the argument to your lawyer. You're not here testifying today."

"I apologize for my client's outburst, Your Honor," Marty said smoothly. "It's just that this is so clearly a frivolous claim. Which is why we are moving to have this case dismissed before it wastes any more of the court's time."

Judge Andrews nodded again, and both lawyers sat to wait for him to announce his ruling. He flipped through the papers before him, taking a few minutes to scan the documents.

Walker sat at his table, maintaining a calm demeanor, as if this whole thing was a walk in the park. In all honesty, though, if he lost this case, it could severely impact his whole company and the future of the entire Just Us Kids Day Care chain. He refused to let some small-town lawyer derail his future expansion plans. Jones Holdings, Inc. was solid enough to withstand this tiny dent, but he wasn't so sure the day care centers could rise above the ensuing bad publicity if the case wasn't dismissed. Walker was in this business to make a profit, not to see it wiped away by some overeager small-town lawyer.

Lindsay Dalton had her legs crossed, right over left, and her right foot swung back and forth in a tight, nervous arc under the table. She whispered something to Heather Marshall, who nodded then covered Lindsay's hand with her own and gave it a squeeze. Heather Marshall's eyes watered—whether for real or for effect, Walker couldn't tell. He'd seen enough people fake emotions in business that a few tears no longer swayed him.

Judge Andrews cleared his throat and looked up from his paperwork. "It's the opinion of this court that there is sufficient evidence to proceed to trial on this case." He put up a hand to ward off Marty's objections, then lowered his glasses and looked at Walker's attorney. "Mr. Peyton, you and your client may think this suit is frivolous, but the evidence Ms. Dalton has offered demonstrates that there are genuine issues of material fact. Now, let's talk about a date for the trial. I realize we had set a date for four weeks from today, but that date will no longer work for me. As part of the joys of getting old, I have to have a knee replaced, and am not sure how long I will be out."

Great. That would just make this thing drag on longer and longer. Walker didn't need the prolonged negative publicity.

"But thanks to a big case settling just this morning, my schedule for next week has an unexpected hole in it and I can hear your arguments on Tuesday morning, after the Columbus Day holiday."

Lindsay Dalton shot to her feet. "Objection, Your Honor. I need more time to adequately prepare—"

"From what I have seen, you are prepared, Ms. Dalton. Tuesday is the date, unless you and your clients want to prolong this case indefinitely." The Marshalls shook their head, and Lindsay nodded acceptance. "Good. I will see you all back here Tuesday at 9:00 a.m. Court dismissed." He banged the gavel, then got to his feet.

Everyone rose and waited until the judge had exited the courtroom, before the lawyers turned to gather their papers. Walker leaned toward Marty. "Temporary setback."

Marty gave him a dubious look. "I told you, she may be new, but we have our work cut out for us."

"Piece of cake," Walker said. "Don't worry."

The Marshalls walked by him, holding hands and

giving Lindsay wavering smiles. The Marshalls didn't look like frivolous lawsuit people, and Lindsay Dalton didn't look like a crappy small-town lawyer hired by her daddy. She looked like one of those ridiculously nice, highly principled people who only wanted to do the right thing to brighten their corner of the world. But Walker knew better. She wasn't here to play nice and he wasn't about to let her win, even if this schedule change threw a giant monkey wrench into his plans.

One that meant there was a very, very strong possibility that Walker Jones was going to be in Rust Creek Falls a lot longer than he had thought.

The mirrored wall behind the bar at Ace in the Hole was good for reflecting a lot more than the alcohol bottles lined up on the shelf, Lindsay Dalton realized. It also showed her own frustrated features. Even now, hours after she'd left the courtroom and her first battle against Walker Jones, Lindsay was feeling anxious, stressed. Yes, she'd won today—a small victory—but that first argument was just the beginning. And her opponent was not who she had expected.

She'd done her research on Walker Jones, or at least she thought she had. An older gentleman—heck, almost at retirement age—who she had thought would be an easy opponent. She clearly hadn't researched enough, because the man sitting in the courtroom today wasn't old and frail. He was young and handsome and...

Formidable.

Yes, that was the right word to describe Walker Jones III. Formidable. He had an easy confidence about him, an attitude that said he knew what he was doing and he wasn't used to losing.

And she was a brand-new lawyer from a small town working for her father's firm. She had convictions and confidence, but that might not be enough to win against experience and attitude. And a big-time lawyer hired from out of town.

"Looks like you had the kind of day that needs this." Lani slid a glass of chardonnay over to Lindsay. Her sister worked at the bar from time to time, even after getting engaged to Russ Campbell, the hunky cop she'd fallen in love a little over a year ago. Lani still had a glow about her, shining nearly as brightly as the engagement ring on her finger.

"Thanks," Lindsay said. "I didn't expect to see you at the Ace tonight."

Lani shrugged. "The bar was short staffed. Annie had a date and asked me to fill in."

Annie Kellerman, the regular bartender. The Ace in the Hole was pretty much the main watering hole in Rust Creek Falls. With hitching posts outside and neon beer signs inside, it was the kind of place where folks could let down their hair, have a few beers with friends and maybe take a fast twirl in front of the jukebox. Since it was early yet on a Friday night, the Ace wasn't too busy—one couple snuggling in a booth, four guys debating last week's football game at a table in the center of the room and a couple of regulars sitting at the end of the bar, nursing longneck beers and watching whatever sport was playing on the overhead TV.

"So, how'd it go in court today?" Lani asked. She had her long brown hair back in a clip and was wearing a tank top with the logo for the bar—an ace of hearts—across the front.

"I won." Lindsay grinned. "Okay, so it was only winning the argument that I brought a valid case to court, but it sure made me feel good."

"Given all the times you've argued with me, little sister, I have no doubt you're going to make a great lawyer." Lani swiped at a water ring on the bar, then leaned back against the shelf behind her. "I talked to Dad earlier and he's proud as a peacock. I'm surprised he didn't take out a billboard announcing the judge's decision."

Lindsay laughed. Their father, Ben, had been ready to burst at the seams from the day she told him she wanted to follow in his footsteps. "It's a very small decision. The big case is yet to come. I have a few days until opening arguments." She let out a breath. "I'm nervous as hell."

"Why? You're a great lawyer."

"For one, I only passed the bar a few months ago. My experience is mainly in cases like whether George Lambert's oak tree is encroaching on Lee Reynolds's potato patch." Because she was so new to her father's firm, he generally shuffled the easy stuff over to Lindsay's desk, as a way for her to get her feet wet. She'd argued ownership of a Pomeranian, defended a driver who took a left on red and settled the aforementioned potato patch/oak tree dispute.

"Which was a win for you," Lani pointed out.

Lindsay scoffed. She'd become a lawyer because she wanted to make a difference in the town she loved. So far, she'd only made a difference for a Pomeranian and a garden. She was worried she wasn't up to the challenge of battling for the Marshalls. But when they had come to her, worried and teary, she couldn't say no. She might be inexperienced, but she had a fire for what was right burning in her belly. She couldn't stand to see anyone get hurt because the Just Us Kids Day Care was negligent. "Score one for the potatoes. Seriously, though, the opposing counsel in this case is…good. Smart. And the owner of the day care center is just as smart. Plus, he's handsome."

Had she just said that out loud? Good Lord.

Lani arched a brow. "Handsome?"

"I meant attractive." Oh, God, that wasn't any better. Lindsay scrambled to come up with a way to describe Walker Jones that didn't make it sound like she personally found him sexy. Because she didn't. At all. Even if he had filled out his navy pin-striped suit like a model for Brooks Brothers. He was the enemy, and even handsome men could be irresponsible business owners. "In a distracting kind of way. He might… sway the judge."

Lani chuckled. "Judge Andrews? Isn't he like, a hundred?"

"Well, yeah, but…" Lindsay drained her wine and held her glass out to her sister. "Can I get a refill?"

"Is that your way of changing the subject?" Lani took the glass and topped it off.

"Yes. No." She paused. She'd been disconcerted by meeting Walker Jones, and Lindsay didn't get disconcerted easily. "Maybe."

"Well, unfortunately, I don't think you're going to be able to do that," Lani said as she slid the glass back to her sister.

"Come on, don't tell me you're going to ask me a

million questions about this guy. Frankly, I'd like to forget all about Walker Jones until I have to see him in court next week."

"I think it's going to be impossible for you to do that." Lani leaned across the bar and a tease lit her features. "Considering he just walked in. Or at least, a man who looks like a hot, sexy owner of a day care chain just walked in."

Lindsay spun on her stool and nearly choked on her sip of wine. Walker Jones III had indeed just walked into the Ace in the Hole, still wearing his overcoat and suit from court, and looking like a man ready to take over enemy territory. "What is he doing here?"

"Probably getting a drink like the rest of Rust Creek Falls," Lani said. "There's not a lot of options in this town."

"Why is he even still here? Why not stay in Kalispell, or better yet, why can't he go back to his coffin?"

"Coffin?"

"Only vampires are that handsome and ruthless."

Lani chuckled. She shifted to the center of the bar as Walker approached. "Welcome to the Ace in the Hole. What can I get you?"

"Woodford Reserve, on the rocks." He leaned one elbow on the bar, then shifted to his right.

"We don't have that," Lani said. "What we do have is a whole lot of beer."

Walker sighed. "Then your best craft beer."

"Coming right up."

Lindsay should have slipped off her stool and left before he noticed her, but she'd been so stunned at the sight of Walker in the Ace that she had stayed where she was, as if her butt had grown roots. Now she tried to take a casual sip of her wine, as if she didn't even see him.

Except her heart was racing, and all she could see out of the corner of her eye was him. Six feet tall—her favorite height in a man, but who was noticing that—with dirty blond hair and blue eyes, Walker Jones had a way of commanding the space where he stood.

She needed to remember that his irresponsible ownership of the day care center was what had made Georgina and lots of other children ill. What if that had been the Stockton triplets? Those motherless newborns who'd needed a whole chain of volunteers to help care for them? The RSV outbreak could have had much more dire consequences—something that Walker might be trying to overlook but that she refused to ignore.

"Counselor," he said with a little nod.

"Mr. Jones. Nice to see you again." The conventional greeting rolled off her tongue before she could recall it. Some kind of masochistic automatic response. It wasn't nice to see him again. Not one bit.

Lani smirked as she placed a beer in front of Walker. "Here you go. Want me to run a tab?"

"Thank you, and yes, please do. I think I'll stay a bit." He sent the last remark in Lindsay's direction.

She still had a nearly full glass of wine, but no way was she going to sit at the bar next to him. Lindsay fished in her pocket and handed her sister some bills. "Thanks, Lani. I'll see you around."

As Lindsay went to leave, Walker placed a hand on her arm. A momentary touch, nothing more, but it seemed to sear her skin. "Don't go because I'm here.

Surely we can coexist in a bar full of people." He looked around. "Or rather, a bar full of eleven people."

"Are you always this exact?"

"Are you always this hard to make friends with?"

She scowled. He was making it seem like this was all her fault. "We don't need to be friends. We're on opposing sides."

"In the courtroom. Outside of that, we can at least be civil, can't we?"

"Well, of course we can be civil." Damn it. Somehow he'd turned her whole argument around. Geesh. Maybe he should have been the lawyer.

"That's all I'm asking. So stay." He gestured toward her bar stool. "And pretend I don't exist."

"My pleasure."

That made him laugh. He had a nice laugh, dark and rich like a great cup of coffee in the morning. "You are not what I expected, Ms. Dalton."

"And you are not what I expected." She fiddled with the stem of her wineglass. "Frankly, I was expecting your father."

"Sorry to disappoint you." He grinned. "I'll try not to do that again."

She almost said, "Oh, I wasn't disappointed," but caught herself. Good Lord, what was it with this man? Was it his eyes? The way they held her gaze and made her, for just a moment, feel like the most important person in the room? Was it the way he'd touched her, his muscled hand seeming to leave an indelible impression? Or was it the way he spoke, in that deep, confident voice, that a part of her imagined him whispering to her in the dark?

He was the enemy. An evil, irresponsible man who

only cared about making a buck. Except nothing about his demeanor matched that description. Maybe he was one of those distracted, charming millionaires who didn't care where his money came from as long as it ended up in his bank account.

Still…he seemed nice. Friendly, even. How could that be the same man who ran a shoddy day care chain?

"And with that," Walker said, picking up his beer and giving her a little nod, "I think I shall leave you to your wine. Have a good evening, Ms. Dalton."

He crossed the room, and took a seat at one of the empty tables, draping his coat over a second chair. When a group of twenty-something girls came into the bar, ushering in the cool evening air and a whole bunch of laughter, Lindsay's view of Walker was blocked, but that didn't stop her traitorous mind from wondering what he'd meant by *I'll try not to do that again.*

Because she had a feeling Walker Jones was the kind of man who rarely left a woman disappointed. In any way.

Chapter Two

Walker didn't know why he'd stayed. Or why he lingered over his beer. Or why his gaze kept straying to Lindsay Dalton.

He told himself it was because he was so surprised to see her in ordinary clothes—jeans, cowboy boots and a blue button-down shirt with the cuffs rolled up to her forearms. The jeans hugged her thighs, outlined the curve of her butt and in general made Walker forget to breathe. He could imagine her wearing the dark brown cowboy boots and nothing else.

Okay, not productive. She was the opposing counsel in a lawsuit vital to the future of his day care centers. They may only be a small piece of the large pie that made up Jones Holdings, Inc., but that didn't matter. Walker was not a man who liked to lose. Ever.

The bar began to fill, and he noticed people glancing at him, either because he was a clear outsider or because word got around. There were friendly greetings for Lindsay but a definite chill in the air when it came to Walker. Clearly, the people of Rust Creek Falls were circling the wagons around one of their own.

Walker had debated flying back to his office in Tulsa after court ended today, but with the trial just a few days away, he'd decided to stay in town. It might be good to get to know the locals, get a feel for how things might sway in court and maybe make a few friends out of what might become a lynch mob if Lindsay Dalton had her way.

The best way to do all that? Alcohol, and lots of it.

Gaining the goodwill of the locals was merely part of Walker's overall plan. He would obliterate Lindsay Dalton's case, then leave the town thinking he was the hero, not the devil incarnate she'd made him out to be.

Walker strode back up to the bar, sending Lindsay a nod of greeting that she ignored. He put a hand on the smooth oak surface. "I want to buy a round," he said to the bartender.

The woman, slim and brunette, looked similar enough to Lindsay that Walker could believe they were related. Especially in a town this small. "Sure, for…who?" she said.

"Everyone." He grinned. "New in town. Figured it'd be a nice way to introduce myself."

"You mean try to convince people you're a nice guy?" Lindsay said from beside him.

"I am a nice guy. My grandmother and third-grade teacher said so." He grinned at her. "You just haven't given me a chance."

"And you think a free beer will change my mind?"

He leaned in closer to her, close enough to catch a whiff of her perfume, something dark and sensual, which surprised him. Oh, how he wished it was as simple as a beer to change her mind, because if they had met under different circumstances, he would have asked her out. She was fiery and gorgeous and confident, and he was intrigued. "If it would, I'd buy you a case."

"I'm not so easily bought, Mr. Jones."

"Then name your price, Ms. Dalton."

"An admission of guilt." Her blue eyes hardened. "And changes in the way you run your business."

Well, well. So the lawyer liked the fight as much as he did. There was nothing Walker liked better than a challenge. "A round for everyone in the bar, Miss…" He waved toward the bartender.

"Lani. Lani Dalton." The brunette leaned back against the counter and crossed her arms. "Sister to Lindsay."

That explained the defensive posture. Okay, so he had two enemies in Rust Creek Falls. He'd faced worse. Besides, he wasn't going to be here long. It wasn't going to matter what people said about him after he left—as long as he won the lawsuit and re-established the good reputation of Just Us Kids Day Care. All he needed to do while he was here was temporarily change public perception about himself. Winning the lawsuit would take care of the rest. So he put on a friendly smile and put out his hand. It wasn't making deals over drinks at a penthouse restaurant, but it would accomplish the same thing. And at a much cheaper price.

"Nice to meet you, Lani." They shook. "I'm Walker Jones, owner of Just Us Kids."

"Your day care has quite the tarnished reputation," Lani said. "Folks here have a pretty negative opinion after all those kids got sick."

Walker maintained his friendly smile. "An unfortunate event, to be sure. I'm hoping people will see that I'm a responsible owner, here to make things right."

Beside him on the stool, Lindsay snorted. He ignored the sound of derision.

The bar had begun to fill since he got here, and the people standing in the Ace in the Hole were making no secret of eavesdropping on his exchange with the Dalton sisters. He could see, in their eyes and in their body language that the angry villagers were readying their pitchforks for the evil day care ogre.

If they thought they could intimidate him, they were wrong. He'd faced far worse, from ego-centric billionaires to feisty CEOs who refused to accept their tenure was done when he bought them out. This small town would be a cakewalk. He'd play their game, make nice, but in the end, he'd do what he always did—

Win.

He got to his feet and turned to face the room. He could handle these people. All he had to do was pretend to be one of them. Charming, gentle, friendly. His last girlfriend had accused him of being the Tin Man, because he didn't have a heart. Maybe she was right. But he could damn well act the part. "Folks, I'm Walker Jones, Hudson's older brother, and yes, the owner of Just Us Kids. I'm here in town to check on things, reassure you all that we run a quality operation. I'd like to take a moment to thank you all for the warm welcome to your lovely town."

Cold eyes stared back at him. One man crossed his arms over his chest and glared at Walker. Another woman shook her head and turned away.

He widened his smile, loosened his stance. As easy and welcoming as a new neighbor. "And I can think of no better way to thank you all for your hospitality than a round on me." A low cheer sounded from the back of the room. Walker smiled and put up a hand. "Now, I know a few beers won't change much, and I don't expect it to. I just want to say thank you. And if any of you have any questions, come on up to the bar. I'd sure like to meet the residents of Rust Creek Falls."

Just as he knew it would, the icy wall between himself and the other patrons began to thaw. A few stepped right up to the bar, giving him a thank-you as they placed their orders.

"I figure it's always a good idea to make friends with the guy buying the beer," said a barrel-chested man with a thick beard and a red flannel shirt. "Elvin Houseman."

"Walker Jones." They shook hands. "Pleased to meet you."

Elvin leaned in close to Walker's ear. "Folks round here are gonna have a hard time trusting you. When those kids got sick over at the day care, it scared a lot of people."

"I'm doing my best to rectify that, Mr. Houseman."

The other man waved that off. "Nobody calls me Mr. Houseman. I'm just Elvin."

"Elvin, then."

Lani slid a beer across to Elvin. He raised it toward

her, then toward Walker. "Thank you kindly. And best of luck to you with the town." He gave Walker a little nod, then walked away.

Walker glanced at Lindsay. She'd either ignored or hadn't noticed the whole exchange. She also hadn't ordered a fresh drink, not that he expected her to take advantage of the round on his tab, but clearly, she wasn't won over like the other folks in the bar, nor did she seem to be intimidated by him. But there was a hint of surprise in her face. She clearly hadn't expected him to outflank her by going straight to the town. Walker headed back to his table.

Before he reached his seat, one of the giggling blondes who had come in earlier stood in front of him, her hips swaying to the music. She put her hands out. "Hey, would you like to dance? Come on, we need a man."

The blonde was pretty, probably no older than twenty-three or twenty-four. On any other day, she'd be the kind of diversion Walker would go for—no real commitment, nothing expected after the evening was over. He'd dated enough of that type of woman to know how it would go—a few drinks, a few laughs, a good time in bed and then back to real life.

He wanted to say no, to tell her he had enough on his mind already, but then he reconsidered. Dancing with the local girl fed into his plan of ingratiating himself with the town, and would also show Lindsay Dalton an unexpected side of him. He wanted to keep the other lawyer as off balance as he could. If she didn't know what to expect from him, the advantage would go to Walker.

So he shrugged off his suit jacket, undid his tie

and the top two buttons of his shirt, then rolled up his shirt sleeves. "Sure."

The blonde giggled again, then grabbed his hand. "It's line dancing. Do you know how to do that?"

"Follow your hips?"

That made her laugh again. "Exactly."

The blonde and her trio of friends surrounded him, and the five of them moved from one side of the dance floor to the other, doing something the girls called a grapevine that they'd learned from that Billy Ray Cyrus video "Achy Breaky Heart." Though he'd never danced like this before, it was fairly simple, and by the time the first verse was finished, Walker had most of the steps memorized.

He had, however, all but forgotten the blonde. His gaze kept straying across the room to Lindsay Dalton, still sitting on the bar stool and chatting with her sister. He watched Lindsay, just to see if his plan was working, he told himself.

He'd done a little research on his opponent in the hours after court. Lindsay Dalton, the youngest of six children, fresh from taking the bar exam and now working for her father's firm. She had been successful with some very small cases she'd argued—a boundary line, something about a dog dispute, those kinds of things. Nothing as big as a lawsuit against a major national corporation, albeit one division of the Jones empire. Yet she hadn't seemed too daunted in the courtroom. If anything, she'd impressed him with her attitude—like a kitten standing up to a tiger.

Though the kitten wouldn't even get to unsheathe its claws at the tiger, her attempt made him respect her. And made him wonder about her.

Across the bar, Lindsay was laughing at something the bartender had said. He liked the sound of her laugh, light and lyrical, and the way it lit her face, put a little dash of a tease into her eyes. He knew he shouldn't—she was the enemy, after all—but he really wanted to get to know her better.

It was research, that was all. Figuring out what made the other side tick so he'd have a better chance in court.

The blonde and her friends circled to the left at the same time that Lindsay started to cross the room. Walker stepped to the right and captured Lindsay's hand. "Dance with me."

Her eyes widened. "Dance...with *you*?"

"Come on." He swayed his hips and swung their arms. She stayed stiff, reluctant. He could hardly blame her. After all, just a few hours ago, they'd been facing off in court. "It's the weekend. Let's forget about court cases and arguments and just..."

"Have fun?" She arched a brow.

He shot her a grin. "I hear they do that, even in towns as small as Rust Creek Falls."

That made her laugh. Her hips were swaying along with his, though she didn't seem to be aware she was moving to the beat. "Are you saying my town is boring?"

Boring? She had no idea. But he wouldn't tell her that. Instead he gave her his patented killer smile. "I'm saying it's a small town. With some great music on the juke and a dance floor just waiting for you." He lifted her hand and spun her to the right, then back out again to the left. "Come on, Ms. Dalton, dance with me. Me, the man, not me, the corporation you're suing."

"I shouldn't…" She started to slide her hand out of his.

He stepped closer to her. "Shouldn't have fun? Shouldn't dance with the enemy?"

"I shouldn't do anything with the enemy."

He grinned, to show her he wasn't all bad. Keep her on her toes, keep her from predicting him, and keep the advantage on his side. "I'm not asking for anything. Just a dance."

Another song came on the juke, and the blonde and her friends started up again, moving from one side of the dance floor to the other. Their movements swept Walker and Lindsay into the middle of the dance floor, leaving her with two choices—dance with him or wade through the other women to escape.

For a second, he thought he'd won and she was going to dance with him. Then the smile on her face died, and she shook her head. "I'm sorry, Mr. Jones, but I don't dance with people who don't take responsibility for their mistakes."

Then she turned on her heel and left the dance floor and a moment later, the bar.

Walker tried to muster up some enthusiasm to dance with the other women—any man in his right mind would have taken that opportunity—but he couldn't. He excused himself, paid his tab then left the bar. The victories he'd had today in court and later in the bar rang hollow in the cool night air.

Lindsay headed home, her stomach still in knots. She rolled down the driver side window of her sedan, letting in the fresh, crisp October Montana air, and tried to appreciate the clear, blank landscape ahead of her and the bright stars in the sky. But her mind kept going back to Walker Jones, to that moment in the bar.

Had she almost danced with him?

What was she thinking? He was the enemy, the one responsible for little baby Georgina's illness and scary hospital stay. Maybe not him personally, but his company, and the lack of standards at his day care centers, was indeed responsible. Not to mention how many of her letters and phone calls to Jones's corporate headquarters had gone unanswered, as he clearly tried to ignore the problem or hoped it would go away. He'd been aware of the problem from the minute the outbreak happened in town, and yet he had done nothing. Hadn't flown in to check on the day care, hadn't responded to the worried parents.

She had no interest in Walker Jones. No interest at all. And that little moment in the bar when he'd asked her to dance had been an anomaly, nothing more.

Walker Jones thought he could buy her town through alcohol and joining in on a few line dances. Well, he could think again. Neither she nor Rust Creek Falls would be so easily swayed by that man.

Lindsay headed into the ranch house where she'd grown up. She'd come back home to live after law school, partly because she needed to save money and partly because she'd missed her family. Now it was just her, her brother Travis and their parents. The house didn't ring with the same noise as it did when Lindsay was young, but it still felt like home whenever she walked in the door.

The scents of fresh-baked bread, some kind of deliciousness the family had earlier for dinner and her mother's floral perfume filled the air. It was late, and her parents would have already gone to bed, but Lindsay saw a light on in the kitchen.

"Hey, Trav," she said to her brother as she entered the room. "What has you home early?"

Travis was the one who was known for partying late, dating a new girl every week and living a little wilder than the rest of the Daltons. She adored her brother, but hoped he'd settle down one of these days. He was a good guy, and in Lindsay's opinion, there were far too few of those in the world.

"My date canceled. She got the flu. Didn't feel like heading to the Ace, and so here I am." He crossed to the fridge and pulled open the door. "Plus I heard Mom made meat loaf for dinner."

Lindsay laughed. "I knew it had to be something bigger than a date canceling."

"Hey, I don't get my favorite dinner often enough." He gave her the lopsided grin that had charmed dozens of women over the years. "Want a meat loaf sandwich?"

"Nah, I'm good. I was just going to grab a glass of wine and head out to the back deck. It's a nice night." Hundreds of thoughts and worries jockeyed for space in her mind. She needed some fresh air, some open space. The soft nicker of the horses in the stable, the whisper of a breeze across her face. Not the confines of the kitchen.

Travis handed her the open bottle of chardonnay from the refrigerator door. "Wine on a weeknight? Must have been a hell of a bad day."

"It's Friday night, so technically it's the weekend." She didn't mention that she'd already had a couple of glasses at the Ace in the Hole. Nor did she admit Travis might be right.

"Yeah, right. You, little sister, are about as wild as a house cat lying in the sun." He grinned, then started assembling his sandwich. A thick slice of meat loaf on top of some homemade white bread, then ketchup and a second slice. "Except when you were dating Jeremy back in college and thinking about running off to the big city."

The two of them walked out to the back deck and sat in the Adirondack chairs that faced the wide expanse of the ranch. In the dark, it seemed like the Dalton land stretched forever. The sight was calming, reassuring. "I never thought about running off to the big city," Lindsay said. "That was Jeremy's idea."

Her former fiancé had been smart and witty and driven. She'd met him in law school and liked him from the start. Then, as they neared graduation, he'd told her he had no intentions of living in Montana. He wanted to move to New York and practice law in a place that made him feel alive. For Lindsay, life was here, in the rich soil, the graceful mountains, the clean air. She never wanted to live anywhere else.

"You know, I still keep in touch with old Jer," Travis said. He'd met her fiancé on a visit to see Lindsay, and they'd become fast friends. "He did move to New York. Doing pretty well up there and working in corporate law."

Lindsay sat back against the chair and looked up at the stars dotting the night sky. "I'm glad for him. I really am."

"And over him?"

She cast a curious glance in Travis's direction. "Yeah. But why are you asking? You have that tone."

"What tone?" He gave her an *I'm innocent* look, the one he'd perfected when he was a kid and always in trouble for breaking a vase or missing curfew. Their mother usually just laughed and let Travis off with an easy punishment.

"The one that says you want to convince me to do something crazy." When she'd been younger, she'd gone along with Travis's ideas—camping overnight by a stream, climbing a tree, catching frogs. But their paths had diverged as she grew up and went to college and Travis…

Well, he went on being Travis. Lovable but irresponsible.

"Last I heard, you almost did do something crazy," her brother said. "A little bird—or in my case, a little blonde college coed I used to date—texted and told me you were dancing with a stranger at the Ace tonight. She was a tiny bit jealous, because, in her exact words, 'I had that man first.'"

Lindsay blew her bangs out of her face. "These are the moments when I do wish I lived in a big city. Geesh, does everyone in Rust Creek Falls know how I spent my Friday night? And for your information, I wasn't dancing with him. He asked, and I said no."

Well, sort of said no. There'd been a moment there when she'd been swaying to the music. She'd been tempted, too tempted, to slip into Walker Jones's arms and swing around that dance floor.

"You should have said yes." Travis got to his feet and gathered up his empty plate. He paused at the door and turned back to face her. "You're a great lawyer, sis. Smarter than half the people I know. But you don't take enough risks, don't get your hands dirty often enough. Life is about jumping in with both feet, not standing on the edge and dipping in a toe from time to time."

Jumping in with both feet was foolhardy and risky, two things Lindsay normally shied away from. But for a moment on that dance floor tonight, she'd been both.

She sipped at the wine and watched the stars, so bright and steady in the sky, and told herself there was nothing wrong with being a calm house cat sitting in the sun. Because in the end, that house cat didn't make foolish choices that brought her far too close to enemy lines.

Chapter Three

Walker watched his brother polish off two plates of eggs and a pile of crispy bacon before he launched into a teetering pile of pancakes. Walker had stuck to a couple pieces of toast and some coffee, his usual breakfast choice. He'd never been much of a morning eater, but his brother Hudson—he could eat all day and still be hungry at bedtime.

The food and accommodations at Maverick Manor, where Walker had decided to stay last night, were outstanding. When he'd spent a night here a few months ago, he'd been surprised. He'd expected something more…primitive, given the size of Rust Creek Falls, but the two-story log cabin–style resort rivaled any five-star hotel Walker had stayed at before. Owned by a local, Nate Crawford, the resort showed the love Nate had for the place at every turn. It had wrap-around porches, big windows in every room and expansive views of the beautiful Montana landscape. He'd almost felt like he was staying in a tree house when he woke up this morning—if a tree house was big enough to hold one of the comfiest king-size beds Walker had ever slept in. The rooms were filled with overstuffed, comfortable furniture, all decorated in natural hues of beige and brown, the perfect complement to the log walls.

There'd been a copy of *The Rust Creek Falls Gazette*, the local paper, outside his door, filled with the usual small-town stuff—birth announcements, cows for sale, missing pickup trucks. It was all hokey stuff, making him wonder if these people were either a town full of Pollyannas or simply immune to the real world, where the front-page story wasn't about a prize mare giving birth to twin foals.

Either way, Walker wanted to leave Rust Creek Falls as quickly as possible. The whole place grated on his nerves. The sooner he got back to Tulsa and the day-to-day operations of his business, the better, which meant not delaying the reason for this meeting, even for pancakes.

"Let's talk about the day care," Walker said. He waved off the waitress's offer of more coffee.

Hudson pushed his empty plate to the side, then wiped his mouth with a napkin. "Things are going great."

"As in, you're there every day and are verifying that with your own eyes?"

Hudson shrugged, avoided Walker's gaze. "Well, yeah, more or less."

Walker's shoulders tensed. He'd trusted his

brother—and had thought it was a mistake from the start. But his father had said it would be a good idea to give Hudson a piece of the family business. Get him more involved, more invested, before their father stepped down entirely. This past year, his father had put Walker in the CEO position, while his dad took on the role of Chairman of the Board. The elder Jones continued to leave his fingerprints all over the company, as if he was still in charge. Walker hoped that once both he and his brother were part of the company, their father would ease up. But thus far, Hudson hadn't displayed the same love for business. Hudson was a good man, a hard worker, but clearly had no desire to be involved with the family business like Walker did. Maybe Walker had read his brother wrong, and made a mistake involving him in the day care franchise.

Walker leased the building from Hudson, who owned the land it sat on. Walker had hired Bella to be a part-time manager, expecting Hudson to fill in the gaps. "What does *more or less* mean?"

"Place pretty much runs itself. Besides, Bella, the manager, is one of those people who likes to keep things in line, so I let her." Hudson took a long swig of coffee.

"Hudson, you bought this property—"

"As an investment." Hudson shrugged again. "You know, pocket money."

Walker bit back his frustration. He should have known his brother would let him down. Their father had hoped, when Walker leased the building on the land Hudson bought, that his brother would actually get involved in the family business. As a fail safe, Walker had hired Bella, hoping she'd serve as Hudson's right hand. Every time Walker had asked Hudson how things were going, his brother had said everything was fine. Implying he was there every day. Now, it turned out that Hudson was off...being Hudson.

"When are you going to grow up, Hudson? Take some responsibility, for once, instead of going from job to job, place to place? Actually settle down?"

"What, like you? Work twelve million hours a week and never date because you don't have time to do anything other than—surprise—work?" Hudson shook his head. "No, thank you. I like to have a life."

"I have a life."

Hudson snorted.

"And just because I work a lot doesn't mean I don't get out, go on trips, date—"

"Name the last time you did any of the above."

Why was Walker feeling so damned defensive? It had to be the small town, which had him out of his element and out of his normal moods. "I went to the Ace in the Hole last night and did some line dancing."

Hudson's brown brows arched. He was a younger version of Walker, with the same facial expressions. "Are you serious? For real?" Hudson said.

"Yes, for real. I'm not all work and no play," he argued. Although Hudson was right. The last time Walker had done anything like that was so far in the distant past, he couldn't even remember it. When he was in Tulsa, his days blurred into a constant hamster wheel of work, work and more work. There were deals to be made, holdings to oversee, marketing to develop, accounting reports to analyze. Jones Holdings, Inc., was so diversified that Walker constantly felt like he was playing catch-up. He didn't have room in his life for anything other than work.

Or at least that was what he told himself. He had a great team working for him, and if he really wanted to, he could take time off. Go on vacation. Pick up a hobby.

Date.

Except he hadn't had a relationship that lasted more than a couple nights in more than two years. Not since Theresa had ended their five-year relationship, saying she wanted a man who invested his heart, not just his bank account.

Walker still didn't know what she meant by that. He'd given her everything he could, or thought he had. The lines had been blurred, though, because Theresa had worked for him, and more often than not, their date night conversations had been about work. She'd wanted more romance, she told him, more of his heart.

He'd told her he wasn't sure he had a heart to give. Work had been his passion for so long, he didn't know any other way to live. Eventually Theresa had given up on him and moved on. Last he heard, she had married an accountant and was expecting their first child. There were days when Walker wondered if maybe he'd missed out on something great. But those moments only lasted a second, because he was smart enough to know he was happiest when he was at work.

Once again Lindsay Dalton sprang into his mind. She was the kind of woman, Walker was sure, who would want the romance and the kids and the house with a yard. She might be all business in the court-room, but he sensed a softness about her, a sentimentality, when she smiled. When she'd been talking to her sister. And when she'd started to dance.

That had made him wonder just how much fun Lindsay was trying to hide beneath those courtroom suits.

"Back to the day care," Walker said, done with thinking about and discussing his personal life. A few days here, and he'd be back to the daily grind. He'd be happier in Tulsa. Less distracted by things like Lindsay Dalton's smile lingering in his mind. "There's a lot of ill will toward Just Us Kids because of this lawsuit. In order to expand the business, I need to turn the tide here in Rust Creek Falls. Even if we win the lawsuit, there are still going to be people who will believe the day care caused that illness. I want to head off the negative publicity from the get-go."

"Something you're apparently already doing," Hudson said. "I heard you bought everyone a round last night."

"How'd you hear about that?"

Hudson grinned. "It's a small town. Everyone knows everything here." He took a sip of coffee, then forked up a forgotten last bite of pancake. "If you want to build goodwill here, the best thing you can do is something that gets you involved with the town. One thing about Rust Creek Falls—it's like a big family. They'll accept you as one of their own—"

"You make it sound like an ant colony. Or the Borg."

Hudson laughed. "Pretty close. I never expected to like this place, but you know, living out on Clive Barker's ranch property and coming into town from time to time…it's started to grow on me. It might do the same for you."

Walker scoffed. "I'm leaving the minute this lawsuit is concluded. Until then, all I'm focused on is winning."

"The lawsuit and the hearts and minds?" Hudson asked.

"All part of the strategy," Walker said.

Hudson sighed. "Why did I ever think five minutes of dancing meant you were becoming human?'

Walker didn't dignify that with an answer. If his brother focused more on business and less on having fun, then maybe Hudson would understand.

"You know, Walker, I'm not this irresponsible screwup you keep making me out to be," Hudson said.

"Then what are you doing with your days instead of overseeing the day care?"

"Going back and forth between here and Wyoming, helping a friend set up a horse ranch. I'm helping him hire people, implement a solid record keeping system, buying the horses…in other words, running a business."

Walker was impressed, but kept that thought to himself. He didn't want to encourage his brother to spend time in Wyoming, not with this lawsuit on their backs. "I'd rather you were running the day care here."

Hudson rolled his eyes. "There is no pleasing you, is there? Can't you start thinking about something outside the family business for five minutes?"

"That family business puts the money in your bank account to do this horse ranch thing. If you were smart, you'd be helping me protect it, not beating me up for not having more fun."

Hudson drummed his fingers on the table for a moment, then sighed. "Okay, if you want to make people like you, do something nice for the town. Something hands-on. This isn't the kind of place that's going to appreciate a bunch of money thrown at it."

Walker scowled. "I wasn't going to do any such thing." Truth be told, he'd thought maybe he could just make a sizable donation to the local community center or a food bank or something and be done with it. He could see Hudson's point. A round of beers only bought temporary goodwill. He needed something bigger. Something involved. Something...

An orange flyer stuffed in the small plastic tabletop sign holder caught his eye.

Rust Creek Falls Harvest Festival!
Get involved now and help make this year's festival the best ever!

The announcement was followed by an invitation for volunteers to meet at the local high school Saturday afternoon. Today.

"Here's something I can do," he said to his brother, spinning the sign toward Hudson.

Hudson laughed. "You? Help with the harvest festival? Have you ever even attended a festival?"

"Doesn't matter. All I have to do is pitch in with... whatever they do to put together one of these things. People will see I care about the town. Problem solved."

Hudson sat back and gave his brother a dubious look. "You honestly think it's going to be as easy as that? This is real life, big brother. It's not some report you analyze or an interview you do with some overly enthusiastic CPA."

"And it's not rocket science, either." Walker dropped some bills on the table, leaving a generous tip for the waitress. "You stay in town for a while this time. Get to work at the day care and make sure the place is so clean and neat, no kid would get sick if he licked the floor. When they call you into court—and I'm sure they will, since you are the landlord—you can honestly say you saw that the place was in order. I'll stop in later, after I check out this festival thing." He picked up the flyer and tucked it in his pocket. "This might just be step one in my campaign to not only beat Lindsay Dalton but build the Just Us Kids chain."

And that would get him out of this town, back to work and away from women who lingered in his thoughts for all the wrong reasons.

Travis had been right. Getting hands-on was a nice change, Lindsay thought as she stacked wood in a pile to start building the vendor booths for the harvest festival. There weren't that many volunteers here today, probably because a lot of people were at the craft fair at the church. The handful of people in the gymnasium had divvied up the various jobs as best they could, but even Lindsay could see they were going to be shorthanded. She didn't mind, really. She'd been spending so much time in the office, working on the court case, that it felt good to do something constructive. Something that didn't also raise her blood pressure because it went with thinking about Walker

Jones. Yes, a little construction project today would be a good distraction, on all levels.

Lani came by, with Russ at her side. The two of them looked so blissfully happy that Lindsay felt a flicker of envy. What would it be like to have someone look at her like that? To take her hand, just because, then smile at her like she was the most precious thing on earth?

"Hey, sis, we're heading out with the landscaping volunteers to do some work in the park. There's a tree that needs to come down and some shrubbery that needs to be pruned." Lani gestured toward the wood. "Are you going to work on that by yourself?"

"I think I can handle a few simple booths." Lindsay flexed a biceps. "I have skills."

Russ laughed. "You sure you don't want one of us to stay and help you?"

"No, no, I've got it. The outdoor work is important. If that doesn't get done, there won't be any place to put the booths." Lindsay picked up the cordless drill and pressed the button. It whirred and spun. There, that should make her look confident. The booths, after all, were pretty much just oversize squares. "I can do this with my eyes closed."

"Okay. We should be back in a couple hours. If you need anything, holler." Lani gave Lindsay a quick hug, then the two of them headed out the door.

Lindsay propped her hands on her hips and looked at the pile of wood. She had a rudimentary sketch, given to her by Sam Traven, co-owner of the Ace in the Hole, of what the booths should look like. A box base, with a long flat piece of plywood to serve as a table, then a frame above it to hang signage from. Like a child's lemonade stand, only bigger.

She had a cordless drill, wood screws and precut wood. What she didn't have was a clue of how to put this together. Okay, so maybe she'd been a little too optimistic when she told Lani and Russ she could handle this.

Lindsay picked up a two-by-four, then one of the shorter pieces. It seemed like this shorter piece should create the sides, then connect to another shorter piece, then another longer one... Okay, one piece at a time. It was just a big box, right?

She put the longest piece on the floor, then got out a wood screw and let the magnetic end of the drill bit connect to it. She knelt beside the two pieces, then tried to hold the shorter one in place while she drilled the screw into it and connected them.

Or tried to. Turned out that holding a piece of wood with her left hand while trying to operate the cordless drill with her right hand was a whole lot harder than they made it look on *Fix or Flip*. The screw whined, twirled into the wood, but refused to go straight, leaving the whole connection askew. Lindsay brushed her bangs off her forehead, then flipped the switch on the drill and tried to back the screw out. It whined and spun but didn't pull back.

"It works a lot better if you use a little pressure," said a deep voice behind her.

Lindsay sighed and rocked back on her heels. "Thanks. Do you mind help—" She cut off her words when she realized who belonged to the voice.

Walker Jones III.

Great. The last person she wanted to see. He

was like a mangy dog, turning up in the least likely places, at the worst possible times. "What are you doing here?"

He nodded toward the wood pile. "Same as you. Helping with the harvest festival."

She scoffed. "Right. And why the heck would you do that?"

"To build goodwill." He shrugged. "I want people in this town to like me. So sue me. Oh, wait, you already are."

At least he was honest about why he was here. But that didn't make her like the idea any more. She wanted Walker Jones gone from Rust Creek Falls, gone from her peripheral vision…just gone. Even if he did looked damned good in jeans and a white button-down shirt with the cuffs rolled up. "You just want to win the lawsuit. Buying a round of beers and helping set up for a harvest festival won't do that."

"Walker Jones?" Rosey Traven, Sam's wife and the other co-owner of the Ace in the Hole, came striding over. She reached out and took his hand, giving him a hearty shake. "I heard you were in my bar last night, buying beers for everyone. That was a really nice thing to do."

"Thank you, ma'am," he said, shaking Rosey's hand as he spoke. "I figured since I was new in town, I should say thank you for the warm welcome I received."

Warm welcome? Lindsay rolled her eyes.

"Well, there's no better way to say thank you than with a couple of drinks." Rosey smiled, then turned to Lindsay. "Hi, Lindsay. Nice to see you here today. We sure appreciate your help with the booths."

"You're welcome. I'm glad to help." She pointed at the convoluted boards. "Once I figure out how, that is."

"You've got some handsome help here. I'm sure he can figure out how to get that together right quick." Rosey smiled at Walker. "I best be going. Sam and I are bringing sandwiches to all the volunteers in the park. You two have fun!"

Which left Lindsay alone with Walker. Again. "Listen, we are on two different sides of a lawsuit," she said, trying to work the drill again and back out the screw. It whined and groaned in place. "Damn it!"

"You're going to strip the screw. Let me help you." Walker's hand covered hers.

She didn't want to like his touch. Didn't want to react. But her body didn't listen to her head. The second his hand connected with hers, his larger fingers encompassing her smaller ones, a little flutter ran through her veins. In that instant, she was acutely aware of how close he was. How good he smelled. How the veins in his hands extended up his muscular forearms.

And how much she wanted to kiss him.

"I've got it." She yanked the drill up, so fast and so hard that it sent her sprawling back. That flutter had been an anomaly. That was all.

Walker's hand was there again, stopping her from hitting the floor. A quick touch, but it sent another explosion through her veins. "Whoa. I said a little pressure. Not a tidal wave."

"I can handle this. I don't need your help." It was a lie—she needed help—but she didn't want it from the man she had sworn to hate. The same man who was—damn it—handsome. And intriguing.

"How many things have you built?" Walker said.

"None." She waved that answer off. "But I can read directions."

"That's great, except some things come with experience, not directions." Walker gestured toward the misassembled corner. "You are a smart, capable, beautiful woman, but you are tearing up that screw head and making it almost impossible to take those two pieces apart. Now, you may not want my help, but I think you need it, at least for a minute."

Had he just called her beautiful? Why did a part of her do a little giddy dance at that?

Lindsay bent her head and worked on the screw again, but the two pieces of wood were not coming apart. The screw refused to go anywhere but in a pointless circle. Lindsay really didn't know what to do with a stripped screw head, or what one even was, only that it sounded bad. She was going to mess this up, and that would mean someone would have to buy more wood. For a festival that was operating on a shoestring budget to begin with, that would be a disaster, and Lindsay didn't want that on her shoulders. She knew when she was beaten, even if the victor was some scraps of wood and a single screw.

She handed him the drill. "Fine. You do it."

To his credit, Walker didn't say *I told you so*. He held the pieces firmly with one hand, pressed the drill into the screw and let the bit whir slowly as he backed the screw out a little at a time. Clearly, the key was patience and pressure.

Pretty much the same thing in a court case, Lindsay

thought. A lot of patience and a little pressure usually equaled success.

"Thanks," she said. The two pieces of wood were still intact, though the screw was worse for wear. Far better to replace one screw than the more expensive wood, which was still fine to use. "I'll admit, I'm impressed."

Walker chuckled. "I can't build a house or anything, but I do have some handyman skills. My grandpa liked to make things, and I was at his house most weekends when I was a kid, so he taught me what he could." His gaze went to someplace far away. Dwelling on memories, perhaps? "I miss him terribly, and every time I see a birdhouse, it makes me think of him. He was a hell of a guy."

She hated that a simple story about his grandpa could make her see him in a different light. She wanted to hate Walker Jones III and his evil empire for how it had mismanaged the Just Us Kids Day Care. Except that was hard to do that when Walker got all sentimental talking about building a birdhouse. "That's...sweet."

"You say it like you're surprised."

"Maybe I am a little." Okay, a lot. For two months, she'd been sending letters and leaving messages for this faceless evil man in a corporate office. But now that Walker was here and in the flesh, she couldn't quite muster up the same feelings of animosity.

"I can tell what you're thinking. I'm not this horrible corporate monster who only cares about the bottom line, you know." He picked up the next piece of wood. "In fact, let me prove it to you."

"Prove it to me? How?"

He waved the wood at her, then grabbed a handful of screws. "Let me help you construct these."

Working all day side by side with Walker Jones? Having him distract her and make her forget that he was the enemy, not a man she wanted to kiss? Lindsay shook her head. "I don't think that's a good idea. I'm suing you, and we shouldn't be talking to each other."

"For one, you're suing my company, not me personally. And for another, as long as we don't talk about the day care or the lawsuit, we should be just fine." He put out his hand. "Deal?"

She hesitated. She knew she shouldn't work with him, especially not with the pending lawsuit, but there were few people in the room, and all these booths to build, and given her track record so far, there wasn't much chance that Lindsay could build them herself. And maybe if she spent some time with Walker she could figure out what made him tick—and use that to her advantage in the courtroom next week.

"Deal." She shook with him, and that same zing ran through her. Clearly, it wasn't an anomaly. Which meant Lindsay might just be making an incredibly big mistake.

But then Walker let her go and started talking about the best method of assembling the booths, and she realized he must not have felt the same jolt. He was being detached and businesslike and doing exactly what he'd promised to do—helping. She had nothing to worry about, as long as she could keep herself in check. Which she could easily do, she told herself.

"Okay, so this piece goes here?" she said, picking up another short one. Work on the booth and forget about the way his touch had seared her skin, yup, that was the plan.

"I'll hold it together. You'll drill a pilot hole first, then sink the screw."

"Me? Drill a what?"

"Here, change out the bit to a drill bit." He showed her how to loosen the chuck then slip in the new bit and tighten it again. "If you drill a pilot hole, it keeps the screw from putting as much pressure on the wood and you have less chance of splitting the wood."

She did as he instructed, using just enough pressure to drill the narrow pilot hole, then back out the bit and change it out for a Phillips head. She poised herself over the two pieces of wood, a little hesitant. "And now we try this again. You sure you have a good hold on it?"

"It'll be fine. Just remember to go slow and keep even pressure on the drill."

She did as he said, and when the screw sank into place, Walker let go. The two sides of the booth held together, perfectly perpendicular. "I did it."

Walker grinned. "You did. Great job."

Confidence filled her chest. Maybe this wasn't such an impossible project. Of course, she was only on the first booth, but still… "Can we do the next piece?"

He chuckled. "Yup. Same idea as before. Ready?"

She grabbed another screw, then hoisted the cordless drill. Right now, she felt like a superhero. She had only built a tiny portion of one booth—with Walker's help—but there was something deeply satisfying about building anything with her own hands that gave her a sudden burst of self-assurance. "Yup."

"You do a mighty good impression of Bob Vila," he said, "only you are way prettier than him."

That made her laugh and flushed her cheeks. Twice now he'd complimented her on her looks. But she told herself the words meant nothing, and she should take his remarks in stride. "I should hope so," she said, laughing them off. "Though if I grow a beard, we might up end up looking like twins."

"Trust me. No one would ever mistake you for Bob Vila."

"Thanks." She ducked her head, hoping he hadn't seen how the flattery pleased her, despite her resolve. Or how tempted she was to keep looking into his blue eyes.

They worked together for a few minutes. Walker was a patient, easygoing teacher who coached her from time to time and made the whole process ten times less stressful. He held the pieces while she connected them, the two of them falling into an easy, unspoken rhythm. They would bump up against each other occasionally or just be within a few inches of each other. Every time he brushed up against her, her heart did a little flutter flip. And then her head scolded her for her reaction.

Soon as the booths were built, she was going to put some distance between herself and Walker. This... attraction she felt for him would lead nowhere good.

In almost no time at all, they had framed the first booth. "Let's get that plywood on," Walker said. He hoisted the heavy piece into place, then handed her the drill. "Just screw down each of the corners, and then we'll put a few more screws along the longer sides to give it more stability."

She did as he said, but her focus kept sputtering. She was acutely aware of the muscles in his hands, the dark scent of his cologne, the broad expanse of his chest and how very, very good he looked in jeans. "There. I think we're done."

They both stepped back and took a second to admire their work. The booth stood tall and straight and ready for business. A sense of pride washed over Lindsay. "We did it."

"We did." He turned to her and smiled. "Seems we *can* work together for the common good."

She laughed. "Don't get used to it."

"Trust me, I won't." He waved toward the pile of wood, and the teasing mood evaporated. They were back to all business about the booths. "How many more to go?"

"Nine." She perched her fists on her hips. The pile of wood seemed awfully high, and the number of hours left to work awfully low. As much as she wanted to get rid of Walker so she would stop noticing his hands and his cologne, she knew she couldn't finish this job on her own. "Think we can do it?"

"Are you inviting me to stay and help?"

Was she? All she knew was that she had a lot of booths to build and working with Walker wasn't as bad as she'd expected. She might even call it…enjoyable, if she was feeling charitable. "Turns out you're kind of handy to have around, Walker Jones." She wagged a finger at him. "Just don't expect any of this to influence how I go after you in court next week."

"Still a bulldog, huh?"

"Of course."

He grinned again. "I wouldn't want it any other way, Ms. Dalton."

"Me, neither," she said, then turned to the next booth. Because the last thing she needed was to let down her defenses and fall for the man who was going to be sitting on the opposite side of the courtroom in a few days.

Chapter Four

Walker hadn't planned on it. Not at all. But it happened. He liked Lindsay Dalton. She was beautiful and funny and smart, but most of all, determined. He liked that best about her. The way she didn't back down from a challenge, didn't find a task too daunting. They were traits that would serve her well in court—

Which was a definite disadvantage to him.

If he was smart, he'd steer clear of her. In fact, every part of his brain was telling him to walk away. Right now. But something kept him there, even as he fed himself the fiction that he was merely trying to gain a better understanding of the opposing side, as part of maintaining his edge over her. So he kept on building the booths with her, one after another, like an assembly line of wood and screws.

But every time she got within a few inches of him, his entire body went on high alert.

Yeah, he was attracted to her. Very much so. He kept trying to pretend all he was here for was building the booths and good community relations and researching the opposing counsel, but really, he'd stopped caring about the festival a long time ago. All he wanted was more time with Lindsay.

"So, did you grow up around here?" he asked.

She arched a brow. "Is this small talk or investigating the opposing counsel?"

She was smart, too, and he'd do well to remember that before he got tripped up on his own plan.

"Neither." He sat back on his heels. "I'm interested in you. Genuinely interested."

She opened her mouth. Closed it again. "We can't… I mean, we shouldn't…"

"I'm not asking you to marry me, Lindsay. Just whether you grew up around here." It was the first time he'd used her given name, and it rolled off his tongue with ease. A little flare of surprise lit her eyes, which told him she'd noticed the name, too. He'd done it only to gain an edge, no other reason.

"And just because I answer your questions doesn't mean I want to marry you, either," she said.

He laughed. "Is everything with you an argument?"

That made a grin quirk up one corner of her mouth. "My mother would say I was born ready to argue."

"My mother said the same thing about me. She used to say I'd argue about the color of the sky on a cloudy day. I was the difficult one, according to her."

"Hmm…" Lindsay put a finger to her lips. "I might have to agree with that opinion."

"Ah, but you hardly know me." He leaned in closer to her, and against his better judgment, inhaled the sweet scent of her perfume, watched the tick of her pulse in her neck. "I'm not as bad as I seem on paper."

"Maybe you're much worse."

He could tell that it was going to take a whole lot more than some beer and booths to impress the lawyer. She was a challenge, and if there was one thing Walker loved, it was a challenge. "Just give me a chance, that's all I ask."

"It won't change anything, Mr. Jones. I'm still taking you to court."

"I wouldn't expect anything less from you." He connected the next two pieces, then tried again. Reminded himself he was here to get to know her, as an opponent, nothing else. "So…did you grow up around here?"

She laughed this time. "You don't give up easily, do you?"

"I suspect neither do you."

"You've got that right." She handed him the next board, then jiggled a few screws in her palm. "Yes, I did grow up here. The Dalton family is as much a part of Rust Creek Falls as the earth the town sits on. I went away for college and law school, and for a brief time, I thought about moving to the city once I got my JD, but I love it here. It's…home."

A soft, sentimental smile swept across her face. Her eyes took on a dreamy sheen. Walker almost felt… jealous.

He'd never loved anything or anyplace as much as Lindsay Dalton clearly loved this town. What would it be like to come home to a place like that? To feel like you belonged?

In that cold, perfect museum his parents had called a home, he had never felt like he belonged. With his father judging everything he said and did, and his mother involved in every cause but her own children, Walker had hated his childhood home. His brothers were the only thing that had made it tolerable. When he'd gone to his grandfather's, where life was simple and the rules were light, he'd felt happy. Like he was meant to be there, building things in the garage his grandfather had turned into a woodshop. The way Lindsay talked about Rust Creek Falls made him think of the scent of his grandfather's cologne, the way the woodsy smell blended with the scent of wood shavings. That gravelly voice giving him wisdom about life and girls, while the sandpaper *scritched* along a plank of wood.

Damn. Now he was getting all sentimental. If there was one thing Walker had learned, it was that sentimentality didn't mix with business. Or lawsuits.

"So what about you?" she asked. "Did you grow up in Tulsa?"

"Nope. In a nearby city, Jenks. My family has never been the small-town type and neither have I. Honestly, I have no idea how people live in a place like this. It's so…claustrophobic."

"Then why open a business here?"

"It made sense on paper." He shrugged. "There are few child care options in the immediate area, it's centrally located and can draw from other towns, and the building needed minimal changes to convert it to a day care."

She looked skeptical. "In other words, the entire decision was based on numbers, not emotions?"

"Is there another way to make decisions?" Walker said. "I'm not going to run my business based on how cute Main Street is." He put a sarcastic emphasis on the cute.

"I'm not talking about cuteness," Lindsay said, her hackles up, fire in her eyes. "But when you open a business in a place like this, you have to realize that it's not just another storefront in a row of strip malls. Any business that operates in Rust Creek Falls becomes part of the fabric of the community."

He scoffed. "Fabric of the community? This is a business, not a knitting circle."

As soon as he said the words, he realized he was undermining his goal of pretending to be one of the people of Rust Creek Falls. If he let his disdain for small-town life show, everything he'd done so far would be undone. "But this town seems like a really great place to live."

"It is," she said. "You'll see that if you stay here for a few days."

I doubt that highly. "I'm sure I will." He gave her a smile that he hoped said he wasn't the evil small-town-hating ogre she thought he was. "I guess I'm a little out of touch with what it's like to live here. I live a couple miles from the corporate headquarters in Tulsa." He didn't add that he would bet a thousand dollars that Lindsay lived in some kind of homey place with a wide front porch, the diametric opposite to his fifteenth-floor apartment decorated in glass and chrome. Everything about this town seemed like something out of an episode of *Little House on the*

Prairie, except with the modern conveniences of electricity and wireless phones.

They worked for a little while, the conversation falling into a lull.

"So, is it just you and your brothers?" she asked after they assembled another booth. "Autry, Gideon and…Jensen, right? And I've seen Hudson around town now and then."

She'd done her homework. "Yes. Even though I have a bunch of brothers, my parents weren't exactly… parentish," he said. "My dad worked a lot and my mother was involved in her charities. We were more often with the nanny than with them."

"That's…awful."

"It's a childhood. We all have one." He shrugged, like it didn't matter.

"I grew up on a ranch," Lindsay said as she held the two legs of the booth together and waited for him to attach them to the brace. "Horses, pastures, big family dinners, the whole nine yards. I still live there now, just while I'm establishing my career."

He finished the next booth and reached for the plywood countertop to install. "I couldn't imagine living with anyone in my family. Working with my father is more than enough together time. He can be a little… hardheaded."

Hardheaded was putting it mildly. Walker Jones II had high expectations for all his sons, but he reserved the highest for his namesake. Walker had done his best to live up to that family mantle, but the times when he had tried to go his own way, his father had lectured him like he was two years old again. The older Walker got, the more he butted heads with his father, over everything from the type of coffee in the conference room to the directions the corporation should take going forward. His phone buzzed all day with texts and emails from his father—which Walker did his best to ignore. As he reminded his father often, Walker was a grown-up who didn't need to be ordered around. But his father rarely listened—to anyone.

Lindsay laughed. "Hmm... Jones family trait?"

"Maybe." She had a really sweet, musical laugh. For a millisecond, he forgot she was the opposing counsel.

He'd done that at the courthouse on Friday, too. When he'd seen her with the baby, he'd seen a softer side, a gentler dimension to the no-nonsense lawyer. There'd also been a degree of tension between them, ever since they started working side by side. Half of him wanted to kiss her—and half of him thought he should back away before he got even more connected to the one woman who wanted to ruin him.

He stood and turned and realized they were out of plywood. This was it, he told himself. His opportunity to leave. So why was he not moving? It was if his feet weren't listening to his brain.

"We'll need a few more sheets to finish up the last few booths," Walker said. "Do you know where the supplies are?"

Where did those words come from? He was supposed to be leaving!

She nodded. "Everything's being stored in that room behind the gym. Four pieces of plywood is a lot to carry, so maybe I should come help you."

Oh, that wasn't good. It meant she'd be spending more time with him, even if it was only the few minutes it took to get the plywood. Being alone with her was definitely not a good idea. But he didn't say no.

They crossed the gym, with her leading the way. She had on jeans and a T-shirt, her hair back in a ponytail again. She looked like the kind of woman who curled up on the couch at the end of the day with a movie or a book. It was so foreign to Walker's life. His evenings were often spent reading reports or answering emails or analyzing financial data. He couldn't remember the last time he'd watched more than ten minutes of television.

In many ways, Lindsay was like Theresa, who had complained about how much he worked, and talked about wanting a home with a fence and a dog. That wasn't the life he led, or the life he wanted.

His attraction to Lindsay was irrelevant. The only thing he needed to worry about was winning the court case.

"Back here," Lindsay said, opening a door at the back of the room. It led down a darkened hallway and into a second room on the right. She patted the wall. "The light switch should be right…here. Somewhere…"

She patted the wall some more. Then turned at the same time he did. They collided in the dark space, skin against skin, her head landing just under his chin, her curves pressed against his chest. "I… I can't find the light switch," she said.

Was she feeling this same weird attraction that he was? This thing he kept trying to ignore because all it did was distract him. She was the enemy, the woman suing him. But in the dark, all he felt, smelled, touched, was Lindsay the woman.

"It might be…" She reached past him in the confined space, her hand tapping the wall. The movement brought her tighter to him, and he shifted to give her more room, but she moved at the same time, and his hands ended up on her waist. She drew in a sharp breath, and he lowered his head.

"It should be…" Her words trailed off, her breath whispering against his jaw. Hot, seductive, tempting. A flare of anger, or maybe it was desire, or maybe both, rushed through his veins. He should leave, he should get out of here, he should remember she was the one on the other side of the courtroom. "Maybe…"

"Maybe," he said, then he cursed under his breath, leaned down—

And he kissed her.

When Walker Jones's lips met hers, Lindsay stilled. Her heart raced, her breath caught in her throat, but her body went very, very still. It wasn't just the surprise—it was the feel of his lips on hers. The whisper of his mouth against hers, tender, sweet, patient.

Amazing.

It was the kind of kiss that started slow, easy, like a summer rainstorm on a wide Montana prairie. For a moment, she forgot who he was, forgot everything. She rose up into his kiss, her arm going around his neck, his going around her waist, pulling her closer. He tasted of coffee and man, and she could feel herself getting swept away.

Then she remembered his words, how he'd called this town she loved *claustrophobic*, how he'd compared it to a knitting circle. Walker Jones had no love for Rust Creek Falls, and no real concern for anything besides his bottom line.

One hot kiss in the darkness behind the gym wasn't going to change that.

She pulled away from him and as she backed into the concrete wall, the light switch poked into her back. Sure, she thought, now she found it. She flicked it on, quick. "We need to get those booths built," she said.

Yeah, that was smart—just pretend the whole thing never happened. The sooner they got back to work, the sooner they would be done, and the sooner she could put some distance between them. Walker gave her a curious look, as if he was trying to figure out what she was thinking. "Yeah, we do."

They grabbed the plywood sheets. Walker hefted two into his arms at once, while Lindsay followed behind with a single sheet. The board was heavy and awkward, which meant it required concentration to wrangle it out of the small storage room and over to the pile of wood. As soon as Lindsay dropped off the first board, she went back and got the last one. By the time she returned, Walker was busy building, and the kiss was behind them.

Or at least that's what she told herself while she handed him boards and screws and they put together the last few booths. They worked without speaking for a while.

That didn't stop her from sneaking glances at his broad back, his muscular arms, the concentration in his features as he assembled the parts. He was one hell of a kisser, and it had been a long time since she'd been kissed like that.

For a second, she'd let that kissing override the fact

that Walker was a corporate shark, with no regard for the things she loved. Even if she discounted that, and the fact that she was suing his day care chain, he was also totally devoted to his business. She'd read his bio. He'd never been engaged, and as far as she could tell, he'd only had one long-term relationship that ended a couple years ago. He'd never been involved in charity work, never done anything but work to build his empire. She'd fallen head over heels for Jeremy back in college, and in the end, he'd chosen his career over her. The bottom line triumphed over the simple life she loved.

The similarity between the two men was not lost on her. In fact, it smacked her right in the face.

Jeremy hadn't wanted to live in Rust Creek Falls. Hadn't wanted the comfortable small-town life she loved so much. He'd told her she was "wasting her talent" being a lawyer here. That had been the last straw, and the end of their relationship. She could have put the exact same words into Walker's mouth a second ago.

Ever since Jeremy, Lindsay had shied away from dating. For one, she knew pretty much every single man in Rust Creek Falls, and for another, she hadn't had the time to do anything besides study for the bar. And now she was so busy with the lawsuit, she hadn't had time to do much more than grab a drink with Lani during the week.

Walker Jones might fit the physical type of man she would be interested in, but he was the complete opposite, morally and every other way. He was driven by money, not by the values that immersed her world in Rust Creek Falls. She needed to remember that his lack of oversight, and his focus on making a profit, had nearly cost Georgina Marshall her life.

They finished the last of the booths without talking much, then stacked them against the wall. Tomorrow there'd be volunteers to paint and decorate the booths so they'd be ready for next weekend. There was still plenty to be done at the park, but building the vendor booths had been a good start.

"That was a lot of work," Lindsay said, "but I'm pretty impressed that we finished all those in one day."

Walker ran a hand over the rudimentary stalls. "I don't understand why they don't just buy some of these premade," he said. "It can't be that expensive to buy a stand like this for a festival."

She bristled. Did he really think people here had the kind of money he did? "Most of the businesses in this town don't have anything approaching a marketing budget. The owners are making do and supporting the town in the process."

"Then why have a festival at all?" He looked around the room, at the stacks of decorations, the volunteers working on hand-painted signs. "Seems to be a waste of everyone's time."

Lindsay tamped down her first response. And her second. "For your information, a festival is not a waste of anyone's time. It's not just about the booths or the sales. It's about bonding as a community."

Walker scoffed. "Bonding as a community? I hate to tell you this, sweetheart, but that's the kind of thing that only happens in novels. People are people, wherever you go, and they're not going to sit around a campfire and hold hands just because you host a harvest festival."

She parked her fists on her hips and stared up at him. "You really are that jaded, aren't you?"

"I prefer to call it realistic."

"This town bonds over more than just a harvest festival, Mr. Jones. When Jamie Stockton's wife died, this town came together to help him take care of his premature triplets. There were people there around the clock, and there still are, for no other reason than they want to help. And when your day care center started making kids sick—"

He put up his hands. "Whoa, stop right there."

She didn't stop. She kept on talking, moving toward him, angry now, at him, at herself, at that kiss. "And when your day care center started making kids sick, this town came together to support the Marshalls and the other families involved. This town isn't like some big fancy city, Mr. Jones, and that is exactly why so many people love it. And why you—" she pointed a finger at his chest "—will never fit in here, no matter how many beers you buy or booths you build."

Then she turned on her heel and headed out of the gym. As far and as fast as she could. The day when Walker Jones headed back to Tulsa couldn't come soon enough.

Chapter Five

Walker told himself he didn't care one bit what Lindsay Dalton thought of him. He didn't want her idealized small-town life, and he didn't care about this harvest festival or anything that happened in Rust Creek Falls.

For God's sake, the place sounded like something in a fairy tale. People coming together to take care of triplets, to support a family with a sick kid—that kind of thing didn't really happen. In the real world, people trampled each other to get the top spot. They looked out for number one.

He'd grown up in a driven, competitive, emotionless house. His father had only cared about what his sons achieved, and if they weren't doing anything spectacular, Walker Jones II had ignored them. Walker had thought that going to work for his father would finally win his acceptance, but if anything, it had only made his father criticize him more.

"You better do me proud," his father would say to him. "I can't have a Walker Jones who doesn't live up to the family legacy."

As if conjured up by the mere thought, Walker's phone began to buzz and his father's face appeared on the incoming call screen. Walker pushed the answer button. "It's Saturday, Dad."

"Just another day of the week," the elder Jones said. "I'm at work, and I assume you are, too."

"Of course." He didn't tell his father about building the booths, something his father would see as a waste of time. If it wasn't producing income, it wasn't worth doing.

"I'm disappointed you didn't get this frivolous lawsuit dismissed," his father said. "This should have been done and handled by now."

The implication—that Walker wasn't doing everything he could. "We go to court Tuesday. I have no doubt we will win. Their case is thin." *But their lawyer is determined.*

His father let out one of those long sighs that said he wished he'd had a son more like himself. More ruthless, more predatory. From the day Walker had started working for his father, he'd tried to live up to impossible expectations, and still failing, despite expanding Jones Holdings, Inc. to three countries and doubling its coffers in the last five years.

If Walker had turned out to be a ditch digger or trash collector, he had no doubt his father would have probably insisted he change his name. Instead, Walker had followed in his father's footsteps, doing everything he could to make his father say words he used so rarely they were like comets.

I'm proud of you.

"Handle it, Walker," his father said. "Quit letting some small-town nothing lawyer dance you around in court."

"Yes, sir." Any argument back would be pointless.

"Don't make me regret making you CEO," his father said, then he disconnected the call without a goodbye. Par for the course.

His mind wandered to Lindsay Dalton. To that kiss. To how it had distracted him from the goal.

No more. From here on out, he would deal with her in court, and nowhere else. *Handle it, Walker.*

And he would. He'd been handling things all his life, and he wasn't about to stop now because of one sentimental brunette living in some Mayberryesque town.

He pulled into the lot at Just Us Kids. The lights were still on, though he'd arrived right at the close of business on Saturday. The day care operated six days a week to allow parents who pulled weekend shifts to find child care. Business had been brisk when the day care first opened in July, but all the bad publicity about the sick kids had really hurt revenue. The bottom line was just starting to climb back into the black in the last few weeks. If he could keep news about the lawsuit from filling the front page of *The Rust Creek Falls Gazette*, then maybe this location would start turning a profit again.

Bella Stockton, the manager he'd hired in the whirlwind couple of days he'd spent here months ago, rose from her space behind the front desk when Walker entered. She was tall, probably five foot nine, and thin as a rail, as his grandmother would say. She had short blond hair and brown eyes, but always a ready smile. Even in the short interview he'd had with her, she'd impressed him as smart, organized and calm. Exactly the kind of person who should be working at a day care.

"Mr. Jones. Nice to see you again," she said.

"Call me Walker, please." He stood in the center of the lobby and looked around. The multicolored tile floor and bright crayon-colored molding were offset by sunshine-yellow walls and several child-size tables and chairs. A ceiling fan shaped like an airplane spun a lazy circle above him.

There were several new additions to the space— pictures on the wall, done by the children who attended the day care, he assumed. A row of flowers made out of handprints, a set of zoo animals drawn in crayon. There were flowers on the front desk and squishy bean bag chairs in the corner, flanked by a small bookcase stuffed with colorful books and a few baskets of toys. It looked warm and inviting, and a great introduction to the kids coming through the door, not to mention a smart way to keep children entertained while their parents were filling out paperwork or settling their bill.

"I like the changes," Walker said. He turned back to Bella. "I know my brother, so I'm assuming these things are all your doing?"

"Yes, Mr.—" She caught herself. "Walker. I just thought the lobby, particularly since it's the first thing everyone who comes through the door sees, needed to be a little more…welcoming to kids."

"I like it. Very much. Before I open the new locations, I should have you come in and offer your opinion." He glanced around again, then nodded. He knew it had been a good decision to hire her. "Nice job. Very nice."

Bella blushed. "Thank you."

Walker was just about to ask where Hudson was when the door opened and his younger brother hurried inside, along with a brisk October wind. "Hey, sorry I'm late," Hudson said. "I had a lunch date that almost ran into dinner." He grinned and gave Walker a quick wink.

Walker rolled his eyes. One of these days, his bachelor brother was going to have to grow up. Hopefully that day was today. Walker couldn't stay here in Rust Creek Falls and babysit this location. He had a merger with another oil refinery to oversee when he got back, along with the upcoming day care expansion to implement. Not to mention the thousand other deals and details he managed at the corporation. If Hudson wasn't going to step up to the plate, then Walker would untangle the location entirely from his brother and open in a new place. Let Hudson find someone else to rent this building, and keep Walker from having to micromanage his younger sibling.

"Now that you're finally here, let's do a walkthrough," Walker said to Hudson. "I want to see for myself how things are being run so I can head off that lawyer before she tries to say we aren't keeping on top of things."

Hudson glanced over at Bella. "You know how things run here. Why don't you take my brother on the big tour?"

Bella made a face. Apparently she wasn't any happier with Hudson's lack of involvement than Walker was. "I'm the manager, Hudson. Not the owner."

"Yeah, but you run the place." He gave her that grin that had undoubtedly charmed dozens of women before. "And you do a damned fine job of it, too."

Bella did not look swayed by the compliment. If anything, she seemed more annoyed by Hudson. Chances were good this wasn't the first time Hudson had tried to flirt with her. And probably one of the few times Hudson had failed to make a woman smile. Good for Bella, Walker thought. She was stronger than he'd realized. And definitely smarter.

"How about both of you show me around," Walker said. "Because apparently I'm not the only one who needs to see how this place is run."

Bella shot Walker a quick smile of agreement, then crossed to the door and flipped the sign to Closed. "Our last child left ten minutes ago, so now's a great time to do the tour." She pulled out her security badge, swiped it against the reader on the wall by the door into the center, then ushered the men through. "We keep a very tight ship here," she said. "Everyone has to have a badge, and none of the children are allowed to run around unsupervised."

"That's good." Last thing he needed now was some kid going missing. He was glad to see that Bella seemed to be on top of the security protocols and procedures he'd set in place.

As Bella ushered them down the hall, Hudson followed along behind her like a happy little puppy, watching her every move. Walker just shook his head.

Bella showed them the individual rooms for the

different age groups of children, the shelves of activities and games, the reading nooks and open coat closet spaces. "We want the rooms to feel as much like home as possible," she explained as she showed off the miniature recliners beside the bookcases. "We also have a variety of activities for all ages and levels of development. Some children prefer crafty things, some like intellectual things. One of our first steps when we take on a new child is to assess their interests and the best way that they learn. It's not school here, of course, but we do like to keep all the children, no matter their age, engaged and learning."

"That's great," Walker said. "I like that."

"We also work with the local elementary school. If one of our children is having trouble in math, for instance, we set up a quiet area for him to work one-on-one with a staff member who can help with homework or understanding concepts."

Walker nodded his approval. Hudson elbowed him. "She's smart, isn't she? Damned glad to have her here. She's always thinking up stuff like that."

Bella ignored the compliment and kept on walking. "We had a good illness prevention program in place before the outbreak of sick children, but since that day, we have increased the number of hand-sanitizing stations and been extra vigilant about cleanliness and disinfecting. We've had no problems like that since."

"That's good to hear." Walker turned to Bella. She was definitely on top of everything that happened at Just Us Kids. He made a mental note to be sure Marty planned to call her as a witness. She'd do a far better job on the stand than Hudson. "Do you think the Marshall baby got sick because of attending Just Us

Kids? Tell me the truth. I'd rather deal with that than be blindsided in court next week."

Bella glanced at Hudson. As his direct report, she no doubt felt he should be the one answering. "Uh, Hudson?"

"You know this place better than I know my own house," Hudson said. "Go ahead. Tell Walker your opinion. He won't bite."

"Yes, please," Walker echoed. "Tell me what you think happened."

"I don't think the first child contracted RSV here," Bella said, her words slow at first, then picking up speed as she realized both men were interested in her take. "We had a few kids come in here after a long weekend, coughing and sneezing. One of those midsummer colds that just seemed to take hold all over town, so it wasn't surprising to see some sniffles around here. We increased our cleaning frequency, instructed staff to wash their hands more frequently and be even more diligent about disinfecting surfaces. It was hard to tell, honestly, if it was just a cold virus or something more serious." Bella sighed. Walker could see she was still troubled about the event.

"We weren't alerted that the first child had RSV for three days. Once we knew, we sent a letter home with all the parents. If a parent brought in a sniffling child, we kept that child separated from the other kids."

To Walker, it sounded like Bella had covered all the bases. He'd read up on RSV enough to know that it did, indeed, start off as a cold, and sometimes developed into RSV in children with weakened immune systems. While the virus was spread through touching germ-filled spaces, the center had done everything within its power to reduce that likelihood. He was feeling more and more confident that the judge would agree.

"Told you," Hudson said to Walker. "She's smart. Everyone who works here thinks Bella is pretty awesome. I don't have any worries when I leave her in charge."

Hudson was singing Bella's praises, but she was not impressed. She mostly ignored Hudson, Walker noticed, and every time she did, his brother tried harder to get her attention. That was what Walker liked best about Bella—she was immune to Hudson's charms.

Which also made her perfect to be entirely in charge at Just Us Kids.

"I'm glad to hear you were on top of it, and covered all the bases," he said to her. "You've done a great job, Bella."

She blushed. "I'm just doing my job. I care about the kids."

"It shows." He glanced at his brother again. Hudson was marginally involved in the conversation—most of his attention was centered on the blonde. Clearly, Hudson had a little crush on Bella and cared more about what she thought of him than what was going on at this day care. "In fact, Bella, I want to make you full-time manager."

He named a significant pay raise, knowing she was worth that and more.

"I... I don't know what to say," Bella said. "Thank you."

"You're very welcome." Walker gave her a nod.

"You two probably want to visit," Bella said. "I'm

just going to grab my things and go home. Thank you again, Mr. Jones."

After Bella was gone, Walker and Hudson walked back through the building to the lobby. At the door, Hudson turned to Walker. "What the hell was that about?"

"What was what about?"

"You making her full-time manager. Not that I don't think Bella is doing a hell of a job, but you made it sound like I'm not even a part of this place."

"You're not. I asked you to oversee things, and protect the family interests. And instead, we've ended up with a scandal and sick kids on our hands. On your watch, I might add."

Hudson shook his head. "Yeah, oversee, not control. I never promised to be full-time, Walker. You knew I had other business interests to manage."

"The only interest I cared about was this one."

"I have been here," Hudson said. "Far more than you think."

"Oh, yeah? Then how come you looked as surprised as I was by the changes in the day care? Can you tell me the procedures for disinfection every night? Do you even know the names of everyone who works here?"

Hudson scowled. "You sound just like our father right now. Doesn't matter what I do or don't do, it's not enough for you."

The reference to their father chafed at Walker. He was nothing like the elder Jones. "I'm just running a business here, Hudson. Nothing more."

"Of course." A look that could have been disappointment, could have been hurt, filled Hudson's features. "It's not about family, it's about profits and losses."

"I'm not that callous and cold."

His brother stood there a moment, looking at the street outside the glass front door. "You know, for a minute there, when you danced at the bar and helped with the festival prep, I thought maybe you were changing," Hudson said. "Becoming more of the brother I remembered before you started working for our father. But I was wrong. You've become just like him. Cold and distant and impossible."

Walker refused to answer that. Refused to entertain the thought that Hudson's words had struck a nerve. He pushed on the door handle, then turned back. "That woman—Bella—is worth more than you think. Take care of her or you'll lose her."

Walker got in his car and pulled out of the lot. As he drove, his mind kept going back to Hudson's words. *It's not about family, it's about profits and losses.*

It bothered Walker that he and Hudson had lost that easy relationship they'd had when they were kids. Of the five Jones boys, Walker and Hudson had always gotten along the best. Maybe it was the four-year age difference, or maybe it was that Hudson's fun-loving personality had balanced Walker's serious, eldest child attitude. But as they'd gotten older and gone their separate ways, their relationship had deteriorated.

Walker had hoped—maybe foolishly—that his stay in Rust Creek Falls would be an opportunity to get back some of the relationship he had lost with Hudson. They were both adults now, and with Hudson's vested interest in the day care property, they had something more in common. But given the look of frustration on

Hudson's face earlier, Walker would put the chances of that happening at zero.

Yet another reason to leave this town as soon as possible. This lawsuit couldn't be settled fast enough for Walker's taste.

Lindsay sat in the Marshalls' living room, holding a cup of tea and feeling the ten-ton brick of their expectations hanging over her shoulders. They had been heartened by the judge's dismissal of Walker's summary judgment attempt but worried that the shortened timeline for going to court was going to impact their case. Lindsay attempted to defuse their concerns. "I think we have a strong case," she told them. "I wouldn't have taken the case if I didn't think so."

While the Marshalls seemed to relax, on the sofa across from her Dr. Jonathan Clifton put his cup on the table and leaned forward. He and his fiancée, nurse Dawn Laramie, who sat beside him, had treated Georgina during the RSV outbreak. He'd agreed to come to the Marshalls' house and talk about next week's trial, given that he would be one of the witnesses she was going to call. "It is going to be difficult to prove that the day care center was responsible, you know," he said. "This isn't a clear-cut case."

Jon had been saying that from the start. Lindsay had talked to several experts, and she knew that Walker had a point—RSV could be contracted easily, especially in children with weakened immune systems. But that didn't make Just Us Kids not responsible. They could have done more, reacted faster. In his deposition, Hudson Jones, Walker's brother and the landlord of the property, had come across as knowing little of the day-to-day details of what was going on within the doors of the center. That alone made them at least partially responsible.

If Walker or his brother had seen baby Georgina lying so frail and tiny in that hospital bed, they would have reacted just as Lindsay had—with horror that something that started out so innocuously could put a vulnerable infant on the edge of death.

"Maybe so, but the day care center should have done more to head off the further outbreak," Lindsay said. "I will argue that their laziness in disinfecting and their slow response to the crisis contributed to Georgina's illness."

Heather Marshall glanced down at her baby, asleep in her arms. Georgina was only six months old, but still so tiny, so fragile. "I just don't want any other parents to go through what we did."

"And they shouldn't. We'll make sure that Walker Jones pays for this. He can't open a day care center in this town and then just walk away from it." Lindsay could feel the fight boiling up inside her again. For a minute there, back in the gym with the booth-building project, she'd seen Walker as a man, not an adversary. She wouldn't make that mistake again.

"We have no doubts you can do this, Lindsay," Pete said. He covered his wife's hand with his own. Georgina stirred, woke up with a happy start, as she usually did, then spied Lindsay. She put out her arms in Lindsay's direction.

Heather gave her daughter an indulgent smile, then got to her feet and handed Georgina to Lindsay. Ever since the first time Lindsay had met the Marshalls' baby, the two of them had bonded. Maybe Georgina sensed all the experience Lindsay had with the Stockton triplets, or maybe she just knew Lindsay was on her side.

Lindsay rested the baby on her chest. Georgina snuggled her little face into Lindsay's neck. She fisted the soft cotton of Lindsay's shirt in one hand. The weight of the baby seemed ten times heavier because it came with all the hopes of the parents sitting across from her.

Lindsay let out a deep breath. "I worry, honestly, that I don't have the experience that you need for a case like this. I've said it before and I'll say it again— I would completely understand if you felt more comfortable with another lawyer."

Heather glanced at Pete, who gave her a little nod. She turned back to Lindsay. "We don't want another lawyer. We want you. You're a Dalton. Your family practically built this town. We know you love Rust Creek Falls and all the people here, and that means you have something a big-time lawyer from out of town wouldn't have. Heart. We know you'll do whatever it takes to win this case."

"Thank you. I appreciate your faith in me." Lindsay inhaled, and the fresh, sweet scent of baby filled her nose. Georgina's fist curled around Lindsay's finger, as if saying, *I have faith, too.* A knot twisted in her stomach. Was she really up to this challenge?

Walker Jones's attorney was more experienced, but the Marshalls were right—he didn't have the heart and soul for this town that she had. Hopefully, that would be enough.

Chapter Six

Walker had never been a big fan of holidays. Everything was shut down—banks, post office, some companies—and that meant he woke up on Monday morning expecting to get to work and realizing his day was already half-shot by the lack of availability of people he needed to talk to. Columbus Day wasn't even a real holiday, he thought, but it was real enough to leave him at loose ends.

He paced his room at Maverick Manor and debated what to do. He had a meeting with his lawyer later this afternoon, just a quick pretrial conference, but beyond that, his day was free. He'd already spent all day Sunday in his room, catching up on documents he needed to read, reviewing financial statements for his company, and cleaning out his email inbox. Even though the room was beautiful, with an expansive view of the lush green valley below and stunning mountain peaks in the distance, Walker didn't relish the idea of another day spent in here, especially when the sun was shining on a perfect fall day.

What was wrong with him? Normally he loved his job. Hardly noticed when he worked sunup to sundown. But there was something about this town— an energy—that seemed to beg him to stop working, smell the roses. Enjoy his stay.

He unfolded *The Rust Creek Falls Gazette*. There was a history of Columbus Day on the front page, then an update on the Harvest Festival preparations. He scanned over the paragraphs and noted a second volunteer event this afternoon. Something about helping with painting the signs.

Would Lindsay be there?

And why did he care? He shouldn't see her. Shouldn't spend time with her. After all, they were going to court tomorrow. Any sane man would stay far, far away from the woman suing his company.

So why was Walker in his rental car driving down the hill and back to the high school gymnasium?

He strode inside, his gaze scanning the room for Lindsay. Disappointment sank in his gut when he realized she wasn't there.

He started to turn away when he saw her coming around the corner with her sister and another man who had the same brown hair as her and Lani. The three of them were laughing at something and clearly teasing each other. The scene looked so happy, so easy.

Envy curled in his gut. He had friends, of course, and family, but he'd never had a relationship with anyone that unfurled as unfettered as a loose ribbon.

Maybe he needed to get out more. Or maybe he needed to relax a little more. Let the mountains and the valleys and the fresh air do their magic.

Or maybe just get back to work, before this whole place wrapped him any further in its lotus-eaters grip.

The happy, unstressed look disappeared from Lindsay's face when she saw Walker, and was replaced with a scowl. "What are you doing here?"

"Helping again."

She shook her head. "Stop trying to play town hero, Mr. Jones."

So they were still on *Mr. Jones*. He'd been hoping she would've rethought that formality, but their kiss only seemed to spur more animosity. Maybe she'd hated that kiss. Or maybe she hated him.

"I'm not trying to play hero. It's a holiday, so I don't have much to do for work. I wanted to keep busy, saw the mention of this volunteer day in the paper, and so here I am."

She shook her head. "It's a free country, so I can't stop you, but I also don't have to work with you. The job board is over there. Go pick anything that doesn't have my name beside it. And please, stay on your side of the gym."

Walker leaned forward and put out his hand toward the man in their group. "I'm Walker Jones, in case Lindsay here didn't already tell you. Also known as the devil incarnate."

The other man grinned. "Anderson Dalton, Lindsay's brother. If she has you on her persona non grata list, it's for a good reason. Although whatever stories she might have told you about me, I was always the innocent party."

"I have four brothers. I know what you mean. There were a lot of crimes committed by Not Me." Walker gave Lani a nod. "Nice to see you again, Lani."

She gave him a barely perceptible acknowledgment. "Mr. Jones."

Two Daltons out of three who didn't want to see him. Okay, so he'd faced better odds.

He would have walked away, but that kiss with Lindsay was still lingering in the back of his mind. Whatever she might be saying now, he was pretty damned positive he'd read interest in their embrace. If there was one thing Walker Jones didn't do, it was give up easily. So he had no intention of leaving the gym. Or, for whatever reason, letting Lindsay's negative opinion of him linger. He didn't know why it mattered to him so much, but one way or another, he was going to prove to her that he wasn't half as bad as she thought.

"Listen," Anderson said, leaning toward him and lowering his voice, "my sisters are awesome, but they're also fiercely loyal to the family, to this town, as pretty much everyone in Rust Creek Falls is. I believe in giving everyone a fair shake, especially people who want to help out and provide some free labor. So come with me and let's see if we can get you hooked up with a job to do. Preferably one I don't want to do."

Anderson and Walker laughed. He liked Lindsay's brother already, and under different circumstances, he could see the two of them playing a few holes of golf or enjoying some bourbon at a fancy bar.

Lindsay shot her brother a glare as he led Walker over to the volunteer sign-in table. Walker gave Lindsay a smile, which she ignored. He wasn't surprised, but he was more than a little disappointed. He turned back to her brother. One Dalton at a time. "So, Anderson, do you live here, too?"

"Yup. I'm a rancher, so most of my days are spent with the horses. Sometimes," he said with a quick nod toward his sisters, "they can be a lot easier to deal with than women."

Walker laughed. "You have that right. Though I don't have a lot of experience with ranches or horses. Give me a boardroom and I'm at home. But on a farm or a ranch... I wouldn't know what to do."

"It's easy. You listen to your heart." Anderson put a hand on his chest. He was taller than his sisters but had the same brown hair and blue eyes. "Your heart will tell you when a horse needs a gentler touch or the land needs some attention. Your heart will tell you whether you're running things right or running them into the ground. And your heart will always tell you if you're in the right spot—or still searching for the perfect one for you."

That could just as easily be a prescription for dealing with women, especially a beautiful, stubborn, bristly lawyer.

Walker signed his name on the page asking for people to mount the signs on posts. Anderson opted to work with him. "Sounds like you found all that here," Walker said. Anderson sounded happy, the kind of deep-rooted happiness that filled a man's soul.

A satisfied smile curved across Anderson's face. "I did. I have a fabulous wife, two great kids, and I spend my days outdoors in this beautiful Montana country. I couldn't ask for anything better."

A part of Walker envied Anderson's happiness. The

contentment in his voice. What would it be like to have that kind of...

Home. Because that was exactly what he saw shining in Anderson's eyes when he talked about his wife, his family, his town. He had found home.

Walker thought of the glass and chrome apartment he'd be returning to in a few days, smack dab in the heart of Tulsa. When he'd rented it, he'd thought it was perfect—great location, great views, great building. But never in the three years he'd lived there had he thought of it as home.

It was just this town. Being around all this...quaintness, with these neighbors straight out of a Hallmark card. This wasn't real life—or at least, not his real life. And he'd do well to remember that before he had some misplaced envy for the misty look in another guy's eyes.

The two of them were ushered over to a pile of painted boards and a stack of stakes, and they spent the next half hour attaching the boards to the stakes, then setting the signs against the wall. Other volunteers came and took the signs in bunches of six or so, to take back to the park for setup.

Lindsay and Lani had chosen to paint signs. They were on the other side of the room, and he could hear Lindsay's laughter from time to time. Everything within Walker was attuned to her, as if an invisible string tethered them together. He glanced over in her direction a thousand times, but she never even acknowledged his presence. Twice, he hit his thumb with the hammer instead of watching what he was doing.

"That's it," Anderson said a few minutes later. He brushed his hands together. "We're ahead of the sign painters, and we'll have to wait for the new signs to dry anyway before we can mount them on the stakes."

"That might take a while."

"Lucky for us, they're just now bringing in lunch." Anderson grinned. "And it's being delivered by one very beautiful woman." He waved to Walker to follow him over to several long tables set up with folding chairs and paper plates. Anderson stopped beside a redhead with blue eyes and a big smile, then gave her a kiss. "I missed you."

She laughed. "We've only been apart for a few hours."

"Long enough for me." Anderson settled a hand on the woman's waist, then gestured to Walker. "Walker, this is my wife, Marina. Marina, this is Walker Jones."

She shook his hand, then shifted back. "Wait. The same Walker Jones that Lindsay is suing?"

"She's suing my company, not me personally. I'm not such a bad guy." He gave Marina a grin, but she wasn't as easily won over as her husband. "Pleased to meet you, Mrs. Dalton."

"I have to finish getting the food set up." She turned away from Walker and placed a quick kiss on Anderson's cheek. "Save me a seat?"

"The one right next to me, of course." He smiled at her and watched her go.

The couple was clearly happy together, still in that blush of new love. Walker could see it in the way their gazes lingered on each other, the way they managed to sneak in little touches of a hand, an arm. Theresa had always been more standoffish, less flirty, and Walker had always thought that was fine. But seeing

Anderson and Marina made him wonder if perhaps he'd been missing out on something all these years.

Was Lindsay Dalton the PDA type?

Before he could question where that thought came from, and why it mattered, he shook it off. Instead, he turned to Anderson. "Your wife is beautiful," he said.

"And unfortunately not a fan of yours." Anderson chuckled. "One thing about this town, and pretty much everyone who lives here, is that loyalty runs deep."

"I'm getting that impression." He let out a long breath. He'd come to the volunteer day hoping to help out a little, connect with Lindsay and keep swaying the town's opinion of himself and his day care center. So far, he was scoring a giant zero in all three categories. "Maybe it's better if I leave."

Anderson put a hand on his shoulder. "Listen, I know there are two sides to every story. And you do strike me as a decent guy, especially since you've shown up twice to help out here. In the end, I'm Team Lindsay all the way, because she's my sister and I know she wouldn't have brought this lawsuit if she didn't think she had probable cause, but even saying that... I think you should stay and have lunch."

"Even if your sister would rather I fall off a cliff?"

Anderson chuckled. "That may be so. Either way, don't let Lindsay scare you. She's a softy at heart."

Lindsay came over just as Anderson was speaking. "Who are you calling a softy?"

"My annoying little sister, of course." Anderson gave Lindsay a faux jab to the shoulder. She feinted one back. "Anyway, I need to go help Marina set up for lunch. Why don't you and Walker get the drink station ready? There's tea and lemonade mixes in the school kitchen, and I left some big coolers down there that you can fill."

Lindsay shook her head. "I don't think—"

But Anderson had already walked off in the middle of Lindsay's sentence, leaving Walker and Lindsay to figure it out. She let out a gust of breath. "Thanks a lot, Anderson," she muttered to her brother's retreating figure.

Walker looked at Lindsay. She had her hair pulled back in a ponytail again today, which had a way of making her look more youthful and, yes, more like a softy. He liked the way the ponytail exposed the curve of her neck, the delicate loops in her ears, the slight V of her T-shirt. She might not want to be here and work with him, but he had to admit he sure didn't want her to leave. Very soon—too soon—they'd be adversaries in court again, so why not use these last few moments without the court case between them to get to know her better? What was the harm in that?

"There are going to be a bunch of hungry and thirsty people here soon," he said. "If you just show me where the kitchen is, I can fill up the coolers."

"You don't look like the kind of guy who knows how to make lemonade." She considered him, one hand on her hip.

He grinned. "You've got me there. The only cooking I've ever done consists of reheating a cup of coffee in the microwave." All his life, he'd had people who were there to make his meals, clean up after him, take care of him. Being in Rust Creek Falls was the most hands-on Walker had ever been.

And, surprisingly, he liked it. A lot.

"All right. We can work together, but—" Lindsay wagged a finger at him and spun toward the exit "—we don't need to talk while we do it."

"Oh, so we're back to that again, are we?" he said, as he followed her down the hall to the school cafeteria. The hall was empty, the lights dim. Their footsteps echoed on the polished tile floors.

"When did we ever leave that?" She pushed open the swinging metal door that led into the kitchen. Fluorescent lights flickered to life above them and bounced off an aluminum cart by the door.

Walker took one side of the metal cart, and Lindsay took the other. Two round orange drink coolers sat on a nearby counter, waiting to be filled. "Did you forget about that kiss?"

Her cheeks flushed, and she cut her gaze away. "We weren't talking while we did that, either."

That made him laugh. "No, no, we weren't. How do you do that?"

Now she lifted her blue eyes to his. They were like an ocean after a storm—tumultuous, mysterious. "Do what?"

"Turn tension into laughter." He walked around the cart, closer to her. "You have this amazing ability." He raised his hand to her face. The edge of her smile brushed against his thumb.

She stepped out of his touch. "A good trait in the opposing counsel."

"Indeed. Though I think it's too bad we are on opposite sides."

"We'd be on the same side if you acknowledged your fault," she said. This was where Lindsay felt comfortable, arguing the law. When Walker had touched her and complimented her, it had knocked her off-kilter. It was as if being outside the courtroom eliminated her ability to think straight.

"As we would be if you acknowledged the truth."

"What truth am I supposed to acknowledge?"

"That you liked that kiss back in the gym as much as I did."

His gaze held hers. She felt like she was on a witness stand, sworn to honesty. "Whether I liked it or not is immaterial. It shouldn't have happened."

He shook his head. "And there you go again, retreating into the law."

"I'm not retreating, Mr. Jones. I'm merely pointing out a fact." Okay, so maybe she was lying. But this wasn't a courtroom and she wasn't under oath and she definitely didn't want to acknowledge how many times she'd thought about that kiss.

"Just like that first day in court. You are so damned confident and defiant—"

"Stop trying to butter me up." She started to turn away, but he kept talking and she stayed where she was.

"But then I saw you playing peekaboo with the baby." He cursed under his breath. "I am not some sentimental fool, believe me. But there was something about seeing you, this strong, powerful attorney—"

"You think I'm strong and powerful?" Why couldn't she turn away? Leave the room? Stop listening?

"I think you're more than that." He shifted a degree closer. "I think you're beautiful and smart and... addictive."

"Addiction can be a bad thing." She swallowed hard, her gaze locked on his.

"It can be," he murmured.

For a moment, the air in the room stilled. Lindsay stayed where she was, breathing in, out, watching Walker. She couldn't think, couldn't speak.

Couldn't understand why she was so attracted to a man who was the opposite of everything she loved in her life.

"I don't know what it is about you," Walker said. "I know I should leave, but I just...stay."

"Me, too." The admission whispered out of her.

He shifted closer. Then he cupped her face with both his hands, leaned in and kissed her.

She curved into him as if by instinct, fitting her soft body against all his hard places, filling in the blanks. His lips danced across hers, drifting slowly at first, tasting her, learning her. Then she let out a little mew, and he opened his mouth against hers, anxious to taste her, to tango with her tongue.

In an instant, their kiss went from slow and easy to fast and wild. Hands roaming over backs, bodies pressing tight together, mouths tasting and nipping. He hoisted her onto the cart, sliding in between her legs.

The cart shifted beneath them, creaking under the added weight. Lindsay jerked to attention and pulled away from him. Her face was flushed, her chest heaving. "We can't do this. It's wrong on a thousand levels."

It was indeed. What the hell was wrong with him? Lindsay Dalton was suing him, jeopardizing the future of the day care franchise. "Not to mention, we'd be foolish to pursue anything, given that in a few days, our business will be concluded," he said.

It was a cold way to phrase whatever this was between them, but the words made it easier for him to take her second rejection.

Her gaze hardened. "You are right, Mr. Jones. Soon enough, our business will be concluded."

The echo of his own words whistled in his mind like an icy winter wind.

Once the lawsuit was over, there was no reason for Walker to stay in Rust Creek Falls. He had a competent manager for the day care and his own business to run back in Tulsa. In a few days he would be leaving—

And leaving Lindsay behind.

She hopped down off the cart and grabbed one of the coolers on the counter. "People are waiting for their drinks. We don't want to let them down. People here have already been through enough."

The hidden message in her words revealed itself clearly. When it came down to brass tacks, Lindsay Dalton's allegiance would always be to Rust Creek Falls. No matter how many kisses they shared, no matter how hot and heavy. Come tomorrow morning he was the enemy, and she was the brave knight out to slay the evil corporate dragon.

Lindsay managed to sit as far away from Walker Jones as she possibly could during lunch. But that didn't stop her from being aware of his every move, of the sound of his voice. Even twelve feet away, she could still feel his presence.

Taste his kiss.

Why did the man have to be such a good kisser? Why couldn't he have been terrible at kissing, one of those sloppy, slobbering, overeager types that she could easily resist?

Damn, he'd been so good. Too good. Making-her-crave-more-again-ASAP good.

She made small talk, laughed at jokes, held babies, talked to her brother about the ranch and the kids, but her mind remained on Walker. In the morning, they'd go back to being adversaries, and she'd go back to suing his company, for the good of the Marshalls and all the parents whose children had ended up sick.

Maybe he was just one of those charmers who tried to win the battle by making the opposition fall in love. Well, that wasn't going to happen to her. No way. No how.

No matter how well he kissed.

For the rest of the afternoon Lindsay remained on the opposite side of the gym from Walker, working on different tasks. As the projects drew to a close and she finished cleaning up, she didn't see Walker anywhere. He must have left when she wasn't looking.

She told herself she was relieved. She mostly believed it, too.

As Lindsay said her goodbyes and walked out of the gym, a misty rain began to fall. She pocketed her keys and headed toward the park, her face upturned to catch some droplets. She loved these fall days, when the air held a sharp chill, a hint of the harsh winter to come. The slight bit of rain added an air of mysticism, like she was walking into a fairy tale.

The park was quiet, empty. Leaves and small twigs crunched under Lindsay's boots, and the trees rustled against the weight of the water above her head. The mist had stopped, and the air began to clear.

She loved taking walks like this. Sometimes she'd walk the perimeter of the Dalton ranch, because the open air gave her room to think, to plan. With the trial starting tomorrow—and all the complications kissing Walker Jones had awakened—Lindsay needed this time to clear her head.

She passed the wooden booths they'd constructed earlier, waiting for the festival in a few days, then skirted the signs advertising the hay rides and hot cider. Lindsay rounded the curved path that led to the back of the Rust Creek Falls Park. Far beyond the swings and monkey bars, there was a little-used grassy area that sported one lone picnic table beneath the spreading arms of an oak tree. Mountains rose like dark sentries in the background, guarding the deep sea of trees below. Lindsay climbed onto the table, resting her feet on the seat, and leaned back, letting the approaching night wash over her.

"What a beautiful sight."

She started at the deep voice behind her and spun around. Walker Jones stood there, impossibly tall and handsome. Her heart did an instant skip beat, and her hormones rushed to center stage to stir up memories of his kiss. "Walker. You scared me."

"Sorry, I thought you heard me come up behind you." He ambled over to the front of the table and gestured to the space beside her. "Do you mind?"

Half of her wanted him to sit there, wanted a reason to brush up against him, but the other half was screaming for her to be cautious. He was her adversary, after all, not her boyfriend. Or even her friend. "We shouldn't—"

"Yeah, I know." He let out a long breath. "But it's been a long day and it's a beautiful view and I don't want to enjoy it alone."

There was something in his voice, something melancholy and lonely, that tugged at her heartstrings. Damn. Maybe Anderson was right and she was a big softy. Lindsay shifted to make room for Walker. "I love this place. I come here all the time when I get stressed out."

"Worried about tomorrow?"

"Nice try, Walker, but I won't discuss the case with you." The last thing she needed to do was tell the man she was suing that she was worried she didn't have enough of a case. That she was going to let everyone down.

That she would fail.

"Fair enough," he said. "So what should we talk about? The origins of Columbus Day? A fact I learned today, thanks to the local paper."

She laughed. Five minutes ago, she'd vowed not to let him get close again, but then he made a joke and broke the tension, and her resolve flagged. "That's big news in this town. Not a whole lot happens in Rust Creek Falls."

He shrugged. "Could be a blessing not many places have," he said. He looked around the park and shook his head, as if he couldn't quite believe what he was seeing. "This town is almost like one of those Norman Rockwell paintings. Or an episode of *Happy Days*. I feel like I'm caught in a time warp or I'm on an alien planet."

She bristled. "Come on, it's not that bad."

He looked back at her, and his eyes seemed to glimmer in the dusk. "I didn't say it was bad, necessarily... just different."

"I take it Jenks and Tulsa aren't like this?"

He scoffed. "It's not as big a city as, say, New York or Chicago, but Tulsa especially has its fair share of problems and crime. It's so busy, it seems to breathe, fast and hard, like a runner rounding a track. Everything is always moving, changing. There's nothing personal or neighborly about it. It's a city, as hard and cold as steel. But this town..." He shrugged. "Rust Creek Falls is different. And believe it or not, I can see how people would like it here."

That pleased her to no end. She loved this town, and to hear someone else say they were beginning to see its good points, too, warmed Lindsay's heart. "Rust Creek Falls has a way of getting in your blood."

He sat beside her, quiet and still, watching the sun's slow descent behind the mountains.

"Can I ask you something?" she said, then let the question out before she thought about the wisdom of getting personal with Walker. "Why open a chain of day care centers? You don't have a family of your own." She'd done her research on him in the last few days and found out he was single and childless, probably because nearly every source referred to him as *driven* and *committed* to his company. "You told me a lot about numbers and research, but you could have found any industry to expand into, rather than day cares. I don't understand why you'd want to get into a business that involved kids."

He arched a brow. "Off the record?"

"Scout's honor." She held up three fingers. "And I was a real Girl Scout for a while when I was a kid. Got my cookie badge and everything to prove it."

He chuckled. "Somehow, I can't see you as the type to take orders and build campfires."

"I'm more of a homebody than you know." She wrapped her arms around herself and drew in deep of the crisp Montana air. It was why she had returned to Rust Creek Falls after law school, why no amount of money and no job or man could tear her away from this place she loved so much. "This land, this air… it's part of my soul. I can't imagine living anywhere else. Maybe because here I can just…*be*."

"I've never known what that was like. To just *be*." The words were quiet, almost as if he didn't realize he'd admitted them.

"Not even when you were a kid?"

He shook his head, and his posture stiffened. "Like I told you, my parents were…uninvolved. We had nannies and a house big enough to fit a Boeing jet, but we didn't have a home, if that makes sense. There were so many expectations and rules and things that could break, that half the time we boys were afraid to breathe. My father was and still is a stern, exacting man, and my mother…well, she figured she did her part by giving birth to us. She got involved in her charities and left everything else up to the staff."

"I had the completely opposite childhood. We were all on the ranch, running around like a bunch of heathens, but we always felt loved." She laid her hand on his arm, for just a second. "I'm sorry you didn't grow up the same way. Every kid should have a childhood that lets them run and jump and be themselves."

He shrugged, as if it was no big deal. "It's part of why I went into the day care business. My father thought I was insane, told me I'd lose my shirt. I still might, but... I wanted to create a place where kids, regardless of what their families were like, could feel like they were at home, for a few hours a day. I researched everything, from the best color paint to the best way to find employees that would embody that spirit. For me, these centers aren't about a profit. They're about giving kids a place where they feel... loved. Like you did."

The evil, corporate-bottom-line-is-everything role she had cast Walker Jones III in didn't fit the man sitting beside her. She didn't want her heart to soften, didn't want to empathize with him, but damn it, it did—she did. There was a chance, of course, that he was lying and just telling her some sympathy-inducing story to convince her to go easy on him in court tomorrow, but Lindsay doubted it. For the first time she believed what he was telling her. This wasn't some line he was delivering, some ruse to ingratiate himself with her or the town. She had a feeling this was her first glimpse of the real Walker.

"What about a family of your own?" she asked. He was, after all, thirty-four, gorgeous, and, of course, wealthy. She figured some woman would've snatched him up long ago and he'd be married with a few kids. But then she realized how forward, how personal that question was. "Sorry, that's none of my business."

"It's okay." He let out a breath. "I met someone that I thought I would settle down with, but...let's just say she wanted more than I wanted to give. I was building the company then and working a million hours, and she wanted me to take time to enjoy life. Sleep in on Sundays and all that." He rested his elbows on his knees and looked out across the landscape. "I couldn't do that. Couldn't, in fact, imagine ever doing that…"

It seemed he was going to say more but held himself back. "Why do I get the feeling there's a *but* you didn't say?"

There was a long pause. The world was hushed, far removed from the houses and streets. It was just the two of them.

Finally he looked at her. "Very astute, counselor." He gave her a slight smile. "Maybe it's the view outside the Maverick Manor, or maybe it's seeing how all those people are coming together for one simple festival, *but*—" he emphasized the word "—this town has me thinking…*re*thinking things."

He hadn't said if meeting her had anything to do with that. And why did Lindsay care, anyway? This man was all wrong for her. Except…

This new Walker she was seeing tonight drew her closer, urged her to open up more, to get to know him better. Made her crave him in new, unexpected ways.

And that was dangerous.

Still, she couldn't stop herself.

"I had the opposite experience," she said. Had they shifted closer to each other or had she not noticed how close they were sitting? "I was engaged in law school, very briefly. I thought settling down would change my boyfriend and make him want to come back here, open up a law practice together, but his heart was set on living in New York and working in some big multi-million-dollar firm. When it became clear we wanted two entirely different lives, I broke it off."

She'd fallen for Jeremy, too, thinking he was one thing when he turned out to be another. She didn't want to make that mistake again, thinking a few minutes of sentiment from Walker Jones meant anything.

"That man was a fool," Walker said, his eyes dark in the deepening evening sky, "for letting a woman as incredible as you slip out of his life."

The words warmed the chill she'd forced into her heart a moment ago, made her think about kissing him again. She held his gaze, inhaled the spicy notes of his cologne. Damn, he even smelled good. "Are you just trying to soften me up before the trial starts?"

He grinned. "Is it working?"

"Nope. I'm not so easily swayed." She feigned affront, but in the face of his smile, it was hard to hold the pose.

He reached up, brushed a tendril of hair off her forehead and tucked the lock behind her ear. His touch lingered on her cheek, and she leaned into it. "Too bad."

"Why?" She could barely whisper the word. The desire simmering inside her was a living, breathing thing, overpowering every sane thought she'd ever had, pushing her closer to him.

"Because if you weren't Lindsay Dalton, lawyer, and I wasn't Walker Jones, owner of Just Us Kids, I think—" his gaze dropped to her lips, then back up to her eyes "—we could have been something."

"But we are those things," the sensible part of her said, even as the rest of her was telling that sensible side to shut up, "and we can't be something."

"In the morning, I'll agree with you. But right

now…" His thumb traced her bottom lip and made her breath catch. "Right now why don't we just pretend none of that exists? Just for tonight. Just for now."

Chapter Seven

Walker had no idea what the hell he was doing, getting closer to this woman, of all the women in this tiny town. He got to his feet, took Lindsay into his arms, then pressed Play on the music app on his phone. A slow-beat ballad came on, the sound a little tinny and distant coming from the small speaker. She looked up at him, her eyes wide but curious. The mist started up again, seeming to shroud them, shut them off from the rest of the town.

"I asked you to dance once before and you turned me down," he said.

"You were already dancing with another woman. Many of them, if I remember right."

He opened his arms. "Right now, you are the only one I want to dance with. So I'm asking you again. Lindsay, will you dance with me?"

She drew in a deep breath, then a smile whispered across her face. "Yes."

He put one hand on her back, clasped her palm with the other one, and pulled her into his frame. Then he began dancing with the woman who was trying to destroy his company.

But she fit so perfectly in his arms, and smelled so damned good, and already he was craving another kiss, craving her. So he danced with her, and kissed her neck, and almost came undone when she pressed into him. The song came to an end, and Walker Jones, a man who never made a move he didn't think about first, whispered five impetuous words. "Come back to my room."

"That…that changes everything," Lindsay said.

"Just being with you has changed everything." He brushed that stubborn lock of hair off her forehead again and knew, no matter what, it was going to be harder than hell to battle her in court tomorrow. Half of him wanted to wave the white flag, just to see her smile again.

"Maybe just for a drink," Lindsay said as the skies opened up and thunder began to rumble. "And only because it's raining again."

Was it? He hardly noticed. "And it's a holiday," he said.

She laughed. "A holiday is a reason to have sex?"

Once she said the two words out loud—*have sex*—his mind raced through a hundred images of them doing just that. "I think a holiday is as good a reason as any, don't you agree?"

A tease quirked a grin on her face. "I think you're giving way too much weight to Columbus Day."

"Hey, it's the whole reason we have America. I don't think the holiday gets enough weight." The rain started falling faster, so he took her hand and they dashed back through the park and over to his rental car, sliding inside just before the storm unleashed its full strength. The wipers raced to keep up with the rain as Walker pulled out of the parking lot and back toward Maverick Manor.

A rare burst of nerves rushed through his gut. Maybe because Lindsay Dalton was unlike any other woman he'd ever met. Maybe because he knew she was right and this was going to change everything, and even he wasn't sure that was a good idea. So he filled the space in the car with words.

"Did you know that Columbus Day has been celebrated since the 1700s? It wasn't made a national holiday until FDR assigned the second Monday of October as the designated day," Walker said. "Just a couple of interesting tidbits from *The Rust Creek Falls Gazette*." The words tumbled in a fast stream, like they were racing to be first out of his mouth.

She laughed. "Is this your idea of wooing a woman? Spouting historical facts?"

He glanced over at her as they pulled under the overhang in front of the hotel. "Is it working?"

"Sadly, yes." Lindsay rolled her eyes. "Either I haven't been on a date in a really long time or you have a way of making history sound sexy."

"I'm voting for sexy history." He leaned across the console, gave her a quick, hard kiss, then got out of the car and dropped his keys into the valet's palm. He came around the other side, then put out his hand to

Lindsay. "Maybe I should tell you everything I know about the life cycle of an earthworm."

Lindsay fanned her chest. "Be still, my heart. I don't think I could handle it."

Damn, he really liked this woman. No, he more than liked her. He was falling for her, for the jokes and the smiles and the way she stood toe to toe with him. She was smart and sexy and funny…and she was staying here when he went back to Tulsa. Before the thought could sour his attitude, he pushed it to the back of his mind. He'd worry about that later. Much later.

They headed inside, stopping by the bar for a bottle of wine and two glasses. "Send some strawberries and cheesecake up to my room, please," Walker said to the bartender.

"Certainly, Mr. Jones," the bartender said, keying the order into the computer. "Right away, sir."

"Strawberries and cheesecake?" Lindsay grinned as they walked away. "You really are trying to woo me."

"The cheesecake here is so good, you might not even notice me after you have the first bite." They took the elevator to the second floor. "Or you may be so overcome with gratitude that you…"

His gaze had dropped to her lips. She was standing a few inches away, and they were alone in the elevator. The warm, enclosed space seemed even tighter now, closer.

"So much gratitude that I do what?" Lindsay asked.

"That you kiss me," he said, shifting closer to her, resting his free hand on her waist, splaying his fingers along the narrow expanse above her jeans, "and don't ever want to stop."

"That would imply you are a very good kisser," she said. Her voice was low, throaty.

"And am I?"

A flush filled her cheeks, and for a moment her gaze dropped away. The shyness entranced him even more. Then she lifted her gaze back to his, all sassy and confident again. "You definitely have skills outside the boardroom, Mr. Jones."

"And you have skills outside the courtroom, Ms. Dalton." The elevator came to a stop, the doors shuddered open, but Walker took a moment to kiss her again, harder, faster this time. Desire surged between them, charging the air.

And then they were tumbling out of the elevator together, a jumble of arms and legs and wineglasses, and across the hall to his room. He fumbled with the key, twice, three times, before the door unlatched and they were inside. All the while, they kept up a heated frenzy of hungry kisses and touches.

He blindly reached for the small table inside his door, depositing the wine bottle and glasses. Then his hands were free to roam over the woman in his arms, up her back, over her curves and along her valleys. He kicked the door shut, then scooped her into his arms and crossed the small living area to enter the bedroom.

The sun had almost finished setting. A soft purple light came in through the windows, casting the room in an ethereal glow. Walker laid Lindsay on the bed, then stepped back to drink in the sight of her.

She had one arm stretched above her head, her chocolate hair in wild disarray and her shirt bunched up above her waist. She was smiling at him, her eyes dark and heavy. "What are you waiting for?"

"I want to savor this," he said. "Savor you."

That made her smile widen. She crooked her finger and beckoned him forward. "Then savor away."

He climbed onto the bed beside her. She slid into the space against his chest and kissed him. Her tongue darted into his mouth while his hand snaked under her shirt and over the curve of her breast. Even through the lace of her bra, he could feel the peak of her nipple. When he brushed one finger over the sensitive bud, she let out a gasp and arched against him.

He took a moment to tug her shirt over her head and toss it onto the floor. She was wearing a lacy white bra, and a part of him wondered if she'd done that on the off chance she would see him today. "I think I should see what else will make you gasp," he said, crooking one finger under the strap of her bra and sliding it down her arm. Her breast bulged above the cup of her bra, as if inviting him to come closer.

He dipped his head and kissed the top of the curve, then the sides, then finally brushed his lips against her nipple. She gasped again, his name escaping her lips in one long, hot whisper.

"Hmm… I think I should see what makes you gasp," she said, then slid her hand down the front of his chest, over the buckle of his jeans, then against the length of his erection. Even through the denim, he could feel the soft firmness of her touch. He wanted more. He wanted her.

"That…" He stopped; he could barely breathe, definitely couldn't think. "That will do it."

"Oh, I don't think so. I think maybe—" She paused,

flicking open the fly of his jeans, then sliding the zipper down before she slipped her hand beneath his boxers and finally—oh, holy hell—along the length of him. "This will."

He let out a gasp. "That…that works. Very well."

"I figured it might." A devilish light filled her smile.

"My turn," Walker said. He reached behind her to unfasten her bra, then slid the other strap down. He followed the path of the lace with his mouth, kissing, teasing, every inch of her neck, her chest.

She arched beneath him, her hands tangling in his hair, her breath coming faster, harder. He reached for the buckle on her jeans—

And there was a knock at the door. Three hard, fast raps.

Room service. Damn it. Why had he ordered the cheesecake?

"Give me just a second," he said to Lindsay. "And don't move." Walker started to slide off the bed when the knocking started up again.

"I know you're in there, Walker," Hudson called through the heavy wood door. "And I think it's about damned time we talked. About the day care, this lawsuit and that damned lawyer. And what the hell you think you're doing with all of it."

Lindsay bolted upright, grabbing her bra and pressing it to her chest. "Did you set this up? Catch the opposing counsel in a compromising position?"

"No, no, that's not it at all," Walker said. "Stay, please. I'll tell him to come back later."

But she was already grabbing her clothes and putting them back on. She smoothed a hand over her hair and let out a curse. "I let myself forget everything," she said. "Forget what's important. Forget why you're here. Maybe that's part of your plan—"

"That's not it, Lindsay. I got just as caught up in this as you did." Yes, getting involved with her was probably a mistake. Yes, he should have waited until after the court case, but damn it, he liked her and he wanted her, and right this second, he didn't care what happened tomorrow morning. "Lindsay, stay. Please."

But she wasn't hearing him. She was already fastened and together and at the door. "I'll see you in court tomorrow, Mr. Jones."

Mr. Jones. That was enough to tell him she was through with him.

Hudson's eyes widened when Lindsay opened the door. "What are you doing here?"

"Leaving. Which is something I should have done a while ago." She brushed past him and down the hall. She never turned back, never gave Walker a second glance.

The rain pattered softly against the windows of the kitchen, like thousands of tiny feet racing down the glass. Lindsay sat in the dark of the house where she'd grown up, eating two generous slices of apple pie. With ice cream. And whipped cream.

"Uh-oh. Must have been a bad day."

She turned at the sound of Ben Dalton's voice. The moonlight outside illuminated his tall, lean frame. "Hi, Dad. Just nervous about tomorrow." There was no way she was going to tell her father that she was trying to erase her feelings for Walker Jones with sugar and fat. Besides, it wasn't working very well.

Her chest still ached, and her brain kept reminding her that she'd been a fool for trusting that man for five seconds.

He'd set her up. Betrayed her. She dreaded court tomorrow, and Walker's lawyer telling the judge that she'd been having a relationship with Walker. She'd been so wrong about him, so wrong about everything. Walker had sweet-talked her and convinced her he was interested, then set up Hudson's appearance.

She'd never imagined Walker would stoop so low just to win a case. Or that she could be so stupid to trust the man on the other side of the courtroom.

Her father switched on the small light above the sink, casting the room in a golden glow, then took a seat on the opposite side of the table. He'd developed a little more gray hair and a few more wrinkles in recent years, but he was still the same kind, wise, patient man she'd always loved. The same man who had inspired her to go into law, to fight for the underdog, just as he had done all his life. "You're going to do fine," he said. "You're prepared, and you have a strong case. And you're on the side of right."

"I'm not so sure about that." She finished the last forkful of pie and pushed the plate to the side. "There is no one event or item to pin this RSV outbreak on. Yes, all the kids attended the same day care, but I don't have an actual definable cause."

"You have enough circumstantial evidence," her father said. "And that will weigh heavily in the judge's mind."

The closer she got to Tuesday morning, the less Lindsay believed she had what she needed to convince the judge. Maybe she shouldn't have promised the Marshalls that she could deliver justice to them for poor baby Georgina. Maybe she shouldn't have agreed to the speedier bench trial, and instead taken her chances with a jury trial. There were a thousand what-ifs that tortured Lindsay. Problem was, she couldn't change or undo any of her decisions. All she could do was try her best on Tuesday.

She looked down at the remains of her pie. All the sugar and carbs and she didn't feel any better than when she'd walked in the door. Damn that man for having a nice smile. And a sexy voice. And amazing kissing skills.

A little doubt tickled at the back of her mind. Maybe Hudson's appearance tonight had been a coincidence, not a setup.

"There's one other thing…" Lindsay rested her palms atop one another. "I've talked to Walker Jones a few times and I'm not so sure he's the kind of guy who would run a shoddy day care."

There. She'd said it out loud. The Walker she had met seemed far from the man she'd imagined—one who protected the bottom line above the children. That was the man she'd been expecting to meet in court last week, the monster she'd created in her mind.

But the real Walker Jones III was far from that man. Either he was very, very good at acting or truly a decent man at his core. Or she was just a naive woman too blind to see the truth.

Her father arched a brow. "You've talked to the man you are suing?"

"He was volunteering for the festival prep events. We ended up working together on a couple of things—"

Ben put up his hands. "Whoa. You shouldn't be doing that. You're involved in a lawsuit against him."

"I know, I know." She sighed. "It happened by accident, really, and then I thought it would be an opportunity to see what makes him tick and maybe use that in court. But…" Her voice trailed off. She glanced at the empty pie plate. Maybe two pieces hadn't been enough to bury her regrets. She should have had three.

"You ended up liking him a little," her dad said, his voice quiet in the dim room.

She nodded, and her eyes stung a little. "Which is why I'm eating a lot of pie in the middle of the night." Not just because she'd ended up liking Walker, but because she had almost slept with him. And moreover, *wanted* to sleep with him even now, even after everything.

She needed more pie. Definitely.

Her father reached out and laid a hand on hers. "I understand. That's happened to me more than once, where I ended up liking someone I was going up against in court."

"It has?"

"Yup. Makes suing someone hard, I'll tell you. You develop a soft spot, and if there's one thing you can't show in court, it's a soft spot." Her father got to his feet, cut a slice of pie for himself, then returned to the table. It was a small sliver, because her mother would be upset if he ate too many sweets, but he'd never been able to resist her rustic apple pie. "I remember one case in particular. Remember Ronnie Hanson?"

She thought a second. "He came to you about a wrongful termination, right?"

"Yup. He worked at AJ's Bookstore for going on

fifteen years. Never late, hardly ever called in sick. One day, AJ just up and fired him. No notice, no real cause. So Ronnie came to me to ask about getting some kind of severance pay from AJ, plus the last paycheck that AJ hadn't given him. He didn't want to sue at first, but when AJ didn't answer any of my calls or letters, we got ready to go to court."

"I vaguely remember this," Lindsay said. "I was a little girl then, wasn't I?"

"Yup. Maybe five or six. Your mom, in support of Ronnie, told me she was going to stop shopping at AJ's store. Come to find out, he'd closed it already and was getting ready to leave town." Ben shook his head. "I was madder than a hornet in a beehive, thinking that AJ was trying to short Ronnie again. So I marched over to AJ's house and demanded he talk to me."

"Did he?"

Her father nodded. "We talked for four hours that day. I'd known AJ, of course, from seeing him around town, but only knew him casually. He was the kind of guy that kept to himself most days anyway. But that day, maybe he needed someone to talk to, or maybe he just wanted to explain, but he invited me in. Sat me down at his kitchen table with some coffee and some pie, just like you and I are doing right now, and started talking. By the time we were done, we'd moved on to pizza and beer—and become good friends."

Her father had always been an aboveboard, conscientious lawyer. She couldn't imagine him making the same mistake as she had and befriending the person on the other side of the courtroom. "How did that happen?"

"AJ told me why he fired Ronnie, why he hadn't sent out the last check yet. Why he was leaving town. As a father, I could understand, and that made my heart go out to him." Her father took a bite of pie, chewed it and swallowed. "Damn, your mother makes an incredible apple pie, doesn't she?"

"That's why it's won ribbons at the county fair." And was the best thing to soothe a stressed newbie lawyer.

Her father took another bite, smiled at the taste, then finished his story. "Turns out AJ had a son with another woman, one he met way before his wife. He hadn't seen much of his son in years. You know how those things go, contentious custody and all that."

Lindsay nodded. "And more often than not, it's the kids who end up suffering."

"Well, his son had been injured in a car accident, really badly. The kind of thing that would need months of rehab. Expensive rehab. This was AJ's only child—him and Beverly never did have kids of their own. So AJ did the only thing he knew to do—cashed in his business and moved to Albuquerque to be there for his son. His son healed, grew up, got married and had a son of his own. Last I heard, the two of them were planning a weeklong fishing trip and taking along AJ's grandson."

This was part of why she loved her father and wanted to be like him. He was a warm, caring and patient man who had always looked for the best in people. If he met Walker Jones, what would her father think of the driven CEO? "That's awesome."

Ben nodded. "And if I had sued AJ like I wanted to, there wouldn't have been much money left for his son's medical care. The stress alone might have given AJ a heart attack. When I saw him, he was a hair away from a nervous breakdown, because he was so worried about his son."

"So how did you settle things with Ronnie?"

"Well, once I got him calmed down—you know Ronnie, he can get as worked up as an elephant in a roomful of mice—he listened to what I had to say about AJ. I explained the situation and suggested to Ronnie that he—"

"Buy the store," Lindsay finished. She remembered this story now. She'd known Ronnie her whole life, but had forgotten how he came to be the proud owner of the local bookstore.

"Ronnie loved that place almost as much as AJ did. He got a mortgage, paid AJ what he needed, minus that last check as a compromise, then took the place over and made quite a go of it. He's still there, every single day, stocking shelves and recommending novels to customers."

"A win all around," Lindsay said.

Her father covered her hand with his own. He'd always been in her corner, always been there for her, for all the kids. "Exactly. Now if you can find one of those for this lawsuit you're in, then maybe that'll bring the Marshalls some peace and bring that smile of yours back to your face."

She tried to smile now, but the gesture fell flat. "Thanks, Dad."

He nodded, then got to his feet. "If there's one thing I've learned from being married, it's that there is no winning when it comes to the people you care about. There's only compromise. And sometimes, sweetheart, that's what you have to do in court, too. Because when it comes down to it, this isn't really about lawsuits and judgments. It's about people. Just remember that, and you'll always steer your ship along the right course."

She sat in the kitchen long after her father had gone to bed, thinking about lawsuits and courses and making the best decision for everyone. And stories that seemed one way on the surface, but were different when you looked up close for the truth. By the time the clock ticked past midnight, Lindsay didn't have any answers. Just a lot more questions—that she hoped would be answered in a court of law in the morning.

Chapter Eight

Walker parked his rental car in the courtroom lot, thirty minutes before he was due to be inside. He started scrolling through his phone, ignoring the texts from his father reminding him to step up, be a man and squash this lawsuit, when a familiar car pulled into the space beside him.

Hudson got out, then rapped on Walker's passenger side window. Walker unlocked the doors, and Hudson slid into the seat beside him. "I wanted to apologize for last night. I was pissed and drunk, and should have handled that better."

"Yeah, you should have. If you wanted to discuss something with me, you should have scheduled a time when we could talk calmly and rationally."

Hudson shook his head. "You know, I just apologized. And now you're sounding just like Dad. Schedule a time, Walker? Seriously?"

"I'm just saying—"

"No. You're just criticizing." Hudson let out a gust. "I know I'm not perfect, but neither are you. What happened to the brother I used to know?"

"I'm still your brother."

"No, Walker, you're not. You're this stranger who only cares about business, and not about people. I realize I let you down with the day care, and I am sorry for that. And I will work hard to try and make it up to you—to myself, even. But it's not like I was sitting in a bar, drinking away the days. I was building a life for myself, for my friend. A life separate from the almighty Jones Holdings."

Walker readied a retort, then stopped himself. He thought back to his words, to his actions. He had been treating Hudson more like an employee than a brother. Which was exactly the way his father treated him, only with impossible expectations. "I'm sorry. But you have to understand—"

"And there you go again, right back to justifying the way you treat me. One of these days, you're gonna look around and realize you have nothing except a cold, impersonal business." Hudson let out a long sigh. "Despite everything, you're still my brother, Walker, even if you are as uptight as a squirrel in a straight-jacket." He opened the car door. "See you inside."

Walker watched Hudson walk away, and wondered if they'd ever have a relationship again. Maybe he'd been a fool for trying to combine business with family, because it seemed all it had done was drive a wedge between the two of them. After this lawsuit was over, Walker vowed to try harder to be a brother to Hudson, not a boss.

A few minutes later, Walker sat in the same court-room, flanked once again by his lawyer, Marty. Instead of arguing a motion to get the case thrown out, they were in trial, defending Just Us Kids Day Care against Lindsay Dalton and the Marshalls. Marty was reviewing his notes, waiting for the judge's arrival.

Walker, on the other hand, was awaiting Lindsay's arrival. That alone was a sign he needed to get the hell out of this town. Since when did his interest in a woman supersede work?

Maybe since he'd met a woman who could stand toe to toe with him. A woman who could make him laugh and drive him crazy, all at the same time. A woman who intrigued and tempted him.

The door opened, and Walker pivoted to watch Lindsay stride into the courtroom. She barely flicked a glance in his direction, as if she hadn't even noticed he was there. But he noticed her. Hell, his entire body noticed her.

She was wearing a dark navy suit with a silky lav-ender blouse. She had her hair back in a clip, a few stray tendrils curling down the slender valley of her neck. She had a briefcase in one hand, a stack of files in thick expandable folders on her other arm and a se-rious, stony expression on her face.

The Marshalls followed Lindsay, and the three of them took a seat at the plaintiff's table. The grand-mother came in next, with a sleepy baby Georgina in her arms. A few other people—witnesses for the plaintiffs, Walker assumed—took seats in the gallery.

"Don't worry," Marty said, following the path of Walker's gaze and clapping a hand on his shoul-der. "I'm going to make sure this small-town lawyer knows better than to mess with a company like yours. She's going to run out of here with her tail between her legs. I'm going to crucify her."

Any other day, hearing those words from Marty would reassure Walker. That was what he wanted to see in his attorney—confidence and a cutthroat, take-no-prisoners approach. But today, the words churned in Walker's gut. They reminded him of Hudson's accusation that Walker was a copy of their father. "You know, she's got good intentions. Let's go a little easy on her."

Marty arched a brow. "What? Are you going soft on me now? I know I was feeling a little shaky myself on Friday, but I'm confident we can win this case, and win it well. That lawyer won't dare to come after you again."

Judge Andrews entered the courtroom. They all got to their feet and waited until the judge sat. "We have the trial scheduled today for *Marshall v. Just Us Kids Day Care*. Are counsel ready to proceed?"

"Yes, Your Honor," Lindsay said, "ready for the plaintiffs."

"The defendant is ready," Marty said.

The judge nodded toward Lindsay as Marty returned to his seat. "Very well, we'll proceed with opening statements. Ms. Dalton."

"Thank you, Your Honor." She stood and launched into her prepared comments.

Walker heard her voice but none of what she said registered on him; he was too busy looking at the woman and noticing how the suit hugged the curves he'd run his hands over last night.

"It is our position that the defendant's negligence

caused an outbreak of respiratory syncytial virus at the Just Us Kids Day Care center," she intoned. But again, Walker zoned out, his eyes drifting down to her shapely calves highlighted by the heels she wore. Only when he heard her speak his name did he drag his attention back to her eyes.

"...Mr. Jones, the owner of the center, failed to correct the dilatory hygiene practices within the center. For that reason, Just Us Kids Day Care Center should be responsible for the sizable medical bills that the Marshalls incurred as a result of the center's negligence. Thank you, Your Honor."

She nodded, then took her seat. She never once looked Walker's way or even acknowledged him. He wanted to send up a smoke signal or pass her a note or something that said *I'm sorry.*

And while he was at it, he'd apologize for his brother's interruption last night, too. Hudson had shown up at Maverick Manor at the worst possible time. Now Walker just wanted a chance to explain, to tell Lindsay it hadn't been a setup, and that he truly was interested in her.

Judge Andrews turned to Marty. "Mr. Peyton?"

Marty rose and cleared his throat. "Thank you, Your Honor. Mr. Jones was deeply saddened to hear that the Marshalls' child had been ill. But Just Us Kids Day Care has always upheld the strictest hygiene protocols and is not responsible for the transmission of a virus that even the plaintiff's attorney admits is highly contagious and easily spread. We intend to present expert testimony that RSV is common and virtually impossible to trace to one contaminant. Blaming Just Us Kids for a virus that could have come from anywhere is like blaming a single daisy for a county-wide hay fever sneezing fit."

That elicited a couple of laughs from the gallery. Lindsay shot Marty a glare.

"We intend to prove that Just Us Kids Day Care was not negligent, and therefore not responsible for this child's illness." Marty thanked the judge, then returned to his seat. He flashed Walker a smug grin.

Any other time, Walker would have been heartened by his attorney's surety, pleased by his attack. But today, winning meant hurting Lindsay, destroying the case she had worked to build. And very likely killing any chance of anything happening between them. His business would win, but his heart would lose.

Okay, so maybe that was being too dramatic. But it was ironic that once again, business was costing Walker a relationship. One that he knew was impossible, because they wanted different lives and lived in different places, and were literally on different sides, but that he still wanted to have.

Lindsay called the teary parents to the stand, one after the other. They each recounted the beginnings of their baby's illness, the scary moments in the hospital with their infant hooked up to machines to help her breathe, the fear that their child might die. Even Walker, who had told himself he was going to remain unemotional through the trial, felt his throat tighten. He could only imagine the stress and worry they'd endured.

"It was the single most terrifying week of my life," Peter Marshall said in a shaky voice. "We love Georgina more than anything in the world, and if I could have traded places with her, I would have gladly given my own breath for hers."

What would it be like to have been loved by parents like that, Walker wondered. To love a child of his own like that? Would he be a parent like the Marshalls, wholly dedicated to his child, or would he be as uninvolved and distant as his own parents had been?

He watched Lindsay questioning them and saw her eyes glisten from time to time with unshed tears. Marty muttered something about the tears being for dramatic effect, but Walker knew better. Lindsay cared—and cared deeply—about her clients, about their child, about this town.

He had no doubt what kind of mother she would be. The kind who would move heaven and earth to protect her child. A mother who would fill a home with warmth and laughter and sweet memories.

She was that kind of woman. The kind a man should marry. Plan a life with.

The thought had come out of nowhere, surprised him. He should be focused on the lawsuit—on the imminent future of Just Us Kids Day Care—and not on the future of Lindsay Dalton.

Marty got to his feet as Lindsay sat down. He glanced at his legal pad, gathering his thoughts, preparing his attack in his head. Walker had seen him do it a dozen times and knew what was coming next. Marty would circle his prey like a friendly hawk, then the second he spotted weakness, he would swoop in and exploit it until the witness crumpled.

Hell, Peter Marshall was already crumpling. He didn't need Marty's help. The father swiped at his eyes with the back of his hand. He shared a shaky smile with his wife, the two of them seeming to have a strong, silent bond.

If I could have traded places with her, I would have gladly given my own breath for hers.

Marty turned toward the witness stand. "Cute kid you have there, Mr. Marshall." Marty gave the sleeping baby in the gallery an indulgent smile. "Bet she's the apple of your eye."

Peter smiled. "You know it."

"Can't say I blame you. Kids do have a way of wrapping you around their little fingers." Marty glanced again at his pad, as if he was recalling a memory or another sweet tidbit. But Walker knew better. Marty was just feigning friendliness before circling closer. "Mr. Marshall, have you taken your baby out in public since she's been born?"

Peter let out a little laugh, as if the question was absurd. "Well, of course we have."

"To the grocery store, friends' houses, things like that?"

"Yes. But not all the time. In the beginning, she was so frail—"

"And when you took her out, did you make everyone who saw her disinfect their hands, maybe wear a face mask?" Marty asked.

Peter's brows crinkled in confusion. "Well, no, that's—"

"So if someone saw your baby, maybe held her or just chucked that adorable little girl under the chin—" Marty made the motion of doing that "—and they had maybe a touch of a cold, you would still let them get that close?"

"Well, we didn't know if everyone—"

"You didn't know if they were carrying rhinovirus germs, did you? Or maybe some kind of upper-respiratory infection?" Marty moved a few steps closer to the witness stand. "Or even maybe RSV?"

"No, but—"

"And yet you allowed those people to get close without taking proper measures to ensure there was no risk of disease?"

Lindsay shot to her feet. "Objection! Mr. Peyton is implying that my client made his daughter sick simply by living a normal life."

"Overruled. Mr. Peyton has a point about exposure, and part of your case, Ms. Dalton, is tracing the source of the infection," Judge Andrews said. He turned to the witness. "You may answer the question, Mr. Marshall."

Alarm filled Peter's face. He leaned forward, his voice earnest. "We didn't think the people who were around Georgina were carrying diseases, Mr. Peyton. We knew everyone—"

"And you knew their medical histories?"

Peter looked to Lindsay, then back at Marty. "Well, no. But that didn't mean—"

"And so you blame Mr. Jones's day care—" Marty turned to point at Walker "—for an illness that your baby could have easily contracted through your own negligence."

Now Peter saw what Marty was doing. Anger filled his eyes. "Hey! We weren't negligent. We were very careful with Georgina."

"So careful that you kept her in a little bubble?" Marty didn't wait for a response. "I didn't think so. You exposed your daughter to the world, Mr. Marshall, and that world is filled with germs. She could have gotten sick anywhere."

"But she didn't. She got sick at day care."

"How do you know that?"

"We didn't go out that week." Peter sat back against his chair, confident that he was disproving Marty's theory. But Walker knew better. Marty wouldn't have started these questions if he didn't have some kind of other knowledge. But Peter went on, oblivious to the defense counsel's plan. "And by Thursday, Georgina had a cough. By Sunday, she was in the hospital."

"So no one outside of yourself and your wife, oh, and the people at Just Us Kids, came into contact with Georgina? No one at all? Not a mailman, a pizza delivery boy, a grandmother?"

Peter's features creased. He glanced at Lindsay again, clearly hoping she'd save the day. But there was no way to undo the words Peter had already said, the admissions he'd made that he had taken his baby out among people who could be sick. Peter let out a long breath, then turned back to Marty. "I forgot that I had stopped at the neighbor's house on Monday night to pick up some cookies they had baked for me. It was my birthday the day before, and I was running home with Georgina from day care. I forgot to tell you, honey," he said to his wife. "I forgot all about it when Georgina got sick and all we thought about was making her well." He turned back to Marty. "I didn't stay long, maybe only a couple minutes."

"And did you know if those nice neighbors were a hundred percent healthy? Or whether they were…" Marty paused, like a hunter about to slay the dragon with a sword. "Sick the week before?"

"No," Peter said softly. Then a realization dawned in his eyes. He gave his wife another look of apology, and Walker could see the pain in Peter's face as he put the pieces together. "The week before, yes, one of their kids stayed home from school with a cold. But we weren't there long, and their son was all better. He was running around and laughing and—"

"You took an infant to a home that could have had lingering illness in it? Germs on the doorknob you touched, perhaps? Or maybe even a few germs on the cookies you surely ingested later? And then you handled your baby, transmitting whatever germs you picked up at the same time you picked up those cookies—"

"No, no. It was the day care center!" Peter leaned across the bench. "I know it was."

"Honestly, Mr. Marshall, you *don't* know that." Marty shook his head. "After all that, can you tell me with one hundred percent certainty that Mr. Jones's day care center was the *only* place, the *only possible* source, of your child's illness?"

Peter hung his head. "No," he mumbled. "I can't."

"No further questions." Marty spun on his heel and returned to the table with a triumphant smile on his face.

Any other day, Walker would have rejoiced with his lawyer. But today, he was left with a sick feeling in his stomach as he watched a contrite and broken Peter Marshall head back to the defendant's table to hug his wife and whisper "I'm sorry" over and over again.

Lindsay called Dr. Jonathan Clifton to the stand, followed by the doctor at the hospital, and made a strong case with each of them that the RSV was contracted at the day care center. Then Marty got his turn, and all of Lindsay's hard work was undone in a matter of minutes. She was a smart attorney, impassioned, but she was no match for Marty's experience and cutthroat instincts. He called Hudson, then Bella Stockton to the stand, along with several other workers from the day care center, and finally Walker himself, all of them making a strong and clear case that the center was clean and up to standards. Lindsay tried to negate their testimony by asking about the disinfection procedures, but in the end, Marty was a more effective questioner.

Which was why Walker had hired Marty in the first place.

But as he watched Lindsay's case fall apart, he wished he had hired a pussycat for an attorney instead of a hungry panther.

The two attorneys made their closing arguments, and the judge recessed court while he pondered his decision. Everyone got to their feet and headed out of the courtroom. Bella told Walker she had to get back to work, and Hudson offered her a ride. "Let me know what happens," he said to Walker.

"I will." He said goodbye to the two of them, then glanced across the hall, where Lindsay was talking to the Marshalls. Once again, Lindsay avoided looking at Walker. She huddled close to her clients, reassuring them in soft tones as she passed him in the aisle.

"I'm going to catch some air," Walker said to Marty. Lindsay had headed away from the courtroom as fast as possible. Her clients were standing in a corner by the soda machine, holding hands.

"Don't go far. Andrews is known to decide quickly.

He's not the kind of judge who likes to think about things for a long time. Cheer up. This is good news. You'll be out of this town before you know it."

"Yeah," Walker said, glancing again at the Marshalls. "That's good news."

He headed down the hall, away from the people milling in the tiled hall. His dress shoes echoed on the hard floor. He kept on walking until he reached a door marked Exit. A second later, he was outside, in the cool Montana air with a bright, happy sun shining on his face.

He leaned against the brick building and let out a breath. He'd never been this conflicted before, never had doubts that he was doing the right thing. It was the right decision for his company—that he knew for certain. If he lost this lawsuit, the entire future of Just Us Kids would be in jeopardy, and his father's prediction of doom for the chain would come true. Yet another black mark against his son.

But if Walker won, the Marshalls were going to be left feeling guilty for their baby's illness, and Lindsay would probably hate him for tearing apart her case.

The door beside him opened, and Lindsay stepped outside. "Oh, sorry. I didn't know you were here."

"Please, stay."

"I should get inside." She started to step back, but he reached out a hand to her.

"Please. Stay." He pushed off from the wall and stood in front of her. "I feel terrible about today."

She snorted. "Really? That's why you had your lawyer reduce my client to tears?"

"That wasn't my intent, Lindsay. I told him to go easy—"

She put up her hands. "Number one, we can't talk about this. It's an ongoing lawsuit. And number two, I don't want to talk about this with you, of all people."

"Then can we talk about something else?" He waved toward the grassy area beside the building. "It's a beautiful day. Come out and enjoy it with me. Please."

She looked over his shoulder. "I just wanted a few minutes of peace before the judge calls us back in."

"That's all I want, too. No reason we can't have those few moments together."

Her eyes met his, and he saw them glisten. "There are a hundred reasons why we can't, Walker."

"We only need one that we can." He stepped back, releasing her. "Share the wall with me, Lindsay."

She hesitated a moment longer, and his heart leaped with hope. Then she shook her head. "I can't. Because I can't be with someone who will destroy a family, all to protect a bottom line."

The door shut with a heavy, hard slam. And the sunny day suddenly seemed to dim.

Lindsay knew what the judge was going to say before he spoke. She stood in the courtroom, flanked by the Marshalls, and felt her heart sink. All that work, all that hope, wasted.

"It is the opinion of this court," Judge Andrews said, "that the plaintiffs did not prove a clear-cut source for their daughter's illness. While the illness was no doubt difficult and scary and nearly fatal, the facts do not support the claim that Mr. Jones's day care center was responsible. Therefore, judgment is for the defendant." He rapped his gavel, and it was over.

Peter and Heather turned to Lindsay. "That's it?"

Lindsay nodded. "We can appeal, but I really don't think we have much chance of overturning Judge Andrews's decision."

"I'm sorry," Peter said, taking the now awake baby from her grandmother. Georgina fussed, and Peter shifted his daughter's weight in his arms. "I really did forget about stopping at the neighbor's until just then. I was so worried about Georgina when she was sick, and when we were preparing for this lawsuit, I was just overwhelmed with work and—"

Lindsay shook her head. "It's fine, Peter. Don't blame yourself." *Blame your lawyer who didn't win today. Blame her for letting you down when you really needed someone strong in your corner.*

"But I do. We have all those bills…" He shook his head and glanced at his wife. "I'm sorry, honey."

She put a hand on his cheek, her gaze soft, her smile understanding. Heather and Peter's love for each other showed in the way they touched, talked, held together, no matter what came their way. "It's okay, Peter. Georgina is well again. We have a wonderful family, and we're just going to move forward from here."

Hearing a sound behind them, Lindsay turned and saw Walker standing there. He was the last person she wanted to see right now, and definitely the last one Peter and Heather wanted to see. "What are you doing here? Gloating over your win?"

"No. I'm here to speak to the Marshalls." He put out his hand, but neither Peter nor Heather took it. Walker let his hand drop. "I wanted to say I'm sorry for all your family has been through."

Heather scowled. "It was your fault, your day care's fault. Regardless of what the judge said."

Georgina started to cry, as if she was agreeing, too. Peter tried to soothe his daughter, but she was having none of that. Heather took the baby, but still Georgina cried. Heather blew her bangs out of her face and tried bouncing the baby and whispering soothing words in her ear.

"Regardless of how things turned out today," Walker said, "I would like to pay your medical expenses."

Lindsay's jaw dropped. "But…but you won. You are not responsible for those bills."

"I want to pay them, and would have, either way," Walker said. "Please, let me do this for you. It's the least I can do."

The Marshalls stood there, stunned and quiet. Georgina, however, was still crying and now reaching, not toward Peter or Heather or even Lindsay, but toward Walker. Her mother tried to soothe her, but Georgina only cried harder, her little hands splaying, arms straining, in Walker's direction.

He glanced at Lindsay, then back at Heather. "Is she…is she reaching for me?"

Heather was having trouble keeping her squirmy daughter in her arms. Georgina seemed determined to go over Heather's forearm and dive into Walker. "I think so. If you don't mind, just for a second, maybe it'll calm her down?"

"Uh…okay." Walker put out his hands, palms up and facing each other.

Heather laughed. "No, not like you're taking a football. Like this." She stepped forward, bending one of his arms to cradle against Georgina's back, then moving his other arm to support her weight, as she shifted the baby into the space created against Walker's chest.

"Heather, I don't think—"

But Peter's words fell on deaf ears as his wife settled their baby in Walker Jones's arms. Georgina stopped crying almost immediately and pressed her head to Walker's chest. Walker hesitated for a moment, then smiled down at the soft, sweet baby in his arms. A look of wonder filled his eyes. "I've never done this before. Are you sure I'm doing it right?"

"She's happy, isn't she?" Heather said. "That's the most important thing."

Lindsay watched Walker's features almost…melt. He was far from a natural with the baby, but within a few seconds, he was swaying gently left to right, holding Georgina against his chest like she'd always been there. Lindsay's resolve to hate Walker crumbled at the sight of the tiny, vulnerable child in the arms of the tall, strong bachelor. For a second, she could imagine him holding a baby of his own and doing all the things a dad would do, singing the songs, telling the bedtime stories, tucking the covers around the baby. Their baby.

Her mind froze. Where had that thought come from? What was wrong with her? She'd just lost the most important case of her young career to this man. How could she let the sight of him holding a baby change anything?

But it did, and she couldn't seem to find it in her to be mad at him another second. "Georgina really seems to like you," Lindsay said. "She doesn't settle down easily with other people."

"But why…" Walker's voice was soft, still tinged with surprise. "Why did she want me to hold her?"

"Our little girl is a stubborn fighter," Heather said. She clasped her husband's hand and the two of them smiled. "And she seems to have a good instinct for people. We might have walked into this courtroom determined to hate you, Mr. Jones, but then you made that generous offer and…"

"And we realized you're not some coldhearted CEO," Peter finished. "Thank you."

"You're welcome." The gratitude seemed to make Walker more uncomfortable than holding the baby. He suddenly shifted Georgina back into Heather's arms, then handed a business card to Peter. Walker cleared his throat, stiffened his spine and went back to being a tough CEO. "Fax the bills to my office and I will pay them as soon as I get back to Tulsa. Out of my personal funds, not my business."

Peter shook his head. "Mr. Jones, that's very generous, but—"

"You all went through a lot, Mr. Marshall, Mrs. Marshall." Walker's gaze included each of them, then paused and lingered on Georgina. A smile ghosted across Walker's face. "And I hope this helps your family heal and move forward."

Then he turned on his heel and left the courtroom. Leaving Lindsay surprised, confused and stunned.

Chapter Nine

Walker should have been on a plane heading back to Tulsa. His work here in Rust Creek Falls was done, the lawsuit settled. Due to yesterday's holiday, he was facing a cramped and shortened workweek, with scores of emails to answer, calls to make, meetings to schedule.

Yet he lingered.

Half of him hoped Lindsay would come back and say now that the lawsuit was over, she wanted to date him. But she had climbed in her car immediately after she left the courthouse and was gone before he had a chance to even wave goodbye.

He couldn't really blame her. He had, after all, won against her in court and was probably the last person she wanted to see right now. His victory rang hollow, though, and left Walker feeling not like he won, but that he had lost something very hard to find.

After thanking Marty, Walker got in his rental car and headed across town to Hudson's house, a ranch he was renting outside of town. He could have headed for the day care, but chances were better than good that Hudson was at home, especially with Bella in place as the full-time manager. That freed Hudson even more from his responsibilities. Walker knew his younger brother, and knew full well "responsible" wasn't on his personal résumé.

As expected, Hudson's car sat in the driveway. He parked, then strode up the walkway and to the door. His brother answered after the first knock. "Hey, Walker. I was just heading out."

"On a date?"

Hudson shook his head. "No, heading to the stables to help with the horses for a bit. When I get stressed, that just kind of re-centers me."

That surprised Walker. Maybe he'd been misjudging Hudson.

"Do you have a minute? So we can talk?"

Hudson hesitated, clearly still leery of another lecture from his brother. Then he stepped back and opened the door wider. "All right. But really, just for a minute."

Walker headed inside. For years, Walker had thought he and Hudson were polar opposites. But in the few days he'd been in Rust Creek Falls, he'd seen changes in Hudson. His brother, whom he'd always thought of as the irresponsible one, was investing in the ranch in Wyoming, in this town. Maybe they had more in common than he'd thought. A part of him wanted to stay right here and spend more time with Hudson, just two brothers hanging out. No business between them, nothing but friendly banter and maybe a couple games of basketball.

What was wrong with him? Was he losing his edge, his drive for corporate success? He held a baby for a few minutes and now he was wondering how he could have it all? He was good at his job, good at running his company. He didn't have time or room for anything else.

Even if, for a brief moment, he'd envied Peter and Heather Marshall and their close bond, as a couple, as a family. Even if when he'd held their baby, he had looked at Lindsay and wondered what it would be like if they were a couple. If that was their baby with soft blond curls and rosy cheeks.

But these were insane thoughts. He told himself he was better off focusing on work, on reality. Not on pipe dreams best reserved for others.

Back on track, he followed Hudson into the living room and sat in an oversize chocolate leather armchair. Hudson seemed antsy and glanced at the door every half second, while Walker, patient and stern, tried to get him to focus. Pretty much the way the two of them had been all their lives.

"Listen, I know you have this ranch in Wyoming you're helping, but I really need you to step up with the day care," Walker said.

His request had nothing to do with business, with the bottom line. It was purely personal. Selfish, really. Because if Hudson took the helm at Just Us Kids, Walker wouldn't have to return to Rust Creek Falls. Wouldn't have to risk running into the woman he was beginning to care for—and who clearly didn't feel the same about him.

Hudson waved away his oldest brother's words. "You hired Bella to do that."

"As a manager. But that doesn't mean you don't need to get in there, too. You should know how the business is running, make sure to oversee—"

"Is this going to be another beat-up-Hudson session? Because I have better things to do." Hudson started to get out of the chair.

"No. I'm sorry." Walker let out a breath. He needed to stop taking out his own frustrations on his younger brother. The fact that his relationship with Lindsay had fallen apart before it even began wasn't Hudson's fault. He rubbed his palm over his jaw and blew out a frustrated breath. "I'm not really here to talk about the center. I came because…" He hesitated. Could he do this? He was far better at weighing assets and liabilities than he was at sharing feelings and worries. But he had come here to do a job, and Walker never backed down from a difficult situation. He took a breath and charged ahead, looking his brother right in the eye. "Because I don't like how things stand between us."

Hudson's mouth opened. Closed. "Okay."

The single word was laced with suspicion. Walker couldn't blame him. Every conversation the two of them had had in the last few months had been confrontational. "You were right, when you told me I was treating you like Dad treats us. I don't mean to. I get so wrapped up in business that I forget about the personal."

"Hey, sometimes I need to be told what to do. And you have a lot on your shoulders, Walker. I wouldn't want to be working for Dad or in charge of his company. I only have to talk to him a few times a year. You see him every day."

Walker nodded. "And he's just as hard on me as ever. I keep trying to prove myself to him, as if that's going to change anything."

"The only one you need to prove something to is yourself. What matters is whether you are happy. Content. Fulfilled."

In the last few days, he could already see a thawing in the icy wall between himself and Hudson. Maybe there was a chance to build a relationship with his brother—if Walker stayed in town long enough. Problem was, the company he helmed was in Tulsa, a company with multiple interests in several industries throughout the world. It wasn't like he could just come here and run the day care. Jones Holdings, Inc. had an oil division, a finance division, a real estate division, and now the soon-to-be-expanded day care division.

Even if he did find a way to bring all that here, there was a woman in Rust Creek Falls who probably wished he'd crawl into a cave. Staying here and watching Lindsay pretend he didn't exist would be painful. Maybe he should leave now. Catch the next flight out. Forget this little town, and forget one resident in particular.

"So, how'd court go today?" Hudson asked.

Walker realized he hadn't told Hudson about the judge's decision. He'd been so focused on getting out of there, away from Lindsay's cold shoulder, that he hadn't even bothered to call or text his brother. "We won. The judge decided that there was no one event the Marshalls could point to as the cause for their daughter's illness, and cleared Just Us Kids of any negligence."

"That's great. So you're completely off the hook?"

"Yes, but…" Walker let out a breath. "I didn't feel right about winning. Those parents had a legitimate worry, and even if you can't blame Just Us Kids, there's nothing to say we *weren't* at fault."

"You saw how strict Bella is with the cleanliness and stuff. Chances are slim that it was the fault of the day care," Hudson said.

"Maybe so. But I decided to pay all their medical bills anyway." Walker shrugged. "Seemed like the least I could do."

And still, it didn't feel like enough. He had this sense of things being unfinished and wondered if there was something more he could do. Something that could have a bigger impact.

"You offered to pay all their bills even after you won the case?" Hudson sat back in his chair and let out a low whistle. "So, Scrooge, where did this altruistic spirit come from?"

Walker bristled. "I'm not a Scrooge."

"You're not exactly Mother Teresa, either."

Walker started to argue, then shook his head. His brother was right. For years, Walker had been focused on the bottom line, the company's net worth, the profit margin. He sought the next takeover, the next acquisition—not the next charitable outlet. But today after court he'd had an empty feeling in his chest. Giving money to the Marshalls had eased it somewhat. He couldn't help thinking that if he gave back more, it would go away totally.

"You have a point, Hudson. I just saw how much

the Marshalls loved their daughter, and thought people like that didn't deserve to be bankrupted by something like this. I have the money to help, so I did."

Hudson smiled. "You did the right thing. That kind of action will go far in a town like this."

"I didn't do it to impress the town. I did it—"

"To impress a girl?" Hudson finished, then laughed. "Hey, I can relate. I'm not above handing over my jacket on a chilly night or opening a door if it impresses a pretty girl."

"Yeah, well, it didn't work." Walker envied his younger brother's easy way with women. Maybe if Walker had a little of that charm and confidence, he could have wooed Lindsay Dalton and not left the courtroom feeling like he'd lost a limb. "That wasn't my intent in paying for the medical bills, either. Like I said, paying for the Marshalls' costs is just the right thing to do. Besides, the pretty girl isn't interested in me."

"If you're talking about that gorgeous lawyer, I think you should keep trying. The lawsuit is done, so…" Hudson put out his hands. "What's stopping you from going after her?"

"She's not interested." If he said it enough, it might stop making his chest hurt.

"She's not interested, or you're afraid to find out she doesn't like your Scroogy self?" Hudson got to his feet and crossed to the door. He put a hand on the knob. "You're fearless in business, big brother, but a scaredy-cat when it comes to women. I saw it when you were with Theresa. You always had this wall up. Like you were afraid to trust her, to really fall in love."

"And you, the poster child for bachelorhood, are the expert on this subject?"

"Hey, just because I can give the advice doesn't mean I have any intentions of taking it." Hudson grinned, the same hapless grin that had gotten him out of more than one scrape. Hudson opened the door. "Now get out of here and go track her down. Before you lose your nerve and fly back to Tulsa."

Walker got to his feet and paused by his brother. "How'd you know I was debating that very same thing?"

"We may not be close," Hudson said, laying a hand on Walker's shoulder, "but we are brothers. And in the end, I want you to be happy, Walker."

Walker met his brother's gaze, eyes so like his own it was almost like looking in a mirror. "Thanks, Hudson."

His younger brother glanced away, as if embarrassed to be caught caring. "It's nothing. Someday, I'm sure you're going to come to me and give me the same speech. Assuming I ever do something stupid like grow up."

Lindsay loved Sunday family dinners on the ranch. It was the one time when all the Daltons were together. But tonight, after her crushing loss in court hours ago, she was doubly grateful for her mother organizing a rare impromptu weeknight family meal. Maybe it would help her forget all about how she let down her clients and how Walker Jones had caught her by surprise.

Why would he go and pay for all the Marshalls' medical expenses like that? For the hundredth time, she wondered if she was wrong about him. If maybe he wasn't a bottom-line-driven corporate shark, but rather, a caring, conscientious man.

No, she knew better. She'd thought the same thing about Jeremy, then discovered he wanted a big-city life and a lot of zeros in his paycheck, not the simple home she had here. The last thing she needed was to let her heart soften toward another man who would disappoint her in the end. It had taken her too long to get over one shattered romance; she wouldn't plunge into another one doomed to the same fate.

Lindsay was in the dining room, setting the table, when her father came up and put an arm around her shoulder. "Sorry about today, kiddo."

Outside the house, a storm was raging, loud and booming. It was going to be one heck of an October thunderstorm, with drenching rains and gusty winds. The perfect night to be tucked inside the house with her family.

She paused in laying out the forks. "I really thought we had a good case."

"You knew it was going to be an uphill battle, honey. But it's okay. Losses teach us more than successes do."

Lindsay scoffed. "Remind me of that when I take on my next clients." She folded a napkin and tucked it under the silverware. "Maybe I'd be better off sticking to working on power of attorney forms and wills."

Her father gave her shoulder a gentle squeeze. "You have the right instincts, honey, and you have the heart of a lion. The legal world needs more of that. You'll win the next one."

"But I really wanted to make a difference for the

Marshalls, and all those families whose babies got sick." Instead, she'd let her clients down. Let Georgina down. Let the evil corporate giant win.

Ben turned her until she was facing him. "You did. You believed them, and supported them, and fought for them. Sometimes, that's all people need."

She sighed. "I hope so, Dad. I really do."

Her father gave her a smile, then headed into the kitchen to help her mother put the finishing touches on dinner. Lindsay finished setting the table just as Anderson and Marina and their two kids, Jake and baby Sydney, came into the house, followed by Travis, then Lani and her fiancé, Russ. There was a flurry of greetings, then the door opened again, and Paige and Sutter walked in with their son, Carter. Right on their heels came Caleb and Mallory, with their daughter, Lily. Everyone shook off the rain and talked about the storm while dispensing hugs and kisses.

The house was loud and lively, all the siblings and in-laws exchanging small talk in a beehive of conversation. It was like the old days, when everyone lived at home and every meal was a spirited adventure. Lindsay's mom, Mary, came out of the kitchen, wiping her hands on her floral apron, then hugged all her grandkids, one at a time.

"Hey, Mom, I thought I was your favorite," Anderson said.

Mary tapped her son on his chest. "You were until I had all these adorable grandkids."

He laughed. "I understand. Heck, all I talk about now are my kids. I've become one of those dads who will show off pictures of school plays and karate lessons to every hapless soul that shows even the slightest interest."

Travis scoffed. "You've become a softy, you big wuss. You won't catch me doing anything like that."

"Anderson is not a softy," Mary said. "You wait, Travis. One of these days you'll be just the same, mark my words. Children are one of life's greatest pleasures and grandkids are twice that and more." She took her husband's hand, then gave her family a misty smile. A second later, she was back to her normal self. "Okay, everyone, dinner's served."

The family piled into the dining room, with the adults crowding around the dining room table while the older kids sat at the smaller kitchen table. There were dishes passed and jokes traded, and the usual hubbub of the Dalton clan being all together. Lindsay plated her share of the roast beef dinner though she didn't seem to have much of an appetite tonight.

Before they dug in, at the other end of the table Anderson tapped his wineglass with a knife. "I'd like everyone's attention," he called out over the din. When it was quiet, he raised his glass. "I'd like to propose a toast. To my sister, a great lawyer."

Lindsay couldn't believe his words. Hadn't he heard what happened in court today? She felt her stomach clench as she looked at her oldest brother. "But I—I lost the Marshall case."

Anderson gave her a nod. "I know."

She looked around the table at her siblings and their families, all of whom were nodding as well. Then she turned to her mom and gave her a smile, now knowing why she'd called this rare weeknight meal. She took a moment to count her blessings for having the best family any woman could ask for. Then she sipped her wine and told them the woeful tale of the court case.

"In the end," she concluded, "my case just wasn't as strong as I'd hoped, and Walker had a better lawyer."

"Nobody in this town's a better lawyer than you," Anderson said as he scooped up a spoonful of mashed potatoes. "Except maybe Dad. And losing a case doesn't make you a bad lawyer. At least you went in there and tried to fight for what was right."

"I don't know about that," Lindsay said. "From what I heard at the hearing, Walker Jones had everything up to par in the day care. And there's a possibility that Georgina got sick from the neighbor's. Maybe my entire case was a waste of time."

"You're still a fabulous lawyer," Travis said, popping a whole buttermilk biscuit into his mouth. "Just do yourself a favor and win the next one."

He flashed her a patented Travis smile, and Lindsay laughed. Her brother was right. She had to put today's loss from her mind and keep on going. She'd done the best she could, and she had tried—and that's what mattered.

Suddenly hungry, she was just reaching for her fork when the doorbell rang. Travis, sitting on the corner of the table, got to his feet. "I'll get it."

Lindsay started to ask Marina about how Jake was doing in school when she heard a deep voice emanate from the foyer. A familiar deep voice. No...there was no way *he* was here. At her parents' house, during family dinner. Lindsay turned in her seat...and there he was.

Walker Jones, still wearing his suit from court, now darkened by rain, standing in the foyer.

Lani whispered, "That's Walker Jones," and the rest of the table fell silent as everyone looked from Lindsay to Walker and back again.

Lindsay shook her head and pushed back her chair. "Excuse me a second."

The only sound in the house came from the kids in the kitchen, oblivious to the tension in the dining room. Lindsay strode up to Walker, hating that just looking at him, all neat and pressed and handsome in a charcoal-gray suit, his jacket and hair wet from the rain, made her heart skip. "What are you doing here?"

"Finishing something." He took a step closer, then another, and she held her breath, expecting him to gloat over the court case or say goodbye—anything other than what he did.

He reached up and cupped her jaw, his touch tender and soft. "I don't want to leave town, Lindsay, not before we see where this thing between us is going."

For a heartbeat, she stood where she was, entranced by his touch, the look in his eyes, the words he'd spoken. Then she heard someone cough, and she remembered where she was and who she was. A Dalton, first and foremost, who remained true to her family, her town and her standards. Walker Jones didn't fit into that equation. No matter how good he looked in a suit.

"This thing, which isn't even really a thing, isn't going anywhere." She stepped back and his hand dropped away, and she told herself she wasn't disappointed.

"Pity. Because I really like you, and I think you like me, too." He drew in a breath, flicked a quick glance at her watching family, then returned his attention to her. "So I came here to officially ask you out on a date."

To ask her out? On a date? The words took a moment to sink in. Her siblings were hanging on every word, not making a secret of their eavesdropping.

"I... I..." She shook her head. Her entire family was staring at her, waiting for her to say something that involved real words. A second ago, she'd had a thousand reasons why she shouldn't be with Walker Jones, but for the life of her, she couldn't remember a single one right now. "I...can't."

Before he could reply, her mother came striding into the foyer. "Mr. Jones, come on in," Mary said, extending her hand to Walker. "We're just sitting down to dinner, but you're welcome to join us."

What was her mother doing? Didn't she know who he was? Before Lindsay could protest, Walker was handing his damp suit jacket to Travis and stepping further into the foyer.

"Thank you, ma'am. Don't mind if I do." Walker gave her mother a smile, then headed for the table. Anderson grabbed an extra chair out of the kitchen and made room for Walker across from Lindsay's seat. Travis got him a plate.

"What are you doing?" Lindsay whispered to her mother.

"That man is interested in you," Mary said. "I can see it all over his face. And I can see the same in yours."

"I'm not interested in him." Okay, so that was a lie. "Not really."

"Uh-huh. That's exactly what I said when I met your father." Understanding softened her mother's features. "That court case is all over, right? So you have no reason not to see where that thing between you two is going, like he said."

"There's nothing going on between us." Well, not exactly... There'd been a couple of kisses. And what had almost happened in his hotel room the previous night.

Okay, so maybe there was something. But it was done now. For sure.

"Nothing?" Her mother just arched a brow. "Then you won't mind if I invite an out of towner who drove all the way to the ranch in this storm to dinner?"

Walker was already talking to her family, with Anderson handing him dishes and encouraging him to fill his plate. He seemed to fit right in, as if he'd always been there. Even Lani had softened toward him. Was this some kind of alternate universe, or was her family seeing a side of Walker that Lindsay had convinced herself didn't exist?

She thought of how he'd paid the Marshalls' medical bills, even though he won the case. How he'd helped set up for the fair, even though it didn't win him any brownie points with the town. How he'd held Georgina with that look of amazement on his face. How all those things had shown her new dimensions of the man she was trying so very hard not to like.

"Go on," her mother whispered, giving Lindsay a little nudge, "and give the man half a chance."

Lindsay returned to the table and took her seat across from Walker. His gaze met hers, and a smile curved across his face. Her heart did that little flip again, and she found an answering smile lifting her own lips. "You may regret this," she said to him. "My brothers are hard on any man who comes here to see us girls."

"That's because none of the guys you dated before were worth much," Anderson said. "Hell, half of them couldn't lift a hay bale or know which end was which on a horse."

"That's your test for good boyfriend material?" Lani said. "Some kind of strong-man-in-the-barn competition?"

"I think it's a good idea," Travis said. "Weeds out the weak."

"Survival of the fittest in dating," Caleb said. "It would make a great reality show."

"Sign me up," Walker said. "There's nothing I like better than a challenge."

"Then you're dating the right girl," Anderson said, giving Walker a little nudge. "And dining with the right family."

The rest of the dinner went on that way, with the Daltons teasing Walker in between asking him questions about Tulsa and his family. She learned he'd never had a pet but he loved dogs more than cats, and, yes, he did know how to ride a horse and hoist a hay bale, thanks to the same grandfather who had taught him carpentry skills. By the time dessert was served, Lindsay half expected her mother to offer to adopt Walker.

The whole time, her heart and her brain went through a tug-of-war. Get close to Walker or push him away? Even if he was here now, he was going to leave eventually. So she hushed her heart and listened to her common sense.

Lindsay opted out of a slice of a pie and gathered

up some of the dishes. "I'm just going to get a head start on these," she said and hurried out of the room before anyone could argue with her.

She stood at the sink, washing the plates, listening to the laughter and chatter in the dining room and the play of the kids behind her. Having her family like Walker so much made resisting him ten times harder.

Give the man half a chance. Her mother's words echoed in her head. But what if she did and he turned out to be just like Jeremy? What if she fell for him and ended up disappointed and alone again? Better to just stay alone.

Lani came in, grabbed a dish towel and started drying the plates. Her sister knew, without Lindsay saying a word, why she'd left to do the dishes. "You know, he's not such a bad guy after all."

"I'm not talking about him." Lindsay circled the sponge around another plate, then rinsed it and handed it to her sister. "What does he think he's doing, showing up here?"

Okay, so maybe "not talking" about Walker needed to be redefined.

"I think he's interested in you, like he said. And you know, men have a weird way of showing that sometimes. Heck, Russ put me in jail." She grinned. "And look how that turned out."

"You and Russ are different."

"How is that? Because he's a part of this town now? Because he fit in with the family?" Lani paused for effect. "Hmm, that sort of reminds me of another man… one who is sitting in the dining room right now, purposely subjecting himself to a lot of Dalton family teasing."

Maybe Lani had a point. Russ had come from out of town and ended up settling here after he fell in love with Lani. He loved their family and had fit in like a missing piece in a puzzle. But that didn't mean Walker Jones would do the same. And why did she care if Walker stayed anyway? She wasn't interested in him.

Okay, well, maybe a teeny, tiny part of her was interested. And flattered that he'd come all the way out here, knowing her family might very well hate him because of the lawsuit, and yet he'd stayed all the same.

"Well, yeah, but…" Lindsay handed Lani the clean silverware, and the objection she had readied on her tongue fizzled away. "None of that makes Walker Jones right for me."

"Just give the man a chance," Lani whispered, echoing their mother's words. "He did, after all, come out in a terrible storm to have dinner with your family. Plus, he survived said dinner. I think that merits at least one date."

Out in the dining room, the men were getting to their feet, saying something about taking Walker out to the barn. Walker caught her gaze and held it for a long second. She could see the heat in his eyes, the interest in his features, and cursed that she felt the same way.

And that she'd just been bamboozled by her own matchmaking family.

Chapter Ten

Walker had grown up with four brothers, but never had he seen Hudson, Autry, Gideon and Jensen act like the Daltons. They were warm and affectionate, loud and teasing, and had him laughing more than he could remember doing in a long, long time. Travis, Anderson, Caleb, and even Russ and Sutter all traipsed out to the barn while the women stayed behind to clean up from dinner. Lindsay's father fell into place beside Walker. The rain had lessened, becoming soft drops instead of the heavy patter from earlier.

"You know this is all part of them making sure you're good enough for Lindsay, right?" Ben said. "This isn't a tour of the ranch—it's a test."

Walker chuckled. "If I had a sister, I'm sure I'd do the same thing."

When they stopped at the door to the barn, Lindsay's father put a hand on the wooden surface and turned to Walker. Ben's face turned serious, his gaze hard and direct. "Lindsay is my daughter, and I just want to make one thing clear. Just because you were invited to dinner and treated like one of the family doesn't mean every single one of us won't come after you if you break her heart."

Apparently the hardest grader in the Dalton family was the patriarch. Walker couldn't blame Ben for being a papa bear with his daughters. He'd do the same for any out of towner who came along, if he'd had a sister or daughter.

"I... I have no intention of doing that, sir," Walker said to Ben. To be truthful, Walker wasn't sure what his intentions were with Lindsay. All he knew was he didn't want to go back to Tulsa without at least finishing the story they had started.

"She's a strong woman and deserves the best," Ben said. "And I'm not just saying that because I'm her father."

"I understand, sir."

Ben held Walker's gaze for a long time, assessing him, measuring him. Finally, he nodded. "Okay, then." He opened the door to the barn.

As Walker followed Ben inside and back to the gentle ribbing by the other Dalton boys, Walker had the feeling he'd passed the first part of the test, but that the jury was still out on whether he would pass the entire exam in the Are You Good Enough for Lindsay Dalton class.

The problem? Walker wasn't sure where this was going to lead or whether he wanted it to lead anywhere. All he knew was that from the second he'd met Lindsay, she had intrigued and tempted him. The business side of him kept telling him to get on a plane to Tulsa, but for the first time in his life, Walker wasn't listening.

Instead, he listened to the Dalton boys riff as they headed through the stables, greeting the horses. This was a family. A real family, with all the inside jokes and shared memories. The kind of family he'd always wished he could have.

Maybe if he stayed in town longer, he could have more time with Hudson, too. Or maybe they were too old, too set in their ways, to develop the easy camaraderie the Daltons had.

He glanced through the stable window, back at the lights blazing in the house. Even through the rain, the Dalton ranch was warm, welcoming. A true home.

The one thing Walker had been looking for all his life, and he'd found it in the most unlikely of places. The very place he was going to have to leave.

The rain had finally stopped. Lindsay stepped out onto the porch and leaned against one of the posts, watching the clouds part and the first stars twinkle. The men emerged from the barn and headed back toward the house. She could pick out Walker's tall, lean frame in an instant among the sea of Dalton boys and the men who were becoming part of the Dalton clan.

She knew she should turn around and go back into the house, but something kept her rooted there as the men drew closer. Walker peeled off from the group, heading up the stairs two at a time to her.

"See you later," Anderson said, giving Walker a clap on the back. "And if you want to go riding tomorrow, just text me."

"Thanks, Anderson. I will."

The other men said good-night to Walker and headed inside, leaving her and Walker outside alone. The only sound came from fat raindrops sliding off overburdened leaves and plopping on the damp ground.

He looked handsome and relaxed, the kind of man she could curl into and feel comfortable and safe with. But Lindsay held her ground, maintained her distance. If she didn't, the temptation to be in his arms would overpower all rational thinking.

"Why did you come here?" she asked him.

"I told you. I wanted to ask you out on a date."

"Why? You're going back to Tulsa any day now, so any 'relationship' we could have—" she put air quotes around the word "—would end just as fast as it began."

He stepped closer. She caught the spicy notes of his cologne. Desire rose inside her, overriding her mind, her common sense. "Are you saying that going on a date with me would be a waste of time?"

"Well…yeah."

"I disagree. And I'd like the chance to prove it to you."

She shook her head. Why did he have to keep trying so hard? Why did she stand here, hoping he wouldn't leave? Why couldn't she just forget this man? "You don't give up easily, do you?"

"Nope. Which is a good thing in business, and in law, as I'm sure you know." He took her hand in his,

his touch warm and secure. "We'll see if that principle holds true when it comes to dating you, too."

Was he implying he wasn't going to give up on trying to win her heart? But more to the point, did she want him to keep trying? What if they ended up apart and alone anyway?

"I'm not so easily swayed." Except right now, she could be swayed into almost anything. A simple touch on her hand and she was ready to melt into his arms.

"I noticed." He gave her hand a little tug. "Come on, let's take a walk. It stopped raining and the stars are coming out."

She hesitated. She shouldn't get any more involved with this man. He didn't want the same things out of life that she did, he wasn't staying in Rust Creek Falls and she had been burned like this once before. But the feel of his hand on hers was so nice, and his smile so inviting, and damn it—she wanted him. He was like the last slice of chocolate cake, something decadent and wrong but too good to resist.

They walked along the flattened path in the grass that led past the stable and over to the corral. It was dark and quiet, and it seemed like the land beyond the ranch stretched forever into the distance. Lindsay drew in a long, deep breath. "I love the way the air smells after it rains. The world just seems…new again."

Walker drew in a breath, too, then nodded. "You know, I don't take enough time to enjoy these kinds of things. I go on maybe one vacation a year but rarely take any time off otherwise. Most days I'm working from sunrise to sunset, and the only time I spend outdoors is when I get in my car. I've spent more time in the fresh air in the few days I've been in this town than I have in the entire past year. Heck, more than I have on any vacation I've ever taken."

"I couldn't imagine a day that didn't have some time outdoors." She drew in another breath of the fresh, clean Montana air. It filled her heart, her soul, and reminded her all over again why she had chosen to live here. "It's part of why I still live on the ranch. Every acre begs you to come outside and enjoy."

He smiled at her and shook his head. "I've never known anyone like you. You're tough as nails in court, and at the same time, you're sentimental and sweet and—"

"You think I'm sweet?"

"You," he said, turning her into his arms, "are very, very sweet."

She shook her head and tried to look away from his hypnotic eyes. "You don't know me very well."

"Then give me the chance to, Lindsay."

She wanted to stay in his arms. She wanted to soak up this night, and this man, and lose herself in his touch, his kisses. But every time she thought about doing that, she circled back around to one very central fact.

Walker Jones wasn't staying.

He might enjoy a few days in Rust Creek Falls as a vacation, but he was not the type of man to stay here long term. And she had too much invested in her life here—in the people of this town—to ever leave.

"Enjoy the evening, Walker," she said as she stepped out of his embrace and pushed down the wave of disappointment in her chest. "It would be a shame to miss such a beautiful night."

Then she turned on her heel and headed back inside. As far away from Walker Jones as she could possibly get.

So, Lindsay Dalton was going to be a challenge. Walker should have expected that from the minute he'd met her. A part of him had hoped that with the lawsuit settled, they could pick up where they'd left off, but she'd made it clear that wasn't going to happen. So he'd left the ranch last night, determined to forget her.

Then he'd walked into Maverick Manor, and for the first time he'd actually taken a moment to look at the mural depicting several local families that had been painted on the wall above the reception desk. Lindsay was in it, along with her entire family. Even in the painting her blue eyes seemed to reach out to him, pull him in like a powerful magnet. And just like that he knew what he had to do. He'd canceled the airplane reservation he'd made and texted Anderson. He wasn't leaving. Not yet.

So here he was again, back on the Dalton ranch, bright and early the next day, helping Anderson with a nervous colt. Walker liked Lindsay's brother. Liked her whole family, in fact. The minute he'd arrived today, Lindsay's mother, Mary, had come out to greet him, then returned with sandwiches and icy glasses of lemonade for both him and Anderson.

He and Anderson had talked about the business of running a ranch, a common ground on which Walker felt comfortable. He was surprised to find how much of ranching corresponded to running a business in general. Just as for him, it all came down to a bottom line and always making sure there was more money coming in than going out. Anderson seemed to be doing a hell of a job running the Dalton family business and clearly loved what he did. He talked with enthusiasm about every horse, every acre and about his plans for the future. If circumstances were different and Walker lived here, he could see the two of them being friends. It made him sad to think about leaving this family behind when he returned to Tulsa.

Walker stood on the gate end of the corral, not really helping as much as playing colt control. Anderson was carrying on a one-sided conversation of soothing, melodic tones with the nervous horse. As he talked, Anderson gradually closed the gap between them. With each step Anderson took, the horse responded by prancing a bit from hoof to hoof. Anderson would pause, but he never displayed an ounce of frustration or impatience. He just kept up his steady *shush-shush* of words until the colt calmed again and they repeated the process. Approach, prance, calm. Until finally he was close enough to lay his hand on the horse's neck. The colt froze, one ear cocked to hear Anderson's murmurs. Another step, another dance of apprehension, more words, then Anderson slipped a bridle over the horse's head. He stayed there a long time, calming and soothing, until the colt was ready to be led around the corral.

As he watched the horse take tentative steps, still wary and ready to bolt at the first sign of danger, Walker realized the moment mirrored his relationship with Lindsay. He'd read definite interest in Lindsay's eyes these past few days, in her kisses, in the way she had leaned into him last night. But every time he tried to get close, she backed away again.

Anderson led the colt into a vacant stall, fed him some extra oats, then gave him one last pat before shutting the gate. The horse was still nervous but far less skittish, which Walker figured was a good sign. For the horse. Would it work that way with Lindsay?

"Let's saddle up a couple horses and take a ride," Anderson said, breaking into his thoughts.

"Sounds good." As much as Walker liked Anderson, though, he would rather be taking a ride with Lindsay. He'd called her this morning and left a voice mail inviting her along, but she'd never replied to his message. Maybe he was fighting a losing battle with her or maybe—

The door to the stables opened, ushering in a long shaft of sunlight—and Lindsay. She wasn't in her work clothes; she'd changed into jeans, a button-down chambray shirt and a pair of cowboy boots. She had her hair back in a ponytail and a well-worn Stetson seated atop her head.

His heart stopped for a second, and his breath caught in his throat while he waited for her to come inside. Right now, he was like that colt, not sure whether to move right or left or go in the opposite direction. So he stood there like an idiot and waited for her to make the first move.

"Don't tell me you're putting someone else on my favorite horse," she said to Anderson.

Someone else. Not Walker. He told himself he wasn't disappointed that she was acting like he didn't even exist.

Her brother grinned. "I wouldn't dare. I was saddling her up for you."

Walker had been so distracted by Lindsay's arrival that he hadn't even noticed that Anderson had been readying a pair of horses, one a tall, stocky roan and the other a strong, lean chestnut. They flanked Anderson on either side, patient and ready.

"Me? I'm not riding today." Lindsay shook her head. "I just came by for a late lunch and then I'm planning on sequestering myself in Dad's home office to get some work done. I have briefs to finish tonight."

Anderson didn't listen. He led the horse up to Lindsay and put the reins in her hand, cutting off her protests. "Do me a favor. Take Walker out for a ride. Show him the property. I've got a…sick filly to look after."

Walker decided he liked Anderson twice as much now. Clearly, her brother was on Walker's side and trying to give him a chance to spend time with Lindsay.

Lindsay's gaze narrowed. "Which sick filly?"

"The one that needs me most." Anderson grinned, then headed out of the stable before Lindsay could argue. Walker and Lindsay were now alone, with just the horses nickering softly from their stalls.

Walker led his horse up beside Lindsay's. "Does this mean you wanted to take me up on my offer to ride today?"

She scowled. "I came home early to work. That's all."

Uh-huh. She could have worked just as easily in her office, he was sure. Maybe the tough-as-nails lawyer didn't want to admit she wanted him as much as he wanted her. He chuckled. "Are you always this difficult to date?"

She raised her chin and stared up at him. "Are you always this stubborn?"

"Yup. Especially against someone so…challenging." He held her gaze until he saw a softening in her eyes and a flicker of a smile cross her lips. "Let's just go for a ride and forget everything else. Okay?"

For a second, he thought she was going to agree. Then the smile faded, and her gaze went to the open stable doors. It was a beautiful October day, sunny and warm enough that they wouldn't need jackets. A perfect day for being outside.

She let out a breath and shook her head. "I can't, Walker. Because in the end, it comes back to the same result. We want different things out of life. I think it's better to not get involved before either one of us has to make some hard choices."

That would mean thinking about what was going to happen when he went back to Tulsa. Eventually, he would have to return. But for now, on this sunny day, Walker didn't want to think about Oklahoma or work or anything other than this beautiful woman.

"I bet you are one hell of a chess player," he said.

Lindsay's horse shifted from hoof to hoof and let out a chuff. She ran a hand down the filly's muzzle and then patted her neck. Curiosity and a bit of a smile lit Lindsay's features. "I like chess, and have been known to play pretty competitively, yes. But what on earth does that have to do with us going for a ride?"

"Because you are always thinking ten steps ahead. Me, I just want to enjoy a beautiful day with a beautiful woman. After that, who knows?"

She shook her head. "I don't live like that, with

no plan for the future. I like to know what's coming tomorrow and the next day and the day after that."

"And I like to take risks." He stepped into one stirrup and swung his leg over the saddle, settling himself on the horse's back. Staying here in Rust Creek Falls and trying to woo a woman who kept on resisting him was definitely taking a risk. He could have taken the safe path of going back to work, but Walker was tired of that. Tired of coming home to an empty, quiet apartment. To living an empty, quiet life. He wanted more. He wanted what he'd found in that dining room last night—and he knew Lindsay was a big part of that. "Some would say opposites attract and balance each other out. So come on, Lindsay, and take a ride with me. Without any idea how the day will end, or what tomorrow will bring. Have fun. Play hooky."

He didn't want to think about tomorrow or next week or anything other than today. About filling this emptiness inside him with a woman whose smile warmed his heart.

She hesitated, her hand on the reins, her gaze on him. The horse nudged Lindsay's shoulder, clearly ready to go. "It *is* a nice day..."

"It's a *spectacular* day."

"And I do have *some* free time this afternoon..." Her mouth twitched as she considered his offer. He held his breath, waiting.

When he'd been a kid, his grandfather had taken him camping one time and taught him how to start a fire. The spark was the first part, but not the most important, his grandfather had said. Anyone could make a spark, but not everyone had the patience to coax that spark into a fire. So Walker waited, hoping the spark of interest he'd read in Lindsay's eyes would become a full-on flame.

A second later, she swung herself up into the saddle and snapped the reins. "Just because I'm going for a ride with you doesn't mean anything has changed." The sliver of a smile on her face belied her words.

"Of course not," Walker said, but as they led the horses out into the sunshine and down the grassy path to the vast acreage beyond the ranch, Walker figured a lot had changed, and he was damned glad it had.

Chapter Eleven

The giant Rust Creek Falls river spread in glistening blue glory before them. Both the horses drank from the water's edge while their tails flicked at the occasional fly. The day shone bright and happy, and as much as Lindsay wanted to say the opposite, she had to admit she was having a good time with Walker.

They'd taken an easy ride around the property while she told him stories about the horses, the Dalton family land, the history of Rust Creek Falls, its namesake waterfall and the river that wound its way through town. He took a genuine interest in what she had to say, in the stories she told about the ranches and mills that had built Rust Creek Falls into what it was today. It was intoxicating to have a man pay such close attention to her, and it made her wish the ride could go on forever. Their conversation—now that they no longer had the lawsuit between them—flowed as easily as water in a creek.

Walker unfastened a plaid blanket Anderson had strapped onto the horse's saddle earlier—probably all part of her brother's matchmaking scheme—and spread it on a grassy area beneath a wide oak tree. "Come on, have a seat. Enjoy the day."

Lindsay did as he asked, leaning back on her elbows and looking up at the dappled sun peeking behind the thick leaves. She was glad she'd agreed to go on the ride, not just because it was a glorious day, but because she was, despite her best intentions, truly enjoying her time with Walker. He was a smart, interesting man, one of the most interesting she'd ever met. He'd told her about his trips around the world, mostly business trips that took him to global destinations. He'd lived an interesting life, one far from the small town she'd inhabited most of her years. "Did you get to enjoy all those cities you went to?"

"Not nearly enough. I tend to get into work mode and weeks will go by before I spend any time outside the office. Now I see what I've been missing by working too much and taking too few vacations," he said. "Maybe I should move the corporate offices to a ranch and make outdoor lunches a mandatory thing."

For a second, she dared to hope he meant he was moving to Rust Creek Falls. But he hadn't said that, and she needed to quit looking for signs that Walker wanted the same life she did. "I try to eat lunch outside whenever the weather is good. My dad does, too. When we're in the office on the same days, we take our lunches over to the park and eat there. It's nice, because I get to pick his brain and spend time with him at the same time."

"Your family is so close," Walker said. "I used to have a friend in grade school who had a family like that. A whole bunch of brothers and sisters. It was always noisy in their house, but a good kind of noisy, if you know what I mean."

"I do." She turned over onto one elbow and looked at Walker. In jeans and a T-shirt, he looked so comfortable, relaxed. Like an entirely different man from the suited one who'd walked into the courtroom. "I was just thinking last night how nice it was to hear that noise in the house again. I've missed having all my siblings home. We're all growing up and going our separate ways."

"But at least you still get together for family dinners." Walker picked up a leaf and tossed it to the side of the blanket. "It's the kind of thing I wished I had growing up. We had plenty of money, a giant house and every single thing we could ask for, but none of us had a true home. There were no family dinners, no fights over the last piece of apple pie, nothing but this never-ending silence, it seemed. Like we were living in a bubble that no one dared break. Your family is loud and loving and awesome."

She didn't tell him that her family liked him just as much. Almost all of her siblings had texted her today to tell her that Walker was a "real catch," and that she should have him back to the house soon. "That warm space is the kind of environment you tried to create with the day care, right?"

He scoffed. "*Tried* is the operative word. Turns out I don't have the first clue how to do that. I talked to all kinds of interior designers and even a child psychiatrist before I designed the first Just Us Kids. And still, I didn't get it right. Bella was the one who added those last few touches that made it seem like home."

"I've been inside the center. It is really inviting." Even when she was suing Walker's company, she'd had to admit that the day care he'd built was far from the sterile, no-personality ones she had seen in other locations. The kids at the day care had seemed happy, too, and the staff was very hands-on and clearly enjoyed their jobs.

"Pretty much all of that was Bella Stockton's doing," Walker said. "Next time I open a location, I'm bringing her in to help with the design. She knew more about how to make it homey than all those high-priced designers I hired. And definitely more than me."

"Bella is a pretty smart woman, and really nice. Her brother is the one whose wife died after their triplets were born." From time to time, Lindsay had run into Bella when she was at Jamie's house, helping out.

"Are those the same triplets the entire town pitched in to care for?" Walker shook his head. "I swear, this town is like another planet."

"In a good way?"

"In a really good way." He rolled onto his arm and traced a line along her jaw. "There are a lot of things in this town that surprised me."

She didn't want to believe him. Didn't want to fall for his touch and his sweet words, but she couldn't stop herself. Her heart melted, and a smile found its way to her lips. "Things like what?"

"Things like…you." His thumb skimmed along her

mouth, then lingered on the bottom lip. He watched her, his eyes dark and unreadable, then slowly, ever so slowly, he closed the gap between them.

He was going to kiss her, and all those intentions she'd had not to get closer to Walker seemed very, very far away. She wanted him now—heck, she'd wanted him from that very first day—and couldn't remember a single reason why she shouldn't be with him. Maybe they were going their separate ways, with him returning to Tulsa and her staying put, but that didn't mean she couldn't enjoy one sunny afternoon with the man who made her heart race, did it?

She leaned in, meeting him halfway. When Walker's lips met hers, the simmering desire in her veins became a heated rush of want, need. His lips moved harder against hers, his tongue dipping in to play. She roamed her hands over his back, down the soft cotton of his T-shirt, over the hard denim of his jeans.

He rolled closer, his torso over hers, and reached a hand between them to cup her breast, but that wasn't enough for her. There were too many clothes, too much in the way. She hurried to unsnap the buttons on her shirt, then reached for the hem of his T-shirt and pulled it over his head. He spread the panels of her shirt, exposing her lacy bra.

He smiled down at her, then watched as he pushed back the cup and brushed a thumb over the sensitive nub. Lindsay arched against Walker, wanting more, wanting everything, wanting him.

His mouth followed the path from her jaw to her neck to her breast, while his hand slid off her shirt and undid the clasp of her bra. He paused a moment to sit back and drink in the sight of her. "You are beautiful," he said.

A flush filled her cheeks. "Thank you."

"Not just beautiful here," he said as the back of his hand skimmed along her skin, "but in your heart and mind, too. You are the most singularly interesting woman I have ever met."

She scoffed and looked away. "You've been all over the world. I'm sure you've met thousands of interesting women."

He tipped her chin until she was looking at him again. "I've never met a woman who could argue with me so effectively and at the same time have such a tender, open heart. You are fierce, Lindsay, in the way you fight, the way you love, the way you live."

Fierce. She liked that description. Liked hearing him say that. "And you are a man who challenges me, in a good way."

"Maybe because I am falling for you," he said, tracing her lips again, his blue eyes locked on hers, "and falling hard."

"Walker..." She didn't want to finish that sentence. Didn't want to tell him not to fall for her. Because tomorrow or the next day, he would be gone, and all this would be nothing more than a memory. A bittersweet memory. "When you leave, where will we be then? We live in different places, have different lives."

"Oh, Lindsay, always the lawyer, ready to argue." He grinned. "Let's not talk about any of that right now. Let's just enjoy this moment." He skipped a finger down the center of her chest. "Enjoy each other."

Her pulse raced. Maybe he was right and she needed to stop arguing, stop debating, and just...be.

It terrified her to do that. To let her heart go, to hand over the reins and trust another human being. But she looked up into Walker's eyes, and decided to take that leap.

"Yes," she said, the word coming out on a breath. "Yes." Then she rose up to kiss him.

He kissed her back, gently at first, then harder, more insistent. She matched him, move for move, and then it was a frenzy of hands on bodies, buttons undone, clothes discarded. She lay beneath Walker and ran her hands along his lean, naked body and thought he had to be one of the best-looking men she'd ever seen.

He smiled at her, a sexy, sweet smile, then started that trail of kisses again. Down her neck, along her shoulders, over her breasts, down the flat of her belly, until he reached the center of her. Her hands tangled in his hair and her breath came in gasps as he brought her to dizzying heights again and again with the masterful stroke of his tongue. When she thought she would go mad with want, he rose up again, took a second to slip on a condom, then slid into her in one long, breathtaking stroke.

She wrapped her legs around his hips and clutched at his back, whispering his name against his neck as he slid in and out of her, deeper each time, seeming to touch every nerve in her body at once. She forgot where they were, forgot what day it was, her mind a dizzying fog of Walker and pleasure.

His strokes quickened, and he leaned down to kiss her as the desire surged between them, faster, harder, until they came together in one long, hot climax. His lips lingered on hers, as if he didn't quite yet want to let go. Then, finally, he smiled at her and held her tight against him while their heartbeats slowed and the breeze cooled their skin.

Walker held Lindsay to his chest and for a long time thought the world was perfect. The birds were singing, the sun was shining, the horses were nickering softly to each other. She was warm against him, fitting perfectly into all the spaces that had been empty for too long.

But it was all only a temporary respite, and he knew that. His business was in Tulsa. He couldn't be away from it for an indefinite period of time. Hell, given how many times his cell phone had buzzed this afternoon, it sounded like everyone in the office was in some state of panic. There were undoubtedly twelve million items that all needed his immediate attention.

For the first time in his life, Walker didn't want to do any of them. He wanted to stay with this woman in this tiny little town and eat apple pie and paint signs for a festival.

He was in too deep. Had fallen too hard. Being with Lindsay Dalton would mean losing track of what mattered, of the company he was working so hard to build and expand.

His cell phone buzzed again. Walker fished it out of his pants pocket. Seven unheard voice mails. Eleven texts. And 110 emails, just from today alone. Not to mention several angry messages from his father about "abandoning his responsibilities." Walker scrolled through the messages and bit back a sigh. So much for his vacation from reality.

"I need to make some calls. We're in the middle of

this merger with another oil refinery, and the seller is talking about backing out. I need to talk to him, and calm him down."

"That's okay." Lindsay sat up and started grabbing her clothes. "We should get going anyway."

"Sorry. There's just a lot going on at work."

"No, no, it's fine." But she didn't look at him as she got dressed, and he wasn't sure what else to say. So he took the easy way out and remained silent.

The aftermath between them was filled only with the sounds of zippers zipping and snaps fastening. He folded up the blanket, tucked it back in place on the saddle, then held out a hand to help her onto her horse.

"I've got it, thanks," she said and swung her leg over the saddle, as cool and distant as she would be with a stranger.

He did the same, and a moment later, they were trotting back toward the stable. He knew he could let this silence continue and it would end here. He'd leave on the next flight, and she would just be a wonderful memory. He thought of the work he had to do, the fires he needed to put out at the office. He should be 100 percent present for all that rather than being distracted by a pretty brunette lawyer in Montana.

Yup, that was best all around.

"Let's go into town and get dinner." So much for letting it go and refocusing on work.

"Sorry, but I really do have some work to do. Maybe another day." She clicked to the horse, increasing the animal's speed. "And besides, you've got stuff you have to take care of, too."

"True. I really do need to get back to Tulsa as soon as possible." Even saying it out loud didn't make the truth any easier to accept. He saw the ranch growing nearer, and his chest tightened.

"I know you do." Her eyes were hidden by the shadows of her cowboy hat. "There's nothing else holding you here, now that the lawsuit is over."

Let it go, he told himself. *Let her go. It's for the best.*

The stable was now only thirty feet away. In seconds, they'd be back, off the horses and back to their separate lives. He'd book a flight and put this town in his rearview mirror. It was what he had wanted from the second he arrived.

Until he met Lindsay Dalton.

He tugged on one of the reins and brought his horse around in front of hers. "I don't want to go back," he said. "I don't want to leave." His phone started buzzing again, vibrating in his pocket, as if disagreeing with what he was saying.

Lindsay shook her head. "Listen, we had a nice time. A great afternoon. You don't have to say those things just because we made love."

"I'm not. I mean it, Lindsay." But work kept intruding—*buzz, buzz, buzz*. He could literally feel himself being torn in two—the half that needed to get to work against the half that wanted to go back to that river and the shady spot beneath the oak tree.

She looked away, her gaze going to someplace far, far from him. Her body was tall and stiff, no longer relaxed and easy in his arms. "We had a nice time," she said again, "but we both knew going into this that it wasn't going to last."

"What if I want more?"

"What *more*?" She swung her gaze back to his.

"Do you want to fly to Montana every other weekend? Skype a couple times a week?"

"We could do that."

"And to what end? You still run a multimillion-dollar company in Tulsa and I'm still a small-town lawyer who doesn't want to leave Rust Creek Falls. It's not like you can just up and move something like that to a place like this."

"It's not impossible," he said. But even he could hear the doubt in his voice. It wasn't impossible, but it would be a major undertaking. He'd have to hire all new staff, rebuild his local network...

Not impossible, no, but not easy, either.

"Do you really want to live in this tiny little town?" she asked, then waited for him to answer. He hesitated. "I didn't think so. And I'm not leaving here. I've already been down this road before, and so have you. You told me yourself that when it came down to choosing between your relationship and your business, you chose work."

"I was new to working for my father, trying to establish myself in his company. Then he made me CEO, and the time constraints multiplied. I couldn't do both. There simply weren't enough hours in the day to be full-time at work and full-time in a relationship."

"And what's changed now?" She shook her head. "Nothing. You're expanding, merging, buying, selling, and so on and so forth. I don't want that life, Walker. I want to stay right here in this little town where the worst thing that happens is somebody's prize pig is stolen at the county fair. I don't want the life you have, and I know that I never will."

He let out a gust. She made it sound like he'd asked

her to get married. He wasn't thinking that far in advance. He wasn't thinking past the pain of not seeing her every day. Couldn't she understand that? "I'm not saying you have to choose my world or yours right now, Lindsay. Let's just take some time together and see where we end up."

"We're eventually going to end up right where we are now. You know it, and I know it. So, we have a choice. We can end it now, after what was a—" her voice caught, the only emotion she had betrayed in the last few minutes "—wonderful afternoon, or drag this out long-distance. I vote to end it now."

He nudged his horse closer to hers. "What are you so afraid of, Lindsay?"

"I'm not afraid of anything. I'm just making the wisest decision sooner rather than later."

"It seems to me like you're running away before you get hurt." He brushed a tendril of hair behind her ear. She held his gaze but didn't betray her feelings. She was stoic, almost cold, not the warm, giving woman he'd been holding a little while ago. "You fight so hard, for this town, for the people you love, for the Marshalls, and yet when it comes to what you want, you back down as soon as it gets difficult."

"I'm being realistic, Walker. There's a difference."

"Realistic? By ending things before we see where they go?"

"Come on, Walker. You know we are different people who want different things. You may say that you want the home life that you see here, the same one you've tried to create in your day care center, but when it comes down to it, you're going right back to that cold, corporate world."

It was true. He could feel the constantly buzzing phone drawing his attention away. Half his brain was already in work mode, making lists, planning next steps. With each passing second, and each email that filled his phone, he could feel the work half gaining strength, talking him out of pursuing Lindsay any further. She was right—they lived two different lives, and no amount of Skyping was going to change that. Still, he wasn't ready to let her go. Or watch her walk away.

"You're just going to pretend today didn't happen?" he said. He already knew the answer, but needed to hear her say it. Needed that…closure. Maybe then he could move on and put Lindsay behind him.

"Wasn't that your plan, too?" She waited a beat for him to answer, and when he didn't she let out a sigh and shook her head. "That's what I thought."

She gave her horse a nudge, and a second later, they were off at a quick canter, into the stable and out of his sight.

Chapter Twelve

Lindsay did a really good job of convincing herself she was happy over the next few days.

After she brought the horse back to the stable, she'd handed the filly off to one of the workers and then beelined it out of there before Walker could catch up with her again. She'd made a huge mistake making love to him—and opening her heart.

Because despite all her best intentions, she had, indeed, begun to fall for the tall, blue-eyed CEO. He was so intriguing, with so many layers and surprises; just when she thought she knew him, he'd shown her a whole other side. Like showing up at the ranch in a rainstorm. Helping Anderson with that nervous colt. Holding Georgina after the trial.

But in the end, the reality was that he was going to leave. She'd been in that boat once before and had no intentions of falling for another man who wanted a life far from Rust Creek Falls. This was her home, her world, her family, and she never wanted to leave.

So she buried herself in her work, staying late at the office, going in early. She had no idea if Walker had gone back to Oklahoma yet. One afternoon she'd seen Hudson crossing the street and had been tempted to run over and ask him where Walker was.

But she didn't. Walker hadn't called or texted her, which meant he had done exactly what she had asked—and severed the relationship before it could go any farther.

Now, several days later, she wished he hadn't listened. Some impractical side of her dreamed of him charging in on a white horse, asking for her hand and then whisking her away toward the sunset.

She really needed to stop watching the Hallmark Channel late at night. Clearly, she'd seen one too many romance movies. To banish the sappy images, she redoubled her concentration on the papers before her, but the words just swam before her eyes.

It was Saturday, the day of the Rust Creek Falls Harvest Festival, and Lindsay was once again at her desk. She had read the same brief three times but hadn't retained a single word. Her mind was on Walker and on what he was doing right now. Was he working on the weekend, just like she was? Was he thinking of her, too?

Finally, a little after three, she pushed away from her desk and gathered up her things. Working was pointless, because she'd accomplished almost nothing in the six hours she'd been here today. She tugged on a denim jacket, locked up the office and then headed downtown. Maybe stopping at the festival would take her mind off everything.

Except the minute she saw the signs she had painted, the same signs Walker had assembled, then the row of vendor booths that she and Walker had built, everything came rushing back to her. The way he'd patiently shown her how to assemble the booths, the kiss in the back of the gym, the moment in the school cafeteria when they'd gone to make lemonade. Her heart ached, like a torn muscle, and it was all she could do to push a smile to her face and pretend everything was fine.

She greeted neighbors and friends as she made her way through the festival. She stopped at the first booth and bought a pretzel from her sister-in-law Mallory and her niece Lily. When Caleb married Mallory he'd become a great father to Mallory's adopted daughter. Lily's Chinese heritage showed in her dark hair and almond eyes, but her cowboy boots and jeans marked her as 100 percent Montana girl.

Mallory gave Lindsay a tight hug, and Lily darted over to do the same. That was one of the things Lindsay loved about this town. At every turn, there was a member of her family. And right now, she needed to be surrounded with people who mattered so she could forget the one who didn't anymore.

"Hey, girls," Lindsay said as she added a little cheese dip to her pretzel. "I didn't know you'd be working the festival."

"We're raising money for my Girl Scout troop's camping trip," Lily said. "So we made pretzels and cupcakes and cookies. Do you want some cupcakes, too, Aunt Lindsay?"

The way Lindsay was feeling right now, she was tempted to eat an entire batch of cupcakes. "Maybe later. The pretzels are delicious, though."

"Thanks." Mallory beamed. "Old family recipe."

"I'll be sure to send lots of people to your booth," Lindsay said, raising the pretzel in a goodbye wave. She made her way through the crowds, saying hello to the Traubs, and several other families.

Peter and Heather Marshall came over to Lindsay. They had baby Georgina in a stroller, all dressed up in a bright yellow coat and a pumpkin-shaped hat. She looked so adorable, and totally befitting the fall theme.

"Lindsay, we wanted to thank you again," Heather said, "for all you did."

Lindsay bent down and gave Georgina's tiny hand a little shake. The baby's mouth widened in a smile. "I wish I could have done more."

"It all turned out great in the end. True to his word, Walker paid all our medical bills, and he reached out to all the other families who had sick children and covered any expenses they had, too," Heather said. "Plus he offered each of the families a month of free day care at Just Us Kids."

She was glad to know he had kept his word. But to do the same for the other families? That went above and beyond.

"He isn't such a bad guy after all," Peter said. "Once we got to know him, he seemed genuinely nice."

Georgina started to fuss. Lindsay tried playing with the baby again, but she wasn't interested. She squirmed in her seat and started to cry.

"Got to know him?" Lindsay straightened. "You mean that day in court?"

Heather handed Georgina a teething ring of floating fish. The baby immediately started gumming the soft plastic circle. "Oh, no, he did more than that. He invited us out to dinner. He said he wanted to hear from us firsthand what we thought about the day care, to see if there were any improvements he needed to make. He went above and beyond, if you ask me."

Peter nodded agreement. "You meet some of these CEOs and they barely know what the right hand is doing with the left in their business, especially in one as big as his, where a single day care is a blip on the screen. Walker, though, is really invested in making his day care chain a success. Not just for his company but for the families who use it."

"He wants it to feel like home," Lindsay added softly. And Walker was doing that, one action at a time.

"That's exactly what he told us," Heather said. "And you know, when you have an owner who cares that much, I think that's half the battle in making a workplace feel like home."

If someone had asked her two weeks ago what she thought of Walker Jones III, "caring owner" wouldn't even have made the list. But the man she'd gotten to know did care and was committed to making things right. If she'd had any doubts about that before, they were gone now.

That only made her heart ache more. He was a good guy—an intriguing, interesting, handsome guy—but also one who lived far away and had no intentions of coming back.

Lindsay started to say goodbye to the Marshalls, then stopped. "Wait. You said Walker took you guys out to dinner. When was that?"

"Two days ago," Heather said, then laughed. "At least I think so. Georgina is getting her first tooth, so no one in our house is getting a lot of sleep lately."

Two days ago. After she'd said goodbye to him at the stable. Was it possible that Walker had stayed in town? That he hadn't gone running back to Tulsa after all?

And if that was so, why hadn't he called her? Texted? Tried to see her?

She gave the Marshalls a hug, bent down and kissed baby Georgina on the temple, then said goodbye before the emotions crowding her head could bring on tears. Maybe she had misread Walker after all. Maybe he was one of those love 'em and leave 'em guys. She was better off without him, after all.

If that was so, then why did it hurt so bad?

She stopped by Nate Crawford's booth, where he was raffling off a weekend for two at the Maverick Manor. He'd done an amazing job rebuilding the manor after he won the lottery and turned the run-down Bledsoe's Folly, as it had been nicknamed, into the gracious and beautiful hotel. With his wife, Callie, by his side, Nate looked like a happy man with a full, rich life.

"Glad to see the hotel is doing so well," Lindsay said.

"I had a flurry of bookings this week. Seems our resident millionaire recommended it to a whole bunch of his friends," Nate said. "And he's already booked a corporate retreat at the Manor for the spring."

He was still in town. Why hadn't he contacted her? "By resident millionaire you mean…"

"Walker Jones." Nate grinned. "He's been one of the best things to happen to Maverick Manor since I opened it."

What the heck was Walker doing? Taking the Marshalls out to dinner, taking care of the other families whose kids had gotten ill, increasing bookings at the Maverick Manor? She half expected someone to come up and tell her he was building a hundred-acre park next. He'd gone from town villain to town hero in the span of a week.

Refusing to spend any more time thinking about Walker, she got a cup of hot cider, bought another pretzel from her sister-in-law and tried to enjoy the festival. A local band was playing at one end of the park, filling the space with the cheery sounds of country hits. Lindsay tried to smile, tried to move to the music, but everything inside her hurt. She tossed her empty cup in the trash, then headed toward home.

The Rust Creek Falls Harvest Festival was in full swing by the time Walker arrived. He'd spent half the day in his hotel room in videoconference planning meetings with his staff. Every time he thought he'd conquered one thing on his to-do list, another twenty sprang up. Any other day, the workload might have exhausted him, driving him to hit the sheets as soon as he got home. This week, though, he'd been energized, staying up long past midnight every single night to send emails, fax signed contracts, make plans.

He had contemplated avoiding the festival entirely, because he wasn't sure his plan would be ready. It wasn't quite there yet, but maybe he could nudge things along in person. So Walker headed out of his room at the Maverick Manor and down to the park.

His phone started ringing. He pulled it out, glanced at the caller ID and decided this was a long overdue conversation. "Hello, Dad," he said when he answered.

"Are you done playing cowboy? Your responsibilities are here, Walker, not in that hick town." His father's voice was harsh.

Walker bristled. "I've worked the entire time I've been here. There are these amazing technological advances called computers that let me videoconference, sign contracts—"

"You are needed here, Walker. In person. I expect you to be back in Tulsa tomorrow."

A thousand times before, Walker had leapt to do his father's bidding, because he'd thought this action or that one would finally make his father see his son as a man to be proud of. But it seemed no matter what Walker did, his father wasn't pleased. "No."

The single word hung in the air between them. The silence went on so long, Walker was sure his father had hung up.

"I am going to pretend you didn't say that," Walker the II said. "Now, when you return—"

"I'm staying where I am. And as CEO, I'm making some changes to how Jones Holdings is run."

"You can't do that."

"I can. You put me in charge, and that means I can do what I want. I've been working with the other members of the board to implement these changes."

"You mean going behind my back to push your own agenda."

"Not at all. I'm doing what I think is best for the company," Walker paused. "And for me."

"You are going to ruin everything I worked for all my life." Disgust filled every syllable.

"No, Dad. I'm going to have the life you never had. I don't want to grow old and realize the only thing I have is a cold, empty business. I want a life. A family." Walker paused. "There's still time for you to do that, too, Dad."

"You're a fool," his father said.

"No. I *was* a fool," Walker said. "I'm not going to be one any longer." Then he hung up the phone and hurried his pace as he entered the park.

The scents of roasting hot dogs and mulled cider filled the air. A tractor with a hay-filled trailer carried loads of kids on a circuitous route outside the park. There were ring toss games and giant hopscotch patterns drawn on the grass, and vendors selling everything from handmade aprons to brightly painted Montana landscapes.

One painting caught Walker's eye as he passed the booth. A landscape of a beautiful stretch of river and the mountains that lay behind it. In the center was the unmistakable Dalton ranch. He could almost see himself and Lindsay relaxing by the river with the horses, almost hear her family sitting down to dinner.

"How much for that one?" he asked the vendor.

The woman manning the booth—the artist, he presumed, given her flowing clothes and chunky jewelry—came around to see which painting Walker was pointing at. She was tall, with wavy brown hair and kind brown eyes. "Oh, sorry, that one's not for sale."

"Everything is for sale." Walker pulled out his billfold, withdrawing a thick stack of twenties. "Name your price."

"There isn't one." The woman smiled and pushed the stack of bills away. "Not everything can be bought."

"That's the Dalton ranch in there, right?" He gestured toward the property at the base of the mountains. He could see tiny horses painted into the corral, some spring flowers on the porch. The sun was just setting in the painting, and everything had been washed with gold.

"It is. My husband's cousin's family lives there." She put out a hand. "I'm Vanessa Dalton, married to Jonah Dalton, and also the artist who painted this."

"Walker Jones," he said. "I've met your husband. Nice guy. Wait. Are you also the artist who did the mural at the Maverick Manor?"

She nodded. "Guilty as charged."

"I thought your work looked familiar." He shook hands with her, then let out a little laugh. "This really is a small town, isn't it?"

"That's what they say." Vanessa smiled again and moved away from the Dalton ranch painting. "Anyway, what about this one?" She gestured toward a painting of the town park, then at one of the mountains. "I have plenty of other landscapes of this area."

"No, this is the one I want." He looked at the painting again and felt that sense of home that he had been missing all his life. "Are you sure we can't come to an agreement?"

"I'm sorry," Vanessa said, "but it's the kind of painting that I'd like to keep in the family."

Walker could see that no amount of money was going to convince Vanessa to sell. He wasn't part of that family and had no right to ask for something that rightly belonged to the Daltons. He was always going to remain where he was—on the outside looking in. Walker said goodbye to Vanessa and made his way farther into the festival.

Maybe he should leave. What was he doing here, anyway? Working some crazy plan that very likely would explode in his face? He wandered down the pathway and thought it might be best to head back to the hotel.

Then he saw her. It was like a bolt of lightning hitting his chest. Over the last three days, Walker had told himself he was doing fine without her, but the instant he saw Lindsay, he knew that was a lie.

He wove his way through the crowds, but she was moving fast, heading for the exit. He increased his pace, then took a shortcut behind one of the booths, rounded it and ended up right in front of Lindsay. "Hey."

As opening lines went, it wasn't his best. Hell, it probably ranked right down there with the worst possible opening line he could ever say. But at the moment it was all he had.

"You're still in town."

Her words were a statement, not a question, and he could hear the hurt in her voice. Hurt that he hadn't called or texted, that he had let her go. He wanted to tell her that he had his reasons, that he'd wanted to be ready to see her, but the words refused to come. "Did you see our booths? They look great all finished."

Worst opening line followed by worst second line ever. Geesh, you'd think he was fifteen again and had no idea how to talk to women. This woman, though, was different, and he didn't want to mess up. Not any more than he already had, at least.

"Oh, yeah, I did see them. You're right. They look great." She started to brush past him. "I need to go."

He put a hand on her arm. Electricity raced through his veins. "Lindsay, wait. Please."

Her eyes glistened with unshed tears. Once again, he ached to undo the hurt from the past few days, rewind the clock, find another way. Hurting Lindsay was the last thing he wanted to do, and the only thing that had been unavoidable. They'd needed time apart—time for him to figure out what he wanted, time for her to regroup and time to pull off what he hoped was a miracle. He could only pray she would understand.

"Can we grab some hot cocoa and go talk?" he asked her.

She shook her head and pulled her arm away from his hand. "I have to go."

"Stay, Lindsay," he said, reaching out and taking her hand this time. "Stay. Just for hot cocoa."

"Walker, what is it going to accomplish? Clearly, we are done. There's no sense in prolonging the inevitable."

"Listen, I'm staying in town for a little while longer while I get a…project off the ground. We can at least be friends, right?"

She winced at the word. "Friends. Yes, of course."

Okay, it was a start. He'd gone about this all wrong from the beginning—trying to be with her when they were in the midst of a lawsuit, then getting scared immediately after they made love. It was a wonder she didn't hate him. "Friends can have hot cocoa. Right?"

"One cup of cocoa won't change anything."

He grinned. "Never underestimate the power of melted chocolate."

She gave him a wary glance. People streamed around them, heading in and out of the festival. The country band played a Randy Travis song. "One cup," Lindsay said. "That's it."

When she finally agreed, Walker felt like he'd won the lottery. "That's all I ask."

And hopefully all I need.

Lindsay should have said no. In fact, she had said no, more than once. But then Walker had beaten her at her own argument and she'd agreed. Not that her resistance was all that strong, anyway. A part of her really wanted to know why Walker was still in town. Why he hadn't called.

It was closure, she told herself. Yeah, closure. With hot cocoa.

They turned back into the festival, heading down the crowded path toward the hot chocolate booth at the back. Every few feet, Lindsay ran into someone she knew. That didn't surprise her. But what did surprise her was how many people said hello to Walker. As they walked, it began to seem more and more like he had met pretty much everyone in Rust Creek Falls. He exchanged a few words with Nick Pritchett and his wife, Cecelia, then said hello to Jonah and Vanessa Dalton. "How do you know so many residents of this town?"

"I've spent a lot of time…wandering around town, talking to people this past week," he said.

Something about Walker's answer seemed suspicious, like maybe he wasn't telling her everything. Or maybe he really had enjoyed his time in town and had made a lot of acquaintances. Word had definitely gotten around about what he had done for the families of the sick babies, because several people thanked him and welcomed him to the festival. Was that it?

Whatever had made Walker so popular, by the time they reached the hot chocolate stand, Lindsay felt like she'd gone through an entire class reunion. She was a little bit jealous that Walker had spent so much time with other people and not called or texted her all week. Why would he do that? And why was he back in her life today? Was it just a chance meeting between friends at the festival?

God, even thinking the word *friends* when it came to Walker hurt her chest. She'd wanted more, but the realistic, practical side of her knew better. No matter how many people he met here, no matter what he did, Walker was ultimately going back to Tulsa and she'd be smart to guard her heart before it got any more broken.

Natalie Crawford, who worked at her family's general store, was standing behind two huge urns filled with hot cocoa. "Hi, Lindsay. Nice to see you and…" Natalie arched a brow as she raked Walker with her eyes. "Whoever this is with you."

A weird little flare of something Lindsay refused to name as jealousy rose in her when she saw Natalie looking at Walker like he was the last bachelor on earth. Walker introduced himself, and Lindsay noticed Natalie held on just a little too long for a proper handshake.

"Two hot cocoas, please," Walker said, then glanced at Lindsay. "With whipped cream?"

"Yes." She was going to need it. That and the cupcakes Lily was selling. Maybe *all* the cupcakes.

"Extra whipped cream on both." He paid Natalie, then took the drinks from her, seeming to barely notice Natalie's attempts to flirt and smile at him. When he turned, his attention was focused squarely on Lindsay. That sent a little thrill through her and cracked the wall around her heart letting in hope. Maybe he did want more.

"M'lady," he said, executing a little bow as he gave her the cup. "Be careful. It's hot."

"Which is probably where it derived the name *hot* cocoa." She grinned at him, then took a sip. The drink was perfect, with just the right amount of whipped cream on top.

Walker and Lindsay ambled over to the playground. The festival ended just a few feet before the swings and slides, and this part of the park was deserted but still filled with the scents and sounds of the festival. She glanced over at him from time to time, wondering why a man who had shown her zero interest in the last few days was suddenly so attached. And did she dare to read something into this?

She took a seat on one of the swings and toed back and forth. Walker leaned against the frame, watching her, an amused smile playing on his lips.

"So, do you want to tell me the truth now about why so many people know you?"

He chuckled. "Why, counselor, that sounds like you're taking a deposition."

"It just seems awfully curious to me that a man who's only been in this town for little more than a week knows pretty much every single resident."

"That's a bit of an exaggeration, but yes, I've met quite a few people here over the last few days." Walker took a sip and looked out over the busy, cheery festival they'd just left. "And you're right. Rust Creek Falls is a really nice town."

She sipped at her hot cocoa and let the swing drift. The chains let out soft squeaks. "And why are you meeting so many people?"

"Well, that," he said as he bent down before her, catching the chain in one hand and bringing her to a halt right up against him, "is something I can't tell you until tomorrow."

His eyes were dark and mysterious. Tempting. She could see the slight shadow of stubble on his chin, catch the faint spicy notes of his cologne. Again today his tailored suit was gone, replaced by well-worn jeans, a thick button-down cotton shirt and a pair of boots. If she didn't know better, she'd swear Walker was born and bred in this town. "What's so special about tomorrow?"

"You'll have to meet me tomorrow morning at the corner of Commercial and South Buckskin Road, at nine. Then I can show you what I've been working on."

Her gaze narrowed. That location wasn't near the day care, so it couldn't be an expansion of the building. "What you've been working on? What do you mean?"

He put his cup on the ground, then grabbed the second chain, keeping her against his chest, so close she could kiss him without moving. "Almost from the second I let you go that day, I regretted it. But you were right—what I wanted and what you wanted were two different things. I thought I could find a way to convince you to move to Tulsa—"

She was already shaking her head. They'd circled right back to the same place. She should have known better than to think it would end differently. "I'm not moving, Walker. I'm sorry. Everything and everyone I love is here."

"I know that." He smiled. "Once I finally realized that, I knew what I had to do."

"What are you talking about?"

"I can't tell you yet. You're going to have to trust me." He caught her chin with his palm and traced the outline of her bottom lip. She wanted to lean into his touch, to kiss that warm spot on his hand, to trust him, but her mind kept telling her to be cautious, to avoid the inevitable heartbreak.

He closed the gap between them and pressed a kiss to her lips. A soft, slow, sweet kiss that tasted like sunshine on a warm spring day. "I opted for another road, Lindsay. And I hope you'll do the same."

"Another road? Walker, you're not making any sense."

He straightened. "Meet me tomorrow morning and you'll see what I'm talking about. I promise, it will be worth your time." He gave her one more kiss, then got to his feet and exited the park, leaving her with cold cocoa and a tough choice.

Chapter Thirteen

Walker had never been this nervous in his life. He'd negotiated multimillion-dollar deals, met with heads of state, jumped out of a perfectly good airplane once, but never had he been as nervous as he was on this bright October Sunday morning.

He had everything he needed, finally. It had been down to the wire, and he'd had to call in more than a few favors, but everything was done and in place. He could only pray that the decision he'd made would be met with the reaction he hoped.

He stood at the intersection of Commercial Street and South Buckskin Road, ticking off the minutes. It seemed to take forever for the hands on his watch to move.

Right at nine, Lindsay pulled up to the curb, parked her car and got out. She cupped a hand over her eyes to block the sun and gave him a quizzical look. "Why did you have me meet you at an empty lot? On a Sunday morning, at that?"

"Because it won't be empty for long. And I wanted you to see it before everything starts."

She climbed up the small grassy hill and stood before him. She had on her cowboy boots again, along with a pair of hip-hugging jeans, a pale blue V-neck shirt and a black leather jacket. She looked sexy and comfortable all at the same time, and all he wanted to do was take her home and explore every inch of her. "What everything?"

"My new corporate headquarters. We're building it from the ground up, because I couldn't find a suitable existing space in Rust Creek Falls." As he said the words, excitement filled him. It had been a long time since Walker had had a business venture that had him raring to start the day. And this one, with this incredible view, and the incredible woman before him, was the best decision he'd ever made. He was glad he'd gotten the support of the rest of the board before he made the move, because it would prevent his father from exerting control over Walker any longer. "It's not going to be some shiny, modern metal building. I'm thinking of giving it a lodge feeling, like the Maverick Manor, so it fits right in with everything else in this town. I should be starting on it next week."

"Next week?" She shook her head, and confusion filled her features again. "Wait, did you just say your *new* corporate headquarters?"

"I've decided to relocate. To right here." He pointed at the ground. "At least during my work hours. After hours, I'll be living in a house in town. A rental, for now, to give us enough time to find what we really want."

She blinked and shook her head again. "I'm confused, Walker. Why are you moving here? And renting a house here?"

"Because I don't want to leave." He took her hands in his, holding them tight. Her fingers were cold, her face wary. He couldn't blame her. He'd been distant all week, afraid to make promises he wasn't sure he could keep. But now, with everything moving forward, Walker was ready to tell Lindsay everything. "I want to stay here, right in Rust Creek Falls, with you."

She broke away from him. "Stay here? What are you doing?"

"Changing my life for the better." He tamped down his disappointment that she hadn't been overjoyed by his news. He'd thought she would be happy he was moving here, happy that he wanted to be with her.

"You don't want to live in this small town, Walker. You've told me yourself how much you love Tulsa. That you couldn't wait to get back to the city. You'll get tired of this place in a few months, and then you'll leave. And this will go back to being an empty lot."

She waved off his attempt to reach for her hand.

"Just quit—" She stopped and took in a breath, then let it out with a shudder. "Quit making me believe in things that are never going to happen."

She turned away and headed back to her car. Walker jogged down the hill and stopped in front of her. "Damn, you are a stubborn woman. What's it going to take for you to believe that I'm serious?"

"You know what I want?" She threw up her hands. "Proof. Something other than words. I've had the words before, and in the end, they weren't true. I want to know you're serious."

He chuckled. "I figured you'd say that." He reached into his back pocket and pulled out a sheaf of papers. "So here, counselor, are your exhibits, proving my case. The deed to this very plot of land. A letter from the building department, approving our architectural rendering. A lease for a rental down the street—"

"How did you accomplish all this so quickly?"

"Well, I paid some of my people very well to work extra hours, but most of the credit goes to the folks in Rust Creek Falls. Everybody knows everybody else in a place this small, and those connections can make the impossible happen." He took a step closer. "Especially when I made it clear that I want to make a long-term investment in this town. One that could benefit everyone here."

She glanced over what he had given her. "You're really doing this, aren't you?"

"That's what I've been trying to tell you."

She looked at the papers again, then at him. Her eyes widened. "You're...you're staying?"

He nodded. "There's more, Lindsay. For this one, I'm going to need a lawyer. A good lawyer, who understands this town and these people and will make sure I do this right." He reached into the opposite pocket and pulled out a handwritten list and handed it to her. "Will you set this up for me?"

She scanned the paper, the notes he'd made this morning, and her brows knitted in concentration. When she lifted her gaze to his again, surprise colored the blue depths. "You're setting up a foundation...and The Just Us Kids Pediatric Pulmonary Center? Why?"

"Because I don't want what happened to the Marshalls to happen to anyone else. Those medical bills, even with insurance, were so expensive, they could have lost their house and everything they had worked for. It could have happened to so many others, too. I thought I'd set up a foundation for the residents of Rust Creek Falls so that no one ever has to worry if they get sick. There's going to be a resource available to them to pay those bills. And a center to take their children to if they need specialized medical care. It's something this whole area needed, not just the town." Even after all he'd done for the families and for the Marshalls, Walker had felt as if he'd left something undone, that he could have done more. "I'm hoping this is a way to give back to the town that will keep on giving for years and years to come."

She softened and tears filled her eyes. "Why would you do something like that?"

He whisked away a tear with his thumb and smiled down at her. "Because you taught me to love this town as much as you do. I want to stay here, Lindsay, and build a life with you. I love you."

She opened her mouth. Closed it again. "You... love me?"

He nodded, and his heart filled with hope and a million other emotions he couldn't name. "I think I have from the minute I watched you argue in court. You were so passionate—about the case, about the people you represented, about the life you have here. And I wanted to be a part of that, with you. But most of all, I wanted to find a home. And I did, here."

"In Rust Creek Falls?"

"No." He took her in his arms. She nestled perfectly

against his chest, fitting into that space like a missing piece. Walker smiled down at her. "Right here. With you. When I see you, I feel like I've come home, and when I hold you, it's like I've found exactly the right place to be."

She pressed her head to his chest, listening to his heartbeat. He held her for a long time, while the world went on, cars passing on their way to church, families going to a big Sunday breakfast.

"I never wanted to fall in love with you," she said. "You were everything I told myself to avoid. Because I didn't want to get hurt again."

"I won't hurt you, Lindsay." He pressed a kiss to the top of her head and inhaled the floral notes of her perfume. "I spent too many years burying myself in my work because I thought what I wanted most didn't exist, and I was afraid to try and find out if it did. Then I came here, and you challenged me to step outside the comfort of my office and to really live. And love." He tipped her chin until she was looking at him. "You changed my life, Lindsay. And now I want to change yours."

He stepped back, then dropped to one knee on the grassy hill. He fished in his pocket for a red velvet box and flipped back the lid. "This was my grandmother's ring. My grandfather said that if I ever found a woman who made me want to be a better man, then I should give it to her. You have made me want to be a better person, a better business owner and most of all a better man. To give more and expect less and to leave the space around me changed for the good."

"I did all that? But...how?"

"By doing it yourself." He held the ring out to her. "So, will you marry me, Lindsay Dalton?"

She hesitated for a long moment, her fingers poised over his hand. Then she sighed and shook her head. "I can't."

The hope he'd held on to for so many days plummeted like a stone. He withdrew the box and thumbed the lid closed. "I'm sorry. I thought—"

She put a hand on his shoulder. "I can't until I show you something. Wait here." She turned and went back to her car, pulled out something big and square, then came back up the hill to him. "Considering you're renting a house here, I think this might be an appropriate housewarming gift."

He unwrapped the paper covering and revealed the painting he had tried to buy last night at the harvest festival. The Dalton ranch, nestled among the mountains and the river. "How did you get this? Vanessa said she would only sell it to a member of the Dalton family."

She shrugged. "We took a vote."

Now it was his turn to give her a confused look. "You took a vote?"

She nodded. "Me and my brothers and sister, and even my parents. Everyone heard about what you did for the kids that got sick at the day care and how you brought a ton of business to Maverick Manor. We decided that someone like that should be an honorary member of the Dalton clan, so we chipped in and bought the painting from Vanessa."

"Thank you." As much as he loved the painting, he realized that seeing it now meant seeing the memories of Lindsay and knowing she wasn't going to be his wife. Could he really look at this image every day and know that she wasn't part of the picture? "Honorary member, huh?"

She nodded. "It's a temporary status."

"How temporary?"

"However long it takes to plan a wedding." A wide smile broke across her face. "You have made a successful argument, Mr. Jones, and provided ample evidence to demonstrate your commitment to this town and to me. And I'm ruling—"

He wagged a finger in front of her. "You're not a judge."

"Might I remind you, this is an empty lot and not a court of law?" She parked her fists on her hips and gave him a stubborn smile. "So the regular rules don't apply."

"Ah, yes, indeed." He made a sweeping gesture. "Proceed, Your Honor."

"I'm ruling that you and I, given that you love me and I love you—" hearing those words made Walker's heart leap "—now enter into a binding lifetime contract. Of marriage."

He laughed. "That's one contract I'm going to sign unread."

She cocked her head to one side. "I don't know if you should. Not reading it first is a big risk."

"One I'm willing to take." He propped the painting against his leg, then took her hand again. "The question is whether you are."

"I took that risk the minute I met you, Walker Jones." She rose on her toes and kissed him. "And I realized I never want to be on the opposing side of you again."

He slid the ring onto her finger and drew her into his arms. "That's one thing that we can agree on."

She looked up at him. "So, about this rental house…"

"It's temporary, just until we find something for the two of us."

"Until then," she said, a devilish twinkle in her eyes, "I think we should go break it in. All part of the housewarming, of course."

He leaned down and kissed her, a long, deep, hot kiss that promised much more to come later. Then he drew back and tucked a stray tendril behind her ear. "Just having you there warms everything, Lindsay."

She smiled up at him. "Welcome home, Walker."

They were the words he had waited all his life to hear. His throat was thick, his heart full, and he couldn't find anything else to say. So he gathered the woman he loved into his arms and held her tight while they stood together on a grassy patch of land that was no longer empty, because now it was filled with hopes and dreams. Home, he thought, had been here all along.

* * * * *

*Look for the next installment in the
Cherish continuity*

MONTANA MAVERICKS: THE BABY BONANZA

*Bella Stockton is completely surrounded by little
ones at her job at the day care center...but she can't
have a baby of her own. Could trust fund
cowboy Hudson Jones be the ideal man to heal
her broken heart?*

Don't miss

THE MAVERICK'S HOLIDAY SURPRISE

by

USA TODAY *Bestselling Author Karen Rose Smith*

On sale November 2016!

MILLS & BOON®

Cherish™

EXPERIENCE THE ULTIMATE RUSH OF FALLING IN LOVE

A sneak peek at next month's titles...

In stores from 20th October 2016:

- **Christmas Baby for the Princess** – Barbara Wallace *and* **The Maverick's Holiday Surprise** – Karen Rose Smith
- **Greek Tycoon's Mistletoe Proposal** – Kandy Shepherd *and* **A Child Under His Tree** – Allison Leigh

In stores from 3rd November 2016:

- **The Billionaire's Prize** – Rebecca Winters *and* **The Rancher's Expectant Christmas** – Karen Templeton
- **The Earl's Snow-Kissed Proposal** – Nina Milne *and* **Callie's Christmas Wish** – Merline Lovelace

MILLS & BOON®

EXCLUSIVE EXCERPT

When Dea Caracciolo agrees to attend a sporting
event as tycoon Guido Rossano's date, sparks fly!

Read on for a sneak preview of
THE BILLIONAIRE'S PRIZE
the final instalment of Rebecca Winters'
thrilling Cherish trilogy
THE MONTINARI MARRIAGES

The dark blue short-sleeved dress with small red
poppies Dea was wearing hugged her figure, then flared
from the waist to the knee. With every step the material danced around her beautiful legs, imitating the
flounce of her hair she wore down the way he liked it.
Talk about his heart failing him!

"Dea—"

Her searching gaze fused with his. "I hope it's all
right." The slight tremor in her voice betrayed her fear
that she wasn't welcome. If she only knew...

"You've had an open invitation since we met."
Nodding his thanks to Mario, he put his arm around
her shoulders and drew her inside the suite.

He slid his hands in her hair. "You're the most
beautiful sight this man has ever seen." With uncon-
trolled hunger he lowered his mouth to hers and began
to devour her. Over the announcer's voice and the roar
of the crowd, he heard her little moans of pleasure as
their bodies merged and they drank deeply.

When she swayed in his arms, he half carried her over to the couch where they could give in to their frenzied needs. She smelled heavenly. One kiss grew into another until she became his entire world. He'd never known a feeling like this and lost track of time and place.

"Do you know what you do to me?" he whispered against her lips with feverish intensity.

"I came for the same reason."

Her admission pulled him all the way under. Once in a while the roar of the crowd filled the room, but that didn't stop him from twining his legs with hers. He desired a closeness they couldn't achieve as long as their clothes separated them.

"I want you, *bellissima*. I want you all night long. Do you understand what I'm saying?"

Don't miss
THE BILLIONAIRE'S PRIZE
by Rebecca Winters

Available November 2016

www.millsandboon.co.uk

Give a 12 month subscription to a friend today!

Call Customer Services
0844 844 1358*

or visit
millsandboon.co.uk/subscriptions

MILLS & BOON®

Why shop at millsandboon.co.uk?

Each year, thousands of romance readers find their perfect read at millsandboon.co.uk. That's because we're passionate about bringing you the very best romantic fiction. Here are some of the advantages of shopping at www.millsandboon.co.uk:

* **Get new books first**—you'll be able to buy your favourite books one month before they hit the shops

* **Get exclusive discounts**—you'll also be able to buy our specially created monthly collections, with up to 50% off the RRP

* **Find your favourite authors**—latest news, interviews and new releases for all your favourite authors and series on our website, plus ideas for what to try next

* **Join in**—once you've bought your favourite books, don't forget to register with us to rate, review and join in the discussions

Visit **www.millsandboon.co.uk**
for all this and more today!